The Assignment

A Novel

By

Craig Mueller

TELEMACHUS PRESS

This book is a work of fiction. Names, characters, places and incidents are either the product of the author's imagination or are used fictitiously. Any resemblance to actual persons, living or dead, or to actual events, locales or entities is entirely coincidental.

THE ASSIGNMENT

Copyright © 2025 Craig Mueller. All rights reserved, including the right to reproduce this book, or portions thereof, in any form. No part of this text may be reproduced, transmitted, downloaded, decompiled, reverse engineered, or stored in or introduced into any information storage and retrieval system, in any form or by any means, whether electronic or mechanical without the express written permission of the author. The scanning, uploading, and distribution of this book via the Internet or via any other means without the permission of the publisher is illegal and punishable by law.

The publishers do not have any control over and do not assume any responsibility for author or third-party websites or their content.

Cover Designed by Samantha Paxton

Cover Art:
Artwork generated with the assistance of ChatGPT AI tools using the following prompt: "A realistic book cover image with a patient file folder laying on a conference table, stamped with the word 'CURED', with a doctor staring out the window in the background, buildings in the distance." Edited and finalized by the cover designer.
© Copyright iStockphoto/1191584971/aoldman
© Copyright AdobeStock/1577988976

Publishing services by Telemachus Press, LLC
7652 Sawmill Road
Suite 304
Dublin, Ohio 43016
http://www.telemachuspress.com

Visit the author website:
www.drcraigmuellerbooks.com

ISBN: 978-1-965121-29-0 (eBook)
ISBN: 978-1-965121-30-6 (Paperback)
ISBN: 978-1-965121-35-1 (Hardback)

FICTION/Thrillers/Suspense

Version 2025.09.11

Acknowledgements

Writing is a solitary experience.
Beyond the fictional world I lived in, my number one fan and supporter was my wife, Lynne. Thank you for listening and for your encouragement.

My dear friend and beta reader, Barb Cooper. Your nuanced insights opened my eyes and helped me improve the story.

Claude.ai, my artificial intelligence companion. Claude helped me edit the narrative elements, answer questions, and make suggestions. There is only one sentence in this novel that I did not write—Claude did. I liked it so much, I kept it.

To Steve Himes and the team at Telemachus Press, thanks for being patient with me.

To my family—for your love, support, and patience—I am truly grateful.

Table of Contents

The Assignment

Chapter One

A silhouetted woman on the monitor said, "My cancer is gone. It wasn't the drugs. It was that machine. Georgia Cancer Institute (GCI) denies it."

The monitor turned black.

A familiar thick Italian accent murmured, "Enough. Find out who—handle them. That woman should be dead." Dr. Marco Tanzilla stared at the screen, remote control in hand inside the GCI Medical Advisory Boardroom.

CEO Stephen James loosened his silk tie and turned to Tanzilla, the salt-and-pepper-haired man in the three-piece suit seated to his right.

"Thirty-seven new testimonials posted on social media this morning," James said. "All anonymous. All claiming something at Georgia Cancer Institute cured their cancer while we're holding out on the world."

The sound of a distant smirk sent Tanzilla's open palm slamming into the conference table. His gold cufflinks and bulky designer watch caught the morning light as he turned toward the source—Georgia Cancer Institute Compliance Officer Donna Sheehan, seated closest to the entrance. "This is on you," Tanzilla growled.

Sheehan smiled and looked at the file in front of her. Her highlighted hair was pulled back in a clip—too long for forty, but she wore it anyway. Sharp cheekbones, dark eyes heavy with liner, and the kind of thinness that looked intentional. Her face hinted at cosmetic surgery that promised perfection but delivered something slightly off-kilter. "Careful, Marco," she warned.

"That's rich," Tanzilla said, leaning in. "You telling me to be careful? You don't scare me. Your incompetence does. The risk you pose to decades of planning—*that* infuriates me."

Josh McIntyre, Director of Communications, raised a hand. "We're tracing the upload sources—"

"Good. But that's not the problem," Dr. Tanzilla barked, eyes still locked on Sheehan. "I've seen the patient files. This started in March. It's August. This should have been caught. What happened to protocol?"

Sheehan didn't flinch and looked up. "Marco, here's protocol," she said. "I don't answer to you. Remember that."

"You will," Tanzilla's voice dropped like a rumble of distant thunder. "You're through."

She met his glare. The corners of her mouth turned up.

"In the meantime," Dr. George Slayton Jr., Director of Oncology at Georgia Cancer Institute and President of the Medical Advisory Board, interrupted. "Let's get through one last interview."

"You want to see incompetence? *This* is incompetence. Thanks to our beloved Dr. Pogue," Sheehan said dismissively and rose to summon Clair Pogue in the corridor.

The morning sun bleached the sterile space. Outside the glass, workers dangling on scaffolding from the twenty-fifth floor fastened letters to the new wing, named after Dr. Slayton's deceased father: *GEORGIA CANCER INSTITUTE GEORGE SLAYTON SR. MD CANCER RESEARCH CENTER*. Thirty years ago, Dr. Slayton Sr. recruited Clair Pogue, the brilliant cancer researcher from John Radcliffe Hospital in Oxford, England, to create and direct Georgia Cancer Institute's Complementary and Alternative Medicine Department. His motivations were twofold: Professional and personal. Deeply personal—intimate.

"This ends today," James declared.

In Midtown, Gus Meier had no idea his life's work had just made him the most wanted man in America.

<center>~~~</center>

Twenty miles away, inside the unmarked building where America's brightest minds conducted research the government couldn't officially acknowledge, the retinal scanner beeped and flashed green. "Admitting Gus Meier," announced the automated voice. Steel doors opened to the Sensitive Compartmented Information Facility, or SCIF. A stark white room with an oval conference table centered in emptiness. Gus dropped his blazer over a leather chair, pushing back his damp, untrimmed hair, steadied his breathing, moved the speaker closer to the keyboard, and waited.

His finger hovered over the space bar before tapping into the session. Three faces appeared on the screen. Lawrence Meier—Opa—his grandfather, speaking Swiss German in his signature white button-down. Helene Kock, his adopted mother, thin blonde hair, pleasant smile. Leif Borgstrom, CFO of Swiss Medical Engineering, peering through wire-rimmed glasses beneath the company logo.

Borgstrom's eyebrow twitched—a new tic, as he called the stockholders' meeting to order. "Good afternoon. Or morning in Atlanta, Gus?"

"Eight o'clock."

"Sorry to intrude." Gus smiled at the man whose loyalty to Opa had aged him before his time.

Twenty minutes of spreadsheets followed. The final page displayed their seven-figure distributions: Opa's majority stake, Gus's inherited portion with Helene's trust, and the company's growth. Two products drove the success— Opa's pacemaker and the implantable spinal cord stimulator patented by Gus's father, Elias, before his death. There were no follow-up questions. The meeting closed. Borgstrom left the call.

"Is today the day?" Opa said.

"I'm going to GCI when I leave here." Gus scoffed, right on cue with his grandfather's predictable concern.

"They resolved their issues?" Opa said.

Gus shrugged. "Still no explanation. I received a call on Monday asking me to appear, with Christian, on Friday at nine thirty."

"You need a haircut," Helena said.

Opa peered over his bifocals. "It's crunch time."

"If I get the data this morning, we'll be fine."

"And if you don't?" Helene said.

Opa inserted, "IEEI is in one week." The International Electrical Engineering Innovation Society accepted two applications for devices Gus designed. Demonstrations were set for next Friday afternoon, each required corroborating data. Projects chosen received marquee publicity and on-stage presentation at the annual convention, which ensured rapid penetration of global markets.

Gus nodded. "Whatever the holdup is, it has nothing to do with me."

"And you'll be home by Christmas?" Helene said.

Gus forced a grin. "That's the plan."

Each month, the same thing. Cat and mouse. Cloak and dagger. Questions felt like interrogation.

"My launch date remains November 7th. Three months from today. The data I get today from the biofeedback will guide my upgrade to the mattress mat."

"How is that coming?" Opa said.

"It has posed problems, but I believe we'll be ready when the time comes." He thought about the second-generation device—his GCI biofeedback code adapted into a thin sensor mat, applied like a fitted sheet to any hospital bed. The perfect evolution of his research. "It will steal the show at the convention. Thousands will be sold and installed, allowing me to monitor data from Geneva and publish the results by this time next year."

"How much data do you need?" Helene said.

"All I can get. And, it has to be unequivocal."

If the data being collected over the past six months at GCI even remotely hinted at a flaw in his source code, clinical trials would fail, requiring a rewrite. He could forget the second-generation revolutionary mat. The lynchpin was his covert code—buried in the parallel software installed in the biofeedback device. Did his code work…on humans? It worked on animals. Did humans react the same to the digitally captured frequencies of substances known to stop cancer when they were electronically transmitted into unsuspecting patients at GCI?

Was his action illegal? Probably. Unethical? Most likely. Essential? Absolutely. People were killed for posing a threat to the medical industrial complex—especially regarding cancer. If there were any possible alternatives, he would have chosen one. As for his timeline? Reliable data dictated. He checked his watch. Time to head to GCI, where eight years of his life hung in the balance.

"You look exhausted," Helene said.

He flashed a quick grin, unable to recall the last time he slept through the night.

"He's young. He's still alive, and I may live to see the end," Opa said.

Helene spoke up. "Are you that close, Gus?"

He blew out a frustrated breath. "I think so."

"Say yes," Opa said. "You've tested it. It worked."

Gus paused. "Not on humans."

Her features softened with understanding.

"That may be why I'm still alive."

She blew him a kiss. "Good luck today."

He grinned, gave a thumbs-up, and ended the call.

One level up, he stepped out of the stairwell, passed two security checkpoints, and exited the building.

Eight years, and he still hadn't told a soul what the code did. The ground beneath his feet felt solid. That didn't mean it was safe.

Behind him, the metal lettering on the brick knee wall read Atlanta Technology & Research Institute.

Chapter Two

Paused at the curb in his late-model white Range Rover Sport, Gus Meier tapped his steering wheel. The high air-conditioned breeze offset the August heat radiating through the tinted windows. The traffic app glowed—red lines snaking across the screen. Given the importance of their meeting and her penchant for tardiness, he'd asked Christian Lawler to wait outside Holder Medical Engineering on Thirteenth Street, a block from Piedmont Park. She wasn't.

He gnawed at his lower lip and checked his mirrors.

She came across the street, knocked on the passenger window, and hopped in. "Sorry. I ran into someone getting coffee."

"Late is late."

The smell of toasted bagel and coffee filled the Rover. Steam curled from a paper cup.

Christian smirked. She and Gus had history: romantic, academic, and professional. A tight rope Gus had walked from his first day at Tech.

In that first semester, he learned she had a mercurial nature—brilliant and focused one minute, emotionally volatile the next. Henry called her a 'tornado of talent and trouble.' Consequently, he never told her about the modifications he made to their device. He wished he could, but his gut said no. He needed her in the role she played. She needed *and* wanted him. He buckled up and hoped for the best, at GCI and with Christian.

He chose the most efficient route to GCI. She ate and sipped.

"Instagram's loving you," Christian said.

Gus's jaw clenched—social media—the last thing on his mind.

"Pictures promoting SCAD's fundraiser next Wednesday. You and The Madonna. It's viral."

Madonna…is that code for jealousy from a thirty-year-old woman?

Gus grunted dismissively. Gina Marchitello—the "Madonna" in Christian's acid nomenclature—was the world-famous fashion designer and daughter of Carmelo's Italian cousin. She was in Atlanta working toward her sommelier certification, and Carmelo had chosen Gus as her guide because he spoke Italian. The arrangement visibly perturbed Christian.

On the edge of GCI campus, the traffic light turned red. A billboard loomed—Dr. Slayton's face, white lab coat, red script: "Georgia Cancer Institute. America's Most Trusted Name in Cancer Care."

"There he is," Christian said.

Gus raised his eyebrows.

"Jesus, Gus. Slayton runs the place. Could you at least *pretend* to care?"

"I care about data, not billboards."

I don't just care about it…my research, my life, depends on it.

"But Pogue said Slayton wanted us here, right?"

He nodded.

"Why?"

"We'll see. And do us both a favor, don't drink any more coffee."

Christian scoffed, "I'm focused. Relax. Besides, they're a month late—it better be because he's amazed by what it does."

Gus turned to her. "The IEEI committee is expecting compelling data. You're a first timer. The data has to be spectacular."

Silence.

"So," Gus added, "Forget about impressing Dr. Slayton."

She nodded, her voice low. "Got it."

"Good. Let's get what we came for. If we need to make changes, make them. Then, you nail the presentation. If you don't, no sales, no royalties."

"Understood. First things first." Her voice carried resolve.

His phone buzzed as he switched off the Rover in the GCI parking lot. Dr. Pogue's text: "Need to see you both before the meeting. Critical." Sent two minutes ago.

The message scattered in his head like startled birds: On Monday, her message telling him to make plans to be at GCI on Friday morning described the inquiry as 'concerning'; on Tuesday, she wrote back to confirm they were coming and that the matter to be discussed was 'alarming'; now, it was 'critical'. Something was wrong.

"Slight change of plans," he said, showing Christian the screen.

She leaned over. "That's...odd. I've left her a dozen messages about the results," Christian said, pulling at a loose thread on her slacks. "What could be critical?"

His pulse shot up—had he been naive? No backup plan.

Sunlight flooded through floor-to-ceiling windows into the gleaming lobby—marble floors, polished surfaces reflecting soft recessed lighting. People in all stages of human existence crisscrossed the space. Despair hung invisible but palpable. Through the glass entrance, workers on scaffolding hung from the twenty-fifth floor, installing massive letters: Georgia Cancer Institute George Slayton Sr. MD Research Center. A frail woman pushed a man twice her size in a wheelchair toward the exit. Her clothes hung loose, shoes scuffed and ancient.

"Anyone with those people?"

Christian's gaze swept the lobby. Crowded. Cold. "Don't see anybody."

Outside an elevator bank, Christian wedged between bodies. Gus followed, distracted.

When the metal doors parted, people squeezed past a wheelchair. The last off: a woman pushing a young man. His red and black Georgia bandanna faced forward, an athletic jacket draped over his shoulders.

Gus said to the dropped head, "Go Dawgs."

The young man twisted, gaunt face turning up. He extended a fleshless hand. Their eyes met. The corners of his sunken mouth lifted slightly.

Gus touched his hand, careful not to squeeze.

The boy murmured, "Dawgs."

The moment struck Gus more than team spirit. More like pure courage.

If this meeting confirms my code works, that kid might have a chance...

The elevator rose in soft silence. The "Dawgs" boy made him recall the posts he'd seen, the whispers he'd heard of shadowy testimonials at GCI. Jolted by suspicions that the rumors pointed to the code he'd created and hidden in the device, he began to perspire. Had they seen the testimonials? Was he walking into an ambush?

~~~

He'd met Dr. Pogue once, last December. The urgency in her message triggered shallow breaths and a droplet of sweat rolling down his torso.
~~~

The metal doors opened to an eerily empty reception area. A sharp contrast from the lobby's bustle. He hesitated to step off. Behind a curved marble counter, a receptionist emerged behind a monitor, her gaze fixed and unmoving. "Medical Advisory Boardroom?"

Gus nodded.

She motioned down the wide carpeted corridor. "Make yourself comfortable."

He chuckled. No one summoned before this board could ever be comfortable.

Brass letters on the wall above the entrance announced their destination. Before they could sit, the wooden door's latch sounded. A thin woman emerged. She moved briskly in a white clinic jacket over a white blouse with a raised lace collar. Her light blue skirt hit mid-calf. Gus knew her age to be seventy-five, but she looked a decade younger.

"Thank you both for coming." Her British accent was as thick as Gus's German. She glanced at her watch. "We don't have much time."

"I'm sorry you have to be here." She sighed. "They insisted." Her lips pursed. "We're in a bit of a predicament here."

Gus raised his eyebrows. "How does that square with your last note calling this pre-meeting meeting 'critical'?"

She exhaled. "You've seen the social media attention we're getting?"

Gus nodded.

Christian said, "I'm clueless."

Pogue continued, "The board isn't. To them, this attention is a critical distraction." She pushed her hair back. "These interviews have become inquisitions."

The boardroom door opened. Pogue paused. A woman with jet black hair peered around, scanning the space. Her gaze locked with Gus's. She retreated, closing the door.

"That was our compliance officer, Donna Sheehan; she will question you. We don't want to keep her waiting," Dr. Pogue said.

Christian touched Pogue's thin forearm and prominent dark veins. "This is not what I imagined."

"None of us did. The CEO, Stephen James, is walking a tightrope, and the ASCO rep, Dr. Marco Tanzilla, is beside himself. The claims being made by patients flummox them. What's worse, the new wing dedication is in one week. This could get ugly."

Dr. Pogue went to stand, and Christian pressed her arm again, her voice lower. "What's ASCO?"

"American Society of Clinical Oncology," Dr. Clair Pogue said. "They're a global network of oncologists. They have the strictest guidelines on research development, implementation/use, and analytics." Her attention shifted to Gus. "Doctors from hundreds of countries developed how treatment pathways work and whether or not to develop them further. They're seeing the posts…and they want an explanation, now."

"They suspect our device?" Christian said.

"Tanzilla can leave nothing to chance. ASCO's offices moved here last month. This place is set to become the Mecca of cancer research. He's just been placed on the Medical Advisory Board. He's the smartest person in the room."

Her eyebrows raised, her glance shifted to Gus, and Christian whispered, "This is nothing like what I imagined."

Pogue's voice softened. "You should be fine. Your device… It's basic. I admit," she hesitated and winced. "Looking back, it shouldn't be in here. I used poor judgment in accepting it." Her eyes widened. "But I did, and here we are; and they have to get to the bottom of this. It's a formality."

The boardroom door opened again.

Dr. Pogue stood abruptly.

Gus and Christian exchanged a look. Wide-eyed. Frozen.

The phrase 'poor judgment in accepting it' echoed in his head.

Chapter Three

Pogue rattled through introductions: Donna Sheehan, compliance director, with a smile as sharp as a scalpel; Stephen James, GCI's CEO, tall, slender, shoulders rigid; George Slayton, oncology chief, with thinning hair and pale skin, proud in his gleaming white coat behind the oval table; and Marco Tanzilla, to Slayton's right, in a designer suit, his steepled hands displayed a thick watch and gold cufflinks.

The movement behind him caught Gus's eye as he cataloged their faces. A man sat cross-legged in the corner, his countenance pleasant. Gus glanced at Pogue and raised his eyebrows.

Pogue leaned toward him, her hand to her mouth, "Josh McIntyre. Director of Communications. Slayton's promo man. On his right, Tanzilla's assistant. Beside her, Sheehan's. They take notes—keep score."

Christian stole a glance at McIntyre.

Dr. Slayton traced his finger down the folder's edge like a surgeon plotting an incision. He did not bother to look up. "Your device. Would you explain it to us, please."

Gus gripped the chair's edge, "That's in the application."

"In your own words, please."

Pulse hammered his throat. Sweat trickled down his spine, each drop a betrayal beneath his blazer.

Slayton looked over his glasses, "Your premise: minimize or eliminate adverse effects from chemotherapy." Slayton paused.

"Is there a question?" Christian said.

Dr. Pogue tapped her foot on Christian's shoe.

Slayton leaned back. "Did it work?"

Gus formed a fist and felt his fingers slide over the sweat.

Christian cut in, "What do you mean?"

Dr. Tanzilla, President of the American Society of Clinical Oncologists leaned in, "Let me, Dr. Slayton." His Italian accent floated across the boardroom, authentic yet calculated.

Gus's throat tightened, years of careful answers scrolled through his mind.

"Your device," Tanzilla said. His eyes darted between Gus and Christian as he spoke. "Did you design it to reduce the patient's reaction or improve the outcome?"

Two unanswered questions made him hesitate: Dr. Slayton's— "Did it work?" and Christian's— "What do you mean?"

Gus took a deep breath and said, "Both."

Dr. Slayton opened his palm and motioned to Gus, "Elaborate."

Gus swallowed, "If I may, let me set this up. Five, maybe six years ago, Mr. James called Atlanta Technology and Research Institute (ATRI) to discuss developing a device that could detect developing bedsores."

Tanzilla wrinkled his face, "Bedsores?"

Gus tilted to Christian. Christian said, "We were told that cancer patients developed the worst bedsore because they were the weakest, thinnest, and in pain."

Tanzilla interrupted, waving his hand and addressed Christian. "Are you also ATRI?"

"No." Christian said. "We're partners in the Georgia Public Private Partnership, PPP. ATRI is the public representative. I'm the private sector representative from Holder Medical."

Tanzilla nodded.

Gus added, "We left the initial meeting focused on early detection of bedsores. When we began brainstorming, we wondered if we could use electrical currents to keep the patient stable—preventing the energy draw down during chemotherapy that made them so sick—so they would tolerate the process better and not have to stay in bed so long. Does that answer your question?"

"Conceptually, yes," Tanzilla said. His head tilted, and he gazed away, thinking. "How is it applied?"

Gus grinned. "Presently, it's a bit clumsy. There are six rubber straps with embedded sensors that we place around the wrists, the ankles, the torso, and the head. The microcurrents from the generator to the patient are imperceptible. They sit or lie down during a treatment."

"For how long?"

Gus shrugged, "They can wear the straps for as long as they want."

Slayton leaned forward and began to ask a question.

Christian spoke first. "We really don't know, yet. The primary objective is to avoid side effects from the chemo. We don't think our device has side effects."

"Why?" Tanzilla said.

Gus said, "Because the sensors detect when heart rate, blood pressure, and respiration deviate beyond set parameters. When that happens, the device automatically sends subtle electrical signals to the brain stem to hold those bodily functions in a normal range. I based it on technology used in the pacemaker."

"Very interesting," Tanzilla said and sat back.

Decades ago, Opa used the information in the tawny notebook in his research, which resulted in him inventing the pacemaker used worldwide. Elias took an interest in chronic pain and applied his insights from the notebook to the implantable spinal cord stimulator to inhibit pain. The inventions launched the family firm into international prominence.

Christian folded her hands on the tabletop, "What. Did. The. Data. Show?"

Donna Sheehan took a deep breath, leaned forward, and claimed the discussion's attention like a prosecutor approaching the bench: "There is no data."

Christian and Pogue gasped. The statement hung, suspended in silence.

The boardroom's polished table reflected their faces like specimens under glass.

Atlanta's skyline ghosted behind them. Towers dissolved in haze, like her chances at IEEI.

Gus flashed back eight years now, to the day after he graduated from Tech. His uncle and Opa, surprising him with the fourth-generation project requiring his extended stay in Atlanta. Blood rushed from his face. With the broad edge of his finger, he wiped his brow. "Why is there no data?"

Donna Sheehan raised her eyes wide, "The irony is, Dr. Slayton and I only discovered your device when you," She looked at Christian, "flooded Dr. Pogue's office with messages about results. Her staff escalated it to Compliance."

Christian's voice firm, "What has this got to do with compliance?" She quoted the vendor application, "Results will be released on or before July 1.' Those results are a requirement for the International Electrical Engineers of Innovation application."

Gus stared at Dr. Pogue, "What's going on? You signed off on this."

Color drained from Pogue's face. "The day before I left. I..." She pressed her lips together, the admission of forgetting a mere device hanging between them.

Sheehan gloated, "The day before Dr. Pogue returned to Oxford was nearly three weeks after the application deadline. The data was linked to the installation." She produced a paper and shared it with Gus. He showed it to Christian.

"That's the application to the Research program. Do you recognize your signature?"

"Yes," Gus said.

She slid another paper across to Christian, "This was completed the day you installed your device. Do you recognize your signature?" Sheehan said to Christian.

"Yes. So, what's the problem? The installation was flawless. I checked it. Everything worked when I left."

Sheehan grinned, "Indeed."

Christian matched Sheehan's smugness, "Then what's the problem?"

"Read the first paragraph of the application, where I circled."

Gus read aloud, "Applications will not be accepted after December 1, no exceptions."

"I highlighted the date next to Dr. Pogue's signature, what is it?"

"December 20."

"Not even close," Sheehan said.

Dr. Pogue turned to Sheehan, "Where are you going with this?"

Sheehan nodded at Christian, "The second paragraph is for you, read what I underlined."

She took the sheet from Gus, "All installations must be completed by December 31 to ensure data collection and aggregation."

Christian looked up, her face pale.

Sheehan smirked. "You didn't do that installation before the deadline, did you?"

Christian shook her head.

"You applied after the application deadline, and you installed after the installation deadline. Our system only collected data from devices installed before the deadline."

"So," Dr. Slayton said, "we have no data to support your application to IEEI."

"That can't be," Gus said.

The room went silent.

"There's more," Sheehan said.

"Jesus. What?" Christian said.

"I am responsible for keeping this hospital compliant with the Joint Commission of Hospitals, aka J-Co. This device was admitted in direct violation of our policies."

Dr. Pogue turned sharply to Donna Sheehan, looking past her to Dr. Slayton, "What's going on here, George? This has nothing to do with why we are conducting these meetings. You're acting as if they are criminals."

Donna Sheehan told Dr. Pogue, "If they are, you're their accomplice. Signing that application on December twentieth made you one."

The muscles in Pogue's jaw tightened. Sheehan's smile never reached her eyes as she slid another document across the polished table. Dr. Pogue looked at the paper and squared off in her seat to face Sheehan, "Who do you think you are?"

"I'm the Director of Compliance, and this won't stand in my hospital."

Dr. Pogue bristled, "Your hospital."

Sheehan raised her hand and her chin to interrupt. Empowered by the minute, she said, "Mr. James understands the consequences of non-compliance." Her glance at the CEO made Gus wonder what leverage she held over him.

Dr. Pogue wrinkled her face and looked past Sheehan and Slayton to see Stephen James staring straight ahead. "Stephen. This is what you regard as important? An application process?"

Sheehan folded the paper folder closed, "We have standards. I'm doing what I was hired to do."

Dr. Pogue pounded her fist on the desk, "No. You are railroading these two young scientists."

"Who can't follow directions," Sheehan snarled. "While you put this institution at risk."

"Me? At risk?" Pogue glared at Slayton's downturned face. "Over a bloody application?" She wheeled on Sheehan. "You're the risk to GCI, not me, or them."

Sheehan cut her eyes to Gus and Christian. "You're expelled from the program." Her clipped tone carried the weight of institutional authority.

Christian moved her hand from Gus's, covering her mouth as her head shook.

Gus glared at Sheehan, hiding behind her bureaucratic shield.

"George?" Pogue's voice held desperate appeal.

Dr. Slayton leaned in. "We answer to JCO, Clair."

Stephen James studied the air above their heads, his silence heavier than any judgment.

Pogue slammed her palm on the table and stood. "Since when in hell does JCO care about a damned application?"

Sheehan's lips curled into a predator's smile. "Standards."

Gus's fingers found Christian's wrist, steadying himself as he rose.

Dr. Pogue's papers were scattered beneath her trembling hands. "You and your nepotist power grab," she hissed through clenched teeth as she made for the exit.

The term "nepotist" jolted Gus. Pogue had torn open a wound—something about Sheehan's corrupt power grab felt deeply personal. Nine-fifty on the wall clock. He fought the rage erupting in him as he passed Sheehan, "I want every unit."

"Loading dock." Sheehan's voice carried the finality of a gavel strike. "Security's waiting."

Gus hesitated and kept walking. Sheehan had no idea what the device did. If she did, why would she give them back? She'd have destroyed them…and them too.

Chapter Four

On the elevator to the lobby, slamming the emergency stop button, Christian glared at Gus. "Don't you dare go silent on me. I know you too well, and you know I need that data."

Fierceness and a trembling voice, barely containing her rage, got his attention. "What just happened in there?"

A raised hand, he meant to calm the moment, coincided with a flashback in his head. The crude introduction to this project—Opa handing him the tawny leather notebook—the faint smell of oil connecting four generations. Then, through Pogue and Holder, he received a research adjunct position in the GCI pathology lab. That's when the lies and deceit began—covert electrical experiments in Pogue's Complementary and Alternative Medicine (CAM) department. He had no choice. He couldn't give an honest answer about his research. Soon, he felt lost. More isolated, he invested days and nights reading and rereading the notebook, assured by Opa that the author had promised, "everything you need is in there." He persisted as his intrigue grew, and ultimately, he prevailed. After years of trial and error, countless prototypes, and acceptance into GCI's research program—no results. What had all the effort been for? Expelled.

When Gus dropped his hand, Christian pounced, "Application late?" She shrugged. "You said, 'No big deal,' Pogue would cover for us."

Gus's jaw tightened. "Christian, why didn't you tell me you missed the install deadline?"

He studied her face. "I can't fix what I don't know is broken." Christian's gaze faltered momentarily. "How would I know a few days mattered?"

"You knew Pogue let us slide on the application." His voice dropped, each word measured, sarcastic. "Did you think that made the installation deadline... optional?"

She smacked the wall in the elevator, then turned to him, her finger pointed. She snarled. "Listen to me. That data exists. I did the damn installation. I did it right. I also built in a backup data collection system. Even offline, those devices should have accumulated usage metrics." She shook her head, clearly frustrated that her foresight was being wasted. "It's somewhere. Those numbers don't just vanish."

Gus squinted, rubbing his temple. "Great idea, but you installed it late. Like you were late this morning. Now—" he spread his hands, "—we have nothing."

"That's bullshit. Listen to me, God damn it."

Christian's chest rose and fell rapidly. She glanced away, blinking hard, then met his eyes with renewed determination. She said, "Holder and Pogue are tight."

"So?"

"Holder is going to find out what's happened. Pogue needs to look for that data."

Gus restarted the elevator. "I'll call Holder. He was in on the late application. mericanHe knew we were taking a risk."

Christian faced forward, shoulders squared. "Do it soon."

~~~

When the elevator doors opened to the lobby, people crowded in. Outside, Gus surveyed the scene. "Does this ever end?"

"It better not."

"Why?"

Christian paused, "Cancer keeps this place going."

His gaze swept the room. She had a point. There was more to being expelled than improper paperwork. "Where's the loading dock?"

~~~

At loading, they found no devices waiting. Security sent a woman on an ATV who dropped off a single box. Inside: five units.

"Where are the rest?" Christian demanded.

"That's all they had at CAM."

Gus stepped forward. "We installed fifty units."

The woman shrugged. "Got the removal order yesterday. I went to the Complementary and Alternative Medicine department. That's CAM, right?

Gus nodded.

The security woman said, "This is what they gave me."

~~~

In the Rover, Gus stared at the box. Where are the missing units?

He said, "We're going back," already moving.

"Good." Christian blurted, "I'm over this bullshit."

She matched his stride through the lobby, past the elevator, to the boardroom.

He opened the door, surprised to see Christian bolt in, her voice cracking, "Where are they?" find

Startled, Sheehan interrupted her conversation with Slayton, "Where's what?"

Christian closed in, forcing Sheehan back, "Forty-five missing devices."

Slayton extended his arm between them. James hurried around the table.

Gus grabbed Christian's shoulder. "Whoa."

Christin scowled, "Turn 'em over."

Sheehan's body coiled.

Gus wedged between them. "Just give us our devices."

"You have what we have," Sheehan growled up at him. "Don't make this more difficult."

Christian's voice cut. She stepped back, "It's your hospital. You find them now, or I'll call the police."

James stepped forward. "Ms. Sheehan—"

Christian rolled her shoulders back, "Who's running this place?"

James froze.

Christian unfolded a paper and stuck it in his face, "I installed fifty units."

Dr. Slayton spoke, "Everyone take a breath."

Christian voice hardened on Sheehan, "You're either incompetent, or you're hiding something."

"Perhaps they're in storage," Dr. Slayton offered.

"Why would they be? I installed them in January." Christian looked to Dr. Pogue. "Who's in charge when you're away?"
~~~

"Dr. Chen."

Christian pivoted to Stephen James. "Then bring me Dr. Chen."

Sheehan scoffed. "Listen to her."

Gus said to James, "That might help."

"He's away. But I'll look into it," James said, his relief visible. "We'll be in touch."

Christian started to protest, but Gus guided her toward the door.

"You have until the end of the day," Christian said, "I know people. You don't want this to get out."

Storming out of the boardroom, two doctors in the hall froze mid-stride. At the elevators, the wide-eyed receptionist's mouth was agape. No one spoke, but everyone listened.

Chapter Five

On the drive off the GCI campus, the traffic light turned red at the Slayton billboard intersection, Christian broke the silence. "I blew that. Slayton does not run that place. And the big Italian guy, Tanzilla, who is he?

Gus gripped the wheel tighter. "He represents ASCO. Their national office moved to Atlanta, on this campus. He's not interested in compliance—I'll bet he was in there because of the social media reports about GCI and cancer."

"And James—some CEO he is. Sheehan ran the show, and he sat there like a puppy."

"Pogue tried to set it up for us before we went in, but James and Slayton? I can't figure that dynamic."

"Like a family argument where the parents are intimidated by their most obnoxious kid,"

Expelled.

So much for eight years of sacrifice, dedication, isolation, and a self-imposed exile to avoid more lies to his friends and colleagues. A matrix of options flashed in his head, like branching circuits.

Christian broke the silence three stop lights later, "Maybe we should forget about Holder and call Pogue." She added, "What if no one used it? What if Chen shelved it? Who is Chen anyway?"

"You met him the day Holder took us there to meet Pogue."

"Damn, that was years ago." She leaned forward. The tension in her voice matched her rolled shoulders. "Is his wife a pathologist?"

Gus nodded.

"Pogue told Holder the four of us were the future in this field."

"Good memory."

While Christian hunted for conspiracies, Gus wondered if they were missing something obvious: maybe the devices were doing exactly what they were meant to do—helping people. Maybe that's what terrified the Medical Advisory Board.

Christian said, "Think she'll talk to us?"

A knot formed in his stomach as he considered it, "Why not wait?" Gus said. "If you tell Holder, he'll be motivated to call her. He's got a lot at stake."

"Him? What about me?"

"Ok. We all do," Gus said.

Christian sighed and fixed her stare on him. "Okay. We wait on Pogue, but you call Holder."

Gus nodded and wagged his jaw. "Did you catch that comment about nepotism?"

"Yeah. That seemed random. Ask Holder about that," Christian said

Gus shrugged and drove through his favorite urban neighborhood, Virginia Highlands, approaching Holder Medical.

"Before I see Holder, I've got to find Bobby."

"What's Bobby got to do with this?"

He lied, "Nothing. I have other projects I'm responsible for. "

"Bobby has really bounced back."

Gus grinned, "He's a rare one."

On the dash, his phone stood in a cradle, the screen flashed, "G-Mar."

Christian said, "Better answer it…Lady Madonna calling."

Their evening plans popped into his head.

"Are you going to answer it?" Christian said.

He punched the keypad, "Hello."

Gina's calmness was a salve to his brain. "Good morning. Is this a good time?"

"Yes." He hesitated.

"*Sei sicura?*" Are you sure?

"I'm sure. I'm driving back from a meeting."

"Buon incontro?" Good meeting?

"Not what I was expecting, but I'll be fine."

"Buono." Good. She asked if his aunt and uncle would object to a specific table location at dinner that evening.

"Are you sitting with us?"

"Si." Yes.

"Whatever works best for you will be fine. They are eager to meet you."

"Grazie. Ci vediamo stasera." Thank you. See you tonight.

"Grazie. I'll see you tonight," Gus said.

"Well, this is getting personal," Christian said.

Gus gave her a blank look. "Don't."

She scoffed, "You can be so dense."

Midtown traffic and pedestrians visiting Piedmont Park crossed in front of them. "I know. I like it that way."

She rested her fingers on his shoulder—their first touch in years. "I'm sorry I've been so…me. I had my sights set…" At the Piedmont light, the sun caught her face. Her fading grin met his sympathetic smile. He told her, "I understand. No inventor wants to watch royalties disappear. Don't get down. You're smart. You'll find a way…I'm not giving up."

On Thirteenth Street, he entered the parking garage between Angelo's and Holder Medical Engineering and shut down the Rover. "I need to find Bobby. If you run into Holder, get us some time. I'll break it to him."

~~~

Inside Holder Medical, they parted at the stairwell, and he withdrew his phone. Sheila, Dr. Lee's secretary, answered. Good morning, Shelia. Is he available?"

"For you, always," Sheila said.

Dr. Peyton J Lee, the director of ATRI greeted Gus. His Asian accent is strong, but his English grammar is weak."

"Good morning, Sir. My timeline has moved," Gus said, "What's the latest on the mats?"

"I call you back."

Gus walked as quickly as he could toward Bobby's office without drawing attention. The blinds were drawn, and the office was empty. A tech in the adjacent lab glanced up. "He's in the Cocoon with Holder and some other guy."

Gus climbed to the third floor, two steps at a time. At Holder Medical, the Sensitive Compartmented Information Facility, or SCIF, was affectionately called 'The Cocoon.'

Credentials accepted, the muted thud of the closing door jarred the three men already inside: Robert Holder, Bobby Blincoe with his predictable grin, and a tall stranger with a ruddy complexion.
~~~

Holder rushed to Gus and announced, "We have an unexpected guest. Gus, meet Connor Keegan, executive director of patient safety at the Joint Commission on Accreditation of Healthcare Organizations. (JCAHO)

"JCO? Was this on the calendar?" The words scraped out of Gus's throat.

Keegan's casual wave twisted the knife of timing. "In town, thought I'd stop by for an update." He leaned forward, eyes bright. "The Liability Insurance Association is pressuring the Joint Commission to mandate a device for accreditation. They don't know we're ahead of them."

Behind Keegan, Bobby's face split into a boyish grin. The same expression he'd worn at every breakthrough.

"You can skip IEEI," Keegan pressed. "We'll buy everything you can make. They want a device like yours on every hospital bed in America—yesterday."

"Every bed." The phrase screamed in his head. The chance of a lifetime… but not on his timeline. And…he had no data to validate his code. No word from Dr. Lee on the new mats. A new mat meant new trials—there was no time for that. Was his life's work crumbling in one morning?

"Quite a win-win," Holder beamed.

Gus's teeth found his lower lip. "Enticing." The word tasted like ash. "The 'I' in IEEI stands for 'International.'"

Keegan's face went blank.

Holder told the ruddy faced red-head, "Gus has the final say. ATRI is the public representative on our PPP projects. That's Gus."

"And having your device on every hospital bed in America is your ticket to international markets. We need to be first." Keegan declared. "Insurance companies are hemorrhaging money over bedsore lawsuits. Like five Category V hurricanes hitting Florida every year. Seriously."

Gus paced toward the far wall, his back to everyone, and turned. "It's not ready."

Bewildered, Bobby Blincoe said, "It most certainly is ready."

Keegan agreed, pleading. "It is. What you have is perfect. Believe me,"

Gus raised his finger, steadier than he felt. "I say when it is ready. And you know this is a material deviation from the timeline in our agreement."

"Oh, man…" Bobby said as Gus and Keegan locked eyes.

Gus said to Keegan, "How many units are we talking?"

"Ten thousand."

His heart raced. The large sample he needed. But he counted on the GCI data to know if it worked or needed tweaking.

He glanced at Bobby, who gave him two enthusiastic thumbs up.

Gus sighed. He'd have to lie. "Sign the contract for ten thousand units today, leave the delivery date and the price blank, and" he motioned to Bobby, "we'll sell you our first ten thousand. Come back next Friday with check writers, I'll fill in those two blanks."

Keegan's smile widened. "They'll be here, and you can name your price. But don't jerk them around. They have to stop the bleeding."

Gus forced his face to match Keegan's exuberance. "I'm committed to putting out the best product. And what you've seen may not be the best. So, they may have to bleed a little longer. We'll see."

Christian appeared in the doorway, catching his last, formidable words.

"Bobby," Gus said, his voice hollow, "walk with me."

It was not an invitation, and he didn't wait for an answer.

Three people watched them leave: one celebrating, one concerned, one clueless.

Chapter Six

Outside the Cocoon at Holder Medical, the afternoon sun beat against the building's opaque roof over the atrium. Gus felt the heat seeping through when Bobby demanded, "What's up with you?"

"Not here," Gus shook his head and kept walking.

"Why? He wants to buy ten—"

Gus cut him off, leading him toward the stairs.

In Bobby's office, thoughts collided, and no viable plan emerged. Ten thousand units by next Friday made his hands tremble. Gus thrust them into his pockets, wondering what was taking Dr. Lee so long.

"What's got you wound so tight?" Bobby said.

Gus stopped at the far wall, studying framed photos—Bobby in Braves gear, squatting behind home plate. "Some recovery."

"Understatement of the year."

"It is, isn't it?"

Eighteen months ago, a home plate collision in spring training left Bobby with a closed head injury. By June, the previous "Rookie of the Year" was back in Atlanta, released, fighting to walk. His engineering degree and one well-placed friend gave him a second chance.

"Just say it," Bobby's voice softened. "What's eating you."

Gus checked his phone, no message from Dr. Lee, and dodged the question. "Lake this weekend?"

Bobby squinted quizzically and scoffed. "Seriously?"

Gina's leaving for California on Monday. I promised her we'd drive up to see Suzanne and Robbie, and to my place for a boat ride."

Bewildered, Bobby said, "Sure, stop by."

Tightness mounting in his abdomen made breathing shallow, then his phone vibrated, and Christian's name flashed. He braced himself.

"I forgot to tell you this," she began. "I put a GPS beacon in each unit."

His throat tightened. "Okay."

"Sorry, but you disappeared for a while back then."

Heat rose to his face and ears. "No worries. Good idea. Have you found them?"

"Yeah. A bunch. They're scattered across the state. The beacon only shows when it's on and for thirty minutes after." Her voice hardened. "Wouldn't Sheehan and Pogue know these devices were removed?"

"You would think."

"I think Pogue's done. As for Sheehan? I don't trust her."

"Agreed," Gus said.

"I'm going to keep tracking them every thirty minutes. I'd love to track Sheehan too."

The call ended. Her contempt echoed like artillery fire…and an idea erupted in Gus.

"Ok. So, what's *really* going on?" Bobby said.

Sweat beaded at his temples. How many times had he wanted to trust Bobby and share the truth? Looking at his best friend, the situation had multiplied to the point where he had trouble keeping things straight: GCI, ATRI, JCO, GPS trackers, Pogue, Sheehan, Slayton, Tanzilla, and social media leaks. Who was behind the leaks? Opa's admonition echoed in his head: Trust no one. Ever. Under any circumstances.

Gus walked to the door, his hand on the knob. "Give me a minute, Bobby. My head is spinning."

<div align="center">~~~</div>

Gus knocked on Robert Holder's office door and stepped in. The meaty hand on the cluttered mahogany desk shot up and motioned him in. "Close the door," Holder said as he ambled to the strategy table, his shirt buttons straining, "Clair Pogue called."

"And?"

"She fumed. The expulsion and missing biofeedback devices have her miffed."

Gus sighed and said, "Christian was right. This is nothing like I imagined. I need someone on the inside."

Holder shook his head, his jowls wagging, "Not Pogue. They've walled her off. Everyone there's rattled."

"About the leaks?"

Holder shook his head, "Damn right. It's a trickle, but they have two major problems: a mysterious device they can't find, and a mole doling out case studies."

"What about Chen?"

"Her protégé?"

"Would he replace her?"

He drummed his fingers on the polished surface. "I'd say Complementary and Alternative Medicine is not going to survive at GCI. It's been on life support for years."

Gus squinted. "Dr. Pogue fought Sheehan's overreach, but Slayton and James, it was unbelievable. They cowered to Sheehan."

"Not surprised. Something strong went down when she showed up. After that, George Sr. and Clair went silent, too. I'm shocked they kept her after George Sr. died."

Gus said, "I have to know who authorized sending the BFDs—biofeedback devices—home and if any data exists. Christian is dead at the IEEI without it."

Holder raised his eyebrows. "Have I got this right? You're behind on her project, but moving on with Bobby's?"

Gus gnawed his lip and nodded, "Not exactly. JCO is ready, but I'm not. They may have to wait."

"Not long or you could lose Bobby. These royalties are critical, Gus."

"My father and grandfather would never make a product release date based on anything other than the product's performance?"

Holder shrugged and shook his head.

ATRI Director Lee's name crossed his phone. Gus thrust it at Holder. "This call is critical," Gus said. "Relax, we'll sell JCO something," his voice steady while his stomach churned.

As the conversation began, Gus left Holder's office and descended the steps to drive back to ATRI. In his faint Asian accent, Dr. Lee said, "The mat is ready. They are expecting your call." Knots in his gut started to loosen until Christian's name popped onto his screen. Gus thanked Dr. Lee and answered. Christian blurted, "IEEI confirmed, no data, no presentation."

"Calm down. There's time," Gus said, exiting the building.

"They're using them, Gus. I've found all but one. They're generating data. It's going somewhere."

His pulse quickened. She was right. If someone had linked the devices to the internet... "Somewhere is a big place."

"Then we have to find it," she exhaled. "Sheehan is not erasing years of our work. And Clair Pogue? She should be on our side wanting that woman's head on a stick."

Gus told Christian, "Pogue called Holder. They're meeting later today."

"About what?"

"He didn't offer, I didn't ask. She's going to speak to James. Holder told me to call him later for an update."

"Not too late, or he'll be drunk. Maybe *she'll* be drunk and spill her guts to him."

"Not Clair Pogue," Gus said. "I'll let you know what I learn. Meanwhile, find that last unit."

In the Rover, Gus scrolled through his address book to find the only person he knew who could do what he needed done.

Gus said to the bass voice on the other end, "Have you had lunch?"

"You know me, G-man."

"How about Fender's in thirty?"

"Oh yeah."

Gus ended the call. The diner near ATRI would work—it would be public enough to be safe and private enough to talk. Finally, however tenuous, a plan was taking shape in his head.

Chapter Seven

ender's Diner was two blocks from ATRI, its neon sign flickering even in daylight. Inside, the aroma of curry mingled with coffee—Mary's special for her favorite regular, Cedric Parikh.

The rotund man nestled in his usual corner booth, tablet propped against the napkin holder, fingers dancing across its screen, had been ATRI's most coveted computer hacker for fifteen years. Some people turned down companies. Cedric turned down countries.

"The mysterious G-man," Cedric said without looking up, his Indian accent warming the words. He offered a fist bump, "I was starting to think you'd gone completely nocturnal in your cubby."

Seated opposite him in the booth, Gus studied his friend's pensive face. The morning's theater at GCI had exposed too many actors—Slayton playing politician, Pogue caught between loyalty and fear, Sheehan wielding power that wasn't entirely hers. Cedric might be able to help him understand who's directing this performance.

"Mary's making samosas," Cedric said, finally setting his tablet aside. "But you didn't come for the food." He leaned forward, beard brushing the table's edge.

"You have that look—the one that says you need to know something that someone doesn't want you to know."

Gus allowed himself a small smile. In his eight years at ATRI, Cedric never asked Gus why he needed his help mapping infinitesimal electrical frequencies. Without Cedric's tutelage in deciphering the notes Gus's father left him, he might never finish and leave Atlanta. "That obvious?"

Cedric's smile spread beneath his beard, the kind of smile that said he'd already worked out half the problem.

He made a subtle scanning motion to check his surroundings and whispered, "Georgia Cancer Institute Hospital."

Cedric's eyes sparkled with interest. "Ah, an institutional archeology expedition."

Keeping his voice low, Gus added, "Emails, reports, data."

"It pains me to say this, G-man."

"Pain is my new best friend, say it."

"You don't know about HIPAA."

"About what?" Gus said.

"The Health Insurance Portability and Accountability Act of 1996. The government's attempt to protect health information. It's added layers I'd have to hack through if you want repeat access, not a one-off."

"I want repeat access."

Cedric nodded, "Of course. Then best to be at a station on site."

"OK. Not what I expected, but it is what it is."

"You'll need a ghost key. Something that piggybacks on authorized credentials but doesn't show in the logs." He sketched something with his stylus.

"Cedric," Gus interrupted. "If I can sneak us in, will you come with me?"

Cedric patted his substantial midsection. "Sneak? G-man, do I look like I sneak anywhere? I'm more of a 'create a diversion' kind of guy."

"Noted. I'll work on getting us inside, if you think you can get into the system."

"Hazard pay?" Cedric grinned.

Optimism surged in him. "Deal."

If Cedric could isolate the data, it should verify patients' radical claims on social media...meaning Gus's years of dedication had successfully merged the cancer-stopping research published by Dr. Beard in 1904, with the work of Dr. Voll in 1938, and the nuances added by Dr. Nicholas Gonzales in present-day New York City, resulting in a drug-free, low-cost alternative to chemotherapy. It would also account for what was making everyone at GCI frantic.

The Rover felt like a sauna when Gus left Fender's. Lunch satisfied him, but not as much as Cedric agreeing to accompany him to GCI.

In the notes app on his phone, he prioritized his tasks: Call GMC—mats. Verify display panels. Call Holder—ask about the nepotism comment Pogue made. And his last item, Angelo's by 6:00.

First, he had to find a way into GCI.

~~~
~~~

Chilled air blew across his face in the front seat, which became his temporary workspace.

"Executive Security Services," the female voice announced.

"Mitch Scales, please. Gus Meier calling."

Pop music filled the minute, each second grating on his nerves.

"Mitch Scales," the faint southern drawl held the "ale" in his last name an extra beat.

"It's Gus Meier."

"Yes, sir."

Scales owned and operated ESS, a firm Opa had trusted for years, when his international business dealings made him a potential kidnapping target. Mitch loved details, and Gus provided them along with his objective: access to the computer network inside Georgia Cancer Institute Hospital.

The response was predictably vague—the ESS team would need to explore exactly when and how to access the hospital. Gus drummed his fingers on the steering wheel. It was another delay, another piece of the puzzle that refused to fall into place.

Focused on his priorities, he called GMC, a niche engineering firm in Dahlonega, owned by three former ATRI engineers. They design and manufacture unique electronic materials and printed circuit boards, mainly for ATRI's covert projects.

"Gus," Patricia Compton greeted him warmly. Her assurances about the mattress mat made his pulse quicken—it would conduct currents faster than anything on Earth.

"We're intrigued," Patricia said, her tone probing.

They were dying to know what he planned to do with such specialized material. "So am I. When can I test it?"

"Tuesday."

"What's your run rate?"

"Too soon to tell." A pause. "How many do you want?"

"Ten thousand."

"Holy shit, Gus." Her voice dropped. "I hope you're not in a hurry."

He shut his eyes and hung his head.

Jones Plastics in Kennesaw was next on his list. Craig Jones, second-generation Tech grad and former classmate, provided the polycarbonate display panels for the mattress mats.

His pulse quickened with each ring.

"Just the man I wanted to talk to," Craig Jones announced.

"Really?"

"Yeah, I need a few mill to retool this place."

"Still a wise guy."

"A blessed one at that. But seriously, I need to retool to keep up."

Gus cringed. "I'm in a bind." He explained his situation.

Jones listened to the explanation then his tone turned serious. "You're way ahead of schedule. I'm not sure that mold is even made."

Gus pleaded his case, more an apology than a reiteration.

"Just the kind of call I love to get on Friday afternoon when half my people are working four tens to get more lake time."

"Including your mold crew?"

"Let me call you back."

"Craig, if it's not ready, could they get it ready in a few days?"

Once the laughter cleared, Jones said, "Tall task and a big ask in today's workforce."

"Money still a motivator?"

Jones chuckled, "Only for some."

Gus swallowed. "I'll pay whatever it takes." His voice softened. "I need this."

Chapter Eight

That same afternoon, thunder growled in the distance as an afternoon storm approached Atlanta, driving the Friday summer patrons out of the beer garden into Chipper's Tavern.

In the corner booth she shared with her best friend, Sarah, the cracked vinyl seat caught Christian's skirt as she shifted. Had she wasted five years, off and on, because GCI wouldn't pull the trigger until they had no choice but to make the investment to stop the lawsuits? After half a million in development costs, her vodka tonics disappeared about as fast as her shot at an IEEI demonstration next Friday.

She pushed her empty glass forward, the condensation leaving a trail like tears on the scratched table. "If it didn't work, I could live with that. But it did. I tested it."

Sarah watched the wet streak, understanding in her eyes. "You were too late."

The barmaid stopped by, and Christian ordered another as she folded her moist paper napkin into small squares. "I knew the deadline had passed." Her words slurred. "Gus said Holder and Pogue were close. She'd let it slide. The new year's deadline is what screwed us up…big time."

"Why'd you ignore it?"

Christian's head shook, her eyes downcast. "He pissed me off. He called to say we were accepted, so I invited him to dinner that weekend to celebrate. He lied. He told me he was leaving for Geneva for the holidays." Her drink arrived. She stirred and sipped it. "Sunday, I saw him having brunch with some woman I'd never seen before."

"Did you say anything?"

"Oh yeah, Sarah…like 'Hi Gus, who's this?' Bastard should have gone with me, had a good time, and left it at that."

Sarah grinned. "Right. He probably knew you…of all people, couldn't leave it at that. With him, you always want more." Sarah chuckled, "You would have wanted dessert, too."

Christian snarled, "What's wrong with that?"

"Christ, he damn near had to get a restraining order to keep you away. You didn't put off the installation to get back at him?"

"Okay, okay, okay, I was furious." She nursed her drink, ice clinking against glass. "I hate Christmas. When all that was over, I was in no mood to do work that made me think about him."

Sarah stirred her martini. "You didn't know you'd be excluded from data collection?"

Christian rolled her lips and stared back at Sarah. "He told me to install them before New Year's. Didn't say why. Just a box to check. And I don't check boxes for liars with brunch dates."

"So, you blew it off?"

"Damn right I did. Screw him."

"Now, if you had screwed him, you might not be here saying 'screw him.'"

Christian shut her eyes, raised her glass, "Screw or be screwed"

Sarah lifted her glass.

Christian's laugh was bitter. "What kills me…those devices are out there. Maybe someone's watching what they do, collecting the proof *I* need?" She tapped through several screens on her phone, showing Sarah a complex tracking interface. "Look. These are active units collecting side effects data. I built them. Me. I can see them…"

"And this is important because…?"

"Damn it, people are using 'em. This isn't random, sweetheart. People benefit from my work, and someone at GCI hides the results. But can I tell that to IEEI? Hell no, I lose sales and royalties. I'm getting screwed again. Or, am I crazy?"

"No, you're brilliant. Call Holder," Sarah said, tapping the table for emphasis. "Make him earn his cut."

Christian's fingers drummed against her phone. "He's probably with Pogue. God only knows what she's selling. Gus said he'd call once they spoke."

"Listen to yourself. 'Gus said he'd call.' Holder is *your* fucking boss. Get your own answers. You call."

Christian straightened. Sarah was right.

She hit his number before doubt could creep in. The ring began. Her pulse quickened.

Chapter Nine

Darkening skies hastened Atlanta's Friday exodus at four-thirty, brake lights already dotting the connector beneath the glass towers. Inside the hotel bar, a crystal tumbler of Macallan 25 sat untouched before Clair Pogue and her manicured fingers traced the rim. Even in the hotel's hushed sophistication, her Hermès scarf and pearl studs marked her as someone who understood the subtle difference between luxury and ostentation—a distinction as delicate as the line between medicine and miracle.

Across from her sat Bob Holder. Seventy on his next birthday, with less hair to comb over each year and more skin sagging around his neck. His open collar, loose tie, and buttonholes strained over his insidious paunch told the story of a man losing interest in appearances. When he called thirty minutes ago, the ice cubes clinking against glass and the wet sound of him slurping his scotch set Gus's teeth on edge. "Come to the Four Seasons. Now," Holder stage-whispered, the alcohol already softening his consonants. "Clair is on her way, and I'm going to get to the bottom of this."

His first instinct was to refuse—he had enough complications without babysitting a tipsy Holder—but then came the kicker: "I want you to ask questions I might not think of, plus, you don't want to rely on my memory to tell you what she says."

He couldn't argue with that logic, drunk or not. With a resigned sigh, Gus packed his laptop in his backpack, his mind already exploding with questions, his palms beginning to sweat.

He found them in the booth, shielded by a curved black leather divider.

"What is he doing here?" Pogue said to Holder.

Gus swallowed and felt the tension forming in his gut.

"He has questions, too," Holder said.

"You're ambushing me, Bob?" Her jaw stiffened.

Holder nodded for Gus to sit beside her, then leaned in, "Clair, if anyone has been ambushed, it's this young man and my engineer. He's ATRI, so someone is going to answer to Peyton Lee. You might as well practice on him."

Flustered, Pogue shifted to put distance between her and Gus. "Dr. Lee already called Steve James. I heard all about it."

"And?" Holder pressed.

"James told Dr. Lee that Sheehan had all the evidence she needed to do what she did. It's their sandbox."

"We'll see about that," Gus said.

Pogue moved her glass. "Listen, I made a mistake. I should have told you no last December."

Holder leaned in, his voice low but stern, "And you could have told us yesterday, or this morning."

Pogue smirked, "I had no idea she was sitting on that."

Holder's tone turned smug. "And I suppose you don't know where the data is or the forty-five missing units?"

"Who says there is any?" Pogue said. "James, Slayton, and Sheehan met with IT on Monday morning." Her fingers tensed around her glass. "The hospital's systems show nothing from those devices. Not a single reading, not one data point. As if they never existed.".

Gus felt sweat building.

"Settle down, Bob." Pogue said, "Steve James knows the score here. He's working to get this resolved. It's delicate because Sheehan's involved. James knows she overstepped. He's navigating the potential political fallout…"

"Stop it, Clair," Holder interrupted, "You guys have issues, no doubt, but remember, life goes on outside GCI. JCO loves this device and another one he's working on. Without the data, IEEI interviews are dead. You know candidates live and die by their data."

"Then you should have followed the directions."

Gus knew she was right. This was not moving him forward, and he had to be at Angelo's in forty minutes.

Holder leaned forward and took Clair Pogue's hands in his. His words carried new weight. "Clair, help us get this train back on track. Do it for George. He brought you here. You two did so much for so many. He's been gone for a few years, and George Jr and his ilk couldn't care less about your department. But I do. Please." He squeezed her hands.

Pogue shook her head. "I don't know if I can." She turned toward Gus, "Did I have any authority this morning?"

"None," Gus said.

"Absolutely none. And the whole Oncology department is bordering on pandemonium."

"Over what?" Holder said.

"This ghost on social media—all these people claiming they are healed. Their cancer stopped."

"Well, maybe it's not a ghost. Maybe it's real. Something in your department." Gus looked at Holder.

Pogue said, "Outcome stats are off. Minimally, but they are never off." Her carefully maintained accent elevated on the last word.

Gus said in a low voice, "What's off?"

"Statistics." The word came out like a hiss. She reached for her scotch and thought better of it. "Drug dosing, advanced imaging, radiation therapy, overnight stays, and all ancillary procedures. That has never happened. Ever. Vendors are noticing. Asking questions. Revenue off. Profits are off. If this goes on, it creates more attention."

Holder said, "And James is worried about the publicity and large-scale implications."

Pogue sat up straight and sipped her drink. "They all should be; they can't explain what's happening."

"Maybe I explained it this morning," Gus said.

Pogue set her drink down. "You stirred the pot. Meanwhile, we've got CEO's and politicians arriving here in a few hours. The stakes are incredibly high. I can't say what they are, but they've been in the works a long time. With a full week of tours, dinners, and ass-kissing, I'm bound to get pressed on the issue and, well, frankly, can't fake it that long."

Gus said, "You really didn't know?"

Pogue shook her head.

"Then why expel them?" Holder asked.

"Save face."

"With who?"

"The big wheels. Sheehan is under the microscope. She needs to deflect to someone else."

Gus watched Holder's head extend slightly, neck craning in subtle recognition, and asked Clair Pogue,

"Why did you say 'nepotist power grab' this morning?"

Pogue looked at Holder and paused. Gus saw the man's eyes widen.

"I can't say," she replied.

Sensing the phrase had struck something deeper than policy. He let it go.

"So," Gus continued, "The department chair responsible for alternative cancer treatments can't explain the online claims."

Dr. Pogue stared back.

"That must be…unsettling. For you. And the powers-that-be."

Pogue opened her palms on the table, quiet.

"Until your explanation, no one could point to anything specific," she said. "But your theory sharpened their focus."

She hesitated. "Tanzilla asked if I could get a device from you. He wants to test it himself."

Gus gave a dry chuckle. "They just expelled us."

A lump formed in his throat. "Why chase the device unless…" He let the question hang.

Pogue's slight nod answered it.

If Tanzilla had the data, he wouldn't want the device. Unless…he did have the data and wanted to reverse-engineer it. Or confirm what he already knew.

Holder reached into his jacket pocket and withdrew his phone. Christian Lawler's name flashed on the screen. He turned his phone to Gus and Pogue, "Keep quiet." He pressed the speaker button, "How's my protégé?"

"Your protégé is done waiting for answers." Christian's voice filled the hushed booth. "Those devices are out there, Bob. I put GPS trackers in every unit."

Pogue's hand froze on her glass—not just shock at being outmaneuvered, but genuine surprise that she'd missed this detail while away.

Holder straightened slightly, professional pride mixing with personal concern. His protégé had out-thought them all, but at what cost?

Gus kept his face carefully neutral, but his mind raced. Christian had proof that someone had authorized sending devices home without proper protocols.

"The trackers show they're in people's homes," Christian continued. "All but one."

Pogue's fingers found her scarf, not so much twisting it as holding on. Everything she'd just confided about falling statistics and desperate administrators took on new weight. Somewhere, data existed that could explain everything—or expose everyone.

"Data is being generated right now," Christian said. Frustrated. "Someone has to know where it's going."

Holder glanced at Pogue, old friendship warring with new complications. "If Dr. Pogue had the data, she'd want you to have it."

Christian sipped her drink. The pause and the sound came through the phone, "I've decided I'd be stupid to be patient. Nobody cares about me or whether or not I get in front of IEEI. If it's to be, it's up to me. The hell with all of them. I'm coming down hard."

"How?" Holder said.

"Can't say at the moment. Someone might be listening in. I don't trust any of those sons-a-bitches."

The call ended. In its wake, Pogue's hands had stilled completely—no more nervous movement, just the absolute stillness of someone who'd realized they were standing on quicksand.

Chapter Ten

An hour after Pogue's unsettling revelations in the lounge, Gus returned to the valet stand and tipped the young man to retrieve his hanging bag from the Rover. He had forty minutes to change and get to Angelo's, shift gears from corporate intrigue to family obligations, and figure out how to keep his project alive while everything around it imploded.

Despite the chaos, a flutter of anticipation welled up in him. Since Gina Marchitello's arrival in May, his time with her had evolved from casual escort to genuine romantic possibilities. His friend Carmelo Marchitello—Angelo's son and the restaurant's proprietor—had asked Gus to guide his Italian cousin during her Atlanta stay, valuing his fluency in Italian and their years of trust.

He ran into Christian and her Holder colleagues at The Terrazza on the evening Carmelo arranged their meeting. Christian, half flirting, half drunk, commented on his unshaven face and uncommonly casual attire. Mid-conversation, Carmelo approached with a woman whose beauty stunned Gus into silence. Christian's eyes widened, and she blurted, "Are you G-Mar?"

Now, months later, he was heading to her culinary debut.

Fat raindrops pounded the Rover as he drove to Thirteenth and Piedmont. Lightning split the sky, illuminating gridlocked streets. He could set aside the volatile day for a few hours and enjoy Gina's triumph.

In the parking garage, he used his pass card to reach a reserved space near the side entrance on the fourth level, where aromas of garlic and oregano instantly lifted his mood.

Then, his phone buzzed. Christian. He considered letting it go to voicemail. Her call to Holder forced him to reconsider.

"Everything good?" he said, keeping his voice level.

The snicker came first. "Your *friend*, my boss, Bob Holder," she slurred, "thinks he can pat me on the head and tell me to be patient?"

Gus pinched the bridge of his nose. "You're drunk."

"What I am is done waiting for men…Oh shit, you're at Angelo's on the red carpet." Her laugh turned bitter. "Must be nice, being Instagram famous with Italy's sweetheart. I'm so over her."

"Christian—"

"Don't. Don't you dare Christian me." She hiccupped. "I'm calling in favors. I am going to drop the hammer!" Her cynical voice softened. "You know I'm right about this."

He refused to answer.

She trailed off, "I'll pick you up seven. She better not be there."

~~~

Through the entrance, servers in the corridor practiced synchronized movements with visible excitement. The kitchen sounded lively. Gina had spent the week teaching staff proprietary recipes she acquired from her friends at Italy's acclaimed restaurants—and paired them with select vintages from the Marchitello estate—a decision that had Carmelo glowing with pride.

As Gus paused at the kitchen window scanning for Gina, Carmelo emerged with vigor. "Augustus!"

The men embraced. Carmelo beamed. "I am a new man tonight."

Gus smiled, letting him savor the milestone.

"I owe all this to Gina. She made me believe and Angelo to see what could be."

"She's a unique woman," Gus added as they moved toward the lobby.

Carmelo paused and took Gus's arm. "You should marry her."

Gus recoiled. "She's made it clear she's not interested in romance."

Carmelo nodded. "You may be very intelligent, but you're not too smart when love is involved."

"Excuse me?"

"That's changed. I notice. Your summer together has changed her."

"Really?"

Carmelo pinched his cheek and shook it briefly. "Trust me."

Atlanta's culinary elite had called in favors to secure tables. Even Angelo, initially skeptical, praised Gina for uniting three generations of Marchitello tradition with a bold vision of the future.
~~~

Roman columns lined the two-story lobby, and frescoes by Italian artists filled the walls and ceiling. Carmelo joined the maître d and head chef in greeting guests from the elevators.

Gus searched the inside bar—a cozy replica of an old-world trattoria with decorative moldings and stained glass—but found no sign of Gina.

On the Piedmont Park side of the Terrazza, Gina stepped out ahead of men carrying wine cases. She moved graciously through the crowd, acknowledging brief comments as she directed the men where to place the cases.

Gus approached. "Is the wine here any good?"

She turned, a gentle grin spreading across her face. "Only the best. Would you like a sample?"

Carmelo's words echoed in his head. Was she flirting?

She embodied Milanese elegance—crisp ivory silk blouse tucked into high-waisted bone-colored trousers, perfectly tailored to elongate her silhouette. A subtle neck tie hung undone, acknowledging Atlanta's humidity. Her glossy center-parted hair was pulled into a low knot. His mind wandered to places untouched in months.

At her motion, he followed her to the main dining room.

"Here is where I put your aunt and uncle, with us." The four-top table near the rear wall held more wine glasses than he'd ever seen at one place setting.

"They'll love it, and they're going to love you."

Gina paused. "Thank you for saying that."

"You're welcome. Does that surprise you?"

"No, it's just sweet of you... When I was nineteen, a photographer kept repositioning my shoulders, telling me to look more 'approachable.' Finally, I asked why. He said, 'People need to feel they could love you, even though they can't have you.'" She turned with unexpected vulnerability. "That's been my life since. Everyone forms an opinion of me from images. It's why I value people who see past that." The simple admission felt more intimate than any fashion story she could have shared.

Henry and Cassie Meier approached, excusing the hostess. Henry's dark suit and conservative tie suggested he'd come directly from his office at the Atlanta Fed. Cassie wore her silver-blond hair swept up, a sleeveless coral linen dress cinched at the waist, revealing espadrille wedges.

By six-forty-five, the dining room filled with Atlanta's elite. The maître d' and head chef joined Gina at the podium, waiting for Carmelo. A photo displayed the steep cliffs of the Italian coast bordering the Marchitello Estate.

"Quite a showing," Henry said to his wife.

"She's delightful," Cassie whispered. "And, she is smitten with you."

Gus glanced at Henry. "I must be a complete dunderhead—" He stopped as Gina approached.

"Excuse me. Might you give a quick look for Carmelo?"

Gus checked the bar and Terrazza. As he prepared to report no sighting, a door opened and Carmelo stepped onto the patio. Before Gus could signal him, men's voices rose.

Gus coughed. Carmelo looked up, and Gus pointed to the dining room. Carmelo darted in that direction.

Gus followed a man in dark clothes as he crossed the room with cavalier confidence, showing no urgency to sit at his assigned table.

The woman beside his seat turned. The dark-suited man bent and kissed her cheek.

Gus froze. The day's crises collided with the sanctuary he'd hoped tonight would be.

Across the room, his aunt and uncle chatted with Gina, oblivious to his upheaval. What business did Carmelo have with the man who kissed Donna Sheehan? His heart pounded. Suddenly, he wondered, was he on the outside, looking in—or on the inside, surrounded? He had to tell himself to breathe.

Carmelo welcomed his guests, credited Gina and Chef Mazzoni, and then invited his father, Angelo, in his signature tuxedo, to the podium. Dapper as ever, the patrons rose in unison. Following a thunderous standing ovation, Angelo told how he arrived in Atlanta in 1946 when this land sat between Atlanta and Buckhead. "But for my brother, I could not have purchased the dilapidated home and three squalid acres to open my kitchen."

When the ninety-three-year-old introduced Gina, he praised his younger brother for sharing his granddaughter's talents.

Gina approached under roaring applause to kiss Angelo. She thanked everyone, especially Gus Meier, for making her stay pleasant.

Hearing his name, Donna Sheehan's head snapped around, her eyes locking onto Gus with cold recognition before she leaned to whisper in the dark-suited man's ear, never breaking her stare.

Chapter Eleven

Before sunrise on Saturday morning, Gus had his bike on the driveway waiting for Christian. Clad in his modified biker garb—black Lycra shorts and a loose tee shirt—he sipped an espresso on his front porch. At seven, his phone dinged. He expected it to be Christian, saying she was late. Instead, he found a text from Helene.

"Did you get your data yesterday?"

"No."

"Are you exposed?"

"Possibly. Forty-five units are missing. No one knows how or why. Curious."

"Does Opa know?"

"No. Lacking details. He'll want facts."

"If you suspect they're on to you, you MUST leave. I can send a plane, or you may go to PDK and take what's available. Put it on my account."

"Not leaving. JCO wants Bobby's mat. NOW. As-is."

"Ahead of schedule? Can you manage that?"

"Yes, and maybe. LONG SHOT!"

"Stall."

"I did. One week. May need more. Much more."

"You/ATRI have the last word?"

"Yes."

"Good. Stall."

"SUPER LONG SHOT"

"It's about shifting the odds. STALL."

"Bobby? The money?"

"Stall. Get it right. Sell it. Leave."

Gus checked the time. Still, no Christian. He sent Helene a thumbs-up emoji.

"Have you told Henry?" Helene texted.

"No."

"Get his take."

"How much does he know?"

"A little. Elias told him. Wasn't supposed to. Brothers talk."

"Does he know details?"

"Not unless you told him. You've kept us all in the dark."

"Opa's rules, not mine."

Gus promised to keep in touch.

At 7:15, tension crept into his shoulders, prompting a text to her. Historically tardy, she never showed up late on Saturday morning bike rides. He called again. More pacing on his porch, eyes fixed on the corner up the street where she would turn as it rang and rang. Voicemail. Something's wrong. A minute later, the Rover's taillights disappeared around the corner.

The only empty parking spot belonged to her. Concerned, he pulled into it, hit redial, and waited. No answer. A neighbor in jogging attire emerged from his unit. The man shook his head; he had not seen her leave that morning, but he said, "…I saw her come in last night; someone dropped her off. She needed help getting inside." He walked to the farthest pot on her porch and uncovered the door key.

The door latch…loose.

Inside, papers littered the entry hall. He stood still. Listened. And scanned the room keenly. An askew coffee table. Displaced cushions—signs of a struggle he'd hoped not to find. If he spoke, would he alert an intruder? "Christian?" The muffled whimper drew him to the living room where she lay on the floor, her wrists and ankles bound tight by silver duct tape, another strip sealing her mouth. Rushing to her, he dropped to his knees and thrust the coffee table aside. Terror in her eyes. Frantic bursts of air whistled through her nostrils. His heart pounded, reverberating through his chest. "I'm here," he said. "Don't worry." He teased the tape covering her mouth, "This will hurt."

She grimaced. Her eyes welled up as he pulled the tape off, taking with it the edge of her upper lip. Blood seeped through the injured skin.

"They came in after I fell asleep," she blurted out.

"Who?"

"Two guys. Strong guys."

He unwrapped her wrists causing similar damage to her skin. The fabric of her slacks protected her ankles. He helped her stand. Exasperated, she pushed her hair back, fidgeted with her blouse and pants and said, "I pissed myself, twice."

Gus nodded and dismissed the remark. "Did you see them?"

She recoiled, scratched her head, and said, "Partly. I didn't hear them come in. Then…a man whispered…I thought I was dreaming…still a little drunk on the couch. He said, 'Laptop.' That's what he said. Definitely."

"How'd you get taped up?"

"The one going through my tote on the chair saw me."

"Did you fight him?"

"No. You idiot… I stayed still, but I lost him in the darkness. Then," Touching her mouth. "His hand…" her head shook, she fought back tears, "Pinning my head down…the other one taped my legs, then my hands," she trembled. "Then a strip across…" She swiped her hand over her face, mimicking how they applied the tape. "Fast and rough."

Despite her ordeal, her fingers managed to systematically check security protocols and run diagnostics at her desktop computer keyboard. Gus stood beside her. Speaking to the screen, she labored to explain, "There are multiple encryption layers. They won't crack that easily." He expected to hear a cool assessment from a security expert rather than a victim.

Cardboard boxes, duct tape, and stacks of books by the wall caught his attention.

"I'm cleaning out. Planned on a new place with the extra income."

Gus nodded and said, "Did you get a good look?"

Shaking her head, she paced through the scattered papers. "No. But, he wore Old Spice, like my father."

"You think this is connected to yesterday at GCI?"

She turned to him, "Don't you?"

Their eyes locked. He said, "I do. They could have come at any time. This is no coincidence."

"Maybe you gave them a reason—your brilliant answer."

"I should have kept my mouth shut."

After a flurry of dismissive waves, she said, "You were being Gus. You were cooperating. We needed the data."

"I'm going to call the police."

"Fine," Christian said. "I'm going to shower. I'm gross."

"You're alive."

An alert appeared on his phone. On the screen, a man in a dark brown jumpsuit stood on his porch. The lettering on his left chest read, "Metro Atlanta Services."

As he rushed to Christian's, he remembered a Metro truck parked two doors away. The man on the screen knocked again at Gus's front door and then walked away.

Christian reappeared in shorts and a loose top, her bare feet silent on the hardwood. She'd pulled her hair back and applied makeup—armor against vulnerability. The familiar perfume reached him as she approached, wrapping her arms around him with rehearsed gratitude. "You're a lifesaver," she said, echoing their past intimacies.

He hugged her back, a resurgent reflex difficult to suppress. Savoring her familiar embrace, he caught himself, surprised by how easily old patterns resurfaced in crisis. When she looked up, poised to kiss him, he paused. "The police are on their way. Look around. You need to tell them what's missing."

On her tiptoes, she stared at him, her eyes glazing.

Don't cry, he said to himself. A crying woman made him as helpless as he'd found her.

She sniffled, "This is what I miss." She leaned in.

"No. No. No…" Gus extended his head. "Don't go there." The buzz in his pocket broke the spell. He loosened his hold, temporarily relieved, and checked his screen. "What the hell…"

A knock on the front door jamb distracted her.

Two Metro patrol officers were appraising the situation.

As they surveyed the scene and questioned her, Gus drifted toward the patio, his phone screen flickering with live footage made his blood run cold. Two men were executing a calculated sweep of his house. His grip tightened on the phone as they entered his bedroom. Every instinct screamed to alert the officers questioning Christian to stop what was happening, but years of discipline held him in check. Stay calm. Think it through. The intruders were too practiced, too focused—this was no random break-in. They were on a mission. For what exactly? Good, they found the virus-laden decoy laptop buried in a dresser drawer. And the baited thumb drives planted in his office desk.

Coordinated break-ins. Stolen data. Christian bound on her floor—this wasn't just about missing devices anymore. The weight of his secrecy suddenly felt heavier than ever, especially now that others were paying the price for it."

When they left, he returned to Christian's living room to hear her tell the police she didn't know anyone interested in stealing her computer. In unison, both officers looked at him. Gus shrugged, "I found her and called you guys."

Standing by the front window, the squad car pulled away.

"Pack a bag. You can't stay here."

She approached, taking his hands in hers, flashing a grin that used to weaken his knees, "What if you stayed with me?"

He lowered his voice, "Don't go there."

"But, Gus…"

He lifted his head, motioning toward her bedroom, "Go pack."

Henry Meier wasn't a fan of Christian Lawler. He'd come between their promiscuous conduct in undergraduate days to refocus Gus on his studies… hence his reluctance to seek refuge at his uncle's home with the same woman. Worse, the events of yesterday and this morning had his calculating mind racing to reinforce the cracks forming in the wall he'd built year by year, lie by lie, to keep everyone associated with him safely isolated. Now, risks were mounting, and isolation wasn't an option.

Chapter Twelve

From the driveway, Gus caught sight of his uncle's silhouette at the dining room window on the second floor, a sentinel figure watching as the wrought-iron gates parted to admit them. Henry Meier's rigid posture, hands clasped behind his back, conveyed the gravitas befitting the Atlanta Federal Reserve Bank President, even in his own home. Cassie, his wife of forty years, waited near the screened porch door at the top of the steps.

Standing at the back of the Rover with the hatch raised, Gus retrieved her tote. Christian scanned the outdoor furnishings on the pool deck and the manicured lawn bordered by an eight-foot wrought iron fence. Security cameras bristled from the shadows of towering pine trees. In a low voice, she said to Gus, "Whoa. Does this bring back some wonderful memories?"

Gus dismissed her reference to their weekend romp during undergrad when Henry and Cassie visited Margo in Palo Alto. The three-day fornication fest had blasted his adolescent psyche wide open, forcing him to see life through an entirely different prism.

"If only they knew," Christian added, a mischievous smile playing on her lips.

Gus shut the hatch and said, "Oh, they know. What I didn't know is that they had installed security cameras before they left."

"No way!"

Gus nodded and smirked, "I found out when they got back."

"They saw?"

"Everything."

"Jesus Christ. You never told me."

"Henry put a stop to me seeing you."

"That was Henry?"

His eyes widened. "You think *I* wanted that to end?"

"Jesus. I must be Satan in this house."

"And now, your triumphant return."

Christian leaned around the Rover to see Cassie motioning them up the steps.

A tote slung over her shoulder, Christian let out a low moan as she climbed each step. They entered the screened porch—a refined Southern retreat where ceiling fans stirred the air above weathered teak furniture. Potted ferns hung from the beams, while plush cushions in muted blues and greens adorned the deep-seated chairs. A crystal pitcher for sweet tea sat on a small antique side table.

"Cassie, do you remember Christian?"

Cassie extended her hand. "Nice to see you again."

Cassie motioned for Christian to go through the kitchen. Gus passed his aunt and mouthed, "Thank you."

Christian quietly thanked Cassie for the cup of coffee as they moved toward the winding staircase. At the library door, Henry extended his hand to Christian. She paused, glanced at it, and took it. Henry said, "I'm sorry to hear what happened. I'm glad you're okay."

Midway up the stairs, Christian saw Gus entering Henry's private sanctuary, the library. As tall as Gus, Henry bent to slide the two solid doors shut.

Gus drifted to the window as if pulled by an invisible current, his mind churning with the past twenty-four hours. The image of Christian bound and soiled on her condo floor collided with memories of her laughing naked on that very pool deck below. The manicured lawn stretched before him as he tried to reconcile the carefree lovers they'd been with the desperate, frightened people they are now. No wild passion—only danger, suspicion, and the sickening weight of unknown threats.

"Thanks."

"You're welcome."

What to say next baffled Gus. He'd always admired Henry's analytical mind—the same precision thinking that had elevated his uncle to the Federal Reserve—but would bringing Henry into this mess help untangle it, or would an economist's perspective only complicate things? Who else could he turn to?

Silence stretched between them until Henry spoke. "Is this personal or professional?"

"Mostly professional."

"Better warm my coffee."

Alone, Gus studied the room: glass shelves displayed economic journals, a sleek monitor glowed on one end of the mahogany desk imported from the Caribbean. The opposite end held a star-shaped microphone/speaker array on the desk's leather inlay, where Henry frequently conversed with national and international bankers.

Coffee mug in hand, Henry returned and moved to his leather chair. "Cassie can handle her. What's this all about?"

Gus nodded, confident Cassie would overlook the past and attend to Christian's wounds. He settled into the couch, holding the yellow and black cross-stitched pillow showing the Atlanta Technology & Research Institute logo.

To set the scene, Gus explained yesterday's call with Opa and Helene, the blowup at GCI, and the bizarre encounter with Sheehan at Angelo's before describing how he found Christian that morning and the two men in his house.

Henry said, "I don't like this."

"What part?"

Both hands wrapped around his mug, Henry's eyes fixed on it. "Your father was working with those two Brits. They were onto something. And then…"

Gus shook his head. "This isn't like that."

A raised chin stopped Gus mid-sentence. "The only thing missing is a yacht and a bomb."

"The guys this morning had every opportunity to hurt her, and me for that matter, but they didn't. They want information."

The leather chair creaked as Henry leaned forward, squinting at Gus. "And what do you suppose they'll do if they don't get the information they want?"

Their eyes locked.

"That's why I don't want to involve you or Cassie."

"Gus, we're involved by knowing you and by you being here. Hell, our names are the same. These people aren't stupid."

"The explosion was an accident," Gus said.

A sneer. "Is that what you tell yourself every time you wash the mottled skin on the back of your neck? You're smarter than that. You may not have been when you were fifteen, but surely to God, you are now."

Silence.

"And you've involved that young woman."

Gus nodded. "She knows nothing about the Assignment."

"Neither did the Brits. Look what it got them and their families."

"That's what bothers me."

"I don't know what you've created or exactly what Elias was working on and left you to finish, but to finish, you'll need accomplices, just like your father did. It's just part of it. You have to see the greater good."

"Geez, you sound like Opa. Everything is for the greater good."

"Hey, more than anyone, you have given your all to this project. You are not motivated by money—you have enough for ten lifetimes. You aren't seeking fame; you treasure your anonymity, which only leaves the greater good. You've hit on something that means a lot to you, haven't you? Well, maybe this is the time to break your silence? Do you want to let me in and see if I can help?"

Gus shifted in his seat. "Do you want to know?"

"Would it help you if I did?"

Help. The word rattled in his head for a long moment. Standing, he walked to the window and suddenly, scanning the lawn and the pool, the memories vanished. "I think it would."

"Okay, then, let's sort this out."

~~~

Christian followed Cassie up the winding staircase to the third floor as Henry pulled the library doors together. Her wrists still burned from the duct tape—red marks circling them like bracelets she couldn't remove. Her lips remained raw from the adhesive.

"You might remember this room," Cassie said, opening a door to reveal a tastefully decorated space in muted blues and grays. "Margo's room."

"I'm so embarrassed. We had no idea…"

Cassie winked and placed her hand on Christian's shoulder. "We weren't seeing you; we were seeing ourselves at that age."

Christian forced a smile, then winced and pressed her hand to her lips.

"I'll get some ointment and lip balm."

Sitting on the edge of the bed, Christian's hands trembled slightly, and she flinched at the sound of Cassie returning.

"Let me see." First-aid kit in hand, Cassie sat beside her. Her touch was gentle as she applied antiseptic cream to the raw skin. "These men who broke in—did they say what they wanted?"
~~~

She grimaced. "No. They didn't say anything. I think I surprised them by being there. They took my laptop. I think it had to do with our Biofeedback device."

"Why?" Cassie's hands paused momentarily.

"We got expelled from the Complementary and Alternative Medicine program at GCI yesterday. A minor protocol issue doesn't justify expulsion."

Cassie resumed tending to Christian's wrists, her silence noticeable.

"I mean, we were in the wrong, but the device did exactly what they hired us to do. Expelling us accomplishes nothing other than wasting years and costing me ridiculous royalties. This thing should be celebrated, not shut down."

"If these people came after you because of that device," Cassie said carefully, "you may be better off walking away. This"—she tapped Christian's ankles as she applied the salve—"is serious business. You're young, beautiful, and brilliant, Gus tells us. There are other research opportunities."

She studied Cassie's face. "But we're so close. The royalties alone are…big. They could set us up for life. Gus and me, I mean."

The antiseptic tube was capped with deliberate focus. "I wouldn't count on that."

Gripping her lip between her teeth, Christian said, "He's different than when we were here. A bit distant. Maybe a bit OCD about his work at ATRI. But there's still something between us; I can feel it."

Cassie formed a circle with her mouth for Christian to copy as she dabbed lip balm on the red spots. When she finished, "A lot *has* changed in his life since your last visit. I'm sure that was a meaningful time and fun, which you may never duplicate, but"—a pause— "knowing what I know, don't get your hopes up."

Christian's gaze drifted around the room, looking for anything to focus on besides the sting of Cassie's words. Her attention settled on a collection of framed photographs arranged on a bookshelf.

"May I?" she asked, standing to examine them.

"Of course," Cassie replied, gathering the first-aid supplies.

Moving closer to the photos, studying family vacations, holidays, graduations—the normal visual history of an affluent family, one caught her eye. She stared at a younger Henry and Cassie on a sleek yacht with their children, "Setting the Pace" emblazoned on its stern. Standing with them were a teenage boy with curly hair, a girl about the same age, next to a broad-shouldered man with thick golden waves and dark sunglasses. A thin woman with straight blonde hair stood with her hands resting on a younger boy's shoulders. They all smiled against the backdrop of a lake bordered by mountains, and sunshine glinting off the water.

"Is this Gus?" Christian asked, pointing to the curly-haired teen.

Cassie glanced over and nodded. "Yes, with his mother Helene and his father Elias. Lake Geneva."

Christian peered closer, noting how carefree they looked, a grin forming. "He's so young and tall. He mentioned living there but doesn't talk about it much."

"Understandable." Cassie's voice suddenly distant. "That picture was taken two days before the accident."

"Accident?"

Cassie's expression hardened slightly. "Never mind."

"Does it have anything to do with the skin on his neck?"

"He doesn't like to talk about it." Cassie's voice dismissed Christian's question.

"He said he got burned in an accident. That was it."

"That yacht exploded two days after this picture. We had just arrived home. Elias and two other men died instantly. Gus was launched by the explosion into water blazing with fuel. He came up for air where the fuel was burning, and some got on him." Cassie's eyes met Christian's. "They labeled it an accident. I had my doubts."

"Why?"

Cassie clutched her upper lip with her lower teeth. "I think the Meier men are geniuses. They only invent things that make radical change."

"That's what Gus said about our device. He said we were going to disrupt the market."

Cassie's eyebrows lifted, and her eyes widened. "Maybe you have? The men who broke into your place and bound you with tape—that has all the makings of a movie that doesn't end well. I've seen it before."

Christian stared at the photo, a doomed yacht named after a family she knew nothing about. "What was Gus's father working on?"

"Don't know." Cassie took the photo from Christian's hands and replaced it on the shelf. "I don't know what Gus is working on. Neither does Henry. You know more than we do."

"Maybe. Maybe not," Christian muttered.

Cassie shrugged. "Whatever you and Gus were developing at GCI—maybe it's time to let it go."

But Cassie's warning had the opposite effect. Christian recalled Sheehan's odd behavior, the men taking her laptop, the non-existent data, and the missing units. She rubbed her index finger on the lip balm; something wasn't adding up.

"I need to get downstairs," Cassie said, moving toward the door. "Rest if you need to. If you're hungry, help yourself to anything in the kitchen."

As the door closed, Christian returned to the photograph. She lifted it carefully and stretched out on the bed, studying the yacht. Accident?

She set the frame on the bed beside her, closed her eyes, and wondered what exactly had she stumbled into. And more importantly—was there more to their device than she realized? Something worth breaking into her home?

Chapter Thirteen

Silence stretched between Gus and Henry like a chasm. Gus traced the Atlanta Technology & Research Institute logo on the cross-stitched pillow, the irony not lost on him. Seventy-three years of family secrets rooted on that very campus. Four generations of Meiers chasing what the notebook owner called The Assignment.

The coveted leather-bound notebook, absconded from the Third Reich during World War II, had set them all on this odyssey. Henry came to Tech to study engineering, but economics suited his aptitude, creating a lingering rift with Opa. His older brother, Everett, chose horticulture in Zurich. Elias, the youngest son, became Opa's next option—maybe his last. Then Elias died, and everything shifted to Gus.

No advance warning on that Sunday morning following graduation. He'd awakened with a future, a life, a woman, a plan. Eight years and three months later, he sat in Henry's library, never more conflicted. Pent-up anger toward Opa—for the manipulation, the arbitrary rules—now seemed justification enough to break his silence with Henry, despite the betrayal it stirred.

His heart pounded. Sweat beaded on his forehead. Images flashed through his mind: the GCI lobby, countless nights in the pathology lab when he'd had only a fantastic idea to guide him. Across from him, Henry waited impatiently, and Gus wondered what his uncle could possibly contribute. Henry had chosen his path forty years ago, built his nice, predictable life.

"You know about the Assignment."

"Vaguely. Elias told me a little."

Gus waved his hands and shook his head. "It's at a point where it's incalculable."

A furrowed brow. "Meaning?"

"You know about Dr. Primack and the notebook?" Gus said, referring to Opa's uncle by marriage.

"Elias mentioned it."

"Primack was working on it before he fled Germany. The notebook has assorted formulas and cryptic notes. There are articles Opa and his father recovered from Primack's home written by a Scottish embryologist named John Beard, who made unprecedented discoveries on cancer."

"This was before the war?"

"Beard? Beard published his research in 1904, before medical training in America was overhauled. The National Cancer Institute wasn't established here until 1937 and expanded by President Nixon's 'War on Cancer' at the end of 1971. Beard published his methods to cure advanced cancers, and guess what?"

"He got killed."

"Close. They shut him down. He was the first to report how injections of the pancreatic enzyme, trypsin, stopped cancer."

The leather chair creaked as Henry moved to the edge. "Please don't tell me you've found a way to stop cancer."

"Why?"

"Because that's not a good idea, Gus."

"Are you kidding?"

"No. I'm an economist. I study economic impacts."

"What's that have to do with stopping cancer?"

"Plenty. What happens to the economy in this city if you stop cancer?"

"Well, people live longer. Less suffering. Fewer medical bankruptcies. Good lord, Henry, anyone can see that. Cassie had breast cancer. That wasn't a walk in the park for her, you, and me. And you're rich."

Eyes shut, head shaking. "You don't get it. There's more to it than that."

Gus sat on the edge of the couch, knees nearly touching. "Spare me some academic answer for why cancer is a good thing. There is no way to spin this. If I can stop it from growing in someone, are you telling me I shouldn't? Is that what you're suggesting?"

Standing, Henry paced to his desk and turned. "Before I go on, tell me—is that what you've done?"

Gus nodded. "I have in animals. In humans? I can't say for sure, but I think I have."

"Geez Louise." The words came out sharp. "This can't get out."

"What? This may be the single greatest medical breakthrough in human history. No drugs, no surgery, no radiation, no insurance."

Henry rushed to the back of his chair, eyes wide, voice rising. "Which means no drug reps, no drug research, no oncology surgeons, no radiation specialists, no anesthesiologists, no nurses, no support staff. How do those people feed cloth and educate their children, themselves? What happens to the medical supply companies, pharmaceutical giants, and the insurance networks." Henry patted his hand in the air around him. "It's one big ripple effect, Gus."

"Jesus, Henry. You're going a little overboard, aren't you?"

"Absolutely not. Your invention, however wonderful, doesn't exist in an idealistic vacuum. We live in a synergistic economy. Sickness is the single greatest contributor to GDP in America. Sickness pays the bills. Cancer equals cash flow."

"You want people to die?"

"People die." Their eyes were locked. "Thank God people die. The economy depends on people dying. You're worried about medical bills bankrupting families—what if people kept on living? How would individuals and families afford five extra years in a retirement home only to die of something else? Dead is dead. You say you don't want medical bills to bankrupt people— what about long-term care?"

"Henry, have you ever seen someone die from cancer?"

"Yes. Two years ago, and I got his job."

Silence.

Looking across the library, Henry sighed. "That may seem cruel, but no one in the cancer complex will let you or this device ruin their livelihoods. Think about that."

"I'm not surprised you see this economically; I am surprised you *only* see it economically. What would suggest if you had a grandchild with cancer? Just what would you trade your grandchild's life for? Factory's close too, Henry. Economies are in a constant state of flux; how many times have you told me that?"

Nostrils flared. "Gradually, yes. But people can't stop dying at once, Gus. Don't play God."

"So, if I find a better way to stop cancer, you think I'm playing God, and all you want is to save Capitalism? Let's let the free markets decide. As an economist, shouldn't you be encouraging me to put this out there to test the markets?"

Henry stood still. His face was blank, sunken. "Gus, the thought terrifies me."

"Why? Did Steve Jobs terrify you? Did the iPhone terrify you? What's the difference? It's an advance in technology. The strong survive. I will win."

"You will die. Mark my words."

"I can't walk away, Henry. What if Opa shelved the pacemaker?"

"It's not the same. Please. Listen to me. Find. Another. Way."

Gus chuckled, rubbing his forehead with his long, thick fingers. "I don't know what to say. How could I stop now? What about the war on cancer—is that one big scam?"

"Don't be naive."

Gus searched Henry's face, looking for his soul.

Henry said, "I'm calling Mitch Scales. You two are staying here for the foreseeable future."

"I called Scales yesterday. Relax, Henry, no one is trying to kill us. They got what they came for."

"You don't know that. They may come back."

Exasperated, Gus shrugged. "I have work to do."

"Gus. Remember how hard it was for you to leave home? Because your father stipulated in his Will that if he died, your care would be entrusted to me. I hated to take you away. And now, I'm asking you to stop. To possibly save your life. Think about it. If you won't stop, then pause. Someone may be onto you. Think about your dad. Helene. Opa."

"All I've done for the last fifteen years is think about them. And for the last eight, the specter of Primack and his damn Assignment have inspired me and haunted me. Henry, it's now or never. I won't be haunted by indecision."

Henry winced. "Gus, see the big picture."

"I do. Just a different one than you."

A knock on the library door preceded Cassie. "Christian just left."

"Left? Where did she go?" Gus said.

"She said she'd be back. She said she'd be okay. She got picked up by a state trooper."

Chapter Fourteen

Cassie stood frozen in the library doorway. Her announcement that Christian had left in a state trooper vehicle sent shock waves through both men.

"A state trooper?" Gus said.

Henry's chin retracted. "What happened?"

"I was confirming lunch plans with a friend when she appeared in full stride. Before I could speak, she was out the door and down the steps."

"Come out here," Cassie said, leading them to the porch.

The screened porch became their conference room. Cassie settled into the wicker chair while the men waited for answers. Gus ran his fingers through his hair, stopping mid-motion to clutch his head. His gaze landed on the ceiling fans' rattan paddles swirling overhead. He shut his eyes. Enough already.

"Did she seem frightened?" Resignation hollowed his voice as his hand dropped to his side. "Like she was running from something?"

"No." Cassie wrinkled her face and shook her head. "She seemed... determined. I asked where she was going, and she barely turned, just waved and said she'd be back, not to worry, she was okay."

Henry's brow furrowed. "That's it?"

Eyes wide, hands lifting in bewilderment. "I couldn't believe it. When she rounded the corner of the garage, I rushed to the dining room window. She marched through the pedestrian gate and jumped in the state patrol car."

"Georgia Highway Patrol?" Moving to the screen door, Gus imagined her rushing down the steps she'd hobbled up just hours ago.

"Yes, the insignia was clear as day. It was there, at the curb. Almost as if..."

"As if she'd arranged it." His voice fell, calculations multiplying in his head. First, Henry wants to throttle his cancer breakthrough. Now, Christian vanishes with law enforcement. Another twist in his convoluted morning.

Pacing the porch length, Henry frowned. "What's her connection to the state patrol?"

Shoulders rising with eyebrows. "Not a clue."

"And why not tell us?"

Eyes darting between them. "She's a strong-willed woman," Henry paused. "She has a plan."

Cassie leaned forward, her expression shifting from bewilderment to sudden realization. "Call her. I completely misread her upstairs. I thought she was traumatized, rehashing what had happened. I think she's planning a counterattack."

He called. She answered on the second ring.

"I heard you left in a state trooper's vehicle."

"Yep. I'm not playing their game. I made a call."

"Okay," he swallowed, "did you call the trooper?"

"I'm so mad I can hardly see straight."

"I know, but where are you..."

"No, don't." Her voice dropped off. "I'm in a dark spot, Gus. If I still had a sponsor, I'd call her."

"Then go to a meeting. You feed off that support."

"I get pissed when people use the program like a band-aide."

She'd leaned on alcohol when emotional burdens overwhelmed her. He'd seen her find support in her Alcoholics Anonymous home group. The decision had to be hers. Experience had proven that.

"But what's with the trooper?"

"I'll tell you later. I've gotta go."

"Wait. Don't hang up."

She acknowledged him.

"Henry and Cassie invited us to stay here until this gets sorted out."

Her voice lowered. "I can't stay there."

"Get over it. Have the trooper bring you back here."

"I've gotta go," Christian said. "I'm proud of myself, Gus. I'm fighting back."

"I'm proud of you and glad you're with a trooper. Please, promise me you'll come here when you're finished."

The lilt vanished. "We'll see."

He set his phone onto the circular coffee table in the center of the planked porch, lowered himself into the wicker chair opposite Cassie, and lied. "She's fine."

"What about the trooper? Where is she going?"

A shift of his gaze from Cassie to Henry. "You're right, she has a plan. And only she knows it."

Resignation washed over him. His shoulders dropped, his hips slid under him, and he propped his feet on the coffee table, crossing his ankles. "We'll know when she wants us to know." His mind went blank for a silent, blissful minute, reveling in the hum of the ceiling fan motors.

"Stay here," Henry said, "for now. She may come back."

Henry and Cassie excused themselves. He had a tee time at ten thirty, Cassie a tennis match at eleven. All of Atlanta would be savoring the cool front moving through, bringing with it a refreshing summer breeze and lower humidity. The clock on his phone read twenty till ten. The plush, tufted cushion on the wicker chair cradled his head like a pillow. Eyes shut, he hoped the humming motors might put him to sleep until tomorrow.

Vibration violated his brief respite. Startled, his feet struck the porch, and his hand flipped the phone, certain he'd hear Christian telling some fantastic story. Gina's name stared back at him. Oh no, he thought. I'm not in the mood to be nice. The vibrations mounted as he debated—answer or not. He answered.

"Am I calling too early for Saturday?"

He drank in the sweetness of her voice like nectar.

"Are you there?"

"Yes. I'm here. How are you?"

"Wonderful, thank you. I wanted to thank you for all of your support. Last night and this morning, we've gotten rave reviews."

"Congratulations. It was fun. I enjoyed watching everything come together. It was really amazing."

"It was. And I appreciate all you did to help. Actually, this whole summer. I loved meeting your aunt and uncle; they're very welcoming. You know she invited me to visit and use her pool deck to study? I will go to their home soon. Will you join me?"

Standing, he walked to the screened door. "I'll be there, but I don't want to disturb you," he said as he descended the steps to the pool deck.

"You won't disturb me." She paused. "I'm ready."

He sat on a poolside chaise, imagining her on the one beside him, clad in a revealing swimsuit, saying, 'I'm ready.' An oasis in his desert of troubles, he blurted, "Ready for what?"

Her chuckle came through distinctly. "My exams."

Did she hear his gasp? Eyes shut, face flushed. "Exactly. Your exams."

"Would you be able to give me a lift?"

Hesitation.

When might Christian return? What if he wasn't there when she did and returned with Gina? "Best if you take an Uber or a taxi. I can send a taxi for you?"

"No need. You've taught me well. I'll arrange my own ride. You will be there?"

He assured her he would be and decided not to mention Christian, calculating she may or may not return. Henry called out to him from the porch. When he turned, his uncle's frantic waving made his stomach free-fall. 'I'll be there,' he promised Gina, cutting the connection and pocketing his phone in one motion as he rushed toward the steps. Henry held the screen door open, tight-lipped, ignoring his repeated questions about what had triggered such alarm.

Chapter Fifteen

Cassie stood by the library entrance in her tennis outfit as Gus followed Henry inside. She slid the doors closed. Henry's look and the soft click struck Gus like the sealing of a tomb.

Henry turned to his right, beside his high-backed leather chair, and inhaled. "Opa called me. Interpol has made a breakthrough in the yacht explosion."

He gasped—yacht explosion. Memories erupted—he was standing on the stern platform, excited to be included, observing the other yachts on Lake Geneva, when the blast launched him, somersaulting, into the lake. Panicked, staring at the fuel-covered surface rolling in flames with the blue skies beyond, he swiped and kicked to get past the inferno without gasping for air and drowning. Igniting fuel spread in all directions. One choice: risk the flames or die. His throat tightened in Henry's library, and his hand swept over his left face, ear, and the mottled skin on his neck.

His legs wobbled. His right arm extended to the desk for support. He caught his breath and settled into the chair.

"That case closed years ago," Gus whispered. His left hand lingered on his neck.

"He'll call back with Helene and the Interpol agent."

"When?" Gus said.

Careful and deliberate, Henry eased the speaker on his mahogany desk closer as if handling something explosive. "Actually, I'm supposed to call him, or Zoom, but only if you want to. I told Opa you were here, but nothing about this morning."

Eyes fixed on the desk. "Okay." A pause, a swallow. "Call Opa, I don't want to Zoom."

Each button tone sounded like a countdown. The familiar ache returned—how often he'd wished he, too, had perished that day.

A somber version of Opa's voice answered. "Henry?"

"I'm here, Dad, with Gus," Henry said.

"Hello, Augustus," Opa spoke in Swiss German.

"Hallo," came the response in his native tongue.

Hands folded on the desktop; Henry sat opposite him.

"Helene is in the other room with an agent from Interpol. She phoned a few hours ago, asking if she could come here, saying she had news about Elias. She wouldn't say what it was—wanted to tell me in person. Then she asked if you two were available. I called Helene to see if she wanted to listen in. Part of me wants to know, and part of me doesn't. I'm old. You two may want to know."

"Not particularly," Gus said. "But I'm intrigued to know what makes this urgent."

Henry nodded and said, "Why don't you get them, Dad?"

During the quiet two minutes, Gus slid low in the wooden chair, hands steepled on the tabletop.

Helene's voice broke the quiet. "Hallo," she said to both men. Then, she introduced Interpol agent Karen Baumann from the Barcelona office.

"Buen día," Baumann said, wishing them a good day.

Helene cleared her throat. "Agent Baumann has information about Elias's death."

"Mr. Meier," Baumann began without preamble, "we've apprehended an assassin in Barcelona who claims to know who killed your son. He says the yacht explosion was not an accident."

Heavy silence fell across the line.

"Go on." Opa's voice was tight.

"Two days ago, a professional long-distance sniper assassinated a pharmaceutical researcher during an outdoor event following the announcement that the European Union approved his breakthrough drug to treat Alzheimer's. Hotel security was at the gathering, observed the attack, and alerted local authorities. He was taken into custody following a foot race and a high-speed chase that led to a collision. During his interrogation, he asked to speak to me alone. He said he wanted to bargain with me for leniency."

Henry and Gus exchanged glances.

Baumann continued, "He teased me with a story about a person under his supervision fifteen years ago, who carried out the explosion on Lake Geneva." Elias Meier, Opa's son, Gus's father, and Henry's younger brother, was killed when an explosion on the family yacht killed him and two engineers from London.

"What makes him credible?" Opa demanded.

"He described the day perfectly. The time, place, the setting."

"That was in every newspaper," Opa said.

"He told me you and Elias were the original targets."

Silence.

"That's true," Opa said.

Baumann continued. "When he saw the teenager, and no senior male, he ordered the operation canceled. But his trainee, the other assassin, ignored the order and set off the bomb."

"Ignored the order?" Henry said.

Gus pressed on, "How did he elude CCTV?" Gus said.

"A high-tech long-range detonator. He provided more details, which I verified. He was there."

Eyes shut, fist squeezed. The information confirmed what Gus stitched together over time. When Opa's wife required hospitalization for acute rheumatoid arthritis, Elias had invited Gus instead.

Henry said, "Agent Baumann, pardon me, but what makes this news urgent?"

"The assassin claims the bomber was reassigned to America. Atlanta."

Gus shuddered. Atlanta?

Henry scowled. "My brother's killer has been in Atlanta as long as Gus? Do you have a name?"

"No name of the bomber, and we're verifying the assassins," Baumann said. "We know he owns a well-known bakery in Lucerne. He's forty-two, single, and…"

"The assassin is a baker?" Helene said.

"Yes. His pregnant girlfriend works there. He says she knows nothing about other life. He told his handlers that Barcelona would be his last job. They proposed one final job after Barcelona. He balked. He said he wanted to remain a baker, get married, and be a father. "

"How touching," Gus said. "He wants to stop killing other people's dads so he can become one."

"Ironic, right?" Baumann said. "

"Who are his handlers? Opa said.

"He claims not to know them. A call comes in, he goes."

"Then what's his leverage for leniency?" Gus said.

"Information. Solving the explosion case is decent, but his chance at leniency hinges on helping us identify his handlers here and…in America"

"Why America?" Opa asked.

"Before Barcelona, the job they proposed is in America, Atlanta. There are two targets, a man and a woman.

Gus stiffened in his chair as the words 'a man and a woman' echoed in his head.

"That's not random," Henry said.

Baumann said, "No, it's not. It's big, but is it enough? Not my call. Personally, I think he's sitting on more. In the meantime, I wanted you to know what he's claiming.

"I never believed it was an accident," Opa snapped.

"I'm sorry, Mr. Meier…" Baumann stopped. "I worked in the Geneva office back then. I assisted Reese Oetken. You won't remember me. Reese mentioned that you and your firm were renowned for experimenting in special projects. Could something your son was working on with the Brits have precipitated the action taken against them?"

"Yes," Opa said.

"I know Reese didn't want to label the explosion an accident. But forensics confirmed the explosion occurred at the fuel pump. I was in the room when you argued that the bomb location was purposely chosen to make it look like an accident. Then you declared his death a murder."

Gus and Henry locked eyes.

"Shit," Helene mumbled.

"Jesus," Henry said.

Abdomen tightening. There it was. Murder. Should he call Christian? She should be safe; she left with law enforcement. When she went to shower at her condo, he conceded his anonymity had been fractured. Now, it felt splintered, like the debris on the lake in the police photos following the explosion.

"When is the hit to take place?"

"That's what makes this complicated. His handlers want him on standby for Thursday."

"This Thursday?"

"Yes. He says they are taking matters into their own hands locally. If they can't finish it, they want him ready."

"So, this is underway?" Helene asked.

"If his account is true, yes, it probably is. Or…"

"Wait," Henry interrupted. "They may not have decided whether or not to act."

"He's right," Baumann's low, soft voice agreed.

"What are you going to do about it?" Opa said.

"We're working on weak intel..."

"It lines up pretty well for me," Helene said.

Replaying the scenes at Christian's condo that morning and at his house—they were easy marks. Had someone wanted to kill them, why not then?

"I know you're in Atlanta, Gus. Otherwise, I know nothing about you or your life there, so this may have nothing to do with you or the person who detonated the bomb. I'm not here to alarm anyone but to inform. And now you know."

Gus said, "Your guy needs to be here, fingering the person who killed Elias."

"We're working on that. I sent the assassin home this morning. I can't raise suspicion if I haven't already. He's under constant surveillance. Two men with him, plus local help. His phone is tapped. Believe me, he's on our side. He wants out. Or, he'll never hold his kid."

"But the order could have been given," Opa said.

"It's possible. That's why I'm here in person. If you are so inclined, based on what I've shared, take whatever precautions you feel necessary. I have no evidence to support this, but you can't rule out that they could use any of you to get to Gus if they are after him. Gus, are you involved in anything that would make you a target?"

A pause. Of all the times he'd lied to save himself, this may be the one time to tell the truth.

"Yes," Helene said.

Baumann said, "Well, the more we know, the better we can prepare to help you."

"I don't see any connection," Gus said.

Henry muted the speaker. "She's trying to help. Why lie? This is serious."

A deep breath.

Henry unmuted the speaker, shaking his head.

"We'll arrange local security," Opa said.

"I took the liberty of contacting the FBI office in Washington," Baumann said. "They have random assassinations similar to ours. They gave me the agent in Atlanta overseeing those. I called him. His name is JD Hile. I'll leave his contact info with Helene. Agent Hile says the hits are random, professional, and all dead ends. Like ours. He hasn't had one for a few years. He referred me to a detective, Udell Suttles, with Atlanta Metro. I called Detective Suttles. He wasn't happy to hear from me. Didn't want to waste more time and money on dead-end cases. If you want or need local help, reach out to Agent Hile or Detective Suttles. When I know more, I'll phone you directly. Meanwhile, our assassin will contact his handler today and arrange to come to Atlanta. On standby."

Henry said, "You better iron out your deal before he leaves. I don't care how good your people are. This guy has evaded you for years; he can lose you between there and here."

"We want to catch the person who detonated the bomb that killed your brother. We want to pin the assassinations on the baker. And we want to know who's running this international firing squad."

"My advice is don't get greedy," Opa said. "Confirm the assassin's targets first."

Exasperated, Baumann took an audible breath. "If he gives us all that, Interpol may very well agree to let the guy make croissants in peace, anywhere he wants, wearing an ankle bracelet or in witness protection. Maybe America."

Gus felt his heart pounding as if he'd made the morning bike ride. By now, his bike-riding friends were at the Flying Saucer eating brunch on the back patio, exhausted in an invigorating way, laughing, talking nonsense, and mapping out their afternoons at Home Depot, a wedding, or tailgating at the Braves game. The only certainty to cross his mind was that none of them could imagine or would believe what caused him and Christian to miss the ride.

Chapter Sixteen

Back in Geneva, Opa said, "I'll show Agent Baumann out."

"That won't be necessary," Baumann said. "Please, keep your seat."

"Let me," Helene said.

"Nonsense," Opa's voice lacked power.

Muffled footsteps and light chatter came through the speaker in Henry's library.

"I guess they both left," Henry said.

Gus stabbed the mute button.

In the abrupt silence, Baumann's comments evoked memories that pressed the boundaries of Gus's mind, and the emotional ground shifted beneath him. Murder—no accident. Who? Why? Steeped in science, he searched for a logical explanation for the raw, unquantifiable feelings festering in him.

He settled back and imagined the bomber's blood-stained fingerprints on the pages of the Assignment notebook. Suddenly, he connected his mysterious past to the sophisticated, unique, and unprecedented computer code Henry feared could destabilize the world economy.

The assassin's eerie account to Baumann sent Gus back in time to his hospital room in Geneva as a fifteen-year-old. Surgeons and nurses probed him like a doll, discussing skin grafts, reconstruction, and outcomes.

Then came the month-long hospitalization. Surgeries and bandages and more surgeries and more bandages. Pain. Uncertainty and loss. More loss.

Next, the postponed funeral—he stood stunned at the graveside beneath a black umbrella as the heavens opened, rain lashing like grief itself, as if all of Geneva mourned. Cold to his bones, he wrestled his indifference toward the American uncle he barely knew, tasked with uprooting his fragile life.

Henry rose from his seat in the library, and his voice snapped Gus back to reality. "That was the most shocking call I've ever gotten."

Gus said in a low voice, "I lied to myself. I knew it wasn't an accident. What good did it do me to call it murder? What was done was done."

"The whole thing was a mess. I was in the dark."

"What about me? I thought you all were lying to me. And I hated you for taking me away. I can still see Helene's stone-cold face. I'm not sure who she hated more, you or Opa."

"I was doing what your father directed me to do, and the court upheld. You were suffering. I just wanted to get you here and start over."

"You all lied about Helene and my mother."

"I thought someone told you. I told your father he should do it sooner rather than later. Same for Opa and Helene. They kept putting it off—stupid."

His biological mother had died during childbirth. A rare vascular disorder that she and Elias were aware of.

Five weeks before her due date, Elias's oldest brother, Everett, had come to the Geneva area from his home in Zurich for a horticulture conference an hour's drive south in Annecy. Elias and his wife drove there for the rare chance to visit. Following a wonderful dinner and catching up with Everett, Elias and his wife retired to their hotel room. Just before midnight, returning to bed after using the toilet, her water broke, and labor began. It came fast and hard, sending both into panic. An ambulance took her to the hospital. Elais ran beside the gurney, shuttling her to the delivery room, explaining her medical condition. The attending physician stopped the gurney and lifted the sheet off her rigid body. Alarmed to find a crowning baby, he announced his findings and declared, "Too late for a C-section."

Elias clutched his wife's hand. They knew the risk.

Minutes after she delivered, with Gus on her chest, her blood pressure plummeted. Multiple blood vessels had dissected and ruptured. She was gone before Elias could say goodbye.

Days later, Helene, the maid of honor in their wedding and the woman chosen to be their child's godmother, arrived in Geneva. Following the funeral, Helene stayed to help with Gus and never left.

Henry reminded Gus, "Had your father married Helene, none of this would have happened."

"Opa could have used his influence…"

"Gus," Henry interrupted.

"My dad is dead, Henry. And I find out my mother isn't my mother, and I'm being dragged off to America." Gus glared at his uncle. "Opa could have found a way. He had lawyers. Surely there was some loophole to make Helene my guardian."

Henry sat still.

"He didn't want me there. He wanted me with you, didn't he? He wanted me at Tech. I was his last chance. He put this project above Helene. Above me." Gus's head shook as if it were on a spring, "That's wrong, Henry."

"That's in the past, Gus. Use the past as a school, not as a prison."

Gus smirked. "Atlanta became my prison. I was all set to return, start my career, and rekindle my relationship with Emiline, when he springs the Assignment on me that morning after graduation. You opened the vault because you were the custodian to the notebook and the notes. You were in on this, Henry."

Henry shook his head, "Now *that's* wrong. I didn't know. Besides, look how far you've come. You say you don't want to quit or leave, so why are you doing all this?"

"Because I've come so far. What I've accomplished is valuable. But I'm still mad that he knew so much and told me so little. A lot of years have passed. He's had chances. I feel manipulated. He used that tragedy to his advantage. What's the end game for him?"

Henry's voice dropped. "I never figured that out. So I built my own life."

The sound of the door closing at Opa's house came through the speaker. Opa said, "We're back"

Prompted by the silence, Helene said, "They may have muted us."

Opa said, "That must have come as a shock to Gus."

A look at Henry. "All those times he reminded me to 'not trust anyone,' and he expected me to trust him.

With a deep breath, Gus released the mute button. "We're here."

"Gus, I arranged a charter at Peachtree Dekalb airport (PDK.) It's ready when you are," Helene began.

The sudden shift to action plans jarred him. "And fly where?"

"Here. Geneva. You can't stay there. You heard the lady."

"I did. Geneva is no haven. I've got the skin grafts to prove it."

"Fly to the North Pole if you want; you just can't stay there."

Opa's voice cut through the tension. "Helene, we have security options in Atlanta. Gus and I will discuss them. I think we're finished here."

She growled, "You don't tell me I'm finished. I buried that boy's mother and his father. I raised him as my own and had him ripped from my arms while you did nothing. I will not bury him. He is leaving, and that's final."

"You can't speak to me like—" Opa began.

"Stop it, Dad..." Henry drowned out his father. "She's right. She has every right to speak her mind. That Interpol agent did us no favors. This news does nothing but rip open old wounds and create new fears. Helene has been his mother twice as long as Elias was his father."

"But he was his father," Opa said.

"Oh, you ungrateful bastard." Helene's voice cracked with fury.

"No. Stop it. Stop!" Henry's bounding voice echoed through the library.

The tone in her voice reflected the scowl Gus envisioned on her face. She said, "Apologize now, or I'll never speak to you again." The words hung like a blade.

Silence stretched like a wire about to snap.

"I'm sorry," Opa's voice cracked.

Her deep sigh came through the speaker.

"I'm so sorry," the old man repeated.

"Let's stay on point," Henry said. "Helene, I share your concerns. Events of the past twenty-four hours prompted Gus to seek my counsel. Consequently, I learned some details regarding his progress on the Assignment—they are remarkable."

"Good," Opa said. "I know what it meant to Elias to have you as a confidant, Henry. Bring me up to speed."

"Hold on a second," Gus said as he struck the mute button again and fell back on his chair, shaking his head. "No matter what I say, it won't make sense. So, what's the sense in going into it all?" Gus waved his hand at the speaker, "I'll figure it out."

Henry tilted his head to say, "It's up to you."

Gus unmuted and said, "It's long and complicated, Opa. Suffice it to say, after seventy-three years, I believe I've figured out what Dr. Primack meant by the Holy Grail."

"You solved the Assignment?" Opa said.

"So it seems," Gus answered.

Curiosity edged into Opa's voice. "Do you understand it, Henry?"

"Well, Dad, as you love to remind me, I'm not an electrical engineer, but he used some Crayons to draw a picture. Yes. I understand what little he told me. I'll leave the details to you two. And we've had a healthy debate on the economic impact of a world without cancer."

"Cancer. That was the Holy Grail Primack was after?"

"I believe so."

"That wasn't on my radar."

"Mine either," Gus said. "It took me years to decipher his cryptic notes. It's a wonder I still have hair. I only persisted, Opa, because I remember you saying Dr. Primack gave the notebook to your father and assured him everything he needed was in there."

"I did. And your father and I scoured that notebook on several occasions."

"Don't feel bad, I didn't see the connection until I read articles recovered from his house, not in the notebook. Then the notebook made sense."

"We dismissed those articles."

"I did too, until they were all I had left. Primack was fascinated by a Scottish embryologist named John Beard, who in 1904 discovered what we call stem cells. After a decade, Beard identified a pancreatic enzyme, trypsin, which an embryo started making when uterine implantation stopped. Beard postulated that the two were connected and not a coincidence. When trypsin levels were elevated, implantation stopped."

"An interesting observation on his part."

Gus said, "What could be the harm in injecting trypsin into people with advanced tumors? The tumors stopped growing."

"Fascinating."

"In the 1960s, an American dentist named Kelly was riddled with tumors and left to die when he came across Beard's work and saved his life using trypsin. He spent the rest of his life stopping cancer in his patients. In the 1980s, a New York physician named Gonzolez was tasked with replicating Kelly's methods and subsequently published articles, wrote books, and made recordings describing his miraculous results. No one at GCI seems to care. They can't afford to."

"You're not giving injections," Opa said.

"No. I found another article from 1938 by a German physician, Reinhold Voll. Primack had it all marked up. Voll developed a way to use microcurrents to acupuncture points. He essentially made a circuit loop out of the person's body, then used an amp meter to detect the amperage coming through them at specific spots. This told him where the energy circulating through the person was congested.”

“Fascinating. Elias was working on a frequency-generating device.”

“I now believe that is what got him killed.”

“But the research and the device were crude,” Opa said.

“You told me in the vault after graduation that the Brits had plans to expand his work. Maybe they, too, were targets.”

Silence.

Gus continued. “After reading what Voll was doing, I believe Primack made the notations in the margins linking Voll and Beard, resulting in his vision of a Holy Grail.”

“What does it have to do with Elias?” Opa said.

His frequency generator may have been crude, but if he ever made the connection Primack had, and figured out how to capture the electrical frequency of trypsin and embryonic stem cells, he’d be a threat worth eliminating.”

“They have electrical frequencies you could record?” Helene said.

“Absolutely,” Gus said. “That’s where I applied what I learned in the pathology lab at GCI. I measured the frequency of trypsin and embryonic stem cells taken from a placenta after a delivery. I stored their binary codes in my computer. Then, replicating what Voll did, I wrapped the straps with embedded sensors around the extremities of diseased dogs and ran the two stored signals through the dogs.”

“Wait,” Helene said. “You didn’t give them the actual chemical, you gave an electrical signal made from it?”

“Yes. Like a recording of a song on your phone. The band isn’t in there,” Gus said.

“And it worked?” Opa said.

“It did. On animals.”

Silence.

Henry said, “This is what you put in GCI?”

Gus nodded, “No one knows. I ran a parallel program with the one Christian made. While her code kept them balanced during chemotherapy, mine was sending and receiving specific currents through them, including the trypsin and stem cells. Christian has no idea.”

“So, you don’t target the individual organ?” Opa said.

“That’s what I was going for initially, based on what Elias left in his notes. The theory being sold today is that cancers occur when an adult cell, like a liver cell, goes haywire and mutates. Beard proved it was these vagrant embryonic stem cells he discovered that led him to experiment with trypsin to stop the process. Dr. Gonzalez in New York got a grant from the National Cancer Institute around 2000-2003 after publishing twenty-five cases that blew their minds."

"NCI knows about this?" Opa said.

"They do." A shake of the head. "They gave Gonzalez a grant based on his initial success, then sabotaged his future research to discredit him. They smeared his life's work. In the medical world, they made him either a lunatic or a fraud. Either way, he was through."

"How do you know this?" Helene said.

"His life is well documented."

"I don't know..." Henry doubted.

"I do," Opa said. "Elias and I encountered the same issue with the pacemaker and the spinal cord stimulator. They say they want new science, but not if it means cuts into their revenue stream."

Henry raised his eyebrows at Gus, "This is exactly what I was worried about. Worse."

"GCI could be onto you. Get on the plane, Gus."

"Not today. There are a lot of kids losing their moms and dads. Some moms and dads are losing their kids. If I lose everything to give a cancer patient anything, it will be worth it."

A moment of solemn silence followed his declaration.

Then, Cassie knocked on the library door and slid it open. Both men turned to her.

"Gina Marchitello is here." Her expression said everything they needed to know.

Chapter Seventeen

Standing in the library, both men said their goodbyes to Opa and Helene, promising to keep them abreast of any developments.

An embrace between uncle and nephew. "I could have done without that," Gus said.

"Me too."

"I used to think my life was F'ed up. It's really one big, 'but-for.'"

"Meaning?"

Hands motioning, balancing the air. "But for one thing, you don't get the other. But for Elias getting killed, I'm not here. But for you remaining here, I'm living with you in God knows where."

Henry said, "But for the Nazis exterminating the Jews, Dr. Primack would not have given that notebook to my grandfather and he wouldn't have given it to Harold Holder, a perfect stranger, in a bathroom in Bern."

"At some level, for some reason, it's connected," Gus said.

"I know I would have never come to Atlanta but for Opa pushing Tech onto me."

"And look at you now." A smile and nod toward the porch where Cassie hosted Gina. "You think it's safe to go out there? Maybe she's the mysterious assassin sent to take out Christian and me?"

Raised eyebrows, Henry said. "Well, she is Italian."

"I know. That's part of the intrigue."

"You could use a little intrigue. Until this morning, I'd say you live a boring life."

"If only I had the time."

A chuckle. "If you change your mind, just remember the cameras."

"No encore performance from me, Gus said.

~~~
~~~

Cassie stood at the screened door on the porch, gesturing toward the pool area with a knowing smile. "Remember the cameras."

"Enough about the cameras."

Near the pool, Gina arranged towels on a chaise lounge as sunlight filtered through the tall pines. Cassie backed away from the door. "We're going to go now."

"Sorry you missed your match," came his reply, barely registering Cassie's response.

After the morning's chaos, the sight of Gina offered a different kind of pulse-quickening danger. The curves beneath her sheer cover-up made a compelling argument for adding the intrigue he and Henry discussed.

Henry said, "Mitch Scales is sending people over first thing in the morning. They know what to do. I told them about Christian."

Irritated that reality had intruded on his momentary escape: "This is no time to be under house arrest." His jaw tightened. "And I hope what the Interpol agent said doesn't drive you and Cassie into hiding."

"It won't," Henry said, extending his hand to Gus. They shook. "I understand what you're doing. I'd use your device. How are you going to charge for it?"

A shake of the head and a shrug. "When the time comes, I'll consult you."

<center>~~~</center>

Butterflies fluttered in his stomach as he approached the pool deck. Gina reclined on a chaise, reading notes in a binder through her sunglasses.

"Am I disturbing you?" Gus asked.

She looked over her sunglasses and smiled. "Terribly. Could you come back?"

He struggled to maintain eye contact, certain he looked as awkward as he felt, and sat on the first chaise. "I can come back. I wouldn't want you to fail your exam on my account."

"That won't happen, I assure you." Struck by the contrast—her radiant presence versus the image of an assassin in Barcelona planning his execution. "Aunt Cassie has you all set up."

Scanning the deck, the seven other chaises, the pool house, and the lawn. "This completely changes my impression of Atlanta. Carmelo needs to move out of that building."

"Maybe. But it is a unique concept."

"Angelo's dream in the 70s."

"Impressive for that time," Gus said. "Speaking of impressive, you stole the show last night."

"Wasn't that fun? Thank you for coming."

"You're welcome. It was amazing. And the new menu goes live tonight?"

A smile. "Yes, and we're slammed."

"Does that excite you or do you dread it?"

"Oh, no. It's a high for me."

"I could tell. You're a performer."

"I don't know about that…people spend a lot of money on an evening out. I try to make it an experience."

"It was an experience I won't forget."

"Danke."

"And tomorrow, it's my turn to return the favor. Maybe not as much wow factor."

"I'm looking forward to it. In Missouri, my cousins took me to a big lake. The Ozarks."

"Never heard of it."

"Very nice. They had a nice house, a boat, rafts, skis—you name it."

"Same on Lake Lanier."

"And we're going to visit Bobby and Suzanne?"

"And Robbie, too."

"Did a...did you," he stuttered, motioning at her ensemble, "design this outfit? Your swimsuit and the cover-up?"

She studied it for a moment. "Do you like it?"

"Very much. It's very... what's the word, chic?"

"Chic? Oh. Have you been preparing for the benefit or reading up on fashion?"

"I'm more than an engineering nerd. Give me some credit."

"Oh, I give you credit. You're not a nerd. I did have you for a geek when we met. I wondered what Carmelo was thinking."

"What? I'm not a geek. I'm a medical engineering researcher."

A chuckle. "You were geeky. Your clothes were a mess? You needed a shave; you gave me one-word answers. You essentially ignored me. At one point, I wondered if you might be gay?"

"Holy crap!" The words were blurted out. "I didn't know you were a celebrity. I've driven you everywhere for ten weeks, and that's your impression?"

"Relax." Gina patted his hand. "You've cleaned up. You shave, you bathe, and you've proven you can speak in complete sentences."

"Still not sure if I like boys or girls?"

"Oh, no. Once I put you and Christian together..."

"Well, thank you. I admit that was a bad first impression. I'd been very busy that day...being an engineer geek, and by the time I realized what time it was, well, I had to go as I was. Besides, Carmelo downplayed the whole thing as some big favor I'd be doing him. He said he felt obligated to help you, not exactly a ringing endorsement."

She removed her glasses. "He said that?"

Gus nodded.

"And now?" She said.

"I find you to be a nice distraction."

"Watch him," Christian said, appearing at the pool gate.

Gina's attention went to her bandaged wrists as she dropped onto the chaise opposite him, with Gina between them. "Could I have a word with Cupid?"

Gina raised her hands and shrugged. "He's all yours."

Christian stood. "Not him." She smiled knowingly, "He belongs to no one."

Christian stopped out of earshot by the driveway at the foot of the porch steps. "I have an idea. And," she raised her index finger close to his face, "before you dismiss me, listen to me?"

"Where have you been?" Gus said.

"I've been working on a way to hack into GCI's network while you're working on getting into her cover-up."

"Please..."

"Save it. And good luck. It's just what you need. Believe me, I can tell." Her face reflected resigned familiarity. "You used to tell me when you needed it. I doubt you're at that place in the relationship."

"Stop it. That's your big idea? Hack into GCI?"

"Yep. We get in, scour their files, and find that data."

A pause and cocked head. "Who put that idea in your head?"

"Maybe I did. Did you ever think of that?"

Hands raised in defense. "Christian, I'll never question your amazing, beautiful mind, but a criminal mind? It's a bit out of character."

"I'm channeling my inner criminal." Her jaw clenched, "I need that data. Are you with me or," she motioned toward the pool, "with Madonna?"

"Have you been drinking?"

"No. But it's on my mind. Right now, *we* need to put our heads together and figure out how to get into that system."

"Where's this coming from?"

She stepped close. A low growl in her voice. "Have you ever had a big man stand over you in bed, plant their hand on your face, and bear down?" Her face twisted. "Didn't think so. I was frightened for my life. As I'm looking at him, horrific images shot through my head. What might he do to me? Then the tape. Thrown on the floor like a candy wrapper. Wetting myself and praying they didn't come back to finish the job? Well, I'm finishing what I started. I'm getting that data."

Agent Baumann's warning blasted in his head: "They may handle this locally."

Christian's smug voice continued. "The only link is GCI. Somebody has it in for me, or us. Who? Why? I don't know. Do you know something I don't?"

Expressionless, fascinated by her assessment, he held his breath.

"The way I see it," she added, "they break in, we break in."

Their eyes locked. A glance toward the pool—could Gina hear them?

Leading Christian farther away. "That's a big risk. Why not go directly to Pogue? Ask her to use her computer. She's got a lot at stake."

"She's irrelevant."

"If you say so. Then maybe she'll go along."

"I think they're giving tours today. A soft opening," Christian said.

"Pogue?"

"Call her." Christian barked. "She likes you."

"I don't think she does." Gus thought back to yesterday afternoon in the bar." But I'll call if it'll make you feel better."

"A cocktail will make me feel better. I need a little brown water."

"No. No brown water for you. Go inside. Sleep. Talk to Gina. Anything to get your head right."

"How about I go tell her about you and me getting touchy on her chaise?" Her sarcasm seeped through.

"Brilliant. While you're at it, tell her about the cameras."

"Oh, right, the cameras. Does she know about them?"

Chapter Eighteen

On the driveway behind Henry's, his mind clamored over Christian's plan to hack into GCI as she climbed the steps to the porch and disappeared inside. When her mind was made up, a team of wild horses couldn't change it. How would she take the suggestions to stay at Henry and Cassie's? He stood still, glancing toward the pool, Gina's foot visible beyond the shrubbery. Would the assassin come to Atlanta? Would he reveal the bomber who'd been reassigned to Atlanta? What are the odds…like getting struck by lightning at the instant he bought the winning lottery ticket? And, while he prepared to go to GCI, where in a chance encounter he crossed paths with the "Go Dawgs" boy in the wheelchair and later met Sheehan, Slayton, Tanzilla, and James. On the other side of the world Agent Karen Baumann was interrogating a professional assassin who, but for being apprehended, would have returned to Lucerne, to his life as a baker and become a husband and father, never divulging the secrets that haunted him.

Faces, voices, ideas—all pressed against his skull like a vise. Peripherally, Gina lifted her foot to cross her ankles and brought him back to the moment, reminding him that beauty and serenity existed. Just five minutes, he thought. All I want is five minutes to forget everything but her.

He lowered the backrest on the chaise beside her. A folded towel became his pillow, and he stretched out.

Gina set her notes aside. "You need a break."

His forearm draped over his eyes, he said, "Is that a question or a statement?"

"Statement." Her voice carried a gentle authority he'd come to appreciate.

"Is it that obvious?"

"As obvious as her bandages."

"She had a rough night."

"And a rough morning?"

Rolling his face toward her, eyes squinted. "Question or a statement?"

"Observation."

"Touché. We're partners on a project that hit a wall yesterday. A big wall. I think it's cracked my head open."

With a commiserating breath, she nodded. "Been there. Perhaps not in the same way as her."

Through half-closed eyes, he said, "She'll heal. We'll get through it. I need to rest."

"I need to study." Gina turned the page in her binder.

~~~

He woke to find her holding his phone, the screen illuminated. Pulse quickening.

"What's going on?" Sitting up abruptly.

She handed him the phone. "You're in demand. It's blowing up."

A text from Scales read, "Still working on GCI access." A missed call from Bob Holder and a voicemail from Craig Jones. Setting the phone down, he did a double-take.

"Did you go swimming?"

She patted water on her forehead, her matted hair exposing her distinct facial features. "Yes. Your phone kept ringing, and you didn't answer, so I got out."

"How long was I asleep?" Holder had called three times. Scales texted twenty-five minutes ago, and Craig Jones called last, the call she reacted to.

Her eyes shifted to his phone. "About thirty minutes. Is Everything okay?"

His business instinct screamed to return those calls. A primal instinct demanded he preserve this moment.

"Fine. Are you getting back in? I'm hot."

"I'd love to...but I have to get back." She tapped her watch. "Remember, we're slammed?"

"Ah. Just a little longer. We've hardly had a chance to talk." He measured her reaction, wondering if he'd exposed too much.

Gina patted his shoulder, her touch lingering. "We'll have all afternoon on the lake tomorrow. I can't wait."

Deflated, he said, "Would you like a ride back?" Gus asked.

"That would be lovely," Gina said and smiled. "Thank you."

Her touch, smile, and voice set his heart racing. Did she feel the shift he felt between them, or was it just his imagination?
~~~

~~~

The drive past the wrought iron gates with Gina contrasted sharply with his arrival and a wounded Christian in the same seat.

Should he tell her he'd taken to following her…online? She'd been quite clear when they first met; while grateful for his help transitioning to the city, that was it. Period. That was months ago. She'd been overly protective, more like defensive. He understood and didn't care, thinking she might be a bit too self-absorbed. As her defenses came down, his opinion changed.

"I've read about you online."

"Really? Anything interesting?"

"I think so. Your family won numerous wine awards, and photographs chronicled your life from the cute kid to the striking young woman, to the most glamorous girl in the world."

She turned to him, her face deliberately dour, "Glamorous, aren't I?"

Gus grinned. Refreshed. Another hint that her guard was coming down. He said, "I saw you as an infant in your grandmother's arms, then in braces, probably until you were in your late teens. Quite the public life."

Facing ahead, she nodded, her smile faded. "Like a subject to the stalkers."

"Really? That bad?"

"It never seemed that way until it did. At seventeen, someone at a wine magazine asked my parents if they could photograph me holding our wine. They refused."

"Understandable?" Gus asked as he checked the rearview mirror. No tail.

"Gradually, I became the Marchitello girl. The face."

"The brand?"

"Apparently."

For these precious minutes, he was just a man driving a beautiful woman, lost in her interesting life story. "At some point, they gave in?" He turned left onto Wesley, approaching Peachtree Street and her church, the Christ the King, the Catholic Cathedral in Atlanta.

"Actually, no. I turned eighteen."

"Ah, bene."

"The decision was mine. The argument with my parents shifted to which designer I would wear."
~~~

"And?"

"They were either too young for my liking or too old for theirs. So, I drew my own and made them with my mother. I wore them on magazine covers, during television interviews, and photo shoots for articles—my business launched. Free advertising."

"Fascinating."

"What's fascinating is that you think I wouldn't notice that wrong turn back there."

Eyes widening.

"I've become proficient at studying maps."

"It wasn't a wrong turn. I wanted to let you finish."

"I know." Gina smiled. "I'm wise to you."

The phone vibrated in his pocket. The real world was calling.

She heard the hum repeating as he pulled to the curb, the parting moment awkward between them. "Go ahead, get that. I'll still be wise to you tomorrow." A smile, watching her step away, then looking back. Tomorrow seemed so far away.

On the phone screen: "Missed call from Robert Holder."

"Hi Bob. Anything?" Gus asked.

"Pogue is spooked." The word jarred him. So did his urgency.

"What happened?" Gus said.

"Don't know. I phoned her a few minutes ago. She shut me out. Yesterday, you saw her; she was on edge. Today, she's mute."

"Why would she do that?" Gus said.

"Why even answer my call?"

"Maybe to get this reaction. You're her friend. You're concerned and calling someone."

"Ya think?"

"Why else? She could be trying to tell you something."

"Will you call her? I want to know if she answers." Holder said.

Face wrinkling as he drove toward Henry's to check on Christian. "Sure. Text me her number, and I'll let you know."

What could spook Pogue? He had no answer, or even a theory. The text arrived, and he tapped the number in. She wasn't picking up when Gina's name popped onto the screen. He dropped the call to Pogue.

Gina started, "That man you asked about last night, with your friend from the hospital."

"What about him?"

"He just dropped off Melo." Carmelo's twenty-something son. "I was coming in the side entrance, and they pulled up, right after you. I noticed Melo, so I waited to let him in. He didn't see me. They kept talking. So, I waited a bit longer."

"Are you sure it was the same guy?"

"Yes."

"Okay," Gus said.

"They looked serious. Maybe they were arguing."

"Hm. And you don't know the guy?"

"No."

"Can you ask Carmelo?"

Gina exhaled. "Hmm, it's not my business."

"True. You're sure it was more than casual conversation?"

"Sì. Definitely not. I could see the other guy's face."

"Danke." Who was the guy, and what was he doing arguing with Melo? He collected himself. "It was nice to be with you today."

"You, too. Danke schön," Gina said and ended the call.

A blaring horn at the traffic light spurred him on, his mind racing through connections between Melo, the mystery man, and Sheehan. Distrust of Sheehan transferred like a contagion to this stranger. Only one thing mattered in this web—Gina. Carmelo had entrusted her to him, and if Melo was tangled with the wrong people, might she have some inadvertent exposure?

He turned right onto Thirteenth Street, pulled over in front of Holder Medical, and redialed Clair Pogue. Voicemail. A block later, at Juniper Street, another try. Same thing. At Peachtree and Thirteenth Street, he called again. She picked up. Startled to hear her whisper 'hello,' he hurried to speak when she added, "Not a good time."

"Holder called me. Are you okay?" Gus said.

Less commotion around her told him she had relocated. "Someone broke into my office."

Blood drained from his face. "When?"

"Last night. I could tell when I arrived this morning."

"Did you tell anyone?"

"No. There wasn't time. I had to get here." She scoffed, "Who would I tell?"

A hesitation. She was telling him. He considered telling her what happened to Christian and the Metro Atlanta guys going through his place. He didn't. Instead, he asked, "Was anything taken?"

"I'm not sure. My desk was disturbed, not ransacked, but someone had been there."

"Security? You could go to them."

"Whoever did this had to know about security."

"Right."

"That leaves Sheehan, Tanzilla, Slayton, maybe Steve James."

"For what? They know more than I do."

"They must think you have more."

"More of what? I'm leaving the hotel now. We're taking guests to the new wing."

"I have a favor to ask."

"Can it wait?"

Hurrying: "I need access to the GCI system to search for our data. Will you let me use your office?"

"I'm leaving." Impatience in her voice and background noise suggested guests were within earshot.

Pressing on: "Will you? IEEI and JCO, both next Friday. We're flying blind."

Pogue tried to sound pleasant. "Oh, let me spare you the trouble." Her voice lowered, "You can't win."

Voices around her became more distinct, with light banter and a few laughs.

Anxiously: "Is Sheehan working with Tanzilla, Slayton, and James?"

"Of course." Pogue sounded enthused momentarily until the space around her went quiet, and her voice dropped. "Stop digging. I know these people. Or they will stop you."

A horn blared. A woman's arms lifted in his rearview mirror, glaring at him. He turned north on Peachtree.

"Stay away," Pogue whispered.

Anxious, he fired off, "Data. Did the data ever exist?"

"I'm not sure."

"It's possible?"

"Yes."

"Did you see any?" he shot back.

A vehicle in reverse beeped near her.

Pogue's voice hushed: "No. Let. This. Go."

"Help me," Gus demanded, cramming his plea into the vanishing seconds of their call.

"Talk soon. Cheers." Pogue ended the call.

Pulling into a gas pump at Starvin' Marvin Mini-Mart, he pounded the Rover's steering wheel.

"If I had an assassin, I'd kill 'em all."

Chapter Nineteen

Clair Pogue's insistence that Gus 'Let. This. Go.' left him in a quandary—of all places—in the parking lot of a run-down Starvin' Marvin's convenience store. Despite his reaction to Opa on the Interpol call and his nagging curiosity about what sustained Opa's motivation for the Assignment, Gus felt compelled to call his grandfather. Gus valued his strategic mind.

When Opa's voice came through, he skipped the pleasantries and cut straight to the point: "Tell me why we're not on the offensive?"

"Meaning what, exactly?" Opa said.

"Whoever killed Elais has an assassin on call. Luckily, we've been tipped off, and I'm too close to the end to leave. So why aren't we capitalizing on our resources?"

"I spoke to Mitch Scales. You and the girl are getting a security detail. Stay at Henry's as much as possible. Don't travel together. If you go anywhere, they'll take you."

Heart rate jumping, though he knew better than to object.

"Done. Why don't we go on the offensive? Nab someone at GCI and get answers."

"That's not how we operate."

"No, instead, we live in fear. Agent Baumann has to get info from the assassin so we can strike back."

"Whoa." Opa's voice softened. "What's wrong? What's changed?"

"My list of suspects is growing."

"You need to narrow it to one?"

"It's not one. It's a group. And time is short. Why not hire some guns and cut them down? That would send a message not to mess with us."

"That would send a message that we're up to the task, which we-are-not."

"Or, look over your shoulder. We're on to you."

"You're talking about striking pre-emptively, and I'm telling you to focus, finish, and move on. Let the Interpol lady do her job."

"What if whoever got to Elias gets here first?"

"Do you want to leave now?"

A pause, "No. I want to consider more aggressive action."

"Focus all your aggression on finishing the Assignment. That is your one and only business. Mind your business."

"But..."

"No buts," Opa interrupted. "Play the game you know. Period. You can't win their game; that's why it's theirs. Scales will have your back."

The firmness in Opa's tone and logic triggered ambivalence. His voice wavered between resignation and reluctance. Gus said, "You tell Scales to make sure his men are armed. Geez, half the people on the street in this city are armed."

Reflecting on Opa's direction, an elderly man pushed against the glass door to leave Starvin Marvin's and limped past as he counted lottery tickets—would extending his life appeal to him? Nearby, young men burst into laughter, full of vitality and oblivious to their mortality. At what age did the fantasy of immortality fade? Yesterday, these strangers didn't exist in his world. Today, they embodied the very questions that perplexed him. Would *he* want to live forever?

If this was what my future looks like—no thank you to immortality. Why extend my life when I'm not even living it? But—the vision is too clear. I can't make myself stop. I want time with my friends—to laugh without calculating every word, to have a candlelit dinner and an honest conversation with a woman I care about. Just one. An evening where I'm not playing a role or protecting a secret. I know it will come. Would tonight be asking too much?

The clock on his dashboard prompted thoughts back to this time yesterday. At GCI, he was unaware of the convenience store's existence. But the old man existed every day, maybe in that neighborhood. Why were their paths crossing? But for the conversation with Dr. Pogue, he would have just driven past?

The car beside him started with a thunderous clap. It rolled backwards, thumping from its missing muffler, wobbling on a substandard spare tire, its front quarter panel mangled, and headlamp shattered, giving pause. Cracked, oil-stained asphalt and a shallow pothole narrowed his focus to contrast. Opa was in the large empty house looking out over Lake Geneva, his dinner finished, his night ending. At this stage, each tomorrow had some uncertainty. Would Opa want this device? He didn't ask for it. Did the fantasy or illusion of immortality fade at some point in a person's life that a thirty-year-old could not yet appreciate? Cool air from a car that no one entering or leaving this establishment could likely afford struck his face. Was comfort the objective?

The voices in his head ticked off in rapid succession, like a carnival wheel spinning: Pogue demanding he stop digging, Opa ordering him to finish, Bobby saying to sell as is, Christian needing cash, Helene wanting him at PDK airport, Henry wishing he'd invented something else, and—he gasped—Gina. Her image flared, then faded. The wheel made one last turn. Opa's voice commanded, 'Play the game you know,' and his heart sank to his belt. Finishing the Assignment depended on what he loathed most: deceit and deception.

Craig Jones's voicemail played on his speaker: "Cash is still king. Triple time. Two teams on your mold. Production on Tuesday. I still need that loan. Later."

Thoughts shifted to Tuesday, his trip to GMC in Dahlonega, and Jones's voicemail. With the right quantities, he might pull off the miracle. Encouraged, a new timeline formed. Do IEEI and the biofeedback data matter? Is that his business? No. JCO mattered. JCO held the keys to his future. Driving toward his house. No more waiting.

~~~

On the apron to the driveway at Henry's house, Gus spied a silver-haired, stubby man in the brick security office beyond the gates. As instructed by Henry, Mitch Scales had installed a security guard who questioned Gus through the intercom, then waved him through.

Around back, unaware that Christian was napping on Cassie's couch beneath the sweep of the paddle fan inside the screened-in porch, his footsteps marching up the stairs startled her.

The gym bag in his hand prompted the question, "Where have you been?"

"Home."

Her eyes widened. "Take me home."

"We're staying here. We're each getting a security detail."

Sitting up, defiant: "I'm not staying here. I'm going after the data."

Her posture, her tone, and her attitude made him cringe. "They're not mutually exclusive. You can stay here, which is smart, and you can keep
~~~

working on getting the data, which is also smart, and more likely to be achieved if you are safe."

She ignored the comment. "What did Pogue say?"

"I caught her at a bad time. She's still an option."

Seated on the edge of the couch, Christian shook her head. "Pogue's done. No one cares what that old lady thinks."

That may be true, he thought, but apparently, whoever searched her office wants something she has.

Gina's name appeared on his phone. As if to justify walking away, he showed Christian his screen and opened the door to the kitchen."

Christian mumbled, "Puppy love," and lay down.

Voice tense and low, Gina told him: "Carmelo and Melo are across the hall in the business office. Arguing."

"I don't know that office."

"It's across from my apartment. It used to be Melo's. He runs their other businesses out of there."

"Okay."

"They're arguing about the guy who dropped him off. The guy you were asking about. His name is Vinnie."

Pacing around the kitchen. The name meant nothing.

"They must be in business together," Gina said.

'Mind your business' played in his head. "Do you feel comfortable listening in on them?"

"Tss, it can't be avoided, they're arguing. Anyone could hear."

"Take notes and tell tomorrow. Thanks for the call."

Gus called Holder, walking past Christian, snoring, toward the pool to talk.

Holder picked up and the words rushed out: "Pogue's upset because someone went through her office last night."

"My money is on Tanzilla and his ilk. ASCO is the NCI hates every CAM department."

"I think she'll be fine, but our IEEI interview may be dead," Gus said. "Don't tell Christian."

"She needs that interview," Holder said.

"What's eating her?"

"Can't say. Swore I wouldn't. She needs the cash flow."

"Personal?"

"Yeah."

Switching subjects: "I'm focusing on Bobby and the mat."

"Glad to hear that. Why stay in this fight if you don't have to? Money is money."

"How well do you know Sheehan?"

"I don't. Pogue has never liked her. She could fill you in."

"Not today."

Their call ended, and he stretched out on the chaise again… the same towel for a pillow. The midday sun fell behind the tall pines opposite the pool, and his overloaded mind went blank. Moments later, asleep, cinematic reels projected in his head like a fever dream. A game table materialized, its jigsaw puzzle pieces erupting into chaos. Pieces shifted in dizzying ways—Carmelo and Melo materializing, at odds with each other, Gina's sophisticated silhouette hovering over the main dining room, Christian at the bar, desperate for money, and a man in a dark suit, dark hair, dark glasses, alone in a corner, seated with a rifle propped against the wall, a wry smile on his face. Mitch Scales entered the elevator as Marco Tanzilla stepped off, looking for him. A faceless man in a black tuxedo approached Gina and said, "He wouldn't listen." Gina walked over to a space between two tables; Bobby and Suzanne, friends and classmates he used to have fun with, were roaring, their plates gorged with food, as bottles lined the table and glasses brimmed over. Bobby raised his glass, "To immortality." Laughter swelled. Gina and the faceless man looked down on him, dead on the floor, his grey hands crossed on his abdomen, a statue of a Trojan Horse in his grip. Gina told the faceless man, "He wouldn't listen to me either."

The dream ended, and he bolted upright, eyes wide, breath coming in gasps as he stared at the motionless pool water. A frantic minute passed. Crashing backwards, he squeezed his face, tracking a descending airliner on the clear blue canvas.

Reality set in, but his heart pounded. His breathing stabilized. He was worried. Life wasn't a dream; it was fragile and anything but boring.

Chapter Twenty

While Gus wrestled with his next moves, in the 19th Hole at the Atlanta Country Club, "Dad" appeared on Henry's phone. Two calls from his father on the same day? Henry stepped outside and said, "Dad? Everything alright?"

"Gus is an exceptional young man," Opa began.

Henry furrowed his brow at the contemplative tone and moved to a quiet spot between the patio and the practice range. "He is."

"My life has been so long, Henry." A twinge of melancholy crept into his voice. "I gave up after the pacemaker. It seemed enough."

"And it was enough, Dad. You have saved countless lives over the years. Don't..."

"I quit, Henry. I could have done more. I should have..

Henry paced toward the end of the practice area. "Dad, don't do this."

Silence hovered. "What Elias and I did is nothing like what Gus has done. Stem cells. Trypsin. Binary codes of their frequency. What on Earth is that," Opa said.

"Yeah, well, you didn't have cell phones to call me anytime, from anywhere either. Times change, Dad."

"Henry. What would happen if people lived longer? Indefinitely? Economically, I mean. Not just with cancer cured, but with cellular regeneration?"

Something in his father's tone gave pause. "Initially? Market disruption across healthcare, insurance, and retirement systems. Eventually, a new equilibrium would happen through all sectors."

"And if I used such a device?" Opa's voice was deliberately casual.

The question landed like a stone. "Dad?"

Heavy silence.

"Is this academic curiosity, or is there something you're not telling me?"

A sigh. "I have stage four pancreatic cancer. Diagnosed a month ago."

Eyes closing, head dropping. The revelation explained too much—Opa's insistence on the Assignment's completion, his unusual urgency.

"Does Gus know?"

"No. And he mustn't." Opa's voice turned firm. "This isn't about me. It never was."

"But if his device works—"

"That's what I'm asking you. I looked into the men he cited, the doctor in New York. Nicholas Gonzalez. His record with pancreatic cancer is impressive. I see Gus based his work on Gonzolez. Should I go see the guy in New York, or would his device give me more time...then, if I decide I've lived long enough, could I just... disconnect?"

Henry stopped. The sound of clubs striking golf balls faded, and his head dropped. On death's doorstep, his father sought his son's counsel, and his learned son felt inept. Wallowing in a crucible of humiliation, the ethical and moral arguments Henry had pounded Gus with had evaporated. His gaze turned to the lush green, manicured golf course, where he'd be but for the Interpol call. Just moments ago, upon arrival, he and Cassie learned a dear friend's father in Tuscaloosa, had lost a long, gruesome fight with cancer that morning. Helpless, all Henry could mutter to his dying father was, "That's a question for Gus."

"I don't want to tell him. He needs to finish."

"Tell him, Dad." Henry thought back to their muted conversations. "He has to hear it from you soon."

"I owe it to him, don't I?"

On more levels than Henry wanted to explain. "You do." Henry recalled Gus's comments after the Interpol call, "But for Gus sticking it out over here, you may not have this option. Thanks to him, it's your best choice."

"They've said they can't do anything for me."

"Dad, do you want to live or are you ready to go?"

"I want to live. I want to be here."

"Then we need to get you a device, either here or there."

"Preferably here. Even flying scares me."

"We'll get it worked out. You call Gus. Tell him what you told me. See what he thinks."

"Thank you, son," Opa said.

Henry stuffed his phone in his pocket and turned to see the activities of the prestigious club unaffected by his life-changing phone call or the welling up in his eyes.

At four-thirty, he carried a packaged biofeedback device out of Holder Medical alongside Gus toward Cassie, waiting in her Lexus LS. At five o'clock, she pulled onto the tarmac at Peachtree Dekalb Airport, where Henry boarded the Geneva-bound chartered jet Helene reserved through her company, Elias Aviation.

~~~

Back at her home with Gus in the passenger's seat, the guard in the gatehouse announced, "Ms. Lawler left with a State Trooper."

"Left? Again?" Gus leaned to his left to see the guard.

The guard said, "A trooper arrived, asked me to notify her, and I did. She walked out, and they drove off."

He checked. No message on his phone. He dialed her.

Cassie pulled around back and parked.

His call went to voicemail. "She's on her own."

"Gone rogue?" Cassie said.

"I can't babysit her. I've got enough on my plate," Gus said.

~~~

Dinner consisted of crunchy fried chicken prepared by Cassie's domestic help, Minnie James. She'd honed her southern culinary skills at Ma Hull's boarding house in Inman Park. When Ma Hull's closed, Henry, a Friday customer, hired her. Their children were young, and Cassie preferred the Junior League at that time. For the past ten years, they provided Minnie with a Lincoln Town Car shuttle service five days a week since her husband, Earnest, died.

The comfort of Minnie's home cooking brought back memories of early days in their home while still grieving and expanding his English with his cousins. Minnie served the chicken warm, not hot, with collard greens, fried okra, and buttery mashed potatoes. She offered one drink choice: the original Coca-Cola in a sixteen-ounce glass bottle.

The sun had not set when his head hit the pillow of cousin Margo's bed on the third floor. Henry had a standing invitation to call if he ran into difficulties.

Margo's room had blackout curtains, an essential part of her migraine therapy, which Cassie never changed. Sleep lasted until seven o'clock. Coffee drew him to the kitchen, where Cassie read the Atlanta Journal-Constitution Sunday Edition.

Looking up from her paper, she sipped coffee and smiled at his casual attire. "Is today Lake Day?"

"Yes, and I may just stay there." Coffee poured black and full.

"You better account for some of them," Cassie said, motioning toward the driveway.

Gus went through the porch to spy two dark SUVs and four of Mitch Scales's security agents.

Inside, he said to Cassie, "I forgot." An exhale.

"Go with it. Besides, your uncle and your grandfather would appreciate it. And Helene and I."

"Has Henry called?" Taking a seat on a stool at the island.

Cassie nodded and sipped her coffee. "Five-thirty."

"He got it hooked up?"

Cassie nodded. "Says he looks better than he expected. He's decided to stay."

"How long?"

She shook her head.

He'd just seen him on Friday during the conference call. He looked tired, but how would he know what an eighty-five-year-old man would look like midday?

Cassie added, "Until he's convinced his father is going to live or die."

He cocked his head, "This may be the most important case study of my life."

Their eyes met. "His, too," Cassie said.

She folded the paper and set it aside. "Henry's worried about you. He told me a bit about your research on top of the Interpol call. How are you doing with all that?"

"It was a kick in the gut." He paused. "I called Opa." He raised his eyebrows and shook his head. "I was in a Starvin' Marvin parking lot." Gnawing at his lower lip, eyes glazing. "He gave me the best advice ever, but he didn't tell me he was dying."

Cassie let the comment hang.

"Yeah, but he called to ask you for help."

"Thanks to Henry."

"Well, he did it. And thanks to you, he's got hope."

An exhale and a blank stare at the newspaper. "If the Interpol lady hadn't called, I would not have let on what I am working on; I had a milestone picked out for when I would tell you all, in a few months. In a few months, Opa would have withered away and died."

Cassie nodded and smiled, "Henry told me a little about your call."

He tilted his head at her. "I just can't get my left brain around how bizarre this is. If this assassin doesn't kill the exec in Spain, he doesn't get nabbed. If he doesn't get nabbed, he has no grounds to bargain for his life and goes back to being a baker. The Interpol agent is none the wiser, and none of this happens. The exec dies, and Opa lives. How crazy is that?"

"I'm not sure it's crazy at all. I always say everything is just the way it's supposed to be. You know why?"

Gus shook his head.

"Because it is."

"Well," he said, "Did you ever think Christian would be sleeping in your house again?"

A snicker. "While I was here? No."

Gus took his mug to the sink, rinsed it out, and looked out at the small huddle on the driveway. "She'll be out for a while. Will you make some more coffee?"

"I didn't hear her come in."

"She had an escort. It may have been the guard at the gate. He practically carried her up the steps. She lost it at the top, which woke me. I came to my door but didn't go out to help."

"You're getting smarter."

"I heard the shower. The guy put her in, talked her through it, then put her to bed."

"And you're leaving her here while you go to the lake with G-Mar?"

An exhale. "Yes. And I am so thankful. Not too keen on the chaperones, but it is what it is."

"Be safe. I'm sure Henry will call if he needs you."

"I'll call them," He said, leaning over to kiss Cassie's forehead. "Thanks for letting us stay here." He headed off to meet the security detail, thinking of Gina.

Chapter Twenty-One

Executive Security service agents employed by Mitch Scales converted the storage room into command central. The space spanned the front width of the house, abutting the garage. They had neatly arranged Henry's lawn equipment and assorted tools in one of the three parking bays. He observed them as he descended the steps. A brunette in black slacks and a pale blue cotton pullover under a linen waistcoat introduced herself, ACE, her initials. Her assistant, a guy about Gus's age, average height, stocky, with closely cropped hair, thicker on top, eschewed the predictable security look. He wore taupe slacks and a cream-colored polo shirt with an ESS logo. Except for the weapon on his right ankle and the bulge beneath ACE's linen coat, they looked like normal people.

ACE explained the arrangement. His role was to do as she told him. No debate. No politics or pulling rank. He was to assume the best if a situation occurred unless told otherwise. She and her partner, Mr. Mop Top, Dan Kaufman, whom she called Danno, would assume the worst. If there was going to be a hero, it was her or Kaufmann, not him. A succinct bio followed. Scales poached ACE from the NSA, where she worked as a threat analyst. "She sees things you and I can't," Danno said. He, ACE explained, earned his shield in corporate security at a California Tech firm, protecting executives and intellectual property.

Opa, no doubt, experience told him, had sent Mitch Scales a sheet outlining his requirements. "May I speak?" Gus said.

ACE gave one quick nod. "Speak."

"You realize this is precautionary? I'm not in any real danger."

Deadpan: "That's what they want you to think."

Loaded into the back seat of the dark grey Chevy Tahoe: "A bit of a cliché, the dark Tahoe."

Kaufman tilted his head toward him. "The only vehicle wrapped in a lightweight ceramic armor and multilayered polycarbonate ballistic-resistant plastics. You'd survive an IED and probably an RPG." Danno shifted farther in his seat. "Never needed this in my tech gig. Different kinds of threats. More digital. Less kinetic."

Gus tapped the window and scanned the interior, satisfied. "I hope I don't need it. But I'm glad to have it."

ACE typed Angelo's address into the navigation displayed on the dashboard.

"The person we're going to pick up is not expecting this."

"Brief them," ACE said, looking in the rearview mirror.

Certain his text would require explanations he wasn't prepared to provide, he typed a message to Gina and hit SEND.

Seconds later, Gina flashed on his screen. "Kidding?"

"I wish. I'll explain later."

Looking in the mirror: "Tell her Danno will come to her; don't come to us."

"Really?"

A stare back. Mind reading time— "No debate. No Questions."

The message was typed verbatim.

The drive to Bobby's property took forty-seven minutes. Forty-seven quiet minutes with texting back and forth, inches apart.

ACE slowed her approach as the GPS route ended at the gravel driveway blocked by a shiny green barn gate. Bobby answered the call, activated the release, and opened the gate. Sumptuous tulip poplars, hickories, and large oaks filled in the flat land. More tranquil than Bobby's description. The sound of chainsaws and woodchippers excited him. His land was cleared. He designed his home, but rarely saw it being built.

Gus shifted to the space between the front seats to point to a place beside Bobby's truck near the mobile home they used for temporary housing.

In the distance, two men with chainsaws prepared to fell a tree. A heavyset man wearing an orange headset maneuvered a mid-sized tractor. He dragged a trimmed tree to the portable mill, where a hoist lifted it to the conveyor platform. The pitch climbed when the blade struck the hardwood, and Gina jumped.

Bobby noticed the unfamiliar vehicle and left the men to their work.

Doors opening.

"Hold it," ACE announced. "We need to identify ourselves."

"I'll introduce you."

"Wait," ACE called out, but it was too late. Bobby had already smacked his old Braves hat against his thigh and created a cloud of dust as he shouted out to his friends.

ACE and Danno stepped out as Suzanne, expecting, emerged from the mobile home, leading a boy no more than three. The women embraced. They'd met once before, two weeks earlier at dinner before a Braves game where Bobby threw out the first pitch. Gina chatted with young Robbie while Bobby gave Gus a manly-quick embrace, and motioned toward the two strangers beside the Tahoe.

Explanations followed, and Bobby's mood shifted from effusive to curious.

"Can we go someplace and talk?" Gus said.

Bobby looked around and motioned toward a patch of ground cleared recently. Whining chainsaws and a buzzing mill prompted Gus to motion to the Tahoe.

ACE and Danno stayed still against the front grill, their eyes tracking the two men behind their aviator sunglasses.

In the back seats, Gus said, "Without going into the details, Christian and I ran into a buzz saw of our own on Friday."

"She told me," Bobby said.

"When?"

"Friday."

"What did she say?"

"That GCI kicked you out on technicalities. She had her conspiracy theory hat on."

After listening to the description she gave Bobby and the amiable tone in his voice, Gus decided there was no way to sugarcoat what he came to say. "Bobby, I haven't told you everything about the mat."

"I figured as much."

Surprised: "Why?"

"Cause you the smartest guy I know, and fair. You heard me out."

If Bobby only knew…

Bobby continued, "I put it out there Friday. You know my circumstances." A nod toward Suzanne. "I trust you. We're more than friends. You're a brother to me. If you see a reason to put the JCO deal off…"

A shake of the head. "I don't…"

Bobby raised his hand and patted his shoulder. "It's okay. It's your call. I just have a request."

Sitting still.

Bobby steadied his eyes. "Buy me out."

He shook his head.

Bobby's shoulder dropped.

Gus said, "Not yet. I'm not saying I won't… I'm saying I won't ask you to risk anything. I believe a buyout right now is an unnecessary risk on *your* part."

"I ain't got no fallback plan." A motion toward the property. "Got this and a decent nut from baseball, but that ain't forever. I'm countin' on them royalties to keep us going."

"I want you to get them…over a distinguished career, and more."

Head shaking. Eyes widening. "You're putting a lot of faith in me, my man."

Tension crossed the chasm between them. "How about this? You come with me on Tuesday morning to GMC in Dahlonega. They're making a fabric mat to replace the current one. Dr. Lee and I designed it. It's the only one of its kind. It will amaze you and JCO." A hand on his chest. "Bobby, I promise. It's worth waiting. See it for yourself, then decide."

Bobby studied his face.

Gus extended his hand. "Decide on Tuesday."

They shook.

Relieved, for the moment, Gus said, "Now show us around." Ready to pretend all was well for the next hour.

~~~

An hour later, ACE turned onto the winding concrete driveway lined by native azalea and rhododendron shrubs.

"Lovely," Gina's voice oozed with appreciation.

Tall Laurels, mature Poplars, and Hickories provided the verdant privacy to the two-story brick home built on the multiple lots the size of a football field. Situated on the street side of midfield, he preferred to call it "a house on the lake" rather than a "lake house." Unlike Bobby's raw property, this landscape contained open grassy space, front and back, that sloped from the road to the water's edge of Lake Lanier. There were three brilliant red, dynamite Crape
~~~

Myrtles near the right corner of the house. The manicured lawn looked like one on a turf commercial.

Kaufman's head nodded gently.

"Explain the lay of the land to me," ACE said.

"Alarm system. Master bedroom, second floor. No basement." Gus pointed. "Garage holds a small SUV, lawn equipment, and bikes.

"Rear of the property?" Danno said.

"Open. Boat on a lift."

"Fences?"

"No."

"Neighbors?"

"Nice people on the right. Never met the people on the left. Can't see their home."

ACE scanned the tree line methodically. "Water access is always a vulnerability. Two approaches minimum—one by boat, one through those trees to the east."

Kaufman checked sight lines to the house.

"Monitor all ingress points. See if you can detect any existing surveillance equipment."

He raised his eyebrows, glanced at Gina, then said, "You think someone's watching? Here?"

ACE maintained her neutral expression. "I never think. I know, or I verify. Better to allocate time to check now than explain a breach later."

"Check the house first, 'cause we're going in. Then, I'm going to drop the boat in the water and head out onto the lake."

ACE looked in the mirror to see his raised eyebrows. He handed Danno the key to the front door. "Security code is 8962455."

~~~

Thirty minutes later. Outside the no-wake zone. The throttles pressed on his twin-engine Grady-White. The force pinned Gina's torso to the plush seat beside him at the helm. Clutching her cover-up and the Atlanta Technology & Research Institute visor he had provided: "That's powerful."

"Too much?"
~~~

Her eyes showed excitement. Head shaking and an accelerating motion with her arm.

Laughter. "I have to show restraint; it's a lot for this lake. I try to get the most of my time here."

She surveyed the landscape, propping her feet on a handhold. "I'm getting a different impression of Atlanta."

A nod.

"And a different impression of you."

A shrug and glance back at the deep wake. In the process, a stolen glance at her, and she stole one back. They laughed.

"What?"

Arms stretching out to the wind. "This is so fun."

As she lowered her arms, she patted his back. Contact. A flinch. Looking over his shoulder.

"Thank you," she said, just loud enough to be heard.

Anxiously: "I hope they're having a good time back at the house."

Eyes rolling. "You're safe out here. I'll protect you."

The next fifteen minutes belonged to the engines' hypnosis. The wind was blowing over the glass-like water, and the temperate mid-morning sun was a quarter of the way off the horizon. Throttle back, the engines purred. "This is my favorite spot. It's called a cove." The ground formed a long tapering inlet. "No one comes here."

Looking around, there were no boats in sight. She looked back and smiled.

The electric anchor disrupted the silence. When it hit bottom, the motor stopped, and silence returned.

Soon, the wide, stable vessel held steady in the faint breeze, and the anchor line pulled taut. Sandals kicked off and a move from under the hard top to the bow. "Shade or sun?"

"Sun, for the moment. Then, I believe I promised you a swim."

A grin, hoping she hadn't seen the conspicuous swallowing motion she had just caused.

"When you're ready, let me know. I'll test the water first."

"What a gentleman."

If she only knew.

Reclined on the bow cushions opposite him, she fastened her hair back, tipped her visor, and adjusted her sunglasses. She had a seductive allure that rendered him speechless. She shifted her hips and hiked her cover up to sun her thighs. A shift in his seat.

His only hope to maintain composure was to bring up Melo and Carmelo's argument.

"They stopped talking right after I called you," Gina said. "I cracked my door to check on them at the same time Melo was leaving with a long box."

"Did you hear anything about the Vinnie guy?"

"Carmelo said, 'I'm done with Vinnie. Whatever it takes. I'm done. Do what you want. I'm done.'"

"Wow. They have something going on."

"They must. But that's all I know." A motion toward the lake. "You want to check the water."

Two floats retrieved, tossed in, and the ladder dropped on the swimming platform. A minute later, bobbing behind the boat: "Perfect."

Positioning herself at the edge. "Here I come."

Giddiness inside.

She loosened her cover-up and let it fall to her feet.

Could he not stare?

As she climbed down the ladder, he admired her with a mix of appreciation and restraint. Each deliberate step she took revealed more of her confidence than her scantily clad body.

A flutter in his chest.

She straddled her float and offered her hand.

He accepted it. "Do you remember all the rules you laid down the first night you thought I was a geek?"

A grin and head shake, jesting. "Standard operating procedure."

Hand waving. "And now? How would you describe this little display?"

A chuckle. "Non-standard operating procedure."

"Good. I didn't want to be accused of breaking any rules."

"Is there one in particular you're considering?"

"No," laughter, "more like one I'm not considering."

"Oh, well, I told you yesterday; we have all afternoon."

Pulling her closer with his legs.

On the boat console, his phone rang. Eyes closing.

"You could let that go," Gina said.

Henry and ACE popped into his head. "I could also check it out and come back."

"Okay."

Climbing the ladder. The call ended. The screen read Missed call MITCH SCALES. A voicemail ding sounded. "We're in at GCI. Today, during the three o'clock shift change. Or, eleven tonight. I have things to prep. Call me ASAP. Timing is crucial." Looking at Gina and replaying the words, 'timing is crucial.' The phone read five till one. Calling Mitch. Scales laid out the plan in great detail, apologizing for the short notice, offering, "I can reschedule it later in the week." A deep breath and imagining Opa dying in Geneva, reminding him to "Mind your business." There was no skipping this. And there was Christian. Maybe it's a bust, and there is no data, but he promised her he'd do all he could. Maybe they get busted in the process. Another look at Gina, who was looking back at him, and saying to Scales, "I'll be there." The call ended with a feigned smile. "Duty calls."

Her face fell, "Am I getting out?"

A nod. "I'm so sorry. This can't wait."

Positioning himself on the platform to assist her. When she stood, he wrapped a towel around her shoulders, and the boat shifted. She leaned into him, her chest touching his torso.

Her face tilted to him, her voice soft. "You've gone from geek to mysterious."

"Me? You're the mysterious one."

Her eyes pierced him. That smile—different now. His heart pounding, his chest tightening. It took all his restraint not to draw her shoulders to him and kiss her. He took a deep inhale, hoping she felt the same way.

Chapter Twenty-Two

Standing at the helm with Gina silently beside him, he texted Cedric to confirm his availability. His message to ACE was: "Heading back. Be ready."

Cedric fired back a black thumbs-up emoji, and his shoulders relaxed.

He could feel her stare. Though tempted to look at her one last time, he kept his hands firm on the helm, his eyes fixed on the bow as he pressed the anchor toggle. The motor whined under strain. Each grinding chain link echoed the weight of the GCI expulsion and Interpol call. The thud of the secure anchor snapped him back to reality. Despite the urgency, the engines hummed with unexpected calmness. The scent of her sunscreen mingled with the aroma of grilled meat on a passing houseboat. He scanned the lake, now dotted with boats pulling skiers, wakeboarders, and children in tubes being slingshot across the water.

She touched his hip, startling him.

Through his sunglasses, he caught her gaze and grinned.

"May I ask you something?"

A nod.

"You said you would explain the security situation. I sense there is more to it. Yes?"

He faced ahead, pondering and raising his index finger, buying a moment to decide. "News that my father's death was not an accident arrived yesterday. Security is a precaution taken by my grandfather."

"Your father was murdered?" Her voice dropped.

"Yes."

"Why? Is someone targeting you now?"

The engines shifted into idle, and his gaze swept across the lake. He placed his hand on her shoulder. "This is why I can't answer your questions honestly. The truth puts people at risk, which is why I lie about my work."

"Wow. From geek to mysterious to deceptive."

His chin lifted in objection. "I prefer 'self-preservation.'"

She considered this, then nodded. "Okay. I can live with that." She dropped her chin and lifted her eyes. "I'm back to mysterious."

They stowed the floats, folded towels, and handed off the packed cooler at the dock with their uneaten lunch and untouched drinks. "We can eat on the road."

Inside his house, he took steps two at a time and rummaged through his closet until he found long chino pants, a solid white pullover, and casual lace-up shoes.

Leaving his driveway, he inhaled deeply and replayed Scales's voice: "We're in at GCI." When ACE passed the turnoff to Bobby's, he imagined how stressful Bobby's life had to be to ask for the buyout. He reached over, touched Gina's shoulder, and squeezed gently. She turned from the bucolic countryside and smiled. "What are you thinking?" he whispered.

She shrugged.

"Are you being mysterious?" Gus said.

She flashed an endearing grin, patted his hand, and turned back to the window.

Just as he was about to doze off, his vibrating phone cut through the monotony of the road noise. Christian.

"Yes," he whispered.

"Where are you?"

"Heading back from Lanier. You?"

"In my office. I've linked every missing unit to an address, except the missing one. Soon, I'll be in GCI's system and contact each patient."

"How? If they catch you now, we'll lose everything—the data, our credibility, any chance of proving the device works."

"You'll see. I'm not waiting for my breaks, Gus. I'm making them."

"Don't make things worse."

"I'm not. We're getting back in at GCI. A complete do-over."

His body stiffened. She had grounds to brag. "Says who?"

"My contact."

"When?"

"Soon."

"I'm working on another angle. In case yours falls through." The call ended. The Tahoe went silent.

He turned to find Gina looking at him. She started to speak, then stopped. A slight grin formed, she raised her hand, and said, "No more questions."

He whispered, "No more lies."

The word "lie" conjured an image of Opa in his mind, which prompted a text to Henry: "How is everything there?"

If Opa died, would he stop? He told himself. Wrong. Opa wasn't going to die because his device worked. He'd seen animals left for dead bounce back. That wasn't enough. A large sample study was needed. The mat study with JCO would accomplish that, and if it worked, he'd sell the mat to healthy people. Wouldn't Henry love that?

Henry responded, "He's weak. Spirits are good. Very grateful to you, both of us. Be careful. The world needs your device. Markets be damned."

Reading the note again, a lump formed in his throat, his eyes welled up and his head nodded imperceptibly.

ACE pulled to the curb outside Angelo's, and glanced in the rearview mirror. "Danno will do this."

Gus started to object.

"Look around," ACE said firmly. "This is the city."

Danno swung open the rear door.

Gina extended her hand to Gus and said, "I can get a ride to the airport."

"Not a chance," Gus said. "I marked my calendar back in June."

"Really, you don't have to."

"I'd like to." He gave her hand a gentle squeeze. "Sorry about today."

She wrinkled her face to say it was no bother. "I had fun."

Danno escorted her to the side entrance.

Mitch Scales called. "We're in a white box van marked Doco's Tacos. Bad weather is supposed to blow through right when we need to be there."

"What's the weather got to do with it?"

"Maybe nothing."

"Hopefully nothing. I need in."

"More important—you'll need a way out. Storms like this take out power. That can create chaos." Scales paused. "The only chaos I like is the chaos I create."

Chapter Twenty-Three

The storm hit on time. Blinding rain and volatile winds pummeled southeast Atlanta, forcing the Tahoe to crawl behind the GCI Medical Complex. Squinting at the radar on his phone, Gus checked the weather pattern. "Not much longer."

"That's it," Danno said when the headlights struck the Doco's Tacos delivery truck backed into the loading dock.

Cedric studied the buildings. "No power."

A call to Mitch's phone failed. No connection.

"Cell towers come back first," Cedric said.

Georgia Power trucks idled on the far border of the lot behind the illuminated hospital. The storm's winds buffeted the Tahoe, rifling refuse bins off the dock. The storm cycled through torrential downpours and brief lulls before finally clearing to unexpected sunshine—a stark contrast to the Sunday afternoon Gus had planned at the lake. Now, he waited, questioning if the plan he'd set in motion still made sense. Did he need to commit a felony when Christian promised to deliver the same information? The rain delay felt like a warning.

The driver of the Taco truck emerged and tapped on the driver's window. ACE lowered it. "You dropping off?"

"Who are you?" ACE asked.

Rolling down his window behind her, Gus leaned forward. "You know Mitch?"

"Gus Meier?"

A nod from Gus.

"Follow me."

Gus and Cedric climbed four slick steps to the loading platform, rain pelting their backs. Pounding on the image of lettuce and cheese in the crunchy taco shell laminated on the delivery truck's door, Gus waited.

The door swung open. Inside, the taco truck's facade gave way to the sleek, modern finishes of a covert operations vehicle.

Scales and his crew, dressed in dark clothes and headsets, huddled near a computer and electronic equipment on a metal desk bolted to the floor.

He turned to see Gus, then Cedric, and frowned. "He's not going in."

"What?" Gus straightened.

"I can't hide him," Scales said flatly.

Deadpan, Cedric told Scales, "My momma couldn't hide me." All eyes traveled to his bushy head, unkempt beard, and imposing girth. "I never played hide and seek. Just seek." His shot at humor fell flat.

Scales said to his team, "Plan B." He motioned Gus to a folding chair. "He sits there." Cedric was directed to a solid metal chair next to the desk and equipment.

"That man is Casey," Scales told Gus, nodding at the lean guy with grey hair walking toward Gus with a headset. "He's my eyes and ears. We talk. You listen."

Casey put the headset on Gus, fastened the battery pack, and did a sound check.

"Casey will meet with our man inside. Get to the Compliance Officer's office. Access that computer." Scales turned to Cedric. "You take over once he's in."

Cedric nodded.

Leaning toward Gus, Scales continued. "You switch with Casey. Get what you came to get, and leave."

Swallowing hard, Gus told Scales, "The files I need may be buried. They may not exist."

Scales stared at Gus. "Once you go through that door, I'm a voice in a truck...driving away if I must, to play another day." Scales paused. "Speed is your friend, time is your enemy. Stay till they open for all I care."

"Base to recon. Power status?" Scales spoke into his mic.

"No power."

Checking his phone, Scales found no signal.

He sat beside Gus and watched him wipe his wet palms on his pants. "You want in the Compliance Officer offices, correct?"

Another nod from Gus.

Scales crossed his legs.

The last time Gus faced Donna Sheehan, she used the element of surprise to pounce on him. Tonight, the surprise belonged to him; if he could help it, she'd be none the wiser.

Outside, blaring sirens announced the steady arrival of EMS wagons.

An hour passed, then two. The van remained silent.

At six o'clock, an update came: "Recon to base. Lots of activity. No power. Cell service is back."

"We need power for routers. Too risky to transmit over cell towers." Mitch Scales said, "Stay or go?"

Rubbing his face, Gus considered his options. Hours ago, he'd been drawing Gina close in sun-warmed water. Now he sat poised to cross a line that could destroy everything—his career, his freedom, any chance with Gina. But Christian's bound and terrified face flashed in his mind, and his promise to get the data echoed in his ears.

"Stay," he said finally.

They continued waiting.

At five past six, Scales's radio crackled. "Power restored in the MOB."

Scales nodded to Casey. "Let's get a move on."

Coming to attention as if being asked to dive from a plane behind enemy lines, Gus felt his heart rate spike.

Scales took him by the shoulders. "You've got this." He and Casey stepped onto the loading dock, and Scales said, "Remember, in and out. Nobody knows you were here."

Looking past him at Cedric, Gus wondered: but are the files there? If ever Cedric could win at hide and seek, let it be now.

On the loading dock, a Hispanic man, no bigger than a jockey, peered through the window in the exterior door at eye level. Casey approached, Gus followed, and the door opened slowly.

"Pedro?" Casey said.

He nodded. "Casey?"

Casey smiled.

They followed him inside. The sight of so many small Hispanic people in tan-over-brown janitorial uniforms shattered his fantasy of a sleek, covert operation. Pedro led them to a utility closet, where they changed into uniforms to match the others. Casey tossed Gus a hat. "Put this on." He pointed at a clipboard. "The guy with the hat and the clipboard is management if anyone asks."

Scales added, "Act normal. Always assume someone is watching."

"Didn't you cut the security cameras?" Gus said.

"You watch too much TV."

Pedro led his crew and their carts off the service elevator on the fifteenth floor. Scales directed them. "Second door on the right."

One crew entered the door opposite the Director of Compliance; Pedro entered Sheehan's. Lifting the paper on his clipboard, Gus pretended to match the name and the room number before nudging Casey forward.

The cleaners stayed in the outer office with Pedro. Gus and Casey surveyed the interior office, similar to Pogue's office.

Casey stood behind the desk chair and snapped a picture. "We leave it the way we found it." Seated at the computer, he jiggled the mouse, made a series of clicks, and in minutes, told Scales, "I'm in. You see me?"

Scales said, "Affirmative. Big man is at the controls."

Sheehan kept two dated pictures of herself and an older man, whom he presumed was her father, in card-sized hinged frames beside her keyboard. On shelves opposite the desk were photos taken at a baseball stadium. Sheehan stood beside a younger man, both holding cups of beer. She wore a navy-blue hooded sweatshirt with Boston spelled out in red letters.

Casey and Gus switched places. "He's in position," Casey told Cedric.

"Gus," Cedric said, "follow along, but stay calm. Whatever steps I take to get in, I'll print it out. You can do this over and over."

Glued to the monitor, Gus watched Cedric work his magic.

"There it is." Cedric said. "That's her username," and he paused. "Wait for it. Here's her password."

"Amazing," Gus said.

"You're welcome," Cedric said. "Now you can get in when you want."

"That's it?" Gus said.

"That's it," Cedric said.

Scales said, "Get what you came for."

Finding the data files of the Complimentary and Alternative Medicine department required navigating labyrinthine corporate directories. Search after search turned up empty folders, archived files with no content, and dead links. The systematic absence of data felt deliberate—surgical.

Scales's impatience came through. "You can do this later, from anywhere, right?"

"Nothing like being on site."

Pedro's head snapped around the door jamb, his eyes wide with alarm. He rotated his wrist frantically—wrap it up, NOW.

A nod from Gus, then he asked Cedric, "How about emails?"

Within a minute, Outlook opened. Cedric mumbled, "She's got a corporate and personal account too." Dsheehan@georgiacancerinstitute.org made sense. The hamitbeav@gmail.com provided no hints.

A smile crossed his face. "Can you access them both?"

"Hold on." Cedric's voice tone shifted.

Scales barked, "Speed this up, fellas. The cleaning crew needs to move."

"I have the password for the personal one too. See right here, where my cursor is?"

"Ladies," Scales interrupted, "move."

"Hold on," Gus growled at Scales. "Ced, you could be a spook."

Cedric opened her private account. "I'll send you all the credentials you need to do this yourself."

Scanning the list, Gus moved his cursor. "Open that one. Let's find out what Omegaman has to say."

Cedric clicked on an email from "Omegaman."

Seconds later, the words on screen sent ice through his veins. The message was brief, but the implications were staggering: *'Stand down until I arrive on Thursday. For once, follow orders. Lives are on the line again. Two wrongs don't make a right. Leave it to me.'*

Heart hammering against his ribs, Gus forced his voice to remain steady. "This is incredible."

"Great," Scales said. "Now leave."

Finishing the email, Gus felt the world tilt slightly. He mumbled to Mitch Scales, "I'm leaving, but I'll be back."

Chapter Twenty-Four

The gravel crunched beneath the Tahoe as ACE pulled up outside Cedric's apartment.

"Wait here," Gus said, his voice tight. "This debrief is solo."

Inside, Gus paced. His footsteps were sharp and urgent. "Ced, I need to get in with the Spooks." The covert and prestigious surveillance team at ATRI.

Cedric's eyes widened. "Da Spooks?" He shook his head slowly. "Son, you be barking up the wrong tree."

"You know them. You know the little guy. I need access. Now."

"Hell, you've barely cracked the files I just unlocked for you. That little guy?" Cedric snorted. "He wants nothing to do with you."

"Tonight was a waste—a mistake." Gus ran a hand through his hair. "I shouldn't have dragged you into this, but now I see clearly what needs to happen."

Cedric lifted a two-liter of cream soda in a silent offering. Gus shook his head. Ice clinked against metal as Cedric filled his Yeti tumbler and poured. "What do you think needs to happen?"

He paused and said, "On Friday, all they told me was 'they could find no data files from my device.'" Gus followed Cedric from the kitchen to the living room, words spilling out as they moved. "Then you get in and—nothing." He perched on the arm of the couch, leaning forward. "So, they were right, I was wrong. No files." His voice dropped. "But then...I saw the email thread. Sheehan's talking to someone about *violence*." He raised his hand. "She thinks she's being cryptic, but she's not. She's targeting someone specific, and the person on the other end is telling her to stand down until he gets here on Thursday."

"That's what's got you all riled up?"

Gus recoiled. "Absolutely. I think I know the person."

Cedric's eyebrow rose, and his whole scalp and mop of hair shifted with it. "Who?"

Gus silenced him with a dismissive wave. "I can't say—There's no time—I need to be listening in. That's why I want the Spooks to help me. They're better than the military or the government. Ced, I need to be eavesdropping inside GCI."

Cedric scoffed. "I'm feelin it."

Gus raised his arms. "Damn right. Ced, I'm feelin it, too. That's why I need in."

Cedric smiled while he stared at his feet on the reclined footrest. He rolled his lip and squeezed the massive armrests with his enormous hands.

While he contemplated his answer, Gus glanced at his setup; three monitors lined the wall where most people would have a TV, with dual keyboards on a side table. This was clearly where Cedric spent most of his time. In Gus's strategic mind, a new plan had begun to take shape. The idea to surveil inside GCI came to him on the drive back from Lanier, during the storm, and while waiting for the power to come on. Getting into the files had merit, but imagine what he could learn if he went all in and bugged the place.

Then came the storm, and Scales, and he decided to go with Cedric, find the data, and be glad. But when Cedric came up empty, and he read Sheehan's emails with Omegaman, he decided to get aggressive or die. Not assassinate aggressive, but pull out all stops aggressive.

Cedric raised his hand, his face brightening with sudden realization. "Shazam. I think you be holdin the card you need."

"What?"

"The Dr. Lee card. You two are tight. I never knew why, but you are. *He's your man.*"

Gus nodded and mumbled, "You're absolutely right. Thanks, Ced. I owe you."

"You know how to thank me."

Gus stood beside the door. "That I do. Please send me the credentials I need to get in. Both emails, too. I'm in for a long night."

Twenty minutes later, ACE paused to let the gates open at Henry and Cassie's, and Gus looked up from his incessant typing into his phone's notepad. After reading Sheehan's email, his pulse quickened. The name Omegaman pulsed in his mind like a warning beacon.

The squall line that had ravaged GCI left its mark—small branches scattered across the lawn. Cassie's rambling roses tore from their anchors along the garage. Her gloved hands worked quickly, and she pulled aside the chaotic tendrils to let the Tahoe pass.

ACE and Danno entered the command center, Gus went to help Cassie.

A minute later, ACE approached Cassie, confounded. "Christian is gone?"

Bent over picking up rose fragments, Cassie said, "Yep. Just left." She straightened, brushing soil from her gloves. "The other team brought her back. She went inside, grabbed her bag, and then left with a guy in a sports car."

Gus shook his head. "I know the guy. He oversees production at Holder." Holder hired him in the Spring. Bobby said he took to Christian right away. Gus thought it might have been the other way around.

Cassie told ACE, "She's not a prisoner. She can come and go as she likes."

Gus exhaled. She might have appreciated Opa paying for her details if she had read Sheehan's email to Omegaman. He dialed her cell. No answer.

Resignation in her voice, ACE asked Gus, "What time do you want us back in the morning?"

"We pick up Gina at seven for an airport run."

"Roger. We'll leave here at six-thirty, sharp."

Sharp was the last thing he felt. His body craved a meal, his skin a shower, and his mind demanded a pot of black coffee.

An hour later, refreshed but on edge, Gus slid open the library doors, hair still damp, wearing loose clothes, with a coffee mug warm in his hands. Kitchen light spilled across the desk and empty chairs—the same chairs where Agent Baumann had blindsided him and Henry on Saturday. The dim room wrapped around him like a sedative, offering momentary peace. Then reality returned as his shaking fingers fumbled with the desk lamp knob.

On Henry's desktop, he opened the credentials Cedric sent. As the program was loading, he recalled all that had happened since the conference call with Geneva from the ATRI SCIF on Friday morning: Expelled from GCI. IEEI likely eliminated. JCO mat deal in jeopardy. Opa on death's door. Henry in Geneva. Christian...well, being Christian and there's Gina...a complicating puzzle all its own.

In his mind, the converging events hadn't just happened to him—they'd transformed him. Had he been set up in some mystical way he found impossible to grasp logically? For what? The Georgia Cancer Institute logo appeared on the monitor, and he shuddered. Was there a way around what he was about to do? None came to mind. He typed in the password and hit Enter.

Clad in her pajamas and a robe, Cassie paused at the library entrance and gave a concerned look.

"I'll be at this a while," he said, his voice fading into a half-hearted apology he didn't really mean.

Cassie gave a faint nod and a knowing smile that spoke volumes. "Henry taught the children, 'An overlooked secret to success is rest.' You might fare better in the morning." The resigned wisdom of a woman who had long ago accepted the Meier men and their single-minded pursuits reminded Gus how much he liked her.

She silently slid the doors closed till they clicked.

Everyone seemed to have a quip.

Alone with nothing but his suspicions and Cedric's access, he set his mug aside, shifted to the front of the chair, and navigated to Donna Sheehan's GCI email.

Interesting. The timestamps showed only today's notes. Then he found it— the Omegaman thread, dating back to March. Sheehan had reached out for 'counsel' about an 'irregularity'—something she claimed was 'probably nothing' yet 'couldn't afford to let escalate.' Her final line: a request for 'objective input.'

To that inquiry came a succinct, "Give it time."

A month later, she stated, "Evidence mounting, not a fluke."

The response was, "Look back to see ahead."

In late July, her third note read, "Have a suspect. Need to talk. Dedication on the horizon. NO distractions allowed."

Omegaman responded, "Patience. Target will grow. Easier to hit."

She wrote, "And the story grows. Easier to link. Why wait?"

Omegaman responded, "Waiting adds to certainty. Then, we'll have to think creatively."

After the July exchange, she stopped writing until Friday afternoon. Sheehan wrote, "Can't wait. The target is impossible to miss. I will handle it." Of course, Christian demanded the results and the missing units and threatened her with her friends in high places.

Omegaman had written his "Stand down" message today at 4:30 a.m.

He sat back, the shock as fresh as when he'd first read it in her office. What 'irregularities' had she spotted back in March? What could she have pieced together in three months? Whatever it was, it demanded full attention. And Omegaman, whoever he was, commanded her respect. He reread the screen, teeth clenching, hands hovering motionless above the keyboard. Those four words burned into his retinas: 'Leave it to me.'

The frustration got the better of him, and he called Cedric.

The TV was playing in the background. Cedric answered, "Don't tell me you're outside."

"No, Ced, I can't find her archive. Her inbox only has today's emails."

Cedric's fingers flew across the keyboard, taking control of Henry's computer in minutes. "Found them. Holy moly, this is an over-the-top organization."

"What is this?"

Before him, Cedric had exposed a digital fortress: nested folder hierarchies, meticulously organized main directories for departments and projects, each housing precisely labeled subfolders with militaristic naming conventions. "Whoever wrote this is one calculated dude."

"The 'dude' is Donna Sheehan."

"Well," Cedric moved his cursor, opening directories, projects, folders, and subfolders. "E-mail is filtered automatically through rule-based sorting algorithms that she likely customized herself. Professional. Methodical."

"You think Sheehan created this?"

"What did her office look like?" Cedric said. "Tidy."

"Immaculate?" Gus said.

"I'd bet she built it."

"Your place is far from immaculate."

"I don't build them; I hack into them."

"Where would you start?"

"Directories, but that won't mean much to you. Go to Departments." Cedric clicked on the screen. "Look in here, or..." He paused over the open projects folder in the Complementary and Alternative Medicine Department. "Drill down. I'll bet what you're looking for is in here. What are you looking for?"

Gus exhaled audibly. "I'm not sure anymore. I wanted data files, but I'm not sure they exist. Then I saw the emails..."

"This looks sophisticated. It's going to be pretty simple or pretty complex. Have fun."

"You want to help..."

"G-man, I been going at it with a Chinese programmer since you left. I break in, they rebuild."

"Seriously?"

"It's a constant chess game with the Chinese." Cedric's voice lowered. "But the way I read the thread that got you riled up, your lady and Omegaman are making all the moves. The 'target that's impossible to miss', I bet dat dude is in da dark bout what's bout ta go down."

"What are you saying?"

"G-man, being a 'target' is not a good thing. When a dude says, 'Leave it to me,' well, dat tells me somethings bout to happen, soon. And, soon ain't Thanksgivin or Christmas. You feel me? Find what you need fast. Like tonight."

Gus swallowed hard, staring at Sheehan's email system. He'd written code that had changed the world, yet this web outmatched him—not just organized but engineered for concealment, each folder a potential trap or dead end. He clicked open the subdirectory and froze. Names leapt out at him—not just Pogue, Slayton, and Tanzilla, but Abernathy, VSchnerr, KSchnerr, and WSchnerr. Unknown players on a board he'd thought he understood. The pit in his stomach deepened. This wasn't going to be the quick dive Cedric had promised, and his list of allies had shrunk to zero.

Somewhere in this digital maze lay what he needed—proof his device worked flawlessly and evidence of why they were determined to bury it. The library's tranquility evaporated. No longer a sanctuary but a deserted island with a hurricane barreling toward shore. His phone glared accusingly: 1:17 AM. He tipped his thermos, watching the black liquid swirl into his mug, and breathed in the rich aroma that promised alertness. Maybe ACE and Danno should take Gina to the airport without him. He'd found his path forward, narrow and treacherous though it was. Another decision with no good answers.

Three Schnerrs. An uncommon name. Where had he heard that name before? Pogue should know if there are three of them in the CAM subdirectory. He didn't relish another run at her, but he'd figure out a way.

It was after seven in the morning in Geneva. Helene would be awake.

"Good morning. Are you okay?" Helene said.

"Yes. A bit tired, but I have a question. Does the name Schnerr mean anything to you?"

Helene uttered a "hmm" and said, "It's a family name, I believe."

"Me too. But where?"

"On Opa's side, I think. After Elias died, I saw a lot of documents. Opa had theories about the explosion not being an accident. He made some tenuous link to his mother's family in Germany. I think her maiden name was Schnerr. That's it. Now I recall. Why do you ask?"

"The name just popped up on something I'm reading. That's all."

"Gus, after Henry arrived and set up your machine, Opa told us about the notebook. That winter night in 1939. His cousins in the back of their car, fleeing the Nazi's. How horrific. The hate. Unimaginable. All for one man's deranged quest for power. And the people…they let it happen. It's a different world today."

Was it different? Power. Hate. Will someone one day wonder how we lived through this?

His eyes were heavy, his back sore, and his dinner had worn off. Who was Abernathy? He thought about saving that search for tomorrow, then pushed forward. Googling the single name, he found a Professor Glenn Abernathy at Caltech, a pianist in the Milwaukee Philharmonic, and the Abernathy Pharmaceutical Company, announcing a breakthrough pain management drug for cancer patients.

He clicked on the pharmaceutical link. The company profile made his blood run cold: a privately held corporation founded in 1967, after a German company based in Darmstadt sold its oncology analgesics division. The VISION tab stated that the forecasted sales in the coming year would pass the billion-dollar mark, thanks to their expanding catalogue of cancer drugs. A photo showed the current CEO and his son standing beside a portrait of the founder, Dr. Aldous Abernathy.

Gus stared at the screen, pieces clicking into place like tumbler locks opening. Three Schnerrs. Opa's mother's maiden name. And now, a pharmaceutical empire with everything to lose if his device worked. Motive. Protect billions in profits. Cash over cure. And, he began to suspect, his own family's blood may be entangled in the web.

His hands trembled as he checked his phone. 1:47 AM. ACE would arrive to take Gina to the airport in a few hours. But first, he had calls to make. The surveillance plan could wait—he'd just discovered something far more dangerous than he'd ever imagined.

Chapter Twenty-Five

At six-thirty Monday morning, ACE kept her word, and they pulled through the gates at Henry and Cassie's. Working on four hours of sleep, he dozed off on the drive to Angelo's.

Standing between two bags outside the residential entrance, Gina looked fashionable in her travel wear. She answered her phone, spotted the SUV, and ended the call with a quick tap.

"I've got this," Gus said to Danno. Before Danno could object, Gus was already out, sweeping her small suitcase and tote into the open cargo bay.

He closed the hatch. "Early call?"

"My mother."

"Checking up on you?"

"Probably. I'll call later."

His mind reverted to the exchanges he'd read between Sheehan, Tanzilla, Pogue, and Slayton. Sheehan wielded more power than her title commanded. The question of why and how she'd acquired such influence made his weary brain misfire.

Exiting the interstate to the Atlanta airport, he broke the silence. "You're going to have a fabulous week."

Gina smiled. "I'm excited."

"Are you ready?" Gus said.

Gina chuckled. "I think I'll manage."

Gus put his hand on hers. "I know you will."

The Tahoe rolled to a stop at "Departures," and Danno stepped out. The automatic doors nearby whooshed open and closed in a steady rhythm. Cars and vans jockeyed for position in and out, leaving an acrid exhaust trail. Travelers flowed in every direction, burdened by oversized luggage, small children and various infirmities.

"Gus," ACE said. "Please stay inside."

Gus smiled in the mirror. "Promise. After this, I'll be good," and he mustered his depleted body to retrieve her bags.

Danno beat him to the luggage. She thanked him for the ride, and Gus motioned to him to give them space.

He found himself closer to Gina's height with her on the curb and him on the pavement. Amid the impatient honks, airport announcements, and police whistles, he held her gaze.

"Long night?" Gina said.

Gus nodded.

"You didn't have to do this, but I appreciate it. And thanks for a fun day at the lake."

"You're welcome. I'll bet California is fun, too."

Gina raised her eyebrows. "Want to join me?"

The thought made Gus laugh out loud. "Bad timing. How about next Saturday? We'll both be free. We'll go back to the lake."

"And spend the night?" Gina said.

His eyes widened. "I hadn't thought of that."

"Really?" Gina contorted her face.

Gus grinned. "I lied."

She rested her arms on his shoulders and clasped them behind his neck.

He added, "Maybe I will make an honest man out of you."

He reached around her waist and drew her close. "We could start now."

Gina raised her eyebrows. "Now?"

"May I leave you with a kiss?" Gus said.

"Oh." Her voice dropped to a whisper. "Please do."

Her lips were soft and full. Light at first, then firm as she pulled him closer, gently.

"That was worth the wait," Gina said.

"You...waiting?"

She nodded.

You could have asked months ago.

"Why now?" Gus said.

"Simple. You asked."

"I would have asked sooner, but you and your rules."

Gina snickered. "This worked out better, don't you agree?"

"I do," Gus said. The words 'I do' made his face flush.

Gina pulled him to her and kissed him again, more passionately.

Weariness aside, his body reacted to her embrace and the kiss. She noticed.

"Is that a yes for Saturday?" Gina smiled.

Beaming, embarrassed, he nodded.

A traffic control officer waved frantically, shouting at ACE to move along. The Tahoe's horn blared a warning, but Gus stood rooted, watching her walk away. She stole a glance over her shoulder and smiled. His lips curved into a smile, hand raised in goodbye, oblivious to everything but her. Holder's name lit up his phone.

"Good morning," Gus said.

"It is not, it's a shit show, and I can't find the little shit who started all this."

Holder's frantic words catapulted Gus's mind back through the predawn hours to last night's discoveries. If Holder wanted to see a 'shit show,' Gus had one to show him, but he couldn't. On Sheehan's GCI email account, he'd uncovered many succinct and cryptic emails between Sheehan and Slayton, James, Tanzilla, and Pogue. Most seemed to either set up a phone call or respond to one or were following up on a previous face-to-face conversation. Her emails were more candid and included Abernathy, the Schnerrs, and Omegaman. He didn't read many before he found himself deep in her matrix, where he discovered copies of patient files and what he suspected might have been the first domino to fall. The excavation revealed layer after layer and left him mentally raw, his eyes bloodshot and heavy, but he could not miss seeing Gina off.

He let his head fall against the vibrating window, eyes closing as Gina's scent lingered on his skin. He wet his lips, reliving the memory of the kiss and her hands against the mottled skin on his neck. For a fleeting moment, he imagined a life where she was more than a temporary distraction—where secret missions and invisible threats didn't consume his days. The thought both warmed and terrified him. Everyone who got close eventually became collateral damage in his family's crusade. And now, despite all his careful barriers, Gina had somehow slipped through. But how could he pull away when her touch had made him feel truly alive for the first time in years?

Gina's kiss had shown him exactly what he was sacrificing—not just romance, but the chance to be himself with someone who cared about him. She'd touched his scars without flinching, asked no questions about the bodyguards. But if he stayed on this path, how long before she became collateral damage like everyone else who got close?

The "Go Dawgs" boy's sunken face flashed in his mind—then Gina's smile as she walked away. Two futures pulling at him. He couldn't abandon his mission, but maybe he was fooling himself thinking he could protect her from it. ACE's watchful eyes in the rearview mirror were proof enough - this wasn't the life for candlelit dinners and honest conversations.

She deserved better than a man who came with surveillance teams and death threats. But God, he wanted to try anyway.

By the time he last saw the clock at two-thirty, terrifying fragments in the emails had caused him to forget the missing data on the biofeedback device. He woke with his head pressed against the mahogany desk in the library. The same unrelenting questions still haunted him: How had Donna Sheehan gained a position of power far beyond her title, and what did she have on Pogue, Slayton, James, and Tanzilla that made them bend to her will?

Holder's voice forced him back to reality. "Are you there?"

Gus blinked his eyes, startled and said, "Yes. I'm here. What's the matter?"

"The PPP Commissioner just called. At seven o'clock on a Monday morning," Holder shouted, then paused to catch his breath. "*He* got a call from the Governor, not his office, the got-damn governor himself. He wants a noon conference with ATRI, my people, being Christian, and the employee and the people at GCI, especially the woman adjudicating matters."

Gus shut his eyes. "Sheehan?"

"Got-damn right."

He tapped ACE on the shoulder and whispered, "Back to Henry's." The pieces clicked into place—Christian's repeated trips with State Troopers, her threats about "friends in high places." The Governor was the head of the State Patrol system. That explained everything.

"Why are you calling me?" Gus said.

"She's not answering. Can you help me find her? I want her by my side when we have that call. Off camera. Quiet."

Holder's ineptness wore Gus thin. "Bob, give it a minute. She'll turn up."

"I knew it. One day, her stubbornness would get her in trouble. Get *me* in trouble. I don't need this shit."

"Bob," Gus said, the firmness in his voice unmistakable. "Listen to me. Christian's right. Sheehan is the problem."

"I don't doubt that. Clair told me that years ago."

"So, I sympathize with your attitude toward Christian at the moment. She's got something going on that I can't put my finger on, but I will, or she'll tell me. I know her. And I saw her stand up to Sheehan. That took guts. Donna Sheehan has issues—some bad F-ing is bad." Gus wanted to drop what he'd read in the predawn hours. "Keep in mind, Christian is making the company money, and you couldn't replace her for a million dollars or in a million years. So do everyone a favor; take a pill and get past your hangover."

"You can't talk to me that way..."

"Bob," Gus smirked, "we both know I can, I just never have. But we're in a tough spot, and Christian and I have a perspective you don't. She saw a lifeline, and she took it. *She* went to the governor. Because of *her*, he's on our side. *That* is what this call is about."

Chapter Twenty-Six

In Monday morning, bumper-to-bumper traffic from the airport to Henry and Cassie's, Gus called Christian.

She answered the first ring and announced flatly, "I heard. He's called three times."

"Where are you?" Gus said.

"Why do you always ask where I am? I'm on the damn phone with you, can we leave it at that?"

"Cassie said you left with a guy in a sports car. Mr. MIT?"

"Let's talk about that call with the governor?" Christian said. "Who's getting shit done, buckeroo? I am."

"Do you remember the night we both met Gina. We were waiting at the bar on the Terrazzo, and you asked me why I went into exile for the past few years." Gus said.

"Yeah."

"You want to know? I'll tell you. I was involved in projects at ATRI that I couldn't talk about. You and our friends always talk about our projects, and I didn't want to lie. This has brought me out of exile..."

"But you still have to lie?"

Gus nodded and continued, "As for the Governor, congratulations, and thank you. We're still on the same team. Work with me."

"Speaking of lying. I think I'll call bullshit on that. Something's off. I know you. You want me close...but on the same team...I'm not feeling it."

"Maybe you shouldn't be sleeping with that guy. You were never this way when...."

"Okay. That's enough..." Christian said, her voice sharp but brittle at the edges. Gus recognized that tone—the same one she'd used when he'd retreated into his work and rebuffed her attempts to rekindle the flame they once shared after graduation. By then, he'd accepted his relationship with The Assignment.

He immediately turned to secrets and lies to proceed, forsaking all professional ties. Now, partners, but not partners, bound by a shared mission to have her biofeedback device sold internationally, but separated by the walls he'd built. Ironically, he needed the trust he had squandered.

Gus changed the subject, swallowing the history between them. "What do you and the Governor have planned?"

"I told him about Sheehan. He patched in the top PPP guy, Welch. I told him what happened."

"What did he say?"

"Just that he would handle it." Christian's tone left no room for questions.

"Well, he's handling it, today at noon. Will you get the data?" Gus said.

"No promises. But I'm getting us reinstated."

"Excellent. Thank you," Gus said, genuinely grateful.

~~~

Back at Henry's, Gus moved like a sleepwalker—alarm set, body collapsing into brief, dreamless oblivion.

At eleven fifteen, he pulled on some of Henry's clean clothes, and ACE drove him to ATRI. He passed through the biometric scanner, humming softly as it read his thumbprint. The pneumatic hiss of the reinforced door releasing its seal echoed in the sterile corridor. He took the stairs to the third floor, each footfall amplified in the concrete stairwell. The quiet on this floor calmed him. This is where the thinking occurred.

In Dr. Lee's office, Sheila, his secretary, greeted Gus while her fingers never paused on her keyboard. With a practiced nod she said, "He's on a call, but he's expecting you."

Waiting outside the director's office, Gus reflected on their evolving relationship—from instructor to mentor and beyond. After graduation, when Gus accepted the Assignment and stayed behind in Atlanta, Lee had become director, and Opa used his influence to gain Gus's acceptance into private research at ATRI. Their partnership deepened when Dr. Lee collaborated on developing the mat material for GMC. ATRI Directors were prohibited from being included on patents, so Gus and Opa had arranged a side deal to compensate the directors. They'd become co-conspirators in ventures that existed in the gray space between government oversight and private enterprise.
~~~

Gus checked his watch. It was 11:45. He texted Christian, chuckling as he typed. "Where are you?"

A moment later, she wrote back, "Jamaica."

"Get back. IEEI Friday at 3:30."

She sent back a smiley face.

If Christian did save herself a shot at IEEI, he and Bobby could focus on the mats and integrating the source code to close JCO. Still too tired to feel relief, he tried to imagine it before Sheehan's emails stole the moment.

If he combined the image created by the emails between Sheehan and Omegaman with the story the Interpol agent told, Christian would need more than a friendship with the governor to save her. For the moment, he didn't see himself as a target.

Regarding the Governor's imminent call, he envisioned Stephen James and Donna Sheehan taking a hit. Slayton and Pogue would be okay. His primary question was what Dr. Chen knew, and when he knew it. Pogue acknowledged Chen stood in for her while she worked at Oxford, and James said he'd ask if Chen knew how the missing units were sent to patients' homes.

Had Chen authorized the devices to be taken home? Surely, each patient had instructions on how to connect to Wi-Fi.

What if they didn't? They would only benefit from Christian's circuit board, not his.

If they did hook up to Wi-Fi, straps around their ankles, wrists, and torso would link them to his program flowing from the server at GCI. The program mapped and recorded the electrical output of every cell, tissue, and organ in their body. In response, the server sent back the cancer-stopping currents embedded in his coding to restore vitality. The patient's data would end up in their dedicated file folders within GCI's system. Cedric could not find those folders.

Gus stifled a yawn, fatigue clouding his thoughts. The machines must be connected to the Internet, and the data files must have been moved or, more likely, deleted.

Christian sent a text to Gus in Dr. Lee's office, "You speak for us. I'm not talking."

He didn't believe it, but he appreciated the note.

"OK," he replied. "Remember, Sheehan's in the hot seat, not us."

"I hope she fries."

"After she turns over the data and the other units?"

"Precisely."

Gus joined Dr. Lee, seated at the head of the twelve-seat conference table. "I need a favor," Gus said.

Dr. Lee turned his attention to him.

"I need to engage the Surveillance team in the basement."

Dr. Lee said, "The Spooks."

The acknowledgment by Dr. Lee triggered tension in Gus's neck.

"Related to this call?"

Gus nodded faintly. "I think you'll understand."

"Let's get through this call."

Dr. Lee connected to the video call. As participants joined—James from Georgia Cancer Institute, Holder, Commissioner Welch, Sheehan, and Pogue—Gus took his position beside Dr. Lee's monitor. Christian and Holder appeared together on a single connection.

Skip Welch began, "Mr. James, have you informed Ms. Sheehan of our agreed-upon protocol for resolving disputes?"

"I have."

Welch said, "Ms. Sheehan, you acknowledge you have no authority to expel a PPP member."

Donna Sheehan cleared her throat, her interlaced fingers fidgeting. "Yes. I am now aware of the relationship between the State and Georgia Cancer Institute."

Welch said, "ATRI and Holder Medical Engineering are hereby reinstated as PPP participants at Georgia Cancer Institute, and agree to abide by all regulations and deadlines. Is everyone in agreement?"

Gus nodded. "Yes."

Christian nodded. "Yes," though the tight set of her jaw suggested otherwise.

The rushed formality of the exchange felt orchestrated to Gus—Sheehan and James clearly hoping to resolve this before any higher authorities became involved. As if on cue, the speaker on the desk beeped, and a female voice announced, "Michael Hettich."

"Good afternoon, everyone. I'm sorry I'm late. What did I miss?"

Stephen James spoke quickly, relief evident in his voice, "Good afternoon, Governor. Mr. Welch handled the issue promptly. I'm sorry to have wasted your time."

"Very good." There was a pause before the Governor continued, "Christian, are you and your partner satisfied with the outcome?"

The direct question to Christian confirmed she had brought this to the Governor's attention. Christian's voice sharpened, abandoning any pretense of agreement, "Not in the least, Governor. Mr. James, now that we've established that Ms. Sheehan has exceeded her authority, let's address the data collected from our device."

Donna Sheehan's expression flickered with alarm as her administrative escape route vanished. She spoke softly, "Mr. Welch, for many years, this research program has set parameters to collect data on devices installed as of January 1st. This device was not installed as of January 1st, another infraction by the PPP members. The installation conducted by Ms. Lawler occurred on January 6th." Sheehan turned to the PPP Commissioner. "Mr. Welch, what do the guidelines say about a partner who knowingly violates the procedures and puts an affiliate at risk?"

Governor Hettich spoke, "Ms. Sheehan, as the Director of Compliance, you claim that the late installation is the reason you don't have data on the device, placing Georgia Cancer Institute at risk, while physicians under Dr. Slayton's direction subjected patients to an unmonitored device for which you are responsible."

Sheehan said, "I did not know it was here."

"Mr. James," Governor Hettich said. "I heard the Chief Compliance Officer admitted to not knowing a device was on premises AND being administered to cancer patients at a JCO-sanctioned facility?"

"Their device did not appear on my report," Sheehan interjected.

"Which you monitored from your desk," Governor Hettich said.

"Correct."

"Did you ever go to the CAM department to verify that the devices on the report matched the devices being administered?"

"That's not my responsibility. Dr. Pogue let them in."

"Oh, not your responsibility? We'll need clarification on *that*. Mr. James, how do you suppose the accreditation committee at JCO would respond to her position?"

The question hung in the air like a guillotine blade. James drew in a deep breath, but the Governor sliced through his hesitation, "If I asked the Attorney General or his office to join us on this call, what crimes might he identify as having been committed by your admission that God knows how many people had this device applied to them with no oversight or consent?"

"Consent isn't the issue," Sheehan interjected.

The Governor snickered, "Ms. Sheehan, patients cannot consent to treatment you did not know existed and the hospital did not authorize."

Donna Sheehan repeated, "That's not my responsibility."

Christian leaned toward her computer screen. "As Compliance goes, so goes the hospital."

Governor Hettich said, "Mr. James, I'm going to arrange a phone call with JCO later today to allow someone there to help clarify where Ms. Sheehan's responsibilities begin and end. You're welcome to be on that call. Meanwhile, you and Ms. Sheehan may want to confer with counsel. In addition to contacting JCO, I will request that the Attorney General investigate this matter to determine if there is potential criminal wrongdoing on Ms. Sheehan's part."

James forced a reassuring tone, "We'll be on the call."

"And Mr. Meier and/or Ms. Lawler," Governor Hettich continued casually, "would either of you be available to explain the situation to the JCO representative?"

Christian leaned in, "I'm available, sir. Thank you."

"Good. I'll have my people make the arrangements." Governor Hettich sighed, "Well, PPP at GEORGIA CANCER INSTITUTE appears to be intact, barring any disciplinary action by JCO. Is everyone up to speed on the rules?"

Stephen James nodded, Bob Holder answered, "Yes, sir," and Dr. Lee showed no reaction.

"Ms. Sheehan, is that a 'yes' from you?"

She nodded.

"I'm sorry, I didn't hear you."

"Yes," she blurted smugly.

Gus leaned forward, one hand raised, "Governor, I have a question for Ms. Sheehan."

Governor Hettich said, "Let's hear it."

"Ms. Sheehan, do you know where the CAM collected research data is stored?"

She pursed her lips and jutted her chin, a fortress bracing for siege. "I'd have to ask IT."

He didn't expect her to know, but he wanted confirmation on record.

"Friday, you stated unequivocally there was no data. How did you arrive at that conclusion?"

"We eventually looked for it."

"We being who? Did you look for it? You said you didn't know our device existed, but you are certain our data doesn't."

Sheehan hesitated. CEO James butted in, "I became aware of the situation when Mr. Holder inquired."

"Mr. Holder?" Gus glanced toward the phone. Mr. Holder, did you call Mr. James to ask about our data?

Holder's voice came through clearly. "No. When Ms. Lawler informed me that she had not received the data due on July 1st, I contacted Dr. Pogue in the UK. She called Slayton, who called Ms. Sheehan."

"So, there's a chain of communication here," Gus said, piecing it together aloud. "Holder calls Pogue, who contacts Slayton, who reaches out to Compliance. And this is when you first became aware, Ms. Sheehan?"

Sheehan's blank expression stalled the questioning. "Yes."

Gus wanted to ask about her comments in the email thread with Omegaman. About taking matters into her own hands. About the target being impossible to miss. He wanted to ask her what she meant in the email to Slayton and James when she told them she would "run the meeting" on Friday and they were to "be seen and not heard." If only he could ask James at that moment. Wouldn't the Governor love to jump on that line of questioning? Gus thought Tanzilla might be fair game. He asked questions on Friday but wasn't invited to this meeting. Why? He read her notes to James and Slayton saying he was not to attend the Friday meeting, but he demanded a seat and James and Slayton told her to work around him.

Sheehan may not have known what the biofeedback device did or even that it was the culprit behind the drop in dosages, procedures, and invoicing, but the emails revealed she knew plenty before the program ended and Christian asked Holder to call Pogue in the UK. If he couldn't bring up the email, at least he could force her to lie to the Governor.

"So, at no time did you know this device existed during the research program?"

Sheehan promptly shook her head. "I did not."

"When did you learn this device existed?"

Stephen James interjected, "When she searched for the application for Dr. Slayton and found what she found, she contacted me."

"Then, Mr. James, you learned about the device and missing data directly from Ms. Sheehan, not Mr. Holder's inquiry," Gus pressed.

"It all began when Mr. Holder inquired," James insisted.

"Save that for JCO," Gus said.

Gus added, "Ms. Sheehan, you've made it clear there is no data on the device, but you reported the application infractions to Dr. Slayton?"

"I did."

"Were you and Dr. Slayton surprised?"

"Shocked," Sheehan said.

"Why?"

"We knew nothing about either of you or the device, so we believed the best course of action was to invite you to explain yourselves."

"Is that part of the PPP protocol? Have you ever called another PPP participant in for interrogation?" Gus said.

Sheehan hesitated. "It wasn't an interrogation."

Governor Hettich asked, "Is there an established protocol for such instances?"

Gus said, "Does the Commissioner have an answer?"

Skip Welch shook his head. "Not to my knowledge."

Gus added, "Yet the Director of Compliance seemed to elevate herself above the CEO, the Chief of the Department of Oncology, and head of the Medical Advisory Board because Mr. James did not ask one question, and when Dr. Slayton tried to, Ms. Sheehan, you cut him off and proceeded to ambush us."

Sheehan said, "Ambush?"

"Governor," Gus said, "Ms. Lawler and I came away with the distinct impression Ms. Sheehan had no intention of allowing us to explain ourselves and every intention to expel us, because the security guard told us Ms. Sheehan ordered her to transfer our devices to shipping the day before."

"That's absurd," James said.

Gus shook his head, ignoring James's protest. "Ask her. And Governor, Dr. Pogue pleaded, she actually screamed at Dr. Slayton to intervene and stop Ms. Sheehan when she announced her decision, and he refused to utter one word."

"Aren't you the arrogant one..." Stephen James said.

Governor Hettich said, "Sounds like a domestic dispute."

James hung his head and sighed. Sheehan's face hardened into marble. Slayton rolled his lip. Dr. Pogue shook her head. Christian smiled.

Gus couldn't resist, "Highly irregular, wouldn't you say, Mr. Welch. It's almost as if they were there to be seen and not heard."

The Governor said, "Steve, Dr. Slayton. I know you each have a busy week ahead, and then the new year will change everything. I would hate to see this throw a wrench into things."

Gus sat back, exhaled, and felt his spine melt into the contours of the chair.

Governor Hettich said, "Is there anything else?"

James shook his head and made a lame attempt to look into the camera. "No, thank you."

"I have one request, Governor," Gus asked.

"What's that?"

"Regarding our data. I would like to bring an IT person from ATRI to Georgia Cancer Institute to search for the files we believe are stored in their system. Mr. James, do you have any objections to this?"

"None. Come at your leisure. I'll have someone in our IT contact you and give you access under their supervision."

"Today?" Gus said.

James's head jerked back as if Gus had slapped him. 'Today?" Defenseless, he said, "I'll arrange it."

"Thank you," Gus said. James told him on Friday that he would find out if Dr. Chen authorized the biofeedback units to be taken home. But Gus smirked; there was no telling what kind of weekend James had.

Dr. Lee's screen turned black. He turned to Gus. "Someone at GCI work very hard to make big drug deal. Going to get too big. May lose autonomy. Bad deal. You see? Governor knows to not bother ATRI. Washington…" Dr. Lee smiled, "They love me. We make things Washington needs. Bigger, is not better, Gus. Better is better. Never try to be bigger if you can't do it better."

Gus smiled and nodded. "Like the mat?"

Dr. Lee nodded, "Exactly. Mat very much better and available to big group." He smiled, "I'll call basement. You call the Governor. Ask for one week of full surveillance. Tell him I say something is very wrong at GCI. He help find it, he look like hero. They not been nice to him."

"I want to spy on them all."

Dr. Lee twirled a pen between his fingers. "Tell him who you want to watch. Start with one week," he said. "I'll send his number to you. If he asks what's wrong at GCI, tell him we have a covert research mission underway and must ensure we have not been compromised."

Gus's breath caught in his throat. The fabricated excuse had struck dangerously close to his buried truth. Did Lee somehow know what he'd built into the device, or was this just a coincidental government-speak ruse?

Dr. Lee misread Gus's reaction and added, dismissively, "Don't worry. He'll want to be a hero. Plus," Dr. Lee smiled, "He knows not to question me. I'm ATRI. ATRI answers to a few Senators and the President. That's all."

"Do you want to call the Governor while I contact the Spooks?"

Dr. Lee shook his head, his face settling into that familiar expression of calculated trust. "You handle the Governor. The surveillance team only reports to me."

Chapter Twenty-Seven

Optimistic and eager to follow the plan he and Dr. Lee had devised after the call with the Governor, Gus moved to Dr. Lee's outer office to review the bullet points the director had dictated. His heart rate quickened, and his respiration increased. Lying to his friends had become second nature. Lying to the Governor of his adopted state brought a touch of anxiety. He inhaled, dialed the Governor from the conference table in Dr. Lee's office, and Lee called the Spooks in the basement. Deflation hit when Hettich's phone blocked the call with an automated message requesting a text instead. Gus complied. Seconds later, Hettich called. "How can I help?" the governor said.

Gus told him what Dr. Lee suggested. Verbatim.

The Governor didn't question him. The call was brief—and encouraging.

Dr. Lee motioned Gus into his office. "You are set. I told little man to treat you like he would treat me."

Gus nodded and grinned at Dr. Lee's calling the guy "little man."

"Did you speak to the Governor?"

Gus nodded, voice steady. "Someone from the Attorney General's office will call soon."

"Soon" turned into right then. His phone vibrated.

"Gus Meier?" the deep voice said.

"Yes."

"Georgia Attorney General, Neville Blakemore. We have some business to attend to."

They exchanged the details and identified the targets. Blakemore conveyed Hettich's directive regarding the scope of surveillance, "as broad as the law allows."

Blakemore asked which government law enforcement agency would supervise the mission? Gus's first instinct was to lie, but he couldn't jeopardize the opportunity. "None."

Interpol agent Baumann sent him two names he found in his notes app. "I have a local agency and a federal one."

"Both."

He read off the names: FBI Special Agent JD Hile; Detective Udell Suttles, Metro Atlanta Police Department.

"I'll send authorization with one restriction," Blakemore said.

"What's that?"

"The Matrix."

"What's the Matrix?"

"Ask Funk."

"Who is Funk?"

"You'll see. He's the big man on ATRI campus."

Excited to leave Dr. Lee's office regardless of the Matrix, the ATRI switchboard texted, "Someone calling from GCI IT department is asking for your contact info."

Gus sent back a thumbs-up emoji.

Moments later, the name Ruben Gerding appeared on his phone. The Director of IT at GCI came off as an affable guy. They settled on a remote desktop protocol...in one hour. Cedric could dive as deep as he wanted now. Gus felt momentum swinging his way and headed for his office in the back of his lab on the first floor.

Before he could gather his thoughts, stepping out of the stairwell, Christian's name appeared on his screen as he and Cedric finalized arrangements to meet in Gus's lab office at 2:15.

Gus caught the call before voicemail.

Christian rushed in, "Holder and I thought you and Hettich scorched her."

Gus kept his stride. "JCO will too. James has to be worried. How was Holder?"

"Surprisingly appreciative. I just talked to Hettich. Boy, does he have a bug up his butt for James."

"Why?"

"Didn't say."

Gus said, "Well, it's obvious."

"Do you have a plan to get the data?"

"Cedric and I will dial into their system in an hour."

"Then we're golden. Cedric can find anything. If it's there, he'll find it."

If only she knew Cedric had struck out last night. With renewed determination, he took the stairs to the basement.

The door to the Surveillance Department was next to the SCIF. Gus paused outside, recalling how straightforward he had imagined his day would unfold when he left the secure room on Friday. Lacking credentials, he provided a fingerprint and a retinal scan to verify his identity in the ATRI system to the operator inside. The door latch clicked; he inhaled and pulled the door open, anxious to meet the little man. A stern-faced woman in goth clothing held up the badge on her lanyard, "Let's see it."

Gus showed his credentials. "I just did the..."

"Scan it," she ordered, nodding to the scanner on the counter. A moment later, her lips pursed, she delivered a second command. "Stay here."

Gus wondered if she'd treat Dr. Lee as cordially.

Moments later, a chiseled man appeared, not quite as tall as Gina. Clad in camouflage pants and a dark khaki tee shirt, with a shaved head, he sported a thick scar from the side of his left eye to his lower lip. Gus estimated they were about the same age. His name escaped Gus as he tried to break free from the man's crushing grip when they shook hands. Gus grimaced. The man cocked his bald head, planted his toe with military precision, pirouetted, then marched away. Gus stayed three paces behind and rubbed his hand. The little man stopped in a brightly lit stockroom.

He pirouetted again, facing Gus and the stern-faced woman. "Per Dr. Lee, you have complete access. If you don't see it, ask."

"How would I know what to ask?"

"What's the objective?"

Gus explained the mission, then followed him around the stockroom, selecting products and presenting each item to Gus without commentary.

"Set them there," the little man said. "There" was a stainless-steel table next to the entrance he hadn't noticed.

Unceremoniously, a detailed description of each item followed. Stunned, Gus wondered if the man might pause at any moment and say, "Just kidding, it won't do that." He never flinched.

The arsenal was comprehensive. High-resolution cameras and microphones embedded in everyday objects—even peel-off stickers—could detect sounds across multiple decibel ranges. Under keyboards, invisible sensors could register every keystroke, capturing passwords, bank accounts, phone numbers, all without a trace. Gus ran his fingers along a seemingly ordinary pen, marveling at the invasive power hidden within its innocuous shell. The shadowy realm made him sweat as he processed fascination and revulsion, blurring the boundary between protector and violator. Were tools like this used to track his father? Might they be used to watch Christian now? His intentions were honorable. Serving a greater good.

He led Gus and the woman down a bright hall into a bunker. There were no windows, only one door. Monitors were across the focal wall. Four chairs behind a long, narrow counter faced the monitors. The man positioned himself between the monitors and the counter. "This is the Watchtower. Here, our people, with your assistance, will monitor phone taps, GPS tracks, and cameras. Everything is recorded and stored in the cloud for twenty-four hours."

Gus raised his hand. "I was given one restriction."

The little man winced. "The Matrix?"

Gus nodded.

"We made it for NSA. It tracks calls ad infinitum. If I'm tracking you, our system tracks everyone you call and who calls you."

"Stretches the rules a bit, doesn't it?"

The little man walked past him toward the reception area.

There, Gus asked the only question Cedric insisted on knowing, "Do you guys have a vaporizer?"

"Yeah. It's on assignment," the short man said.

Gus squinted. Is he serious? A vaporizer? It was a joke, wasn't it? He recovered, "Dr. Lee told me to ask if you have anything under development?"

The short man left and returned promptly with a box containing six smaller boxes. He opened one, took out a pair of eyeglasses, and handed them to Gus. He examined them and put them on. "What's the big deal?"

"They record everything you see and hear. The camera is built into the nose bridge, and the microphones are here," he pointed to the edge at each end of the frame.

"Where is it captured?" Gus said.

"The cloud. Real-time monitoring is available in the Watchtower or accessed remotely."

Gus examined each pair of glasses and settled on a casual pair, a formal pair, and sunglasses.

The short man stepped to the door and called a name. Five staffers, three guys, two girls, appeared. "This is Babe and her team. They'll do the installation."

Gus interrupted, "That's not necessary, but…I've forgotten your name."

"Funk."

A grin came to Gus. "Funk? Is that a first name, last name, or rank?"

None of the five staffers smiled.

"Just Funk. Anything else?"

"Well, Funk, I'll take care of installing this where I need it."

Expressionless, Funk said, "We do installs."

Gus hesitated and grinned. "You don't have to. I'm grateful for the equipment."

Funk ignored Gus. "Give Babe the details. We like a two-hour notice." He turned to leave, then pivoted to Gus. "I wouldn't let Dr. Lee do an install."

The little man disappeared, no crushing handshake.

Babe wrote the details.

Mission accomplished, Gus checked the time on his phone. Five minutes until the GCI call with Cedric and Ruben Gerding. He headed to the steps, his pulse racing, and a chuckle rose in him. Never, in his wildest dreams, could he have imagined planning a first, let alone a second, break-in at GCI and that the man leading the charge in his absence would be named Funk.

Climbing the steps to the first floor, he texted Scales his plan, requesting a second entry later that night. As he exited the stairwell and the pulse of ATRI beat on all around him, confidence returned to his stride. Something in Ruben Gerding's comments, perhaps his tone of voice, sparked a thought in Gus's mind about how he might find the files. Quickly. But for someone at GCI playing this cat-and-mouse game, Christian would not have called the Governor, and he would not have been compelled to hack into GCI last night, which led him to this night. Where would all this lead?

In his lab, Gus passed engineers working in pairs at various workstations. No one acknowledged him. Focused on the glass-walled office at the back, he saw Cedric seated opposite his chair, repositioning the computer screen and keyboard. Gus opened his laptop, brought up his original code for the installation, and found what he thought might solve the mystery. He gnawed on his lower lip and called Gerding on his desk phone, pressing the "Speaker" button. Instantly, Gus heard Gerding's voice. Did he detect a touch of arrogance? What had he been told?

Gerding and Cedric took a few minutes to connect the computers. Gus drummed his fingers on the desk as Gerding navigated the system to the address on his acceptance letter.

"This is where the files would be if they existed," Gerding said. "These are all the files we are collecting research on," his tone condescending. Gus would not have been surprised if he patted himself on the back and said, "Satisfied."

Gus turned his laptop screen toward Cedric, revealing a single line of code. "Type this in."

Cedric squinted and typed, his fingers clicking on the keyboard like a metronome counting down the seconds. The air conditioning hummed to a stop, leaving the room in sudden silence.

"Search," Gus said, his voice barely above a whisper.

"Whoa. What do we have here?" Cedric said.

"What's that?" Gerding said.

A yellow folder icon labeled Meier/Lawler Biofeedback Device appeared. The folder Gus created and Christian installed in January.

Gus smiled. "How did this get here, Ruben?"

"No idea."

Cedric double-clicked on the folder, and Gus felt his body shudder as the blood drained from his face, reading the bold letters: ACCESS DENIED. He caught his breath. "Explain that, Ruben."

Ruben scrambled for an answer. Then Gina's name appeared on his screen. His finger hovered over the answer button for a fraction of a second before pulling back.

Ruben said he'd never seen that sign, ever.

"Voicemail" appeared on his screen, then vanished.

"Who could deny access to a file?" Gus demanded.

A text followed. "Call me. Urgent."

Ruben Gerding's explanation faded to a blur of white noise. Urgent. The word pulsed in Gus's mind, drowning out everything else.

Chapter Twenty-Eight

Y ou're going to do it. Understand?"

"I've never done this. I've never even seen this. So scream all you want. I've got to make a call."

"Who to? You're the head of IT."

"McIntyre. Our comms guy. He might know. But calling the governor won't help."

"Oh, really? You realize we found what everyone told the Governor does not exist? You and I are speaking because the Governor wants us to see what's in this denied file." Gus lowered his voice, "Ruben, you get in or you get ready. Cause when I call him, I'm pinning all this on you."

Gus flashed his phone at Cedric. "Missed call" from Gina. "I've got to step out. You got this?"

Cedric smirked, "You got him where you want him, G-man."

The shade from three Pin Oak trees couldn't save him from the smothering humidity as he sat on the wooden bench fixed to the ATRI lawn.

A text from Gina followed. "Urgent."

He couldn't not call—but 'urgent' had only one meaning: trouble. And he already had enough.

"I got your text." He stood and paced. "What's wrong?"

"My father called. There's a problem at home. He asked me to fly home."

"When?"

"As soon as possible."

Shocked into stillness, he waited for her to continue, but her silence stretched between them.

"That sounds dire."

"It is."

He imagined the worst and resisted the urge to ask why. "Are you going?"

Her voice softened. "Yes."

He exhaled. "When?"

"That's what I wanted to discuss with you."

"Why me?"

"I'm conflicted."

"About?"

"Well," a heavy exhale came through his phone. "You."

His chest tightened. "Oh." He sat. "What about me?"

She paused. "You're different…in a good way." She chuckled, "No one ever asked to kiss you."

"Rules, you know"

"And you're sweet, in a geeking sort of way. And we've made plans—the lake. Saturday night." She hesitated.

Gus said, "Mama Mia. I've read you all wrong."

"No, you read me perfectly. I put a wall around me. It's a reflex anymore."

"Understand."

"That kiss. The first one. It meant something. I felt it like nothing before."

He swallowed, a subtle head shake emerged, and his face became distorted, "My life. Gina, it's complicated."

"*My life* has its hurdles, too. Right now, I want you thoughts on whether I stay or go."

"I thought you were going?" His voice lifted, "Given the choice, I, I want you to stay more than anything, and…"

"And?"

"And I want nothing more than a weekend at the lake with you."

"There's a but coming."

"But." Gus paused. His voice softened as he exhaled, "There's trouble at home, whatever it is, your family needs you. I understand. Believe me, I do. It would be selfish of me to ask you to come back."

"Selfish?"

Gus measured his response. His thoughts returned to when this odyssey began; Opa asked him to stay, 'one year at the most.'" "It's part of my complicated life. I can't explain right now, and I'm not going to lie."

"I've decided. I'm coming back," Gina declared.

"What? Why?"

"I'm keeping my schedule. I'll call my parents. I'll be back in Atlanta Wednesday at 4:30."

"And what do you expect to happen when…?"

"The situation at home is tense. I completely understand why they want me there, but a few days won't make a difference like it would here. I have commitments to honor. The SCAD benefit. The dedication celebration is on Friday. The lake on Saturday - I'll leave Sunday."

He exhaled slowly. "I don't know."

"What don't you know?"

"It's all good, but..."

"But what?"

He gnawed at his lip. She represented a rare connection untainted by his obsessive mission and the requisite deception. Their kisses set him free from the years-long web he'd spun around himself. Knowing she would leave the following day, the idea of a night alone felt wrong—at least not wise. He'd been in a similar situation with Emiline. He had to choose: stay and complete the Assignment to appease Opa, or decline and return to build the life they envisioned, letting all the hope the Assignment possessed die. He stayed; Emiline left. The hurt lingered. I would again.

"I don't think I can do," the words caught in his throat, "'Goodbye-sex'."

Gina pleaded, "Why are you calling it 'good-bye'?"

What else could he call it? It's what happened with Emiline. In the convoluted, corrupt world encapsulating him, the only truth he knew was that once they crossed that physical, emotional point of no return, there was no going back. He knew himself, and he respected Gina. She'd be in Italy, dealing with whatever was calling her back. He may very well be dead, or in exile on some remote, uncharted island in the Pacific or the ice-covered continent down under, Antarctica. He hung his head, searching for an answer.

Before he could speak, the screen on his phone flashed, "Cedric."

Startled back to his complicated life, he said, "Gina, I need to take this call. Let's talk later."

"What's wrong?"

"Nothing, really. I've got a lot going on."

"Maybe I moved too fast."

No red-blooded man would accuse you of moving too fast.

Gus chuckled, "That's funny. Seriously. A lot is going on here. Let's talk again. Soon."

He looked at the screen just as the words "Missed Call from Cedric" appeared.

He stared at a squirrel busy eating on the ATRI lawn. The oppressive humidity clung to his shirt, matted to his back. His mind traveled to Geneva.

The voicemail ding went unnoticed.

Hearty laughter from two women leaving ATRI broke his trance. He cocked his head and smiled. When had he last laughed that way?

He imagined walking with Gina through sunflower fields, skiing the Alps, and cruising Lake Geneva. A lump formed in his throat. Everything he imagined with Emiline. That evaporated like the hot steamy Might his last memory be their kiss on the curb?

When he stood, the earth tilted beneath him like a carnival ride. Colors smeared across his vision as the tree canopy and sky merged into a nauseating swirl. The copper taste of fear flooded his mouth as his peripheral vision darkened to pinpricks. His knees folded without warning, joints suddenly liquid, and he crashed to the dirt with a sickening thud. The impact sent shock waves through his body, gritty soil pressing against his cheek. Somewhere distant, birds continued their indifferent song, the normalcy of their chirping a surreal counterpoint to the thunder of blood in his ears.

The laughing women rushed over; one splashed bottled water in his face, one smacked his cheeks, jarred his shoulders. She lifted her face and shouted for help. No help came, but Gus came around. On the bench, he declined emergency care. Three young men from his lab appeared and accompanied him to his air-conditioned office. They provided a snack and a power drink, and he assured them the heat had drained him, that he was 'overtired' and 'needed some sleep.' Otherwise, he was 'fine.' They left, reluctantly.

His mind reset, fixed on his sudden vulnerability. By Friday, running the gauntlet lined by those who meant him well and those who meant him harm would require all his energy, physical and emotional. He listened to Cedric's voicemail, asking him to call ASAP.

Gus pushed his desk chair aside, lay on the floor, soothed by the cool air, and called Cedric.

"Ruben hit a wall," Cedric said, "But I may have a way in. Hold up on calling the Governor."

"How?"

"I'm looking for a place in the code where someone could switch the file access off."

"Ruben should know that?"

"Not really. I'd say isolating a single folder is uncommon for them."

"Who could do it without him knowing?"

"Beats me."

"When will you get in?"

"Later. That's going to take a minute, and I'm behind on something big."

"This is big, Ced," Gus said, then added, "By the way, the little man, his name is Funk. He and his crew are going in tonight."

"Funk? That's his name?"

Gus nodded.

"Awesome. Neat guy, right?"

Gus grinned. "With a good grip."

Gus checked his phone for a text from Scales. Nothing.

Henry's name flashed on his phone. Approaching 9:00 in Geneva.

Gus answered. "Henry?"

"Gus. Opa's getting worse."

Still recuperating on the floor, his body tensed. "Worse?"

"He started out fine, but he's getting a fever."

Gus rose, slammed into his chair, and found the data folders in the cloud. Two minutes passed.

"I see his readout. Damn. He's getting toxic. The unit is stopping the cancer, probably killing it, or his immune system is, but he's not eliminating the waste."

"What do I do? Call the ambulance?"

"Not yet. Give him a pint of water. Make a large pot of coffee with purified water and call Helene. Have her go to the pharmacy and buy an enema bag. I'll send you the directions. You have to give him a coffee enema."

"You're kidding?"

"No. It's the best way to eliminate the accumulating dead cells. It triggers his liver and gallbladder to excrete them."

Gus remembered the first time he read that recommendation from Dr. Gonzales, an esteemed infectious disease specialist. He thought the medical establishment might tar and feather him. In time, they did worse.

Reflecting on his code, Gus had no specific frequency to facilitate the elimination of the dead cells and the chemicals they released into the person's circulation. He assumed the body would somehow handle the situation. A lump appeared in his throat. Had many succumbed due to the toxicity created by his device? If any had died, his method would be no better than traditional chemotherapy.

Heavy in his chair, elbows on his desk, Gus sighed and rested his forehead on his palms. What if his device failed on the one person he most desperately wanted to save?

Looking ahead and prioritizing, he scrapped the commercial future of the biofeedback device. No IEEI demo. The mattress mat was all that mattered, but he couldn't risk flawed code. His breathing stopped. Suddenly, the GCI data he began to equivocate over was invaluable, for a different reason than Christian and IEEI.

A new question stabbed his mind: was the person hiding the data keeping it from Gus or from GCI? Each digital barrier felt personal, not just technical obstacles, but deliberate attempts to thwart the mission his family had sacrificed everything for.

Laser focused, Gus texted Perry Michael at GMC: "Mat demo still on for tomorrow?"

He texted Bobby the same, adding: "Confirm Keegan's group will be here Friday?"

A second text went to Scales. "We need to get in GCI tonight. Can you clear it?"

Impatient, he punched in Mitch Scales's number. Before it rang, he ended the call, set his phone down, and thought, wait. What if Funk went to GCI and couldn't get in? What if Cedric hit another firewall? Emails and files weren't enough to run the gauntlet ahead. He had to know what Sheehan, Slayton and Pogue were saying behind closed doors.

Inside, he screamed at himself. 'Stop worrying. Focus.'

Mat. Bobby. Christian—keep her alive.

The thought of keeping Christian alive yanked his mind back to Sheehan and Vinnie. Opa's voice rang in his head: 'Mind your business.' Maybe, he thought, those two deserve more attention than I'm giving them.

Funk's text lit up Gus's phone: "Going in at 5:00."

Stunned, he looked at his phone: 3:50.

How did he pull it off?

"What about Mitch?" Gus texted back, "Cancel my guy?"

Funk sent back a thumbs-up emoji.

He fired off a text to Mitch: "Abort mission."

Chapter Twenty-Nine

At four thirty on Monday afternoon, the desk phone in his lab office rang. Dr. Lee announced that an FBI agent and a Metro Atlanta detective were in his office and would like to speak with him.

A man who could have played linebacker at Tech in his day, with tight salt-and-pepper hair, sat at Dr. Lee's conference table, his back to Gus. He stood, turned casually as if Gus had interrupted a conversation at a cocktail party. "Special Agent John David Hile, FBI." He offered no handshake."

Watching the show, a man of his height stood nearby. He had dark skin and nappy, prematurely grey hair. He didn't look healthy, with the bags beneath each eye. The dated brown suit hung on him. The collar on his dull white shirt was loose around his neck. The tie looked older than Gus. He extended his hand and offered a shallow, warm smile. "Detective Udell Suttles, Metro Atlanta Police."

Finally, Gus thought, a decent person.

Seated at the conference table, Hile explained they'd received notice of his surveillance application. Gus shot a glance at Dr. Lee. Lee nodded.

"The Bureau sees all material collected under the Patriot Act," Hile said. "It's reviewed electronically for keywords and word patterns. It flags suspicious activity."

Suttles added, "You may use what you collect in court. We make all law enforcement decisions."

Gus nodded, mentally cataloging the implications.

Suttles continued. "If the Bureau detects anything concerning, they will notify me, and I will work directly with you. Understood."

Gus's head shook subtly, "Yes, but..." Gus paused to check his words to Suttles. "Why is any of this your concern?"

Suttles looked at Hile.

Hile said, "Let's just say, 'We're on the same team.'"

"How is that?" Gus said.

Hile said, "Interpol Agent Karen Baumann brought us up to speed on our predicament."

The name hung in the air. So did the word. Predicament.

Gus swallowed. His heart rate quickened. His palms began to sweat. He nodded at Hile.

Suttles broke the tension: "It's my concern because I'm the local contact for ATRI surveillance requests."

Gus glanced at Dr. Lee.

"He here before me," Dr. Lee said.

Gus feigned a grin. Maybe he could lean on this guy. The situation was broadening in his mind. The edges were blurry but recognizable.

Hile said, "We have oversight."

"Oversight?" Gus said, glancing at Suttles.

Gus thought he saw a sincere grin. Suttles said, "We've got your back."

The FBI introduction lasted minutes. The implications would last longer.

Hile had spoken to Baumann about the assassin, no doubt, but was the assassin actually coming? Was he already here?

Were they going to speak to Christian?

~~~

The two men left. His teeth clenched; impulses lurched inside him. Text Christian, "You're staying at Henry's. Please. Talk soon."

Outside his first-floor lab, he texted Henry. "How's Opa?"

He texted Cedric, "Progress?"

Texts from Bobby and Perry Michaels, The M in GMC Engineering. Each confirmed the meeting for tomorrow morning to conduct the mat demonstration.

In his office, he straightened chairs and cleared his desk. Routines to calm the chaos in his mind. He pulled up the mat source code on his screen and confirmed what he knew: there was no specific toxic elimination code to change. His assumption had failed, leaving the entire project hanging in the balance. Opa was lucky to have Henry. He sighed. The device was not yet a self-contained one-size-fits-all cancer-stopping device. Would it ever be? Maybe. Critics would
~~~

feast on that fact, as they should. But, as disappointing as the toxicity news was, postponement stared him in the face, and the code pulsing through thousands of people in JCO beds persisted in clouding his objectivity in decision-making. Meanwhile, he'd break Ruben Gerding. His desperation to get into the denied data folder made him appreciate how desperate someone was to keep him out.

His phone vibrated.

"Hello?"

"Gus Meier, Josh McIntyre, Communications Director at GCI. There's breaking news on the internet about the Governor intervening at GCI on behalf of PPP, and the Compliance Officer and the CEO being suspended. Do you know anything about that?"

Gus scoffed, "How would I know?"

Silence.

Josh said, "People know things."

"Josh, what's the big deal?"

"The big deal is people on social media continue to claim miraculous results in GCI cancer patients. They want to protect the device GCI expelled—your device. That's why I'm calling. GCI and Donna Sheehan are taking incredible heat."

"Still no data?"

"No. So these claims are baseless. However, Ms. Sheehan strongly believes that Ms. Lawler knows more than she's telling."

"Why not me?"

"She regards you as a stuck-up ATRI nerd. This is beneath you."

Gus smirked. Now he's a nerd.

"I called the Governor's office to request that they issue a conciliatory statement. They won't."

"How many people?"

"Enough for a CNN producer to call and ask me what's going on."

"Hm," Gus said.

"Slayton and Tanzilla were going on their morning show, *New Day*, tomorrow morning to talk about the new wing, cancer care in America, and what contribution GCI is making."

"Why are we talking, Josh? I'm busy."

"You're listed as the designer of the device. Do you have a response to these claims people are making?"

"You mean you want me to tell you what the Chief of Oncology and the President of ASCO should say when the host asks them to explain the claims? Is that what you want?

~~~

He checked his watch; it was 5:00. Funk was in at GCI. Hile's men were monitoring. Kip and Carley were in the Watchtower. Soon, he'd hear and see for himself.

He and Bobby would see the mat demo in the morning.

Where was Cedric on the data? He needed to get into those files.

He squeezed his forehead. Could he integrate the rest of his code into the mat and hope Opa's toxicity issues were a one-off problem? The answers: probably not and probably not.

Aromas from the restaurant filled the room. He needed food. His gaze drifted to Gina's apartment door. Then to the business office, where Melo had removed the legal box. His thoughts drifted back to Josh McIntyre. What motivated that guy? Everyone seemed to be hiding something. Gina. Melo. Christian and Sheehan. But the cancer patients on social media weren't hiding—they were exposing the truth about their reactions to the device. He had a truth of his own...he wanted anonymity.

His phone buzzed with a text from Funk: "We're in. Audio/video live. What you see will change everything."

Gus stared at the message, his pulse quickening. The surveillance operation wasn't just beginning—it was about to expose secrets that could destroy everything he'd worked for. Or save it.

Either way, there was no turning back.
~~~

Chapter Thirty

Tuesday morning, in his bed at Henry and Cassie's, Gus bolted up from a nightmare. Panting and sweating, his jaw trembling, his eyes darting wildly in search of orientation. A flailing hand smacked the clock repeatedly to silence the alarm and defend himself if it wasn't a dream after all.

He fell backwards onto his bed. His heart was still pounding, and the fear was still real. Covered in sweat, he swung his feet to the floor and fixed his eyes on a family photo Cassie kept on the dresser.

Scalding water hit his body. Too relaxing. He flipped the lever to cold and braced against the wall, shuddering as it struck him in the bull's-eye on his back.

What might it feel like to be shot?

His mind vacillated between standing on the thin metal fence and the stories Josh told about saved patients speaking out. He could understand one side not wanting the news out, but not both. He didn't want it out. Who was he in the dream? The irony of people being saved by his device, which placed him at risk, weighed on him. Was Sheehan the masked entity grabbing at his ankle? He thought about Funk, Kip, and Carley. Had they recorded her calls? Would more men in black masks appear on CNN *New Day*? The dream faded, and he wondered about Opa. Gina? Her birthday? He'd need some time to complete a thought.

A single sheet of paper on the desk beside the bed held the scribbles he made at 2:00 a.m. A meteor shower of ideas, strategies, and options tormented his sleep. There. The sequence. The route forward. Verify Mat. Recover Data. Update source code. New PCB, Integrate. Demonstrate. Sell. Distribute. Monitor. Analyze. Publish.

The shower stopped. Less brain fog, more focus. Not on the entire sequence but on the critical first step: verification. Without proof the mat worked, why risk his life, or Christian's?

Move on. Stay safe. Come back later.

The mat would conduct frequencies ten times faster than the biofeedback device. The circuit board in his backpack needed to confirm to Bobby and JCO that the wait was worth it. He gnawed on his lip. His breath quickened. Reality hit him. The future of the Assignment and the future of cancer care hinged on this trip to GMC Engineering. He had his doubts.

He followed the aroma of coffee down the stairs. Cassie stood at the island, newspaper spread, looking annoyingly alert. She nodded at the headlights outside and pushed the carafe toward him. "You're out early."

Gus yawned. Glanced out to see ACE had backed in, always prepared. He powered his phone on and set it on the island. "Got to get a jump on the fun."

He poured and took a burning sip.

His phone hummed, dinged, and played successive short melodies signaling texts, emails, and voicemails.

Cassie looked at the phone, then at him, ignoring the phone. He shrugged and exhaled audibly, "They've been there all night, what's another few minutes?"

She turned the newspaper page.

"Question,"

Cassie gave him her attention.

Gus opened his phone and turned it to her.

"Who is Antonio Favolini?" Cassie said, referring to the attribution to the photo of a teenage Gina, arms linked with a dark-haired boy, laughing, carefree, ankle-deep in a wooden vat, wearing grape-stained pants rolled up to their knees.

"Old flame?"

Cassie repeated the caption under Happy 30th Birthday. "Crush is not the same without you. Still here. Always yours."

Crush—the annual grape harvest ritual they'd clearly shared—gave context to the wooden vat in the image. He felt an unexpected tightness in his chest, his eyes steady on her carefree smile, as Antonio's arm was wrapped possessively around her waist; both of them laughed, their feet stained purple. The intimacy of the moment captured in the image yanked at his heart. In her, he saw happiness personified.

"She didn't tell you?" Cassie's voice pulled him back to the present.

"About her birthday or the wounded boy back home?" He tried to keep his tone light, but the picture stung on many levels, past and present.

Cassie grimaced. "She's mature beyond her years. I'd bet she didn't want any fanfare."

Gus agreed. "Just an odd way to learn about it."

Cassie retrieved an insulated cup from her cabinet, poured a fresh cup of coffee, put the top on, and handed it to him while nodding toward the door to the porch. "You've had some odd lessons lately."

He accepted the cup. "I've had an odd life."

Cassie smiled, hugged him, and added, "And you wouldn't trade it for anything."

He hugged her back, glanced down at her pleasant smile, and lifted his coffee cup in a small toast. "I think that chance has passed." His lips curved into a weary but genuine smile as he squared his shoulders and headed out.

Danno opened the back door for him. ACE met his eyes in the rearview mirror, a slight nod acknowledging his readiness, her gloved fingers tightening imperceptibly on the wheel. She pulled through the wrought iron gates and past the guard on duty. He checked the map app on his phone and texted Bobby his ETA. The rendezvous point was The Smith House restaurant. A quick breakfast, strategic review, and onto the demo at 8:15.

The drive would take ninety minutes. Gus thought he'd rest his eyes and think about something he relished, Gina.

His dreams were sweeter, and the interruption less abrupt with the phone he'd stashed under his thigh vibrated.

"Henry." Appeared on the screen.

"Good, you're up," Henry said. "I'm on the line with Agent Baumann."

He froze. What? No nice update on Opa.

Agent Baumann spared him the pleasantries. "Negotiations have taken a turn. My people wouldn't deal. They upped the ante, convinced he had more to offer. He did. Much more. The person who detonated the bomb is now involved in a prescription drug ring in Atlanta. I've spoken to Hile and his local detective. His story checks out. Negotiations are back on."

Gus gripped the phone tighter. "Why the gamesmanship? Get the names, shut it down, and let me finish."

"He's not stupid." Baumann's voice hardened. "He's holding details."

Gus's tone hardened too. "He's holding all the cards. That's what you're saying?"

Baumann eased up, "Not all of them. Listen, I want him inside. I *need* him inside, working for us. I'm going to bust his people here *and* there *and* stop some bad shit in America. This is not just about you."

That explained the gut punch.

Gus shook his head, staring out the window at the passing landscape. "Got it. What's next?"

"He'll be there Thursday morning. When he arrives, authorities will fit him with surveillance gear. At some point his handler will announce the targets." Baumann paused. "We're working on a meeting with the detonator."

"Like an assassin's reunion?" Gus scoffed, running his hand through his hair.

Baumann continued, unfazed. "His freedom hinges on his helping us accomplish all our goals. That's what he bargained for. If we succeed, he can make croissants wherever he likes."

~~~

After breakfast at the Smith House, Bobby rode with Gus, ACE, and Danno to GMC. The conversation Gus and Bobby had over breakfast brought a sense of calm. No anxiety. No mention of the buyout. A genuine eagerness to see the mat process data.

Before they reached the facility, Bobby received a call from Suzanne. The slight fever their three-year-old, Robbie, woke with had shot up. A small seizure followed, then another, lasting longer. She called EMS, now Bobby. After relating the story, ACE drove him back to the Smith House, and he left. As Gus watched him rush away, he felt certain he knew what mattered most to Bobby and thought back to his father's excitement when he had invited Gus to join him on the ill-fated yacht cruise. Please, he said to himself and to any source or Spirit that might intervene, spare Bobby and Suzanne the weight of the grief he had known.

~~~

At GMC Engineering, Perry Michael and Patricia Compton led him to the operations fabrication room. On what reminded him of an oversized drafting table, Michael unrolled the thin, opaque plastic sheet.

Gus took the material between his fingers. "So sheer. Almost fabric. Amazing."

Patricia Compton smiled. "It is."

Gus pinched the fine, end-to-end hairlike graphene microfiber strands embedded in and reinforcing the sheer plastic. "This is what's patented?"

Perry Michael said, "Yes. You, as the designer, Dr. Lee, and you are the creators, we are the manufacturer."

A bulky man approached and smoothed the opaque plastic over a three-inch foam mattress pad.

"Welcome back, Gus," said David Grace, the "G" in GMC. "I'm your final examination."

Apprehension crept in as Grace lay on the sheet. He rolled side to side, and Gus winced.

"Relax," Pat told him. "The graphene in it won't allow ripping."

Gus opened his laptop and connected to the WiFi.

Pat Compton installed the PCB, which Gus had removed from his backpack.

Real-time images and information appeared in five blocks on the monitor.

"Verblüffend," Gus whispered the German term for amazing and stepped toward the screen, "Lightning fast."

A high-resolution infrared image appeared. It captured the heat patterns emitted from David Grace's massive body, which moved in unison with him. In the right margin, his vitals were displayed: blood pressure, heart rate, oxygen saturation, and body weight—three hundred and seventy.

The system continuously monitored all metrics in real-time. Any deviation outside preset parameters triggered an alarm. Most importantly, thermal sensors formed an image to expose a forming bed sore. Hourly data was uploaded to a cloud account for one month, and all alarms were recorded in the patient's electronic medical record.

"Beautiful," Gus smiled. He scrolled down to find what he called the Trojan Horse data, his cancer-stopping source code sent to independent private access spreadsheets. Empty. No Trojan Horse. He toggled back between pages. Load, damn it. Nothing. His stomach dropped, and a cold sweat broke across his forehead. His fingers typed frantically. To no avail. Bobby's data came through; his didn't.

The three partners watched disappointment wash over his face.

"This may be the fastest processing material on earth," David Grace said. "You expected a complete redesign of your PCB, right?"

Gus furrowed his brow, stared at the empty spreadsheet, and told himself to stay calm.

"When is IEEI?" Pat asked.

Dazed, Gus didn't waste his time mentioning three days.

"Maybe next year?" David said.

He thanked them and left, holding the lone mat.

~~~

Danno escorted Gus to the Tahoe. Gus scoffed at the attention. All the security for what?

ACE left Gus alone with his thoughts for five minutes. She glanced in the rearview mirror and coughed, "You had several calls."

He collected his phone, expecting news from Bobby.

Nothing from Bobby. There was a call from Josh McIntyre, Christian Lawler, and Bob Holder. All three called twice. All three left voicemails.

Christian's first. "Unless you're dead. Call me the instant you get this."

Bob Holder sounded a bit more conciliatory. "These testimonials are amazing. Your father would be proud. I know your grandfather is. So am I. And, for the record. I'm not surprised."

Josh McIntyre whispered frantically. "Mr. Meier—Gus, this is Josh McIntyre. Slayton and Tanzilla went on the CNN morning show, New Day, this morning. You may have heard about all the claims on social media that GCI is withholding a cancer cure. I specifically told the producer questions about those claims were off limits. After they cover the new wing dedication, the host ends with that! Tanzilla went off the rails. He called patients mental cases, religious zealots, and even dropped the antiquated term, spontaneous remission. Social media is crucifying him and GCI. They know Donna Sheehan expelled you. They know you by name, and Christian Lawler. Get ready."

Get ready? For what? Was McIntyre expecting the media to link his expulsion to the cancer claims? The muscles in his entire body seized. His mind went to his euphoria when his first animal experiment saved a Jack Russell Terrier named Bob. He didn't want any media attention.

The voicemail continued, "CNN has called me six times. They are getting calls from around the world. We are too. James just left my office. He spoke to the people at CNN and Dr. Lee. CNN has asked if you and Sheehan would appear on New Day tomorrow and clear the air. Set the record straight. James and Sheehan fought it, but they've been under extraordinary pressure to go on. Dr. Lee says it's up to you. Gus, you need to do this. I'll prep you. We've got to put out this fire. As soon...."
~~~

The voicemail timed out.

Gus stared at his phone screen and slammed the phone on his thigh. It wasn't his fire to douse. Sheehan started it.

The story being told raised his suspicion…A wannabe morning talk show host hoping to land a journalistic coup defies direction and goes off script on two prominent physicians? Who does that?

What made Josh think he'd go on CNN after that stunt? Gus didn't need to ask. Every researcher knows to control the controllables. Plus, Sheehan had a hidden agenda. He saw no upside. Worse, publicity put his face to a name and a name to his device. No, thank you. Instinctually, ideas darted into his head. No sequence made up for the failed source code verification in the new GMC mat.

Helene came to mind. With a phone call, a plane would appear at PDK airport by the time ACE arrived in an hour. Nothing would please her more. He opened the notepad app on his phone and began typing a new sequence of ideas, should he decide to leave.

To Josh—Deflect. Make up possible links between the device and outcomes. Share with CNN host

Possible Zoom from Geneva to deflect attention from Christian

In Geneva or in exile—monitor how Sheehan, Josh, Tanzilla, Slayton, and James react/respond to the patient claims

Reaction dictates when to return/resume integrating new mat w/ new source code

Leaving now is a delay—not defeat

The mass distribution opportunity is most likely gone.

JCO happy—decreased bed sore infections. Charge premium. Bobby royalties huge.

Christian gets free publicity. Sets her own price. Great royalties going forward.

A long exhale preceded the distinct relaxation in his neck and shoulder muscles. He set the phone on his seat. The plan had merit. Tranquility reigned.

Call Helene or wait? Wait. Rest first, then call.

A call roused him. Kip Richardson in the ATRI basement. The Watchtower.

Kip's words tumbled out, rapid-fire. "You got my messages?"

"Yeah."

"Sheehan must not sleep," Kip said, urgently edging his voice.

"Calm down. Just the highlights, Kip."

"Last night—" Kip spoke faster now, barely pausing for breath. "She had a long conversation with New England Analgesics in Boston. They refer to that call as Boston. Then she called Vincent Schnerr at Consortium Security, Stone Mountain, Ga. His brother is Klaus Schnerr. Her brother is some guy named Bo."

"Kip," Gus interrupted. "Stop. What's valuable?"

"I'm getting to it. Listen to this recording," Kip said, his voice dropping to an intense whisper. "It's Vinnie Schnerr talking to Sheehan. She's called Boston rather than calling Klaus. I can't tell why she is supposed to. Maybe you can. Vinnie tells her to call her brother."

"About what?" Gus asked.

"I don't know. I wanted you to hear it and tell me," Kip said. "We have the whole conversation. This is just a portion."

A man's voice said, "Did you call him?"

"That's Vinnie Schnerr," Kip said.

The woman's voice responded, "No, I called Boston instead."

"That's Sheehan," Kip said.

Agitated, the male voice said, "You're gonna get me killed. Why call Boston? You know better. This is Klaus's call to make."

"Well, your brother is a condescending prick that won't listen to me."

"No shit. Cause when you don't follow the rules. You put him in a bad spot, which puts me in a bad spot."

"And now, Tanzilla…"

"Jesus," Vinnie shouted. "Tanzilla is a lunatic with his own agenda, and he's not your boss. Klaus is. You know it. So what the fuck?" The man took a breath. "I gotta call Klaus."

"No."

"Yes. You and Boston are *way* out of bounds, and I'm linked to you."

Sheehan scoffed, "Geneva and Boston go way back."

"No one gives a shit. Geneva will tell Boston to follow the fucking rules. I'm sorry, but I gotta call."

"Wait. Save time, save face. Send a couple of your guys to pick her up."

"Pick her up? And do what? My guys don't do that. The rule is, I see or hear anything suspicious, call Klaus. That's the rule. Period."

"But your guys could pick her up, right?"

Vinnie chuckled, "You're not listening. Then what?"

"Get her to turn over the source code. I may be able to decipher that code."

"Why didn't you get it when you had them?"

"I didn't know Tanzilla would want it."

"Now what, you want my guys to beat it out of her?"

"Intimidate her. She'll lead us to it. If I get it, decipher it, all is forgiven."

"Wrong. Tanzilla may be happy, but Klaus? He'll be pissed. And Klaus puts targets on targets, so shut the fuck up and let me do what you should have done a long time ago, unless you wanna put targets on us."

"Vinnie. Calm down. Okay. Klaus runs the show, but you and I will never be targeted: We. Make. The. Money." She laughed. "I wrote the damned program. Everyone's fat because of you and me, including Klaus, right?"

Vinnie's tone calmed, "Alright, alright. But you should get Bo involved."

"That's not Bo's thing."

"Not his thing?" Vinnie exploded, "He's our fucking mole. Klaus went to great lengths to save your ass and put him where he is. He might put a slug in your head while you sleep."

Sheehan exhaled audibly and paused, "OK. Relax. Don't call Klaus. I'll call."

"Well, I gotta call Klaus, but I'll tell him you got it down to two suspects to keep the scene clean, and you're working with Bo to get the code. He can't think I'm going rogue. He sure as hell can't think you're going rogue, again."

"Give me till the end of the day tomorrow?"

"No. Not smart. Every minute I wait is risky. If he knows you called Boston, the longer I wait, the worse it is for us."

"Maybe Bo can't get close enough. You think he can."

"How should I know? He's your brother. Call him up. I'm calling my brother."

Kip said. "That's it."

Gus replayed what stuck out in his mind. "The brothers know the hierarchy."

Kip said, "Yep. Her brother is the wild card. Not sure where he is. I found a Consortium Security office in Geneva that must be linked to the Schnerrs. The Schnerr brothers' father is Wolfgang. He stepped away from the company recently. Cancer. There may be a succession soon. Vinnie respects his brother's status. Sheehan resents him."

"But they make the money. What's that all about?" Gus said.

"I'm not sure, but she seems to think it puts her above reproach. Something's got to give."

Gus stared at his phone, processing the surveillance recording. Christian was in immediate danger. His escape plan suddenly felt like cowardice. He thought of Opa lying weak in Geneva, fighting for his life with a device that might fail without the missing data or an upgrade. He thought of Christian, unaware that people planned to "pick her up."

Too many crises converging at once—the failed mat demo, the CNN exposure threat, Opa's deteriorating condition, and now this direct threat to Christian. His mind couldn't process it all, but one thing was clear: he couldn't abandon her now.

He deleted his escape plan and began typing a new message to Christian: "We need to talk. Now. You're in danger."

His pulse quickened. *Call Bobby. Trust Christian. Everything you need is here. Stay the course. Play the game you know.*

He clenched his teeth and imagined what life may have been like seventy-three years earlier when the Jewish engineer handed off his notebook and this project, certain that death awaited him and his family. His parting words to his great-grandfather echoed in his head, "This must not fall into the wrong hands."

Chapter Thirty-One

Tuesday's third attempt to organize his action steps appeared one letter at a time on his phone screen. Item one, 'Consult Opa.'

Six hours ahead made it 5:00 p.m. in Geneva.

Henry answered. Gus felt relieved hearing Opa had shown improvement, particularly in his mental acuity and alertness.

"Thanks for being there, Henry. I need to speak to him," Gus said.

Henry shared more details as he made his way to Opa. All were encouraging.

Gus studied the landmarks outside the tinted Tahoe window. They were near the 14th Street exit.

"Go ahead, Gus," Henry said.

Gus hesitated and looked ahead. "Hold on."

Traffic slowed. A flashing road barricade pointed to a single lane.

"Pull into this parking lot, please," Gus said to ACE.

She did.

"Would you both step out? I need privacy on this call."

ACE peered in the rearview mirror. He moved his head toward the door.

Alone, he said to Henry, "The mat demo failed."

"How?"

"I don't know what I was thinking. I knew better. I can't rush this. The new mat is too fast. I should have told JCO I have to stick to the original timeline."

"But you didn't."

He scoffed, "They're like a dog in heat. They want it now. Bobby's version is fine. This ship is sailing, with or without me."

"Can you fix it——integrate your code with the mat?" Henry said.

"That's why I called. Is Opa on the call?"

"Yes."

"Opa, I need some advice."

"On what?" Opa asked.

"Trust. To have any chance at pulling this off, I have to put my trust in someone."

~~~

When Gus walked in, Christian and Bobby sat opposite the entrance at the conference table in the Holder SCIF. Their expressionless faces did not soften as he set his backpack on the desk and began. "Did either of you see the CNN program?"

Christian slid her phone across the table. "It's on YouTube. Watch the last minutes."

"I haven't," Bobby said, walking to Gus and looking over his shoulder.

Dr. Tanzilla and Slayton looked relaxed on the CNN set. The clip began with Tanzilla giving an upbeat answer about the new wing dedicated to Dr. Slayton's father and the progress he expected in cancer research at GCI.

Then, with no warning, the host said, "What can you tell us about the claims that GCI is sitting on a non-pharmaceutical cure for cancer now?"

The doctors openly glared at the host, then at one another. The host pressed them about the Complementary and Alternative Medicine Department. "These are serious claims, and the number of people making them is not insignificant."

Tanzilla clenched his teeth. Slayton nodded and said, "It's an exciting time in oncology. My father founded the CAM department with Dr. Clair Pogue. We are a research facility. As glowing as these accounts are, science is not founded on anecdotes. It demands rigorous study."

"Then why did you expel the device all these individuals have claimed to have healed them?"

"That hasn't happened," Dr. Tanzilla declared.

The host's face broke into a wide grin. "Your denial is exactly why there is talk of a coverup, a conspiracy to hide a cure for cancer."

Tanzilla seethed.

The host glanced at Dr. Slayton. "Dr. Slayton?"

Slayton froze. "I'm not the one to ask."

"If not you, who?" The host asked.

Tanzilla stood before Slayton could answer.

"Incredible," Gus said as he stood and returned Christian's phone to her.

Christian accepted, her eyes locked on Gus, "Are you the one to ask?"
~~~

Gus held his ground and paused. His glance shifted to Bobby, who waited. "I've reached a crossroads."

"And?" Christian said.

"And I've decided to cancel our appointment with IEEI on Friday."

Christian gasped.

Gus said, "On behalf of ATRI, I cannot release the biofeedback device at this time."

"God damn, you," Christian blurted. "Who got to you? You sold out. Like Slayton sold out Pogue. Jesus Christ."

He swallowed. His chest tightened, but his voice remained steady. "It's not over. Just not now, Christian. But Bobby has a deal on the table with JCO. It bypasses IEEI, and it closes on Friday. It requires all my time and energy."

Christian turned to Bobby.

Bobby raised his hands. "I didn't see this coming."

"Bullshit," Christian said.

Bobby tilted his head at her and cringed. "Who you talking to?" He paused. "We go back, girl. Gus and I got a deal. I don't know nothing about your deal. We're jus doin some tweaks, that's all."

Christian stood, "Well, Bobby," she mocked, "I ain't got no deal." She walked to the door, her hand on the knob and turned to Gus, "Come out here."

They stepped into the corridor, Christian's footsteps quick and determined. She led Gus to the railing overlooking the atrium. Sunlight streamed through the glass ceiling, patterns shifted on the walls, and the persistent rush of water fountains below created a wall of white noise to keep their conversation private.

Christian's grip firm on the brass railing, her words barely audible, she spoke in a low, demanding voice, "Be honest, does this thing really help people with cancer?"

He honestly considered being honest and trusting her, but he couldn't. Not yet. Not her. Not entirely. "Something is happening....no one can pin it down."

Her jaw tightened, her head shook, and her eyes closed. "God damn it. You're still a horrible liar to me. Lie to Bobby, to Holder, to anyone, but" she faced him, "You can't lie to me."

He chose silence.

She said, "I see the miraculous claims people are making. Maybe this, maybe that, or maybe it's not GCI hiding something, but you." Her voice cracked, her eyes closed. "I'm an idiot. I trusted you. Now, no IEEI. No royalties."

"In time."

"I don't have time. My father is dying from cancer."

Gus held his breath; the burden of his recent lie suddenly became heavier. "I'm sorry."

She swallowed and covered her mouth for a long moment. "They don't have much. She's in terrible health. They can't stay at home. I can't take them. My sister and little brother can't. I was counting on the royalties to pay for a nursing home."

Gus nodded. He'd met them in undergraduate days, when he and Christian were close. He recalled feeling like a prize she had won when around her family. "They were kind to me."

Christian faced the atrium, rested her arms on the railing, and planted her face in her hands.

Gus started to set his palm on her back, hesitated, then gently set it on the sturdy physique she once shared freely with him. "I understand. You know about my father."

She turned to him. A tear rolled down her left cheek. "John is not my dad. He's my uncle. She's my aunt…my mother's sister." Christian said, her voice cracking. "My real father is dead. My mother killed him. And his lover. She's on death row at Arrendale."

The Women's correctional facility was ten miles past his exit to the house at the lake. He felt as if the floor had disappeared beneath him. His throat constricted. This revelation explained so much about her—the drive, control, and carefully constructed walls.

She wept uncontrollably. He drew her close. His eyes shut tight against his own sudden emotion. Her body trembled. Each sob reverberated through him. The scent of her lemony shampoo sent rushing memories through him.

He'd last seen her cry when, at Henry's insistence, following the weekend romp caught on camera, he'd declared an end to their promiscuous relationship for the sake of good grades. Her pain then had seemed disproportionate, dramatic. Now it made brutal sense—another abandonment, another rejection by someone she'd allowed herself to be vulnerable with. The revelation hit him like pieces clicking into place. Her control issues. The walls. The drive and determination. Years of erratic behavior. Now it made sense. Another abandonment. Another rejection. She had suppressed her past, buried her secrets. He'd been blind. She kept him blind. And he had kept her blind, too. He wished he could go back and know her better, more honestly, sooner. They were both suffering now.

He squeezed her firmly and whispered, "I can help."

A call interrupted their exchange. Gus found his phone, glanced at the screen, and tilted his head down to her. "Take a unit to him. Today. Show him how to use it."

"Will it work?" Christian asked.

Gus nodded, grinned and waved his phone at her. "Trust me." He began stepping away, "I have to take this."

She took several quick steps toward him, pulled his face toward her, rose on her tiptoes, and kissed his cheek. In a low voice only he could hear, she said, "Thank you."

~~~

Josh McIntyre said, "Do you have a second?"

"Yes," Gus said, turning into a stairwell.

"Mr. James has charged me with calling you on behalf of GCI to ask if you, on behalf of ATRI and the PPP, would be willing to join Donna Sheehan on CNN News Day tomorrow morning to address your device and the news regarding its expulsion from GCI?"

"Why would *I* go on CNN?"

Kip Richardson flashed on his phone screen. "Josh, give me one second."

"Kip?" Gus said.

"Have you talked to the guy from GCI?"

"Who?"

"Josh."

"He's on hold right now."

"It's a total cluster over there. Tanzilla and Slayton got decimated on CNN. People are screaming for an investigation into a cover-up at GCI. James has called in outside PR help and law enforcement."

"Why law enforcement?"

"Patient records? Hackers. Conspiracy to harm GCI. With the dedication coming up, he's being proactive." Kip scoffed, "That Josh guy is pushing to have you and Sheehan on together to clear the air."

"Me? Clear the air?"
~~~

"They want you to lie. Tanzilla wants you to say there is no correlation between the claims people make and your device." Kip said.

"Why me? Why not Christian?"

"Image. ATRI credibility. Josh told Tanzilla CNN wants you and Sheehan. I can't verify that."

Gus remembered the earlier call between Sheehan and Vinnie regarding Tanzilla—*his agenda, the source code*—and switched the call back to Josh. "Josh? Tell them I'll do it. I'll go along." Gus embellished his reasoning, "Sheehan was perfectly within her limits, and I'll simply share what I said in the meeting Friday morning as to why I think the people are getting better.

"What's that?"

"Classic complementary medicine. It's perfect. It's what makes GCI so wonderful and unique. My device..."

Josh gasped, "Jesus. Don't say that. Tanzilla wants you to say emphatically that there is no correlation between what people are claiming and your device."

"Really? Has that been concluded?"

"They have nothing to support the claims being made."

"Did they find our data?"

"Listen, Gus, don't be a wise guy." His voice dropped, "Hold Sheehan up as honorable and conscientious, and portray yourself as a meager research engineer, not a physician."

"Hum. Okay," Gus said. Meager? He would go one step farther. *The source code. Perfect bait. A peace offering.*

At last, a rare moment of encouragement that he believed would disarm Tanzilla and Sheehan, deflect her vendetta from Christian, and resuscitate the mat project, on life support.

In a hurried walk, he returned to the Holder SCIF to enlist Bobby's help. Recalling the terrorizing dream he'd woken to that morning, Gus imagined taking some shots at Sheehan on national TV. Let her see how she liked it.

~~~

In the SCIF, Bobby sat where Gus had left him twenty minutes ago.

"How'd that go?" Bobby asked.

"What?"

"Christian?" Bobby said.
~~~

Gus chuckled at how much had transpired since she had called him out. "Fine. She has a lot going on."

Bobby shook his head. "She must." Then added, "About this morning. I'm sorry I couldn't be there. That business with Robbie, that was wicked scary."

"I can imagine. Glad he's okay." Gus inhaled. "The demo. It didn't go the way I wanted. The mat, you're going to love. But the PCB has to be redesigned."

Bobby flinched and shook his head. "Naw, man. It works."

Gus grinned. "Bobby, I'm going to give you a chance to manage in the big leagues. I need an all-star team to integrate the source code into a new PCB. Fast."

The quizzical look on Bobby's face gave Gus pause. Don't force the issue, Bobby. Please.

"I got talent, but not ATRI talent."

Gus grinned. "I need the best you have. You're my Bobby Cox managing the Braves. Pick an all-star lineup. Everyone gets a handsome bonus, win or lose."

Bobby raised his eyebrows and shook his head. "JCO liked what I showed them. I ain't losing. This new wrinkle wasn't part of the deal."

Gus sighed.

Bobby knew the score.

Gus had to lie. "Dr. Lee and I designed the mat specifically for this project. JCO is requesting an accommodation to our timeline. Dr. Lee and I agree that request is not in the best interest of the end product. JCO is trying to make their problem my problem." The part about Dr. Lee was the lie. To Gus, the rest was the truth.

Bobby began making recruiting calls. Engineers respected Gus and signed on. They would meet in the SCIF at 7:00 that evening.

~~~

In the Holder Medical parking lot, Gus surprised Danno by knocking on his window, startling the bodyguard awake.

"I feel extra safe with you two sleeping on the job," Gus teased, his mood lighter for realizing how he'd play Sheehan on TV. He met ACE's glance in the mirror. "To ATRI. Make haste."
~~~

At the red light at Tenth Street and Piedmont, the same afternoon sun that had lulled Danno to sleep now found an even easier target in Gus. Already worn thin from nights of restless sleep and strange dreams, he felt the warmth streaming through his window like a sedative. His exhausted body surrendered immediately—eyelids that had struggled to stay closed for weeks now grew impossibly heavy, the heat amplifying his bone-deep fatigue.

ACE drove to the rear entrance at ATRI. Danno jumped out, surveyed the area, and opened the Tahoe's rear door. Gus gave up on telling Danno to stay in his seat, insisting he could manage alone, and swiped the ID card on his lanyard to access the building.

Through security, he caught a glimpse of the stairwell to the basement, but instead, he went to his office to zip and transfer Christian's source code in the biofeedback device. *Tomorrow's offering.*

Once the thumb drive began, he rested his eyes with his head back on his chair. *Let them chase half the puzzle.*

The vibrating phone on his desk jarred him. He instinctively reached for his phone. Gina. He sighed. Answer or voicemail? His day had momentum, albeit slight, a conversation with Gina could change that; he hated to admit it. The realization kept his eyes glued to the screen for one more ring.

He couldn't resist.

"Hello, Gina," Gus said.

Chapter Thirty-Two

"Oh, I'm glad I caught you," Gina said.

Caught. The word snagged his cluttered brain. Her voice carried warmth but rang thinner now. Facebook post. The endless stream of birthday wishes. Antonio. Regardless, the events of the day and the timing of her call had dimmed the afterglow of their kiss and everything they'd planned for the weekend.

"Really? More news?"

"About the same, actually. If Carmelo and my father did not need me, I'd suggest we come here for the weekend. It's spectacular. Today, after our examinations, a few of us drove to the most wonderful vineyard, Kuleto Estate. Small by my standards, 760 acres, but quaint. Adorable and incredible wine."

As he listened, he sighed. A heavy sadness weighed on him as he considered her suggestion for the weekend, wondering how to end their call and make his way to the basement.

"Did you have a happy birthday?"

"Birthday? Oh yes. Yes, I did. Thank you."

"Lucky me. I learned like millions of your Facebook followers."

"Would you like to have known?"

The question and her tone took him aback. "It crossed my mind."

"It crossed my mind too, at the airport. I prefer that to be private. Anonymity is priceless, a fact I didn't realize until I lost it."

Her reflection and tone resonated with him. He'd overreacted, having witnessed her celebrity firsthand. But old photos with expressions of unrequited love? That was new.

"I saw a fantastic photo of you when you were younger," Gus said, sincerely.

He heard her chuckle, "Antonio posts that photo every year, along with the caption."

"Sweet."

"Our families are neighbors." He sensed her hesitation, but it was not long enough for him to respond. "We were once engaged before I ran off and became famous."

"Wow. That's serious?"

"A story for another day. I'll only say we were young. The good lord saved me."

"Will he be there when you return?"

"Yes. My father told me his grandfather is dying."

"And your examinations?"

"Finito, Completato, Eccellente." Finished, Complete. Excellent.

Gus said, "Sehr guet." Swiss German for very good.

"Can you accompany me tomorrow night?"

Gus reassessed his feelings instantly. "I will. And I'll pick you up at the airport. Did you call for anything in particular?"

"Yes," Gina said. "I wanted to hear your voice."

At his desk, he scratched his head, exhaled long and slowly, and imagined Gina, so far away, the first time since they'd met in late Spring, now wishing to hear his voice of all the voices she could want to hear.

~~~

Christian called. Relief in her voice. "The FBI just left."

"Left where?"

"Here, at Holder. Two agents interviewed me regarding the biofeedback testimonials on social media. They're looking for the leak."

"What did you tell them?"

"Exactly who was in the room. I didn't know the names of the people behind us."

"I know the guy, but not the two women."

"That was that. Weird. GCI can't find our data, but they launch a federal investigation to find out who's saying nice things about us on social media."

"GCI doesn't think they're nice."

"What do you make of all this hoopla?"

"Interesting. I'd know more if I had that data."

"They'll be by to see you, I'm sure."

~~~

The temperature had dropped noticeably in the basement as Gus swiped his credentials and pushed through the Surveillance security door. The soft pneumatic click behind him sealed out the normal world on his way to the covert operation on display in Watchtower. The air carried the distinct smell of electronics running hot—ozone, plastic, and the faint metallic tang of cooling systems working overtime.

He found Kip, Carley, and the staff, headsets on, focused on the wall of monitors that bathed the room in an eerie blue glow. The light pulsed subtly with each data refresh. The kaleidoscope of shifting information cast ghoulish shadows across their faces. Their headsets hung heavy on their ears, their expressions grim and focused as their fingers typed in near-silent bursts as required.

"Mama Mia. Busy," Gus said, his voice sounding unnaturally loud in the room designed to absorb ambient noise.

Kip's face begged the question Gus asked, "What's wrong?"

"Too damned many loose ends on these calls." Kip's fingers tapped nervously on the counter. "They make calls to blocked numbers. The people clearly don't want to be tracked."

Funk stepped in. "That's why we made the Matrix. Sorry. The most valuable information will not be between the three phones you are authorized to track. It comes from the down-line conversations."

Kip whispered to Gus, "I don't know what to share with you because I can't always tell who's talking."

Funk said, "Filter keywords."

Kip's wide eyes turned to Gus. "What are they?"

Gus shrugged and narrowed his brow, "I'll get the AG to add Tanzilla, McIntyre, Vinnie, and his brother, Klaus."

Funk said, "Better have good reason."

Gus nodded at Kip. "Do I have any good reasons?"

Kip picked up a short stack of papers from Carly's desk and motioned for Gus to follow him.

As he followed to the reception area, Gus asked, "Any mention of my data files? Is anyone plotting against me or Christian?"

Kip pulled a chair from the round table and handed Gus the transcripts, his hand visibly trembling. "They plan to use you and Sheehan as damage control. Josh is going to call to rehearse the show."

"Josh and I already discussed what they want."

Kip nodded, "Okay. Not surprised. But did you know how much Tanzilla hates Pogue and her CAM department? And, he hates Dr. Slayton Sr., over a secret agreement the Board made with them and Sheehan when she joined the GCI staff. Pogue and Slayton Jr. made reference to that agreement on one of their calls."

His voice dropped even lower. "Everyone has a secret."

"Sheehan says she and Vinnie have the financial advantage."

"I heard that. What about the program she wrote?"

Kip Richardson shook his head.

"Did Sheehan call her brother?" Gus said.

"Yes. One of the blocked numbers. Couldn't trace it, but" Kip's eyes narrowed. "Sheehan wants your source code. She sounded desperate."

He could feel them closing in like a hunted animal feels the hunter's footsteps. Years and years of isolation, innovation, and just when he's ready to launch, the results he fantasized about achieving, might lead his father's killers back to him? The air in the basement thickened by the second.

Kip returned to the Watchtower and left Gus to flip through the transcripts. An hour later, hunched over pages of conversations, his heart beating like an uphill jog, a phone call jolted him.

Josh McIntyre. Not a surprise.

Josh announced, "James, Tanzilla, and Sheehan would like you to get on a call with them in 15 minutes."

"Sure," Gus said, and he stood, moving in circles, inhaling and exhaling to the point where he nearly hyperventilated.

Kip appeared from the Watchtower and set a highlighted transcript on the table. "Read this. Came in after CNN this morning."

Gus scanned the document:

TRANSCRIPT #27B—SLAYTON (George, Jr. MD) to HAMILTON (Michael, FDA Director) JAMES (Stephen, CEO Georgia Cancer Institute Hospital)

HAMILTON: "What the hell is happening over there? I've had calls from six board CEO's and everyone on our board."

SLAYTON: "It was an ambush, Mike."

HAMILTON: "What did you expect? You have to find out where this is coming from and stop it. You and Tanzilla looked like fools. The guy cited outcomes and data, and all Tanzilla could say was that data doesn't exist? Does it, or doesn't it?"

SLAYTON: "We're containing it."

HAMILTON: *"Is that what you call this. Every news agency and every name on my contact list is asking if you're suppressing a cancer breakthrough. A scandal is fatal. Hettich's office…they leaked the suspension too."*

JAMES: *"We don't know that."*

HAMILTON: *"Wake up, Steve! Of course, they did. I cut Hettich out, and he's getting me back. Go ahead, say it, you were right. My transition team wants to cut you and Sheehan from the selection committee."*

Gus looked up. "Is this from this morning?"

Kip nodded.

"What selection committee?" Gus said.

"Beats me. Hamilton runs the FDA, it has to be connected," Kips said as he slid Gus another sheet. "And this one's from thirty minutes ago."

TRANSCRIPT #42F—TANZILLA (VINCENT) to KLAUS SCHNERR in the office of G. Slayton, Jr., MD.

TANZILLA: *"It's a goddamn wildfire. Patients have contacted the press. The networks are all over this."*

SCHNERR: *"We're going back on CNN. If the host goes rogue again, I'll waste him."*

TANZILLA: *"Get the ATRI kid. He's bright. Tall and handsome. His story made sense. We'll say it's like an off-label drug. We're looking into it. It's too soon to say. We have to convince the public we're putting their best interest first. That we're being responsible."*

SCHNERR: *"I like it. Have him dazzle 'em with engineering bullshit and while Sheehan pleads her moral and civic duty to play by the book in the interest of public safety and JCO regulations."*

TANZILLA: *"That's good. The kid will say this is delicate science. That no one is hiding anything, and these few people—don't make them out to be nuts—are simply telling their version of a much larger story. Sheehan and the kid must show cooperation. We're together on this—investigating in the interest of public safety. We'll look responsible... like we actually give a shit."*

SCHNERR: *"Good. Cause the guy caught you flatfooted this morning, and now we're getting crucified."*

TANZILLA: *"Well, that's your department's problem."*

SLAYTON: *"Mike Hamilton says his folks want to cut James and Sheehan from the Committee."*

TANZILLA: *"Fuck Mike Hamilton. We need the fucking source code. Then we'll claim it as our own. Then we send them where we send everyone else that fucks with us."*

SCHNERR: "Do me a favor...do yourself a favor, learn to say no comment. My phone is blowing up. Boston is panicking."

TANZILLA: "Boston should be panicking. I knew this was a bad idea fifteen years ago. When she got here"

SCHNERR: "That may be corrected soon."

TANZILLA: "Not soon enough."

SLAYTON: "That's the God damned truth. She a scandal all her own."

TANZILLA: "Klaus, this is trial by fire, I know. You've got your hands full with your dad so sick and your brother so close to Donna...."

SCHNERR: "Wolf is in the dark. I can't burden him with this. He'd go off on Vinnie, and Vinnie might kill him. It falls on Donna; she waited too long."

Gus's pulse quickened, blood pounding in his ears as the implications crashed over him. His grip crushed the page as he muttered more to himself than to Kip, "Why's the FDA involved? What's the 'correction' Schnerr said was coming soon?" The words hovered between them, ominous and loaded with threat.

He ran a hand through his hair, mind racing to connect these new puzzle pieces. The room seemed to shrink around him, the air growing thinner. "They're losing control," he said finally, voice steadier than he felt. The realization was both terrifying and exhilarating—their chaos meant his opportunity—and increased danger.

"That's not all." Kip's face had grown paler, a slight tremor visible in his hand as he handed over another sheet. "This came in just before I came out here."

TRANSCRIPT #51A—SLAYTON (GEORGE) to POGUE (CLAIR)

SLAYTON: "It's worse than we thought. The PR team counted. Eighty-seven patients who've come forward."

POGUE: "Eighty-seven? They issued fifty units."

SLAYTON: "Eighty-seven."

POGUE: "Your father would love this."

SLAYTON: "It's ironic, for sure. Soon, Schnerr is going to unleash the dark side and start slitting throats. They exist to protect the Consortium."

POGUE: "We know where they should start."

SLAYTON: "They should start with her, but they can't. She's the devil, with whom they made the deal. And, to save you, my father made the same deal."

POGUE: "If only he knew what all that led to."

SLAYTON: "What do you make of these terminal people's claims on social media? They say they used the device. Cancer stopped. And we're covering it up."

POGUE: "That's not entirely untrue, is it?"

SLAYTON: [PAUSE] "Clair, for God's sake, not on the phone."

POGUE: "I'm seventy-five, George. We don't even know what we're covering up. What's Klaus going to do to me? Kill me. They stuck the knife in a long time ago. It might be a relief. What can James say to the Board of Directors without becoming a target?"

SLAYTON: "Nothing. He's in the crosshairs. They want Sheehan's head."

POGUE: "Too bad. They can't have it. None of them know the real story we're tied to."

SLAYTON: "Tanzilla's solution is to get the source code. Spin it that it was ours, they stole it, then make them disappear."

POGUE: "Sounds like Marco. Good luck. The Genie is out of the bottle."

Kip pointed to a notation he'd made at the bottom. "Look. The CNN producer has been calling everyone at Georgia Cancer Institute. They want patient interviews for tomorrow's segment with you and Sheehan."

Gus glanced at his watch. Josh would call any minute. He sighed, took deep breaths, and thought about how quickly the GCI situation had deteriorated. A single morning news segment had snowballed into an international story.

Funk emerged from the Watchtower, noticed Gus, and snapped his head toward the open door to an office, "A word." Gus stepped in, Funk closed the door.

"You're getting close to fire." Funk's voice was flat, clinical. "The Schnerrs."

"You know them?"

"I know them."

"How do *you* know them?"

"I know people who have the skills the Consortium hires out. You're getting airtime. You're their type of target—a threat to pharmaceutical intellectual property. They eliminate threats."

"Like a cancer treatment that doesn't require drugs?"

Funk nodded, "From the surveillance I see and read in the Watchtower, the son in charge might not survive this. Desperate people behave desperately."

Gus resembled that remark.

"What about the other son, Vinnie?"

"Vincent." Funk's expression hardened. "I consulted with him on digital security for the Consortium before returning to ATRI. I figured it was a program his girlfriend wrote. She was dark, but bright, if you know what I mean. I had access to the intellectual property."

"You didn't report what you found?"

"Who says I didn't?" Funk's scar twitched. "How do you think your FBI friend Hile's been building a case for years. He can't get close enough; they keep changing it up."

"Her program siphons drugs?"

"From what I remember," Funk nodded. "They described it differently, but I knew."

"So, they're the next generation?"

Funk nodded. "This was right after the Twin Towers came down. I remember thinking how fucked up it was, the country took a kick in the crotch, and all they could think about was buttoning up the software and flooding the streets with drugs. All cash. I suppose they still are?"

"Big money?" Gus said

Funk wrinkled his face and nodded. "Like printing it. All cash. They got to launder it somehow, but knowing them, they did."

"You connected to them anymore?"

Funk smirked and shook his head, "ATRI is the best gig."

Gus nodded. "You get to live on the edge...on the good side."

Chapter Thirty-Three

Alone in the surveillance reception area, his phone rang precisely .t the fifteen-minute mark. Josh McIntyre said, "Gus, are you there?"

"Yes," Gus said as he dashed to the stockroom and softly closed the door.

"Excellent. I'm here with Mr. James, Dr. Tanzilla, Dr. Slayton, Ms. Sheehan."

No niceties.

James spoke first, his voice tight with controlled anger. "This, whatever you want to call it, a leak, a conspiracy, blindsided us. I'm sure it has blindsided you, Mr. Meier."

Gus said, "Completely."

James said, "I'm getting calls expressing curiosity and panic from, of all places, the Mayo Clinic, Johns Hopkins, MD Anderson, Sloan Kettering, and Dana-Farber. They all want to know about this 'breakthrough device.'"

Tanzilla said, his voice gruff, "The servers are struggling to keep up."

Josh said, "Gus, people are begging for what they were told didn't exist. Even if the outcomes are accidental, no event has brought this much attention to GCI, ever."

Tanzilla continued, "We need to turn this around. Make it positive. God damned people are posting videos every damned place. A woman in Buckhead claimed we gave her six months to live in January, and now she's cured. Clear scans. Normal labs. No evidence she ever had cancer. She swears it's all due to your device, Mr. Meier."

Gus started to respond, but Josh cut him off.

"CNN wants to put the Buckhead woman on tomorrow, and others. I'm not sure a nuclear bomb would be a bigger scoop for them." Josh added. "I spoke to the producer. They can't handle the calls wanting more details and more patients have asked to appear. I offered to bring the two people at the heart of this story to the studio. You and Ms. Sheehan."

Tanzilla's voice hardened. "That's genius. We need a unified message."

Gus recalled the transcript. Were they reading from it?

Slayton said, "Gus. Dr. Slayton here. Young as you are, you know the value of solid research. The viewers won't. I want you to come at this not in complete denial, but as someone as fascinated as they are. Once we get past the news that you were expelled, you explain that you did in fact error in the application process, and that's behind us. Going forward, we need larger-scale controlled studies."

Gus felt his heart leap in his chest. Large-scale controlled studies. JCO. Precisely, his plan for the mattress mat.

Dr. Tanzilla added, "These people were asking us to take a stand without irrefutable evidence. We have a duty, a responsibility to public safety. Would you agree, Mr. Meier?"

"Yes," Gus followed along. "This sounds like something the NCI would love."

"Indeed it is. Make a note of that, Josh. Perhaps we scrap Donna here and get someone from the National Cancer Institute to come on and talk about doing research to bring science to these claims. NCI's reputation is above reproach. That should give the impression we are leading the charge toward the truth."

Josh recoiled, "I'll call, but will they agree to do research on this?"

Tanzilla scoffed, "Yes. And in the process, they'd find fifty ways to sabotage it, then publish that the process didn't work, saying all the claims were scientifically unsubstantiated. It's just what the NCI does in instances like this."

Gus heard Tanzilla chuckle. The bravado shocked him. A near-exact account of what the NCI did to Dr. Nicholas Gonzales's research under the auspices of duplicating his outcomes. Their devastating meddling sabotaged him.

"As for all the people making these claims, our people will handle those details."

Josh wrinkled his face. "Who are our people?"

Tanzilla leaned back, referring to the Consortium, and told Josh, "They're not your people." He lifted his arm toward James, Slayton, and Sheehan. "They're our people."

Gus heard complete silence.

Tanzilla said, "Mr. Meier. We'll come up with a script and get it to you tonight. You stay on script, understood?"

Gus paused, feeling the weight of everyone's attention on his answer. "Will you send it soon? I'd like to rehearse."

"You'll be reading a prompter," Tanzilla snapped. "It's all scripted. We'll script the host, you, and Donna. Read it before to be familiar. To sound natural. That's it."

Gus swallowed. "Understood." Yes, he understood he had every intention of deviating from the script to offer the source code to Sheehan. Nothing he heard contradicted his plan.

Donna Sheehan added, "We leave the Governor out of this. Read what we send. Don't get cute. Got it?" Gus found her voice suspiciously calm.

"What if the host gets cute, like this morning?"

"He's been warned," Tanzilla said.

The sternness landed like a swat to the back of Gus's skull. Warned.

Dr. Slayton said, "He's kidding, Gus. The public cannot be fooled into believing this or any other device has any bearing on cancer. We cannot afford a crisis of faith in what we do here. Medical science is what we need people to believe in."

Gus flashed back to the Sunday morning Opa introduced him to the Assignment. The details were scarce but the message indelible, "Science isn't something you believe in like a religion. It's a method—a way of testing reality that invites doubt, demands skepticism. If something can be disproven," Opa said, "it should be. That's the point."

Yet there sat Dr. Slayton, the mute from Friday morning, who had found his voice. The same man who sat silent while Sheehan executed her ambush now revealed what truly mattered—not patient outcomes or truth, but faith in a system. The religion of medical orthodoxy. Beneath Slayton's carefully chosen words, Gus heard the real message: Protect the church. Preserve the status quo. Years of grants, studies, protocols, careers built on incremental progress—all threatened by a device that might render them obsolete overnight.

"Just say what Josh writes. Okay?" Tanzilla said.

"Sure," Gus said.

~~~

Gus rushed to the Watchtower. What were they saying in the aftermath? His eyes darted to each office on a monitor. All three offices were empty. He slammed his fist on the counter. There were no cameras in James's office.
~~~

Beside a perplexed Kip, Gus exhaled, deflated. "How blind can these people be?"

Kip gave a nervous laugh, "Maybe they're not blind. They genuinely cannot allow this to happen."

Gus rested his hips on the cabinet behind the counter, staring at the monitors. "This surveillance started as a data retrieval operation, and now we're tracking people who 'make others disappear.'"

"Gus, have you ever heard of an IPOTA?"

Gus snapped his head toward Kip. Grinning. "Is this a joke that's supposed to make me feel better?"

"Maybe. Professor Murray taught this. An IPOTA stands for Inverted Pyramid of Theoretical Application. The apex is the theory. The subsequent mass stacked above is predicated on the theory being proven. What happens if the theory is not sufficiently challenged? What happens if, after time has passed, a prudent person tests the theory and determines it was wrong? How then do they undo all they have built on a false premise? I think you are exposing their IPOTA."

Gus nodded. The IPOTA theory struck a chord. His device had proven what Tanzilla and Slayton did not want him to expose to the public. Their treatments, protocols stacked on protocols, careers, and reputations were balancing on an inverted pyramid; his work threatened to topple it. No wonder they were terrified.

Gus nodded. Looked at his watch. His eyes widened. "Cool story, Kipper. I have to call Cedric."

<div align="center">~~~</div>

"Come in G-man," Cedric said.

Gus hurried in. "You found everything?"

Cedric said, "Score one for the G-man."

"How?"

Cedric nodded at the cluttered chair.

Gus shifted papers and periodicals and sat.

"Ruben Gerding traced it to whoever denied it."

Gus bolted out of his chair, his arms bracing him on Cedric's desk, "Who?"

Cedric's head shook. "Forget it."

"I should lean on him."

"The dude might jus' snap." Cedric said, and motioned Gus behind his desk chair.

Gus obliged. His eyes locked on the screen, scanning the data intently. His heart raced as his understanding crystallized. His spreadsheet filled. Patient identification numbers, baseline recordings of each patient's electrical vibrancy followed by successive columns showing the microcurrent frequency feedback his program chose to send through them. Data only he could interpret.

Patients were gaining electrical vibrancy—not overnight, but progressively over days, weeks, months. They were healing. His breathing quickened, a surge of validation rushing through him like a narcotic. Science proved his theory; the Assignment was finished. Vindicated in rows of undeniable data.

"Can I..." Gus motioned to the keyboard. Cedric relinquished his seat. Gus sank down, fingers flying across the keys as he navigated deeper. He found the toxicity cells—Opa's undoing—located the pattern, and his euphoria vanished.

Undeniable. Opa's vibrancy had increased, toxicity followed, and then his vibrancy plummeted. Would the people raving about their progress on social media face unsuspecting and devastating reversals? Had others already experienced this and kept quiet? His triumph was rendered hollow by this critical oversight.

Humility rocked his arrogance. Being brilliant at code didn't make him an expert in biology. Each cancer and body had its own electrical signature—and a chemical complexity he had unintentionally disrespected. Lesson learned. Doubly painful this close to the end.

He clicked on a particularly revealing cell, hoping to access the formula. The message hit him like a physical blow:

READ ONLY.

His body shuddered, and he exhaled while he clenched his teeth. "Damn."

Cedric leaned in. "I didn't try to open it, sorry. It's frozen on that page. Someone really wants this data withheld."

Gus stared at the screen. "I can see the erratic numbers." Age? Most likely.

"Can you make anything out of this?"

"Possibly."

"At least you can see the column to give you the clue."

Gus gnawed his lip, nodding. "But for my uncle calling me, I would have missed this completely..."

Cedric paused. "Can you fix this in your coding?"

"Honestly, I'll need medical help. I don't know enough about the body to make the change. If I could see the formula driving that column, I might be able to make a reasonable guess." Could he risk a call to New York, to Dr. Gonzales? Or had the NCI intimidated Gonzalez to stay away from the likes of him?

"Time to lean on Ruben," Cedric said.

"He's going to feel me," Gus said.

Cedric stared at his determined friend as the door closed behind him.

Descending, his vision cleared. Everything now hinged on Ruben Gerding, an unsuspecting man he'd never seen.

Chapter Thirty-Four

Gus ordered pizza from Izzy's while ACE drove them from ATRI to Holder Medical Engineering. With his head against the window and eyes closed, he imagined where he'd insert the solution to toxicity in the source code. But for Henry observing Opa, the toxicity would have gone undetected, potentially crippling his large-sample research if JCO installed ten thousand flawed devices. To make the proper repair required, time, research, and trials—a daunting task. His head hurt thinking about it.

Stuck at another red light, he resisted checking his backlog of messages and instead thought of Gina, his favorite therapy.

On their way to the Holder SCIF, Bobby explained all six of his stars. Well credentialed. Impressive. Eager to work on a Gus Meier project. He'd meet them in forty-five minutes.

At the Holder SCIF security pad, Gus stopped, tapped Bobby's arm, "Before we get in there..."

Bobby stopped, curious.

"First, thank you. I appreciate your help."

Bobby nodded.

Gus said, "One more thing."

Bobby chuckled, "Damn, you always got one more thing. What now?"

"This program. The one we're here to integrate with the new mat." Gus paused.

Bobby tilted his head. "What?"

"It's not yours."

Bobby scoffed, "Geez. Gus..." He paced back and forth. "What are we selling, JCO? Or do I even wanna know?"

"It's a code I designed and wrote."

"Damn." Bobby stopped. "Like Christians? Do ya jus go round hiding code inside shit?"

Gus raised his hands. "When I have to."

Bobby's eyes fixed on him. "You have to?"

Gus nodded. "This is big, Bobby. You will never be a part of anything this big in your life."

Bobby pursed his lips. They locked eyes. "This is bout all the noise on social media? Don't you be getting me in no trouble."

Gus tilted his head. "You could get hurt. Even killed."

Bobby swiped his ID card and pressed his finger onto the fingerprint recognition pad to access the SCIF. Inside, the lights were bright. Twelve chairs around a long oval cherrywood table. Bobby motioned for him to sit with his back to the screen. On his side of the table, Bobby motioned to the empty chairs. "I'll put them here."

Gus went where Bobby told him.

Seated opposite him, Bobby said, "What have you gotten me involved in that'll get me killed? I got Suzanne and Robbie to think about."

"I'll tell you, and you decide..."

"That's what you said about the mat and here we are..."

"Bobby," Gus raised his voice loud.

Bobby froze.

Gus lowered his voice and said, "My code stops cancer."

A long moment later, Bobby's head nodded deliberately and slowly as the thought. Perhaps their entire past made sense to him. "That's big. That's really big. Somebody might want to put a cap in your ass for that."

Gus leaned in, his clenched fist thumping the table, "And it may save Christian's father's life. And my grandfather and people you and I will never know. It may save Suzanne, Robbie, or you. I need the huge sample JCO can provide. But they can't know."

Gus paused.

Bobby stared back.

He shook his head. "No one can know, Bobby. No one. Not now, probably never. But I wanted you to know. You have a stake in this if you want. It's your call. If you leave, please promise to keep this between us."

Neither man moved. Gus nibbled at the inside of his lower lip. Bobby's breathing increased. His nostrils flared. The minute seemed like an hour. Gus waited. He needed Bobby. A friend. An outlet. Bobby had responsibilities that Gus didn't. He could not coax or cajole him. The decision was Bobby's to make.

Bobby nodded, "I get it. I'm in. We fix this, here and now. Sell it and let it go. You get what you need, JCO gets what they need, and sick people get well. As for money, there should be plenty for everyone. How could that be bad?"

Gus scoffed, "I agree. Lots of people don't. Thank you."

Bobby's simple reframing lifted his confidence in a flash. There and then, Gus decided that, until it was over, there would be no more lying, cheating, sneaking, denying, and conniving.

"Let's roll," Bobby said.

"We need to overhaul the data handling routines," Gus said, sketching on the whiteboard. "The new sensor array will generate many more inputs."

Bobby nodded. "Got that covered. Malika for threading, Darnell on buffering to prevent bottlenecks, the twins for sensor fusion algorithms."

Gus raised an eyebrow. "Load balancing?"

"Rajiv wrote the parallel processing for the Mars rover. Your mat's in good hands."

Gus hesitated. "I'll handle the frequency calibration for toxin clearance myself."

Bobby's smile faded. "That's the trickiest part. You sure—"

"I'm sure." Gus's tone closed the subject.

Bobby shrugged. "Your call, coach."

By 7:30, no one spoke. The rhythmic clatter of keyboards filled the room as engineers worked in focused concentration, monitors glowing with lines of code and data visualizations. Gus heard the occasional "um" and "ah," followed by murmured discussions about algorithm optimizations and sensor response thresholds.

At 8:30, Gus and his partners had extracted data from a paltry eighteen patients. The team had split terminal windows running parallel analyses on age demographics and response variations. Just before nine, a slight trend appeared in the toxicity response patterns. Not enough to bet a code update on, but more than he had.

At ten, his eyes were heavy. The trend continued to emerge as data points populated their scatter plots. The coffee Bobby brought in didn't help. At eleven, he called it quits. Experience taught him to draw the line and move forward tomorrow rather than press on and risk failing tonight.

~~~
~~~

ACE and Donno's shift expired. The Scales replacement team out front drove Gus to Henry's. On the screened porch, he found Cassie sleeping in the breeze of the fan. He jostled her. "Still like for me to wake you when I come home?"

Cassie smiled. "I do."

She told him Henry had called and given a good report on Opa. He and his father were enjoying their time. He sounded optimistic.

Christian arrived back at 9:30. Cassie said she was "Quiet." She thought she looked exhausted and went up to bed. Despite that, Cassie noted she seemed less edgy, bordering on kind, with a hint of gratitude.

"Sounds about right," Gus said. He understood why.

Upstairs, he checked his silenced phone. A missed call from Josh McIntyre. "Oh my God," he blurted, then found the script email with text: "Confirm you got this. See you at 7:30." He sent a thumbs-up emoji.

He quickly triaged the rest: texted Holder about Bobby's team, noted Craig Jones's voicemail about plastic housings, Special Agent Hile wanting to discuss "conversations," Dr. Pogue with "something to consider." Facebook showed Gina on a stone veranda, mountains and vineyards bathed in an amber sunset.

Josh's script was pure corporate speak—admitting nothing while sounding conciliatory. He'd follow it long enough to establish credibility before offering Sheehan the thumb drive with Christian's code. Would she take it publicly? Would that force Tanzilla's hand? Either way, it bought time for Bobby's team to finish the mat integration, shifting focus away from Christian.

Lying in bed, staring at the ceiling, he sorted tomorrow's battles: CNN with Sheehan, mat integration with Bobby's team. Hile would wait. And Pogue... her message nagged him. What could she possibly offer now? As fatigue claimed him, one image persisted—Gina on that veranda, bathed in amber light, a world away from the danger closing in. Why did her father call her home? Too much to ponder.

Sleep came suddenly, like a system crash. His last thought was of the alarm set for 6:00 AM—less than six hours away. Outside, the first hints of a thunderstorm rolled in, nature's warning of the tempest to come.

Chapter Thirty-Five

Gus woke before the alarm on Wednesday morning. Sleep had been elusive, his mind shifting between rumbles of thunder, flashes of lightning, and persistent thoughts about facing Sheehan on New Day. Through the window, debris was scattered across the pool deck. The chaises where he and Gina had sat were barely visible beneath fallen limbs and branches. That tender memory felt distant now, fragile against the harder edges of the task ahead—incompatible with the mindset he needed to appease Tanzilla—deceptive, coerced, adversarial.

As if the morning weren't complicated enough, the rest of the day demanded equal precision. Gina's flight arrived at 4:15. The benefit at Savannah College of Art and Design (SCAD) began at 6:00—cocktails first, then dinner at 7:00, with the program starting at 8:00. Given all the attention on her, and now on him, he needed to be sharp.

In Henry's borrowed suit, he found Cassie in the kitchen with her newspaper spread before her and coffee already prepared.

His formal attire raised her eyebrows. "Wedding or funeral?"

"CNN."

"Taking a tour?"

"Don't I wish. I'm a guest on New Day."

"I was afraid of that," she said. "I heard yesterday's show."

"I'm damage control."

Cassie smiled knowingly. "How ironic."

Gus nodded. "And possibly a strategy."

Cassie glanced upstairs toward Christian's room. "Does she know?"

He shook his head. "Her father is dying. Cancer."

"She's going to find out."

"Her mind is elsewhere," he said, sounding hollow even to him, another rationalization in a growing list.

As he descended the steps to the driveway, ACE held her gaze on his suit. Danno said, "Uh oh, this is serious."

On the drive to CNN, he reviewed the emailed bullet points, patted the thumb drive in his breast pocket, and ignored his coffee. The calm before the storm. Part of him suspected Sheehan would cancel, the other part itched for the confrontation.

A bubbly New Day production assistant welcomed him at reception and navigated him through the studio maze to the ready area outside Studio B.

She introduced him to the producer—Anita something—who broke the news: Sheehan had canceled.

Josh McIntyre arrived a moment later and joined them, exasperated. "I just found out. It's a cluster. She said it wasn't in her best interest."

"I'm not going on," Gus announced.

Josh and Anita exchanged glances. Her eyes widened, her cheeks filled. Holding her breath.

"You're going on," Josh said.

Gus lowered his voice, firm, and told Josh. "This was rigged in her best interest." His mind jumped to Kip in the Watchtower. Transcript? "You scripted it and you couldn't make her deliver her lines

"Tanzilla is livid," Josh said.

"Of course he is. She told him, *again*, she doesn't answer to him. Apparently, she answers to no one. Well, this isn't in my best interest either."

Josh's shaking head resembled a seizure. His hands raised to Gus. His voice was frantic. "No, no, no. You have to go on. It's been promoted. People are watching. We can't cancel. We can't hide."

"This is not my problem," Gus said.

Josh's put his face beside Gu's ear, "It will be. And it will be mine too. Trust me. You are in no position to walk away."

His head retracted, "What?"

Josh shook his head. "Trust me. I'll explain later. Right now…roll with it."

Gus squinted.

"Do this. Be the star."

"What about the script?" Gus said.

Josh moved close to him, "Stick with 'You're not a physician. There is no data linking your device to stopping cancer."

"Do you know that to be true?" Gus said.

His face blank, Josh turned to Gus, "Yes. It's honest, and the audience will believe you."

Skeptical, Gus put his hand on McIntyre's elbow and whispered, "What's going on, Josh? She never was coming, was she?"

Josh shrugged. "You're on in ten minutes. I scrapped the teleprompter. Tanzilla wanted it, but it was stupid. Rehearse your lines."

His phone vibrated. Kip Richardson. Gus stepped aside.

"Kip?"

Kip blurted, "Remember the conversation where the FDA chief, Mike Hamilton, said his committee members didn't want Sheehan and James? She found a way back on and bowed out of this show."

"What committee?"

"An important committee. She ghosted Tanzilla and McIntyre to stay on it. It must be worth the fallout."

"This happened this morning?"

"Hamilton himself called her last night. I listened to it this morning. It was cordial. Very matter-of-fact. He said it boiled down to optics. All of hers were bad, and he was told to end it. She pulled out to save her spot."

"Who gives the director of the FDA orders?"

Kip said, "People with a stake in whatever's about to happen at GCI?"

"The dedication? That doesn't make sense." Gus said.

"Has to be someone above James and Tanzilla. She told them separately this morning, unapologetically."

That explained why Tanzilla was livid.

"And?"

"James understood. No objection."

"Tanzilla?" Gus said.

"Furious. Said he was taking heat."

"From?" Gus smirked.

"Oncology groups."

He patted the thumb drive in his pocket. Sheehan undermined his plan to make a peace offering on an international stage to misdirect GCI. In the distance, Josh and Anita were huddled. Josh turned toward him and waved to come to the set.

"Thanks, Kip. Talk soon."

Ambling toward the couch on the studio set, McIntyre instructed him, "Forget about everything else. Say your lines. No matter how contrived they sound. Show Tanzilla you are on his side."

"Why am I on his side?" Gus said.

"It's the right side to be on," Josh said.

Something about Josh McIntyre told Gus to do as he said. It wasn't trust, it was a hunch.

Positioned on the curved couch he'd seen countless times on television, Gus faced a male host—not the woman who'd interviewed Tanzilla and Slayton yesterday. With the lights dimmed and staffers making last-minute adjustments, the host and Anita explained to him that the segment would run for six minutes instead of the original eight.

The first question confirmed that Sheehan's absence prompted a script change he hadn't counted on. He asked if Gus had abused his ATRI status to get his device into GCI? He admitted he had. How did the Governor get involved? This gave him the opportunity to introduce Christian and her personal relationship with Hettich's son on his journey to sobriety. The questions were not close to what he'd rehearsed. His abdomen tightened—his breaths became shallow. Klaus Schnerr's comment echoed; he'd waste the host if they went off script. Next, the host asked who reported Sheehan and GCI to JCO? Gus threw shade at GCI CEO Stephen James for self-reporting, which led to him being asked whether or not he felt validated by Sheehan and James getting suspended. He downplayed the suspension as a legislative requirement and assumed responsibility for putting Sheehan in a no-win situation. On the wall opposite his seat on the curvy couch, the clock turned close to the six-minute mark. Relieved, ready to hear the call to commercial break and the lights to dim again, the host set the noose and broached the onslaught of social media claims that his device stopped or cured cancer.

In seconds, sweat formed under his collar. Nervousness made him digress, and rather than recite his lines verbatim, he went off script by saying what he'd said last Friday in the Boardroom——precisely what Josh told him not to say. "If my device has any role in these recoveries, it would come from complementing traditional medical approaches." The line flowed calmly. He thought he sounded credible.

The host pounced. "I've personally spoken to over thirty people since Monday. None are on chemo, and each says your biofeedback device is the only treatment they use. Explain that."

Gus flinched. "Did you contact those patients, or did they contact you?"

"I did." He gloated. "I'm known for my investigative reporting."

"How did you get their contact information?"

The host recoiled. "That's confidential."

"Precisely, medical records are confidential. So, how did you get them?"

The host balked and said, "We'll come back to that. Why does every person say your device is responsible for their recovery? What's unique about your device?"

"I can't say because I've never spoken to any cancer patient at GCI who used my device. But you have. Have you seen the data collected on my device over the past six months…because I haven't. I'm not discounting the claims people are making. I believe they are improved; that's not the question. The question is how? I'm not a physician, nor are you. GCI is dedicating a new cancer research wing on Friday. It seems prudent for GCI to research the claims being made, and for the JCO or the FBI to investigate you and CNN regarding the files you reviewed."

When the lights dimmed for the commercial break, the host hurried off the curved couch. Anita and Josh swooped in while someone unclipped his mic. "Lively," Anita remarked with professional detachment. Gus stood and walked past Josh, expressionless.

The production assistant escorted him to the reception area, where calls already flooded the switchboard. He imagined similar scenes at GCI and ATRI.

Gus rubbed the mottled skin on his neck. Had his answers planted a bomb at GCI? He could only watch and wait.

~~~

Near the CNN parking lot exit, ACE slammed the brakes. "Jesus Christ."

Thrown forward, Gus looked up to see Anita, the producer standing with arms raised in the Tahoe's path. ACE lowered her window two inches.

The producer peered into the back seat, "Gus. We've got to talk."

"No. I'm through. Drive," he told ACE.

Anita grabbed the edge of the window, moving with the vehicle.

ACE stopped and ordered her with authoritative calm, "Remove your hands."

"Gus. Five minutes. I can explain everything. It's important. It'll make sense. I promise."
~~~

"Pull over," Gus instructed, curiosity overcoming his irritation.

Anita waited at the window. Gus opened the door behind ACE. "Get in."

Her panic had intensified, "You are someone's worst nightmare."

Gus studied her, calculating her next move, and told Anita, "You have four and a half minutes to tell me everything, or she drives to a remote location, and I become your worst nightmare. Clear?"

Anita leaned closer, her voice dropping to a conspiratorial tone. "I get calls. I get emails. Anonymous. The top execs won't let me air everything."

"Your host went rogue?"

"I told him to. And I'll tell you and the FBI everything I know. I'll show them everything I have. And believe me, there's plenty, and it's not good for GCI."

"What isn't?"

"Public scandal. It could kill their standing with the FDA."

Gus raised his hands. "What is it with the FDA?"

"Oh. You don't know that part—I've said enough." Anita started to leave.

Gus touched her arm, "Wait—any idea who's sending this to you?"

Shaking her head. "None."

"That's a lie. Who?"

She continued denying.

"Ok. Then, what's their endgame?" Gus said.

"I think they want to create a scandal at GCI. Expose them. Stop them."

"Stop what?"

Silence.

"Whatever." Resignation in his voice. "That has nothing to do with me."

Anita's eyes widened, "Oh yes, it does. Whoever is behind this has specifically named you. They provided the files. They say people at GCI will stop at nothing to find out why these people are cancer-free. I have a list of people at GCI to investigate if anything happened to you."

"So, you wanted me on the show?" Gus said.

Anita nodded,

"Now what?" Gus said.

"I'm going to contact the FBI. "

As ACE pulled away, Gus sank into his seat, the weight of what he'd learned settling over him. So much for offering an olive branch to Sheehan on national television—a peace offering with no recipient. Now he needed another way to deliver the message—and the code—without compromising his position. If

Sheehan and the Schnerrs wanted the code so badly, there were simpler ways than this national cable media circus. He would have given it freely—under the right circumstances. Now what? Friday loomed like a deadline painted in blood.

Chapter Thirty-Six

Leaving CNN, Ace guided the Tahoe past Centennial Park, where morning sunlight dappled through the trees. Gus watched children playing in the fountain, his heart still racing from the interview, strategic thoughts ricocheting in his mind. The scene triggered memories of his first visit to the area with Henry, Cassie, and his cousins fifteen years ago. His cousins now lived in the American West while he ground out eighteen-hour days in Atlanta, increasingly tangled in a web of danger and deception spun by shadowy figures he'd rather avoid if he couldn't evade.

Yet as one landscape faded from his consciousness, another emerged. Cassie's breast cancer. At fifteen, new to his American family, he'd glimpsed raw fear in Henry's eyes. For the first time, his aunt, uncle, and cousins experienced the precariousness he'd been living with.

Only now did he realize how far he'd drifted from that boy who once swam freely in Lake Geneva with the Alps as his backdrop.

His phone rang. Henry. Cassie had tipped him off.

"I saw the show. Things are heating up," Henry said, his voice deliberately casual. "Are you reconsidering coming home?"

"Oh. So, is that home now? And it's suddenly safe?" Gus couldn't keep the edge from his voice.

"Maybe a holiday? Helene would love it. See your star patient. He's improving. Well, let's say he's less bad. We watched your interview. He cheered you on."

Gus felt a smile. "I wish I could say I'm less bad."

"Someone is stirring the pot. Be vigilant," Henry warned.

His phone flashed an incoming call. Kip Richardson. "I've got a call. Talk soon. Regards to Opa."

Kip came on the line, voice tight with excitement. "Did you ever see a guy go over Niagara Falls in a barrel?"

He shook his head, "Kip. I don't know what that is."

"If you were here, you would. This place is nuts. But before it got nuts, it got scary."

"What does that mean?" Gus said, a cold feeling settled in his stomach.

"Thank God the AG signed off on letting us tap more phone numbers. Last night, we recorded a call between the Schnerr brothers and their father. The dad knew nothing about Sheehan, and your device or the past months at GCI. He's been in Texas getting his cancer treatment. Why would he go to Texas and not GCI?"

Gus scoffed. "It depends on the cancer."

Kip paused to find the name. "Has a sarcoma in his left forearm."

"If it's there, it could be everywhere in a man his age. Better treatment at Anderson or Methodist, in Houston." Gus said, his thoughts going to how his device might help the man combat the aggressive cancer.

"He's back. Taking a break or giving up. His name is Wolfgang, and he's catching things on the news like the CNN show yesterday. In the call last night, he and Klaus got tense. Pharmaceutical CEOs are going around Klaus and calling Wolfgang personally about all the social media attention at GCI. The old man is pissed." Kip's voice rose. "They all acknowledge there is a leak at GCI and they are screaming for Klaus to find it. The dad moved on to Vinnie and a 'restructuring' that sounds like it's been in play a while—including a break with Angelo."

Gus felt his body shudder. "My Angelo?"

"He has a son named Carmelo? His grandson is Melo?"

"Yeah."

"That's him. Angelo's out. Wolfgang and Vinnie want Melo." Kip paused, "Gus, you can listen to the recording, but it sounded like Wolfgang was getting his affairs in order before he died. He had an edge telling Klaus how to keep the members happy?"

Members? Gus's mind raced back to Angelo's last Friday night—Vinnie and Carmelo emerging from the stairwell, tension evident. Then, on Sunday, Gina spotted Vinnie and Melo in a heated conversation at the curb. Yesterday's surveillance showed Sheehan and Vinnie debating over calling their brothers.

Kip continued, "Wolfgang had no stamina. He faded."

Bobby beeped in. "Thanks, Kip. See you soon."

"We're at a crossroads here," Bobby skipped the preamble.

"Why?" Gus straightened, immediately alert.

"The mat processors are blowing past the timing controls in the code. The signal is degrading. We're getting noise. Failure to communicate."

Gus's mind shifted to computer programming and made an instant diagnosis. "You need new drivers to talk to the peripherals. Mix in resistors and conductors. That will change the clock speed and interrupt the latencies. That should work."

"We already thought of all that. The crossroads is, do we repair or rebuild? Repair comes with risk. Rebuilding takes time. Your choice"

At the intersection, Gus noticed people in the crosswalk—their lives continuing normally, some of them dealing with cancer, oblivious to the stakes of his mission.

"Bobby, imagine this is a baseball game. It's late in the game. We're down. Defense only keeps the score from getting worse. We need to put runs on the board, right?"

"That's why I'm calling. Who steps up to the plate."

"You're the manager. Do we have the time and talent to rebuild?"

"Everyone here thinks it's the best for the product."

Gus declared without hesitation, "Then start over. You have the talent. Pick your lead engineer. Break it down. Assign tasks. And if you need more people, cherry-pick whoever's available. I don't care if it takes the whole company. This is going to be one for the ages."

"What about Holder?" Uncertainty crept into Bobby's voice.

"What about him?"

"What do I tell him? What if he won't let me."

"Bobby." Gus lowered his voice. "Never mind. I'll tell Holder. Don't worry, he won't get in the way."

On a side street, three police cruisers blocked the road. A helicopter hovered overhead. Gus leaned toward Danno, "What's going on back there?"

"Probably a drug bust," Danno replied.

The comment sparked a connection. FBI Agent JD Hile. He found the number in his phone and called.

Hile answered on the second ring.

"You asked me to call," Gus said.

"Suttles and I would like a sit-down with you. Soon."

"I'm heading to Holder Medical on Thirteenth and Piedmont now."

"Meet you there," Hile said and disconnected. What could these guys want?

His mind drifted to the CNN host. The guy had gone off script in spite of Josh. Gus thought he'd recovered well enough to satisfy Tanzilla. While savored the tactical victory, Christian rang in.

"My phone is ringing non-stop." Her voice was controlled but tight. "Someone just leaked more damn video testimonials. And these are not like the first ones; these are professionally done. These are real cancer patients. Their families and friends are on there, saying this little BFD saved them. Our names are in the intros as the creators."

"Damn. Where?" Gus asked.

"Everywhere. YouTube. Facebook, Instagram, Twitter. News outlets are flooding the streets. Holder's losing it. The switchboard's swamped."

"Where are you?"

"In my office."

"OK. I'm on my way there."

"Are you going to make this go away?" Her voice hardened. "You caused it."

"Turn your phone off. If you want, go out the second-floor entrance to the parking garage and go through Angelo's to the street and catch an Uber to Henry's and stay there."

A long pause stretched between them. Christian said, "I've put some pieces together and I know not to relive everything with you, but I'm fielding calls I can't answer. What have you done?"

"Some pieces to a complex puzzle. I made each piece, and I'm not sure I can put them together. If you can't answer the questions, don't answer the phone."

Vulnerability broke through the anger. "I'm grateful this thing might help my father. I am," Christian said, her voice softening before hardening again. "But the rest? God damn it. I feel like a fricking pawn in your clandestine-ATRI world." Her voice dropped lower. "I could just spit." She stood abruptly, chair rolling back. "You think giving me a device for my father fixes everything? Your charity makes us even? I was counting on those royalties, Gus. Real money. Independence. Not sitting around hoping you'll throw me another bone when you feel generous."

"I can't live like this—wondering if you'll change your mind, cut me out again when it suits your mission. You want to play God with cancer? Fine. But don't play God with my life."

Media trucks lined both sides of Thirteenth Street. ACE diverted to Angelo's parking garage; her expression grim. She swiped Gus's credential card and drove to the second-level entrance to Holder.

Gus told Christian, "I've got a meeting on the third floor. We can talk later. Don't worry."

Inside, Gus spotted Hile and Suttles in the lobby, and walked to the conference on the next level while ACE retrieved them.

Across the atrium, Bob Holder stood at his office entrance, his usual bluster muted. He caught Gus's eye and gave a subtle thumbs-up.

On the third floor, Hile opened without preamble. "We intercepted communications your people haven't."

Gus's brow furrowed. "How could that happen?"

"Filters. We dial into specific language parameters. Got lots of hits."

Intrigued, Gus leaned toward Suttles. "I didn't know which terms to use."

"Depends on what you're trying to surface," Suttles said with a hint of a smile. "Street talk has its own language. Most folks miss it entirely."

"We think we've reached an intersection between our investigation and your situation." Hile's gaze never wavered.

He furrowed his brow. "Connection?"

Suttles gave a slight nod.

"My situation is..." Gus paused deliberately. "It's not related to drugs. Not street drugs. Chemotherapy...indirectly."

"Donna Sheehan, part of your problem?" Suttles said. His tone remained flat.

He nodded once.

"Vinnie Schnerr?"

"Potentially."

"We have confidential informants on the street. Intelligence coming back links Schnerr to our trafficking operation." Suttles said.

Hile continued. "The network is large and sophisticated. Schnerr could not orchestrate it independently. If he's involved, she's involved." Hile's words carried certainty.

"You're just now getting this? After how many years?"

"There's change afoot." Suttles twitched his eyebrows. "Change brings change. My guys are picking up on the chatter. We worked it back to Vinnie."

"What's this got to do with me?"

"We need to link him to this ring. We need internal access. You're positioned to facilitate that."

A guarded smile came to Gus's lips. "The Schnerrs and Angelo Marchitello are connected, going back four decades."

His throat tightened. Swallowing took effort.

"We want to know all we can about these long-term business associates," Hile added.

"I don't know Angelo."

"You and Carmelo have a relationship."

He hesitated. "Sort of. He's no drug dealer."

Hile dismissed the comment. "He selected you as the companion for his notable relative," Hile said.

Silent, a chill crept up his spine.

Suttles' tone was almost paternal. "Son, your interactions with Gina Marchitello are documented across multiple social media platforms." "But your academic credentials don't extend to criminal deception."

Really? Deception had served him remarkably well. "What exactly do you want?" Gus asked.

"Documentation and financial records."

"And just how would I access those?"

"Through your girlfriend. Gina Marchitello." Hile delivered the name with perfect pronunciation.

"She's not my girlfriend," Gus said, a smirk tugging at his lips. "You should approach her directly. Or Carmelo."

"Let's not dance," Suttles said, shifting forward. "Would your path forward be better if Sheehan and Vinnie Schnerr were gone?"

"Gone?" his body tensed.

"Yeah. Gone. Would that help your... project?"

"Yes." The word screamed inside him, but he remained silent.

Suttles read his face and smiled. "Sounds mutually beneficial to me. How bout you?"

Gus swallowed hard. "I still don't see how I can help you."

"We'll pick this up tomorrow," Suttles said and stood. "Discuss it with her after you collect her at the airport this afternoon."

Gus stopped breathing. His eyes shifted between the agents.

Hile said evenly, "Don't underestimate federal resources, Mr. Meier."

Gus's phone vibrated. With numb fingers, he retrieved it. The message read: "At the San Fran airport. Flight is on schedule. Looking forward to seeing you."

He stared at the screen, then looked up at Suttles, who returned his gaze with unnerving calm.

Dell Suttles said, "Let me guess, your girlfriend?"

Chapter Thirty-Seven

On the second floor of Holder Medical Engineering, ACE, Danno, and Gus watched Hile and Suttles exit through the front doors, navigating the journalists lining Thirteenth Street. The drooling media couldn't see past the manufactured drama to the real story that had just brushed their shoulders.

Gus checked his watch. 10:10. The SCIF. The toxicity code. Damn.

He moved, and ACE followed. Gus stopped. If looks could kill.

"We're your shadow," ACE said, her voice low and steady. "Non-negotiable."

"Jesus," Gus spun toward her, fingers clenching. His eyes darted between her and Danno. "What can happen in here?"

ACE used silence as a balm. "You heard Josh. These people are pros. You got a rent-a-cop on that door."

"Call Mitch," Gus ordered. ACE stared back, jaw tightening. "Please. Let's beef it up out front and pretend it's all crowd control."

Danno took his cue from ACE. She said, "Call Metro, too. We'll handle it inside and have them handle the street. Tell them Suttles told you to call."

ACE asked about possible building openings. Gus called Funk. In minutes, Funk sent a smart print summary—an electronic blueprint highlighting every entry point, vulnerable spots glowing red. Danno would post the expanded detail there.

They followed him to the SCIF and stood watch, backs to the wall, scanning the corridor.

Inside, the team worked quietly in pairs. No one looked up, faces locked in concentration, keyboards clicking in the stillness.

Bobby said, "We're all pulling in the same direction. Max is the team leader," nodding to a guy in a dark hoodie with voluminous curly hair.

Bobby crossed to Max, whispered something that made the man's head snap up. He followed Bobby toward Gus, wiping his palms on his jeans.

After a quick handshake, Gus asked the heavy-bearded man, "What's the prognosis?"

"Guarded. The program is sizable. The mat is lightning fast," Max stared at the screen, fatigue ringing his eyes. "Requiring a circuit board substantially more layered than what you have now. I can't say it will fit in the unit."

Gus told Bobby, "Figure that out. I'll be back. Going to look in on Christian."

Bobby said, "You need to get going on the toxicity piece. I want it ready when the time comes. I can't wait for you."

One more demand on his time. Gus nodded and exhaled. How could he be in multiple places at one time?

At the exit, Bobby added, "I did some cherry-picking. Holder told me, 'Whatever Gus wants, Gus gets.'"

Gus smiled faintly and left. The SCIF door hissed closed.

On the third floor, outside Christian's closed office door, he paused. What did he hope to accomplish by engaging her?

While he contemplated his decision, Kip called from the ATRI Watchtower. He stepped away, out of earshot.

Kip declared, "There's a call coming from Vinnie Schnerr to Christian. Vinnie's in Sheehan's office at GCI. Christian is in her office at Holder."

Gus turned to face her office, moved toward the door, turned the knob gently, and peeked in.

She glared at him, papers clutched in her white-knuckled hand, eyes red-rimmed. She jerked her hand for him to come in. He sat and mouthed, "Speaker."

Her slightly trembling fingers poked at the speaker button.

"Clever." Vinnie's voice oozed contempt. "You, the real brains on this project, pulling the strings while you hide behind Gus Meier."

"I guess I should say, BINGO, you figured it out." Christian's voice cracked.

"You played the Governor. Nicely done. I'll bet Meier didn't know about him any more than he knew about the device you developed."

"Nothing gets past you."

Vinnie chuckled, voice dropping. "I know a little bit about developing programs and coding. I know the last person to handle the device is the developer.

That's you. When news leaks like it has of late, you hide behind his ATRI credentials and send the schoolboy onto TV to do your bidding. Slick. Only one problem. I'm not buying what he's selling."

Gus mouthed to her, "Too bad."

Christian shook her head, "A smart guy like you wouldn't."

Gus scribbled a note and showed her.

She read it and improvised, "So, we agree we're two smart people. You would understand how I would naturally want to protect my overtly simple biofeedback device that is obviously a pawn in someone's covert attempt to expose Donna Sheehan as incompetent."

He heard Vinnie breathing.

Gus flipped a paper.

Christian said, "She struck me as a woman who could have a few enemies."

Vinnie's response took a split second longer. "Your device is curing people."

Gus shook his head. She took the hint: "You may know more than I do if you think my little device has healing capabilities."

Vinnie paused.

Gus wrote.

Christian read. "I'm the decoy. Someone is going to great lengths to get to her."

Silence.

The call ended with a sharp click.

The color drained from her face.

Gus pursed his lips. Well played.

Christian's hands shook against polished wood.

He nodded. "I pulled that out of thin air."

"No, you didn't. You pulled it out of your ass. Don't they say that where you come from? Well, that's where it came from, and frankly, oh, Jesus. His reaction? His sphincter could pinch a penny."

Gus wrinkled his face. "You know who that was?"

"How the hell would I know?" She stood abruptly, chair rolling back to hit the wall.

"I do, and he's bad." Gus leaned forward, voice dropping. "But I think you put him on his heels."

"That, or I put a red dot on my forehead." She leaned onto outstretched arms. "He knows shit I don't want him to." Her voice broke, the first crack in her armor.

Gus felt his chest heaving. Should he tell her the truth? How much? Opa said the time had come to trust.

"It's a damn good thing you walked through that door when you did. Why are you here?"

"Would you believe an angel sent me?"

She nodded frantically. "That's about the only F-ing explanation. I need a drink."

Gus lied, partly. "I was in the SCIF rewriting code for Bobby's project. I wanted to check on…"

Her eyebrows rose, a bitter laugh, "Oh God. Tell me you're not dragging poor Bobby into this? He's got a family. Not that I don't, and not that you care."

Gus stood to leave, shoulders tight. "I know who that was. And just to be safe, I'll have my detail relocate yours to the second level. You leave out that door when you go home…to Henry's. I'll see you there later."

A text hit her phone.

Christian read it, eyes narrowing. "I see your every move, and your brother and sister too. Have a nice day."

"It's a bluff," Gus said.

She pointed at Gus, her finger trembling, "If this goes South. My blood is on your hands."

As he opened the door to leave, a neatly outfitted, bulky man with a short-cropped beard greeted him affably. "Hi. Is she busy?"

Startled, Gus propped the door wide.

"Thank God," Christian said as she moved around the desk, shoulders dropping. "A sensible man if ever I knew one."

He headed to the SCIF, calling Kip. The corridor seemed longer than before.

"What prompted Vinnie to call Christian?"

Kip's voice thrummed with excitement. "Klaus. He wants him to intimidate her to turn on you. The media is pummeling GCI. This call was strategic. Planned. Even if she doesn't turn on you. She might talk to save her family."

Gus remembered Pogue's call. "Keep an eye on Pogue. I'm going to call her now."

"Ok. By the way. Sheehan made one call to the blocked number. I think it's her brother. She told him to pull out all the stops."

"Has she heard from the FDA?"

"No. Just Klaus. Which led to the call to Christian. The FDA guy and a few Senators are pounding Stephen James. But, honestly, Gus, this is so far beyond listening in to find your missing data, it's impossible to keep up with all the calls and who's saying what. Reams of transcripts, but no time to read them."

His phone vibrated. Gina.

"I just saw your picture on someone's iPad at the airport. You're popping up on all my feeds. I'm being linked to the man who can stop cancer. Is there a connection?" Her voice held none of its usual warmth.

A text from Bobby distracted him. "Conner Keegan called. Saw you on CNN. Eager to see what we have. Call today to review the Terms Sheet."

"Gus," Gina said. "Are you there?" Impatience edged into her tone.

"Yes. I'll explain when you get here." He pinched the bridge of his nose, headache building.

"I'm not exactly anonymous."

"When is your flight?"

"In an hour. I'm beside a vending machine with my back to everyone." Her voice dropped. "People are looking at me. I hate this. I should have skipped this."

"Hold on," Gus said. He punched at his phone screen, sweat beading on his forehead. "You're in San Francisco?"

"Yes."

He scrolled on his phone, stopping at the Golden State Executive Charter website.

The line went silent. He heard terminal announcements echoing faintly.

"Get directions to the Golden State Executive operation. By the time you get there, I'll have a plane waiting."

"How do you do that?"

"My mother owns Swiss Executive Aviation. I'll put this on her account."

"Thank you. Now, what about this cancer business?"

"When you get here."

He heard her breath change as her pace quickened, "From geek to mysterious to intriguing. And now, my travel agent." The warmth he desired had returned.

"I do what I can," Gus said, filling out the Golden State Executive Charter payment information on his way to the SCIF. "Please, let me know if you need anything."

Kip rang again. "Talk to me, Kip," Gus said, patience fraying.

"We just intercepted a strange call to Klaus Schnerr from a cell phone at a hotel in Zurich, Switzerland. No name."

Zurich? Klaus and the Assassin? "Do you have a transcript?" Gus said, forcing himself to stay calm.

"Check your inbox."

"Ok. I'll call you if I have questions." Standing in the corridor, he opened the attachment, words jumping off the screen.

*TRANSCRIPT #64C—KLAUS SCHNERR to UNKNOWN CALLER ZURICH

KLAUS: "Yes?"

CALLER: "I arrive Thursday morning. 7:30 local time."

KLAUS: "I see that here. Look for the placard."

CALLER: "No need. Holly will pick me up."

KLAUS: "Holly? Don't use that name. And why would you do that?"

CALLER: "Why not? I let her know I was coming."

KLAUS: "Did you tell her why?"

CALLER: "Visiting family."

KLAUS: "Did she tell you about being engaged to my brother?"

CALLER: "No."

KLAUS: "She is."

CALLER: "Fine. I'll phone you when we're through."

KLAUS: "No. My driver will pick you up. I'll let her know. And I'd like you to dig around about their plans."

CALLER: "Such as?"

KLAUS: "The business. Wolf isn't long for this world. Those two are a power couple."

CALLER: "Okay. I'll dig."

Phone in hand, it fell to his side. Involuntary short breaths accompanied cold sweat glazing him. Klaus and Tanzilla weren't waiting. His pounding heart slammed against his ribs. The 'power couple' occupied space in Klaus's head. But why?

Christian. Should he alert her? Who was Holly…the detonator? Could he get his hands on Carmelo's business records and stop them before they stopped him? The options made his head spin. Confusion sucked at his energy.

Kip texted, "Klaus just distributed burner phones to Tanzilla, Sheehan, Slayton, James, and Sheehan. Eavesdropping may be over. Still have visual and audio in three offices."

A tactic of a man who sees his margin for error narrowing. Gus could relate.

Chapter Thirty-Eight

Still standing in the corridor on his way to the SCIF, when Kip dropped the transcript from Zurich, confounded, Gus did the only logical thing that came to mind: he called Detective Suttles.

"The Assassin is on his way?" Gus said.

"Yes. We know. Hile is coordinating with Baumann at Interpol."

"He's meeting with someone named Holly. Is she the detonator?"

"I can't say."

"I'd like to be at that meeting."

"Why?" Suttles said.

"I need to defuse the focus on me."

"Given any more thought to getting those records?"

"Plenty."

"And?"

"My brain hasn't spit out an answer yet."

Suttles said. "You mean you haven't figured out how to play it?"

Gus said, "Is that what I mean?"

"Uh Huh," Suttles said.

"Can I ask you something? Personal."

"Uh-huh."

"Do you have a lot of friends?"

"Uh-huh."

Gus grinned and nodded. "Why is that?"

"Never asked," Suttles replied.

"Uh-huh," Gus said. Something in Suttles's laconic way quelled his mounting anxiety. "When I figure out how to play it, I'll let you know."

Gus waited for the 'uh-huh.' Instead, Suttles said, "I know you will, Gus."

He continued down the corridor to the Holder Medical SCIF.

Outside the entrance, his phone vibrated. Pulse quickening, he read 'Pogue' and groaned as he exhaled. The voice in his head screamed, "Leave it. Bobby is waiting." But…she must have news, otherwise…he turned to the railing overlooking the atrium, and answered.

"I'd like a word," her delicate British accent calmed him instantly.

"Go ahead."

"Face to face. In one hour?"

"About what?"

"Where are you?"

Damn. She did have news! "At Holder. "It's a media madhouse."

"I'll come to you."

"Go to the second floor of Angelo's parking garage, the side entrance."

"I know it well."

Gus exhaled. "I'll have someone there."

Staffers were leaving through the front entrance, where they wove through the media, hoping to see him and Christian. A small group sat conversing with their feet up on an ottoman near the waterfalls. How many times had he and his young colleagues occupied the same seats discussing the day's work, planning for tomorrow? How important their tasks seemed then. Times had changed, along with the stakes. Was Clair Pogue coming of her own accord, or had she been sent? Klaus? Perhaps. Why else would she drive across town at rush hour—-privacy. What she was coming to say, were for his ears only.

His phone vibrated. Resigned, not angry, he read Kip's name and braced himself.

Kip told Gus, "That call from Pogue…she's on a mission. GCI is unraveling."

"What's unraveling?"

"The mystery surrounding the FDA. Funk showed me how to use filters like the Feds. I plugged in your name and the term 'data.' What just popped up explains why they're worried, and they should be. I'm sending you the transcript. Read it now. This is what needs to be leaked rather than people being healed."

Exasperated, Gus said. "Details, Kip. Help me."

"Check you're email. It's complicated. Whatever you do, don't let her know that you know. It may blow our cover."

A siren on Thirteenth Street intensified when the doors opened as Gus rested his forearms on the railing and read the emailed transcript. Startled by classified information beyond their authorization, he surmised that the FBI had to know. Suttles said they read everything. Did they? Or did they rely on filters, like Kip? Regardless of Pogue's intentions, the transcript illuminated the motivation driving Tanzilla, James, and Klaus.

At last, inside the SCIF, the overhead lights were low. Recessed rope lights accented the room and soothed him. His gaze laned on Bobby who gave a glance at the clock on the wall, then tapped the watch on his wrist to stress the urgency.

Max approached Gus. "It's fast and big. If you had to choose size or speed, which would it be?"

Gus shook his head.

Max raised his eyebrows. "If you want it to fit and you want it tomorrow, you have to choose."

Gus tilted his head forward, raised his eyebrows to match Max. "The folks at GMC say my drop-dead time is six o'clock Friday morning. Can they keep at it?"

Max pondered the timeline. "They're too old for all-nighters," he said, "but they love the challenge. The reality is, you could give them a year, the circuit board required to drive the amount of code in this new mat…, it won't fit." A blank look came to his face.

Bobby glanced around the SCIF, "They all agree. You have to cut something."

Gus nodded and waved them away. He needed to think.

Bobby told the team to step out.

"Let me call Cedric," Gus said. The big man told him he'd hacked into the GCI code to look for a line where someone could have switched off the access code to the data files, adding, "I suspect your data exists. There's jus no tellin where to look."

"What about Rueben Gerding?" Gus said.

"Nothing. They may have shut him down. Stalling," Cedric said.

Gus imagined Gerding in a room with Tanzilla, being threatened by the big Italian to defy the Governor and ignore the order to cooperate.

~~~

The hour passed quickly. ACE called to say Dr. Pogue had arrived.

Gus directed her to the third-floor conference room. Time to meet the messenger.

Danno escorted Dr Pogue onto and off the elevator. Gus turned the blinds and told ACE and Danno, "Note anyone looking this way, who walks by, or
~~~

does one thing the least bit suspicious." Tucked in the back of his mind was the comment Vinnie emphatically made to Sheehan on their first panicked call, "He's our fucking mole."

Moles were rare at ATRI. That only left Holder.

The conference room served as a meeting place for research and development teams. A square table, eight chairs, two on a side, a whiteboard, and a dorm-room refrigerator. Gus went for water and offered Pogue one; she declined; he guzzled half the bottle and sat catty-corner to her. Her penchant for propriety reminded him of his grandmother, except Pogue's fingers weren't twisted by rheumatism.

Dr. Pogue began in a measured, slow, and deliberate cadence. "A consensus is building that I underestimated your device."

Consensus? Keep quiet. She was sent here.

"If media accounts are true and your device is pivotal, and cataclysmic..."

Cataclysmic?

"I underestimated you." She paused, holding his gaze without blinking. "I also believe you are ignorant of who is on the opposing side and how they operate."

"I knew your father—through Holder. I liked him. I like you..." Her left elbow propped on the table, her open posture implied truthfulness. "His death did not surprise me; it hardened me. Would you like to know why?"

"I would," Gus said.

"Two months after his death, I was called before the Board of Directors— not the Medical Advisory Board—as if I'd committed some infraction." Her voice began to crack with suppressed rage. "My department was told that research related to cancer was being discontinued. Not temporarily, but permanently."

Her fist slammed the table. "That bastard Tanzilla and his ASCO cronies! They made me the same deal they made George Slayton Sr.—huge salary, fall in line, or else. They tripled my salary and threatened to destroy my reputation if I left."

"For fifteen years, I've watched them turn GCI into their personal money machine while real treatments get buried!" Her British composure cracked completely. "They hired Sheehan to make sure no one strayed from their revenue protocols. She's not compliance—she's their enforcer!"

"Why are you here?" Gus said.

"To save both our necks," she said, lifting her chin. "Sell your source code and walk away."

Shocked, a nervous chuckle escaped him.

"I'm disappointed," Gus began. "You know my device isn't capable of what they're claiming. Why are they in such a panic?"

"Because the social media stampede has them terrified!" Pogue's nostrils flared. "Tanzilla is convinced you and I are colluding against them."

Gus squared himself on the table, forearms on edge. "Then he's stupider than I thought. But you—you went along with this willful blindness for fifteen years. You knew better, but you took their money and stayed quiet while real treatments were buried."

Her face flushed crimson. "Willful blindness? You think I had a choice? Do you know what happens to doctors in complementary and alternative medicine who don't play along? Every year, a hundred of us are killed—car accidents, heart attacks, suicides. All very convenient."

The room went silent. Gus felt the weight of her words.

"George Slayton Sr. knew this. That's why he signed their deal. That's why I signed mine. It wasn't willful blindness—it was survival."

"And now?" Gus said quietly.

"Now they want me to help them eliminate another threat. You." Her voice cracked. "And they think if you just sell and disappear quietly, it will all go away."

"For how long? You think appeasing them after fifteen years of abuse will suddenly make you safe?"

She crossed her arms defensively. "What choice do I have?"

"The same choice my father had—fight back."

"And look how that ended!" she snapped. "Your father was threat number 101. They don't just suppress treatments, Gus—they eliminate the people who create them. You naive fool—you think logic matters to these people?"

Gus's eyes narrowed. "You think surrender will save you? There's a whistleblower behind the testimonials, feeding information to CNN. Even if I sell, they'll still be exposed."

"What whistleblower?"

He raised the transcript Kip had sent. "Seriously? A whistleblower inside GCI is orchestrating the social media campaign. They're not just after my device—they're after the FDA designation."

"What designation?" Her face blanked.

"The Breakthrough Therapy Designation. The one that gives GCI authority over emergency drug approvals. Public scandal is the only thing that can disqualify them."

The slight space between her lips slowly closed. Her eyes shut. She drew in a long, deep breath.

"You didn't know the full scope, did you?" Gus said more gently. "They don't trust you. And they're willing to make me the scapegoat."

"I should drive to the airport and never look back," she whispered.

"And leave the whistleblower to expose everything anyway?" Gus shook his head. "Don't you see? Selling my device won't stop what's coming. The moment they announce a deal with me, the whistleblower reveals the FDA corruption. Tanzilla's in checkmate."

Pogue stood and gripped the back of her chair, her expression desperate. "Then what do you suggest?"

"Go back to GCI. Tell them they have a bigger problem than Gus Meier." He paused. "Tell them the whistleblower knows about the selection committee— about how Sheehan's the public representative who gets a vote in deciding which cancer drugs receive emergency approval ahead of well-researched alternatives. You can bet the whistleblower is going to name every company that stands to benefit. Then tell them to ask themselves: what's it going to be?"

Pogue said nothing and left.

For the first time, lying felt good.

Chapter Thirty-Nine

From the third-floor railing, Gus watched Dr. Pogue exit to the parking garage shared with Angelo's. Behind him, the SCIF engineers filed out. Surprised, he stepped into the empty room.

"Bobby, what's going on?"

"We're done…until you decide what to cut."

Stunned, Gus leaned his weight onto his outstretched arms on the table. His head hung. His clenched fist pounded the table and his head shook. Silence yielded to his heavy exhale. More silence. Head still hung, Gus said, "I'm sorry, Bobby."

Silence.

Bobby rested his hips on the edge of the SCIF conference table, his face registered his concern, "I've never seen you like this."

Still hanging, his head nodded. Following a series of deep breaths, he looked at Bobby and chuckled, "I've never been in a situation like this."

Silence.

Gus snickered, "I can't believe my life has come to this." Facing his friend, he added, "Truth is stranger than fiction."

A slight grin came to Bobby. "I understand. No one's leaving. They're just getting out of this room."

He exhaled and paced around the table. "You think JCO would move the demo to Monday or Tuesday?"

"No. Conner Keegan called again to confirm we were still on track. I know it's tight and tried to buy us some time, but his people are set on Friday."

Gus kept circling the table as he called Cedric. Cedric delivered bad news— all his calls to Rueben Gerding had landed in voicemail.

Gus asked Cedric to send him the Excel spreadsheet, hoping to identify the toxicity frequency range he'd programmed. But as he thought about it, he realized guesswork wouldn't cut it. "Actually, never mind," Gus said. "Guessing got me into this situation."

Dr. Chen? He knew about the device. Would he risk speaking to Gus and helping him identify the specific frequency range to eliminate the toxicity issue? Even if Chen did help, they'd still need to bypass the read-only version to analyze the data to confidently know what to cut from the source code to make the circuit board fit. He thanked Cedric and phoned Gerding directly.

"Reuben, you have until ten o'clock to release the read-only file. After that, I'm going to drive down to CNN and blow this wide open. I've had enough."

He handed Bobby a credit card and asked him to take them next door for a nice Italian meal. "Give me two hours. If I'm still stuck, send them home."

They left the SCIF together. Gus stopped at the railing. Bobby delivered the news to his team. Their smiles were a consolation.

A text on his screen brought him back to his frenetic world. It was from ACE. "ETA 2 minutes." Following her earlier call about Dr. Pogue's arrival, Gus had asked her to meet Gina's private plane at Peachtree Dekalb Regional Airport at 5:15.

He called ACE, "Everything go right?"

"Yes."

"May I speak to her?"

"Hi Gus."

"Hi. Do you have a minute to talk before your event?"

"A little, not too much."

ACE parked by the entrance that Pogue used. Inside, they hugged, exchanged a quick kiss, and sat on comfortable club chairs in an open area, the waterfalls serving as a soothing backdrop.

"Nice flight?"

"The best. Thank you."

Gus smiled. "I have to tell you something."

"About cancer?"

"About Carmelo."

She looked puzzled.

"He's in business with a bad person."

She listened.

"Did you know this?"

She hesitated.

"What do you know?"

"My grandfather and Angelo are brothers."

Gus nodded.

"I set up Zoom calls for them each Saturday. I hear what they talk about."

"And they talk about their business?"

She nodded.

"Which is?"

She hesitated. "Real Estate."

"Real Estate?"

"Parking garages, like the one outside. Angelo built that with them many years ago. They have them all over."

"Who is 'them?'"

"I think it's the man you saw at dinner and the one with Melo."

"He's pushing Carmelo out. Can you confirm or deny that?"

"I think that's right."

"Does the name Schnerr mean anything?"

She nodded, "That's the partner. Angelo's partner. He told my grandfather his sons are pushing Carmelo out."

"Partner?"

"Yes."

Gus hesitated. "Can we go see Angelo?"

"Yes. I was going to call him anyway."

"When?"

"I'll call him now. I was going to ask to visit him in the morning."

Gus grinned, "Good. I'd like to go with you."

She reached Angelo and set the appointment. One statement made his heart race. "I'm leaving Friday night, so I won't be able to have coffee on Saturday."

Her plans had changed again. No stay-over at the lake…

When she ended the call and noticed his expression, she said, "I'm taking the midnight flight to Rome."

"No lake trip?"

She shook her head.

"No good-bye-sex?"

"Maybe welcome-back sex some other time."

<div align="center">~~~</div>

ACE and Danno accompanied Gina to the Savannah College of Art and Design benefit.

At seven o'clock, Bobby texted, and Gus instructed him to thank the team for their diligence, and he would see them the following morning. Alone in the SCIF, scouring his source code for possible places to trim, hoping Dr. Chen would return his call after hearing his two voicemails, he wondered why Chen hadn't reached out. Had Tanzilla and James gotten to him? The Schnerr's?

At 9:15, his phone vibrated. "Good," Gus thought, someone is getting back to him.

ACE. She said, "Gina's gone."

While ACE gave her accounting, another call interrupted.

Gus answered. "Are you listening?" a techno-synthesized voice said.

Startled, Gus said, "Who is this?"

"Listen up. Here's the deal...."

He listened. Pogue had given them his answer. This was their counteroffer.

He called Dell Suttles. They planned to meet at SCAD.

Gus roused Bobby, who was sleeping on the loveseat inside the second-floor entrance in the event Gus had a breakthrough.

"Can you drive me to SCAD?"

Disoriented, Bobby said, "What's up?"

"Gina's been kidnapped."

~~~

Suttles and his partner were in the campus security office inside the student union hall.

"Coordinated strike," Suttles told Gus. "No close parking." Pointing at the monitor, "Here, this couple in formalwear approaches her. There's ACE, heading for the truck. Now, watch. Danno moves to give them space. He's standing guard. But as Gina takes a few steps the man leads her out the door."

"What now?"

"Did they say what they wanted?"

Gus mumbled. "No cops. They want my source code. I zoned out when I heard they had Gina."

"They're impatient. They called too soon. This will go fast. Are you going to give it to them?"
~~~

"Had Sheehan shown up at CNN, I was prepared to give it to her on TV to get the focus off me."

"Good. This will be quick. They'll call; you turn it over. Everybody's happy."

"What now?" Bobby asked.

Gus looked at the clock on his phone, 10:45. He checked his email. No message from Reuben Gerding. "Let's go to CNN."

~~~

In the same lot where he'd started his day, Gus strategized. Inside, he'd invoke the name of Anita, the New Day producer. If they got her on the phone, she'd get him in. Bobby parked his Toyota, and they set out.

His strategy worked. Security called Anita, who heard his story and passed him through to a crew ready to take it down digitally. Anita would contact Suttles to confirm the details and air it in the morning.

On the way out, his phone vibrated. Rueben Gerding texted, "Sorry for the delay. You're unlocked. All clear. Good luck. Here are your credentials."

Gus looked at his watch: 11:40. He was frazzled. Humbled by the overwhelming confluence of motivations and personalities he could not have foreseen, he said to Bobby in a low voice. "Drive me back to Holder. Have the team ready at 8:00. I'll get it cut down. It'll fit. You head home."

Bobby studied his friend, "We're in extra innings. The game's not over."

"Well, we're going to need coffee."

They rode in silence for a few sacred minutes. Gus phoned Carmelo. "I think they're using her to get to me," Gus said.

"Why? What do they want?"

"A scapegoat."

~~~

In the Holder SCIF on the third floor, Gus typed the credentials Gerding sent and accessed the notebook of spreadsheets buried in the GCI system. He searched through cells methodically, hunting for the toxicity code and identifying which frequency codes the system rarely accessed. The data confirmed what previous researchers had found, and he observed when using biofeedback on animals and Opa—cancer patients' bodies consistently chose the embedded frequencies from trypsin and embryonic stem cells. They were like the one-two punch that stopped cancer.

But as he dug deeper, his enthusiasm turned to dread. A pattern emerged in the mortality data. Like Opa, elderly patients initially showed improvement, but it then suddenly reversed. The timeline was unmistakable.

His device was taxing them. The very frequencies that helped younger patients proved toxic to older ones. Had Henry not called, Opa might have died.

Shame and guilt washed over him as the scope of his oversight became clear. Dr. Chen would get a visit first thing in the morning.

Bobby kept his coffee full and hot and took down notes Gus dictated regarding changes Max and the team would make. By 1:00 a.m., the rigidity in his body softened as hope appeared on the horizon.

Then his phone rang. Blocked caller.

The same techno voice said. "Make it easy. Turn over the source code."

"Who is this?"

"Listen." The techno voice demanded. "Put a hard drive in a box of Sarah's Doughnuts. Have them delivered to the visitor's desk in the main building by ten o'clock tomorrow morning. When we have it, you'll receive a call with the location where she is. She's fine. If you play this right, she'll stay that way. If you don't, she'll vanish, without a trace."

Chapter Forty

Hours later. delirious at three a.m., Bobby said, "I'm going to have to call the game."

"I'd say we won," Gus said and yawned. He'd made enough cuts to boost his confidence that the printed circuit board (PCB) would fit. He had more to do, but he liked his chances.

Bobby walked to a closet. "We have four cots. I've never had to use them, but I know where they are."

They slept in the SCIF on nylon cots with synthetic blankets and foam pillows that could pass for bricks.

~~~

Bobby jostled his shoulder at 6:30, Thursday morning. "Coffee?"

Gus first reached for his phone. No missed calls from the kidnappers. No text. He rolled to the side of the cot, sipped his coffee, and reflected on Gina, the thumb drive, and the donuts. As he made his way to a leather chair around the conference table, his phone vibrated. It was 7:00.

"Detective Suttles."

"Hile said you could sit in the surveillance van."

His heart rate rose, knowing he'd be eavesdropping on the assassin. "Where and when."

As Suttles spoke, he typed the time and location into his computer, then ended the call.

His code cuts were working. He felt ready for Max and the team.

Bobby returned to the SCIF. "I'd better order the donuts."

"No. I'm going to go get them and deliver them."

Bobby sat beside him. "You don't have to do that. You need a base hit, not a home run."
~~~

"What I need is to score."

"You score by letting a stranger deliver the thumb drive in the box of doughnuts."

"They'll get the thumb drive from me." And while he was at GCI, he planned on seeing the elusive Dr. Chen.

~~~

ACE met Gus on the second floor of the parking garage at 7:45.

Just after eight, she pulled the Tahoe behind a step van on Northside Drive with "RW Smith Company General Contracting" emblazoned on its sides. Gus exited the Tahoe and entered the van through the passenger's door and the cutout behind the seats. Hile greeted him and introduced the technicians and the driver. Minutes later, they were in stakeout position in the Caribou Coffee parking lot at the corner of 10th and Piedmont, facing the Flying Biscuit.

Hile informed Gus, "Two agents inside. Their waitress is one of ours. The ceramic dish is our mic."

"Is your man wired?"

Hile shook his head. "We tied into their security cameras." He's using a pair of your glasses. First time we've used them."

Gus put on his AV glasses and told Hile, "I'm going in."

Hile raised his hand to Gus, settling it on his chest. "This is as close as you get."

Gus shook off Hile, "You get him these glasses, or I will. I'm leaving nothing to chance."

Hile put a hold on his elbow and said, "Follow directions."

"Remove your hand," Gus said.

Hile let go and growled, "Look at the monitor." Hile growled.

"It stinks," Gus said. "He needs these," and removed the glasses.

A technician at the desk announced, "They're here."

He recognized the phone tracker on the screen.

The technician relayed the outside agents' words: "Subject is in a late model, navy, Porsche Cayenne. Headed North on Piedmont. Two passengers. They've stopped. The passenger has exited."

Gus said. "Who goes in, you or me?"

Hile used binoculars to see through the side window in the van door. "That's him."
~~~

Gus leaned toward the windshield to see a man approach his favorite breakfast spot. His father's killer. A lump formed in his throat. His breath caught.

"He's in position," the tech declared.

The man appeared on the monitor—poor image from that distance, and the lighting. The waitress set down menus. The opposite-facing camera showed an empty seat.

"Hile. You or me? Three, two, one."

"I'll go. Give me the damn things."

Agent Hile exited the rear of the van, darted across the street and shot into the busy dinning area. As quickly as he went in he came out. Gus brought the program linked to the glasses up on his phone. Remarkable.

Winded, sweating, Agent Hile came in the rear doors and took his seat.

Gus flashed the phone screen in front of him. "Look."

Hile did, then looked at Gus. "Everything you record is mine. This is an international operation."

Gus nodded. The image on his screen jostled as the assassin adjusted the glasses. Gus then mumbled to Hile, "Where's Holly?" The assassin told Klaus he was meeting Holly. Gus had imagined this moment countless times—facing his father's killers.

Customers entered and left through a narrow glass enclosure.

On the monitor's top left image, an indistinguishable woman stepped forward and scanned the restaurant. She stopped momentarily, then walked to the assassin and slid in opposite him.

"Zoom in on image 5."

The image zoomed in on her face. Gus squinted, repositioning himself so that he was square with the monitor.

"That's her."

"Oh my God," Gus whispered.

"What's wrong?" Hile said.

Gus pushed his face toward the monitor and squinted.

The assassin said, "Holly?"

"Oh my…Holly. Yes," Gus whispered unconsciously

"You know her?"

Gus ignored Hile.

Is this guy Omegaman?

The assassin said, "Is that you?"

Sheehan nodded.

Staring. Blankly. Then, standing abruptly. His hands settled gently—delicately—on her shoulders. Leaning, the camera on the glasses framed emerald-green eyes.

Gus gasped.

Erik, the assassin, smiled and said softly, "Hi."

She smiled, faintly.

He drew her close, embracing firmly, her face rested on his chest.

Staff and customers squeezed past them. The bustling of the restaurant enveloped them.

Gus stared at them, her dangling arms unresponsive for a full breath before she wrapped them around his waist.

Peering over Hile's shoulder, he furrowed his brow. Was she crying?

When the hug ended, he moved his hand intentionally toward her long bangs, and her head extended to evade his touch.

"Don't. Please."

Nodding apologetically, Erik said, "Sure."

They sat opposite one another.

Erik leaned forward against the table and took her hand. "They wouldn't let me visit."

She nodded.

"You look… wonderful."

She feigned a grin. "Different."

His grin widened, encouraging, "Your eyes…your smile…they're the same. I see you. Just as beautiful."

She lowered her eyes modestly. "This was a mistake."

"Grasping her hand on the tabletop, he shook his head and said, "No, it isn't. Don't say that."

Gus could hear himself breathing. Hile shifted to give him space.

"Holly," Erik paused, lowering his voice. "What happened?"

The surveillance camera caught her contemplating her response. Gus leaned in.

Sheehan was Holly, the detonator turned compliance officer, and a murderer?

Gus felt short of breath, and his heart raced.

"I'm sorry. I should have listened. But," she hesitated, "I've thought of this a million times…I couldn't help myself…so arrogant, so immature. I know that now. I had to push the button. I had to see the boat explode. The power. The control. Then, when it didn't happen,...." Her eyes wandered off.

"Why? Why didn't it happen? You were standing by the sea wall, then you took off running," the assassin said.

A pause before she delivered the verdict. "The detonator didn't work."

He took in a deep breath and held it.

She continued, "I thought I might be too far away. My jogging suit was the perfect decoy. I'd look innocent. As I jogged closer, I kept pressing the button, but nothing happened. I thought I could be useful and report that the detonator had flaws. I could run past and you would pick me up on the other side. It never occurred to me it would go off when I got next to the wharf."

"Oh my God." The words came out before he could stop them.

Her face wrinkled. "I still have nightmares of flying into the plate glass of the storefront." Her voice trailed off. "My face sliced open...conscious long enough to see the blood pooling under me."

An imperceptible nod, Erik whispered, "I thought you were dead."

"I wish I were."

The assassin stayed still.

In the van, Gus and Hile could see and hear him taking deep breaths. His glasses focused on her—hollow eyes, flickering eyelids,

"Two months in the hospital."

"I know. I kept up with you."

She looked away at people going about their busy lives. "Eight reconstructive surgeries...No one claimed me."

Erik's composure was completely gone now. His face showed everything— guilt, horror, helplessness. "They sent me to Lucerne."

Lips pursed, eyes welling up, she nodded, still looking away at nothing. "I got sent here."

"And I hear it's worked out," Erik said.

"Some great scheme by my father and your uncle, Wolfgang."

He nodded confidently, "I was told you were easy to hide here. Wolfgang was here; your family was not far. They found a place to use your training."

She nodded. "I stayed in Wolfgang's home...Following my last surgery...He got me a new identity, training, and a job. It's all been a sham."

"To move their drugs."

"Oh, yeah," Sheehan said. "We own the streets."

Jesus—she just confessed to the prescription drug ring.

"Klaus told me. I asked about you."

Sheehan scoffed, "You abandoned me."

"Holly. I did not abandon you."

"May 19th was fifteen years. When did we end? I get blown up, and you get reassigned. That's not an end, Erik, that's an escape."

Gus recognized the bitter version of Sheehan.

She leaned in. "I pleaded to come back to Geneva, to be with you, but Klaus said no because Vinnie and I took over the region and he was lapping it up." She lowered her voice, "That drove me further into the shadows."

"But you and Vinnie became something."

"Erik!" She leaned in, her teeth clenched, and her fists on the tabletop. She lifted her long bangs. "Hair can hide those scars. But it's my heart."—she sat back and swallowed, nodded, swallowed again and said faintly, "The scars on my heart cripple me most." She raised her hand to say, Please don't talk right now.

Erik nodded.

She continued, her voice cracking, "Vinnie doesn't soothe my heart, Erik. You do."

Eril seemed to gather himself, falling back on practical questions. "Why not leave?"

She scoffed and turned her head. "And go where? Klaus has essentially told me this is my life."

"Or else?"

"You know what else," Sheehan shook her head and scanned the restaurant.

"He told me you're making changes. That's good, right?"

She sighed loudly, "We are." Her voice hushed, "We're ready to expand to hospitals throughout the east coast."

"You and Vinnie? Not Klaus."

Sheehan's face hardened. "Fuck Klaus. It's our gig."

The business records from Angelo's. Gina. What about Gina?

Erik shifted in his seat. "That's more than I need to know. What's the problem you wanted to talk about?"

Just then, the waitress appeared, asking if they wanted the check, her tone insinuating the people crowding the entrance would appreciate the table.

Sheehan motioned with her hand to Erik. "It's changed. I got a new problem. Let's free up the table."

She can't have a new problem?

They walked to her Mercedes in silence. Behind the wheel, Sheehan drummed her fingers on the steering wheel, then turned to Erik.

Erik turned to her, the camera on his glasses framed her face perfectly, "This is no bullshit. Vinnie and I are in this together. The target is Klaus."

In the van, Gus swallowed, and his palms began to sweat. Erik held his head still—she stared back. "I'm serious."

Perfectly framed still, Erik said, "You may have guessed, I'm here to do a job for him."

"I know who he's after. He'll tell you he's cleaning up for me...AGAIN. He's such a prick."

"And when I do. I'm finished. This is my last one. Promise."

"That can only mean one thing: there's a woman."

Erik nodded.

"Children?"

"Soon."

Sheehan looked away. Erik held the camera on her. A sad, forced grin came to her as her head bobbed in resignation. She looked into Erik's eyes and the camera, "Do what he wants, then do me a favor. The whites of her eyes turned pink. "If ever I meant anything to you, and you want to help me live in peace, kill Klaus…as a parting gift."

Erik's face went carefully blank. His professional mask sliding back into place.

Chapter Forty-One

Reeling from the Flying Biscuit surveillance in the van with Hile, Gus remembered Sheehan's eyes—his father's killer—now a drug kingpin, who wanted Klaus eliminated.

Sheehan had not shown any sign of recognizing his name or connecting him to the dead man on the yacht. *Amnesia? Abandonment? Disinterest? Guilt?*

Approaching the Tahoe where ACE and Danno waited, Gus read a text from Bobby, "Are you at GCI?" A thump in his chest felt like Bobby had punched him. Gina. He patted his pocket—thumb drive safe and sound.

Agent Hile broke the silence by declaring Sheehan had not confessed to a crime he could prosecute. Without the business records between the Schnerrs, the Abernathys, and Angelo's family, Hile said, "our case is weak."

A glance at his watch triggered anxiety and confirmed he'd skip the donuts. He had what they wanted, and they had what he wanted.

He left the van through the back door and hopped into the rear seat of the Tahoe. "Georgia Cancer Institute, Cancer Center," he told ACE, checking his watch. The thumb drive felt heavy in his pocket. Twenty minutes later, ACE made an abrupt stop outside the medical complex.

He made for the revolving doors, pushed the bar handles firmly, and stepped out to survey the lobby he and Christian had panned six days ago.

Images of the "Go Dawgs" boy, Dr. Pogue, Sheehan and the Medical Advisory Board raced through his head as he took in a deep breath and looked for the information desk and suspicious eyes tracking him.

In the center of the chaotic lobby, he spied a round fixture with a white counter, marked "Information." The enthusiastic volunteer finished speaking to a guest.

He smiled, "Are you expecting a delivery of doughnuts?"

She eyeballed his empty hands. "Yes."

"I'm from the bakery. There's been a mix-up. Who are they for?"

"You don't know?"

"That's the mix-up. Can you help me?"

"You don't have any donuts."

"They're in the van."

Less enthusiastically, she told him, "I just have a number to call when they arrive."

"Great." Gus took out his phone. "Will you call that number?"

As she did, Gus's phone vibrated.

The techno voice said, "No donuts?"

"I have what you want. Come get it."

"Don't make this hard."

Instinctively, he gripped his lip between his teeth and scanned higher positions overlooking the lobby.

The techno voice said, "You won't spot me. And you won't see her again if you don't wise up and leave it on that counter."

Select faces in the crowd focused on him, moving closer—some men in security uniforms, others in street clothes.

"Leave it and leave, or she vanishes."

Scanning every direction. They had the place covered. He conceded. They had a contingency plan. He didn't.

From across the counter, observing his paranoid head movements, the concerned volunteer eased backward. He locked eyes with her and slid the thumb drive across the counter, under his cupped palm, and waited for her to trust him. When she came to it, reluctantly, he told her, "Call the number again. Give this to whoever the voice on the other end tells you to."

Twenty minutes later, Gus paced in short lines in the Cancer Center basement. The plaque beside the door read N.E. Chen, MD, Pathology. Dr. Chen's wife. Chen was late, allowing his nerves to settle enough to call Carmelo and speak clearly.

"I paid what they wanted. Watch for Gina."

Carmelo said, "Understood."

Their call ended.

Soon, Gus would have to explain this to Gina—if she were there.

Fluorescent lights outside the lab buzzed overhead. Antiseptic smell sharp in his nostrils. Pacing. Flashing back to Pogue.

He played the whistleblower card.

His fists clenched against his thigh.

They played the kidnap card. Would Gina pay for his miscalculation?

When they tested Christian's biofeedback source code on the thumb drive, they would confirm it only controlled severe swings in bodily functions during chemotherapy.

But they didn't care about the truth. They needed a scapegoat to offer the media.

That's all this was. His jaw tightened. *A performance to shift blame.*

With the thumb drive delivered and Carmelo duly notified, Dr. Chen, the oncologist, had his undivided attention. Somebody authorize those units leaving GCI—an indefensible violation of the research agreement.

But why?

He checked his phone. He had no calls, no texts, and...no choice. He had to stay, pace, and wait.

Feeling rare vulnerability, a pit formed in his stomach. Chen knew more than he did. He'd treated some of these patients.

Now fifteen minutes late. He called Chen. No answer. The pit in his stomach morphed. Bigger. Tighter.

Footsteps echoed in the stairwell. Chen's voice, speaking an Asian dialect into his phone.

Gus leaned against the wall, tilted his head back, and let out a long, forceful exhale—**PFFFFFWWWW**—the sound of steam escaping a pressure cooker.

Dr. Chen rounded the corner, still talking rapidly. When he saw Gus, he ended the call abruptly and approached with his key card.

"Back where it started," Gus observed as they entered the lab.

"Very different now. Sorry, administrative call ran long." Chen's English had improved since they'd met years ago.

The small office brought back memories of his early research on recording electrical frequencies of tissue samples Dr. Chen analyzed. An upgraded electron microscope occupied the same space on the station, along the wall opposite the door. He sat in the familiar chair beside her desk. Dr. Chen moved directly to his wife's chair, opened the laptop, and began typing.

Sitting still, studying Chen, questions rocketed in his head as he unconsciously gnawed the edge of his lower lip. One question mattered: what tissue should his program stimulate to prevent toxic buildup?

While Chen typed, Gus retrieved his vibrating phone. Carmelo texted: "Home safe and sound. Thank you."

His shoulders dropped. Gina must be home.

Chen looked up. Ready. He turned the laptop toward Gus to read the files of the elderly patients who had regressed at some point during treatment.

Gus said, "I've seen these files. What tissue should I program into the code to eliminate toxins created by the treatment?"

Chen paused. "Lymphatic tissue and spleen. My best estimate."

Gus nodded, relieved, and said, "I have those frequencies in my catalogue."

Chen turned the laptop toward himself and added, "You know about this?"

Chen typed, then turned the screen back to Gus, who had returned to his seat. Chen pointed to columns of data.

"These. They not dying from cancer."

"That's good, right?"

"They not dying. Period."

Ice water hit his veins. Gus gripped the desk edge.

"What?"

"Program make stem cell stay viable. Stem cell not degenerate."

Silence. His breathing changed.

"You're saying—"

"As cancer stops... aging stops."

His breathing stopped.

"You plan for this?"

"For what?"

Chen raised his eyebrows, his slanted eyes widened, "Immortality."

Dumbfounded, his mouth agape, Gus stared back. Even in an Asian dialect, the word elicited a rumbling shudder.

His phone buzzed. Ignore it. More buzzing, grab it. Bobby: *Call ASAP. Stuck. One way out—you won't like it.*

Stuck? Bobby's engineering crisis felt like a mosquito bite compared to the atomic bomb Chen just detonated in his skull. Sorry, Bobby. At the moment, immortality dwarfs circuit boards and JCO demos. Chen's revelation may have just brought the Assignment to a close.

"Jesus Christ." The words came out as barely a whisper. Gus stood and turned in the small space, his mind reeling. Immortality. The word echoed in his skull like a death knell—or birth cry. "No other researcher mentioned this possibility."

Would each person who used my device be condemned to watch their loved one's age and die?

Chen said, "They not put person in electric envelope with all right frequencies. You do. This not surprise to me. Perfect energy medicine."

Gus shook his head, rubbed his hands, wagged his jaw, and pondered Henry, Opa, JCO...then said to Chen, "You figured out what the device did?"

"I asked my wife if you tested frequency of stem cells."

"She told you the frequency of a stem cell?"

Chen nodded, "I study results they not let you see. Then, I knew what energy is going into the person."

Chen stood. Moved toward the door.

Gus moved quickly. Positioned himself in front of the door.

"Who would not let me see?"

Chen froze. Silence.

Gus said, "You told someone. That person instructed you to remove the biofeedback devices. Who?"

Chen's face went blank. "I say too much."

"Who told you?" Gus studied his panicked face. "Tell me. I'll call the FBI. You're involved, Chen. Are you a spy?"

Chen shook his head violently, "All authorized. I document everything."

"How do you account for 87 testimonials from 45 units?"

"I don't—"

Gus leaned in, his teeth gritted, "People are sharing this. If you sent devices home, that's on you. You'll lose your license. Go to jail. Do you understand how much trouble you could be in?"

Chen shifted uncomfortably.

Gus pressed harder. "Give me a name."

Chen made a move toward the door. Gus cut him off.

"Was it Pogue? She could authorize it. But she wouldn't." His mind raced as fast as his heart, breath coming short. How far would Chen take this? How far would Gus let it go? He closed the distance and fixed his stare. James, Tanzilla, Slayton—they wouldn't want this out. "Who, Chen?"

Silence.

"WHO?" His tone shifted from bullying to pleading as Chen resisted. "Stephen James told Christian he'd look into who authorized this. Did he contact you? Did you two decide to gamble on ignoring her?

Stares still fixed, Chen's head shook ever so slightly. "I never tell you."

"I need to know," Gus demanded...then relinquished his position.

Chen paused at the threshold. "And I never tell on you."
Silence.
Chen added, "What you do next, is on you."
The door closed. Gus stood alone.
His fist slammed the desk. "God damn it."
Immortality or mortality? His choice. His responsibility.
AHHHH. He screamed into the empty lab.

Chapter Forty-Two

At the curb outside the Georgia Cancer Institute, Cancer Center, ACE positioned the Tahoe. Gus settled in the seat behind her, burdened by the recurring scene in the lobby and immortality. He said, "Angelo's, please."

Bobby texted. "Call me."

Not now. Bobby already said I wouldn't like his solution. I can't handle another crisis.

His world was growing increasingly surreal, as if he were watching someone else's calamitous life unfold. Through the window, Druid Hills rolled past—tree-lined streets, a jogger, a mother pushing a stroller, and two white-headed women conversing on a front porch. *Normal life continues, oblivious to immortality and assassination plots.* A moment later, ACE pulled to the shoulder of the road to honor a funeral procession. He studied the faces of the people in the passing cars. Solemn. Solemn. Solemn. In that moment—clarity. *Finish the mat, which meant calling Bobby. And Bobby had bad news.*

I'm too exhausted to think clearly. Gina first. Then figure out the rest.

~~~

A parallel scene of Klaus with Erik in a room at the Consortium building. Elevated so Klaus can see everyone through glass cubicles—no one hides.

"Was it the homecoming you'd imagined?"

"No."

"You wanted something specific?"

"I wanted nothing, just my target. My last one. Then you and my brother can have the Consortium."

"Very well. Here is the dossier on your target," Klaus said, and slid the folder across the table to Erik.
~~~

~~~

On the curb outside Angelo's building, ACE spied a parking spot. Danno didn't get a chance to open his door when Gus hurried to the residents' entrance.

Inside the stairwell, a glance at the stairs, and he punched the elevator call button. Inside the common area, she opened the apartment door before he knocked. Red-rimmed eyes. Hands shaking slightly. Still beautiful. Still here.

Their hug was brief—chilly.

As sincerely as he had ever spoken, he said, "I'm so sorry you were dragged into this."

Her eyes searched his face.

His hands raised to embrace.

She pulled away.

"Don't," Gina said.

"Are you hurt?"

"Hurt?" Her voice was steady but sharp. "No, not physically. Terrified? Yeah. Mostly, I'm confused. I want answers, Gus. No, wait. I want one good reason not to pack my bags and leave right now."

What good reason did he have?

"What in God's name did I walk into when I came to this city?" Her head jutted forward. "Angelo's has been perfect, you too, perfect. But in the last twenty-four hours, I found out I'm in an alternate universe. So, please, help me, Gus. Explain this to me. And don't lie. I'm not part of *whatever* this is." A deep breath. "I trust you. You can tell me the truth, and I'll believe you. Prove my instincts right."

Trust. Truth. Instincts.

Mesmerized. Might his eight-year odyssey alone be ending? Here stood a woman—fierce, declarative, magnificent—traumatized, her family calling her home, yet she offered him sanctuary—creating space for truth. She's not afraid of who I might be. She seems to know.

He scratched his head. "There's a lot to tell."

She sank into the chair across from him. "That sounds like an honest start."

He sat heavily on her couch. "You saw the news story at the airport."

"A mysterious cancer breakthrough and a coverup?"

His lips pursed. He nodded. Here goes... Breaking the seal that kept him alive—and alone. He said, "That was me."
~~~

Silence.

"You created a cure for cancer."

He nodded, "And more."

Eyes squinting, she dropped her head slightly forward. "More?"

His eyes widened, "You probably won't believe it."

"How long have you known?"

"For a fact? In humans? Last night, while you were in captivity."

Gina lifted her chin. "And not searching for me."

Was she being cute?

"There was nothing I could..."

"Gus...I'm kidding. How does someone set out to cure cancer?"

He grinned. Relieved. "That..." Should he really go there? Yes. "My great-grandfather was given a notebook by his Jewish brother-in-law in 1939 with theories about using electricity to stop cancer. Someone in my family has been working on this for seventy-three years. I just happened to be the one who figured it out at Atlanta Technology & Research Institute."

"You're thirty. So, you graduated about eight years ago?"

"Yes. I was ready to get back to Switzerland. I had a career and a girlfriend waiting for me."

"Never made it?"

His head shook. "The morning after graduating, my grandfather and uncle showed me the notebook from 1939. I heard the whole story of our family history, and before we left the vault, my grandfather had convinced me I was the last hope to finish it. He said it would probably take a year."

"I'd think curing cancer takes more than a year."

"My father and grandfather didn't know the Assignment was to stop cancer. I studied all the documents and figured it out." He shrugged.

She said, "You couldn't quit?"

"No." He paused, "I'd be killing those people and dying a death I imagined being worse than cancer."

Gina's breathing changed, but her gaze never wavered.

"That's a lot to tote in your backpack."

A slight nod. "It got heavy—you're the first person I've told."

Incredulous. "Ever?"

Another slight nod. "My father was killed while working on it. I kept it top secret. I chose to live in the shadows, a self-imposed exile, to avoid having to lie to friends about what it was I was working on. Now, someone is leaking testimonials like the one you saw. They are accusing GCI of covering up a cure."

"Who would know this?"

Gus shook his head and shrugged.

"They are covering up, right?"

"More like holding off...on saying anything. They can't confirm what's stopping the cancer. Yesterday, someone from GCI came to me and asked me to sell. I refused. Within hours, you were taken."

"So, the people who took me wanted your secret formula. Later, you gave them what they offered to buy?"

"Yes. Well, honestly, that's what they *think* I gave them."

"You lied to my kidnappers?"

"I didn't lie...more like a calculated risk. I gave them what they wanted, but they can't tell if it does what they think it does."

She shook her head. "Ok. What's the 'more' part? What could be more?"

He ran his hands through his hair. "Stopping death."

Confusion erupted on her face.

Gus nodded slightly, his face blank.

He said, matter-of-factly, "An unintended consequence may be—immortality."

She stared for a long moment. When she spoke, her voice was barely a whisper. "Immortality is forever. You just saw the results last night. When did you start testing this thing?"

"January."

"Where?"

"Georgia Cancer Institute."

"That's a strange unintended consequence. You seem troubled by it," Gina said.

He gnawed his lip discreetly and nodded.

Her voice went low as she thought out loud, saying, "It would trouble me." Staring off, pondering, she added, "Did you tell the people that might happen?"

Gus exhaled. "I didn't know. They didn't even know the device targeted their cancer."

Her face wrinkled, "No one knew? No consent?"

"It was purely to help them tolerate chemotherapy."

"This was unethical. Those people should have been told."

Shifting to the edge of the couch, firm, he said, "In that alternate universe you find yourself in, telling makes sense. But in the real world I live in, ethics is not an issue. Where is the ethics in killing or kidnapping anyone who threatens their revenue stream?"

"I just...I can't imagine how a place like GCI would stand for this."

"You can't say it's 'GCI.' It's people. A few people in authority are pulling all the strings...for the whole world. Is this making sense?"

Gina studied his face for a moment, then walked to the window, looking down on a staff person setting up on the Terraza.

"I can imagine this in Italy. I didn't expect this in the United States. Sick people all over would love to come here for health care." She turned to Gus. "What a shame. People's trust—violated."

Gus stepped close, "It's a crime. Like a war crime against humanity. According to Dr. Pogue, about a hundred times each year, researchers like me, are killed."

Her head moved slowly side to side.

"Guess who owns the security company that does the killing?"

More head shaking.

"The Schnerr family. The family that's in business with Angelo and Carmelo."

"Really?"

Gus whispered, "Funded by the pharmaceutical companies. Wolfgang Schnerr runs the company."

"This would be a good place to lie."

He shook his head, slowly, steadily.

"Angelo is partners with them, and they're after you?" Gina said.

He nodded now, slow and steady.

"Mama Mia."

"You wanted the truth. Well, that's it."

Her forehead furrowed. "Do you retreat? Regroup? Take your research someplace else?"

"No. There are too many lives at stake. I have to see this through."

"You couldn't quit?"

"Could you?"

"Let me say, there is an art to quitting. I quit modeling and designing clothes. High profile, big money. I tell myself that I won by quitting. Quitting is not bad, so don't think it is. Sometimes, it's the best choice. But this is, as you say, more. Much more. And, I think you have a good hand to play. Don't you?"

Gus sat back on the couch. His hands behind his head, eyes on the ceiling. He said, "I do—if the chips fall my way at ATRI before six o'clock tomorrow morning."

"What about the immortality issue?"

Leaning forward, his forearms on his knees, he looked up, "I'm not totally at peace with it."

"But you're going ahead?"

"I am," Gus said.

"Ethics be damned."

"More like ethics aside, intimidation be damned. Lives are on the line."

Gina grinned, "I'll pray for you."

"Ok. But don't mention any of this to Fr. Moser during confession."

She grinned, "I confessed all my sins last night—including what I was going to do to you when I got my hands on you."

"That will have to wait. We're supposed to see Angelo, remember."

"Oh," Gina cringed. She'd forgotten.

Gus stood and offered her his hand. She stood, bodies touching, their faces inches apart. He said, "This appointment with Angelo is critical. It could alter the course of my life."

"I hope it does. This conversation sure has altered mine."

Chapter Forty-Three

At the curb on Piedmont Avenue in front of Angelo's, Danno stepped out to greet Gina, exiting the resident's entrance. Gus followed. Danno hugged Gina and told her he was glad she was unharmed.

ACE turned in her seat and apologized profusely.

Behind Danno, Gus withdrew his phone. Bobby texted, "I'm convinced your mat is better than mine. But we have a problem. ANSWER ME. It's now or never."

He told ACE, "Pull around to Holder—second floor." He looked at Gina, "Can you reach Angelo and tell him we're running late?"

Gina nodded. "How late?"

"I don't know."

On the ramp to the second level entrance, he said to ACE and Danno, "Come in if you like." She parked. They stayed in the Tahoe as he punched in the security code and disappeared inside.

The atrium's open space felt different now—calming, grounding. After sharing with Gina, answering her questions, he was ready to dive back into the fight.

He took the steps two at a time to the third floor, punched in his SCIF credentials, and saw the room—empty—save Bobby Blincoe.

Bobby let him approach, then told him the bad news. "The new housings arrived. The program has to be rewritten, using sophisticated techniques the team knows about but doesn't know who."

"Who does?"

"That's the rub. They all agree on who can."

Gus detected the tone shift in Bobby's voice.

"Christian?"

Bobby nodded, "I know she's upset and she..."

"I know. That's on me," Gus interrupted. He thought about the Lymphatic and Spleen frequencies. Rather than go to his lab at home, he said to Bobby, "I need to access my cloud account." Bobby opened a laptop and turned it toward Gus. His fingers rattled the keyboard. A minute later, he nodded at Bobby. "The team is right. I was blind...Christian is the best person." He pointed to the screen. "I need these frequencies added to the only unit in circulation. She knows how. The ones that work will bring the other's up to baseline. The ones that don't will cause the others to deviate up or down. Only integrate the ones that keep the others at or near level."

Bobby said, "I got it."

Gus faced him, "This project dies without her."

Bobby nodded.

"She's a partner or I can't ask her to help."

"If I'm the GM of this ballclub, I'm drafting Christian. I'm all about winning."

Gus said, "Good. Here's my idea on making her an offer..."

When Gus finished, Bobby called Christian's office to ask her to come to the SCIF. Gus called Gina to give an update and say he'd be twenty to thirty minutes. Angelo was waiting; there was no rush, but she had to get back to prepare for the evening. The clock in the SCIF read 12:50.

Christian came to the SCIF in short order. Gus stood to greet her, then Bobby.

"There's a new deal on the table," Gus said to her, then looked at Bobby. "I have had to redesign the source code on this device." Gus pointed to the image on the screen. "It's like the BFD, only larger. This was my plan. However, I did not anticipate having to do it so quickly—but we have JCO coming tomorrow. They are coming to buy ten thousand units. The ones we *can* sell are inferior to this one—if we can get the code on a board that will fit in the existing housing. Everyone agrees that you're the best developer and only you can make this a reality."

Christian let the compliment pass and crossed her arms on her chest. "And?"

"And, Bobby and I want you to be our partner."

"On what? I don't even know what this does. I already can't answer questions on the BFD. Why would I write code for something I don't know what it does?"

Gus thought back to Opa and trust. The time had come to trust Christian. She'd earned it. He understood her better and announced, "I'm going to tell you what I designed these devices to do, what I've seen in terms of results, and what needs to be done to sell to JCO."

Over the next twenty minutes, Gus revealed once-tightly held secrets, inserting key pieces into Christian's puzzle. Bobby nodded as the image in his head took shape as well. He explained the immortality issue tangentially, having decided to place limits on individual application time by asking Christian to install GPS trackers and a remote shut-off code. Gus told her about Gina being kidnapped and all that he, Bobby, Max, and their team had done. He saw her defenses coming down. He knew her—she loved the game, the team, the challenge—especially the vote of confidence from her colleagues. He explained his objective to her on the laptop. He identified where in his design he anticipated the changes—leaving the final decision to her. When he finished, he sat back and let her navigate the program. As she did, his heart rate jumped. The team had accurately estimated her abilities. But could she make it fit in time? She closed the laptop, turned to him, and lifted her hand to shake it. Then she shook Bobby's and the pact was formed: victory or bust.

He said, "We're all taking on risk, understood? What happened to Gina could happen to you or your family."

Bobby nodded. "I don't want anyone to know I'm working on this."

Gus said. "One hundred percent. While you all work here in secret, I'm going to do what I can to assist the FBI in stopping the people who want to stop us."

Leaving Holder Medical Engineering, Gus took his seat in the Tahoe behind Danno, savoring a rare sensation—gratitude for restored friendships through honesty rather than manipulation. The weight of prolonged secrecy had lifted. He looked at Gina, who looked back at him differently —not as someone he had to protect from his truth, but as someone who chose to stay with him after he had spoken it.

~~~

In the new wing of Georgia Cancer Institute's research complex, Dr. Marco Tanzilla sat behind his carved Italian desk, phone pressed to his ear. The unmarked office still smelled of fresh paint, but his usual boisterousness had curdled into rage. "You take that thing apart layer by layer and tell me if it does what I think it does. This ends today. Or I'll lead the campaign to have your
~~~

head on a stick. Do you understand, young man? You'll be through. We'll all be through."

Through the speaker on his phone, a female voice announced, "Dr. T, FDA Director Hamilton is holding."

"Jesus Christ."

~~~

In the assisted living section of Renaissance on Peachtree, a slight elderly man sat alone at a four-top in the main dining room. Gus surveyed the space—no other residents at 1:45.

Gina put on a happy face and made introductions. A waitress offered coffee. Gus declined; Angelo ordered a cappuccino, and Gina ordered a cappuccino and a sandwich.

Gina explained she'd be leaving tomorrow night. Angelo acknowledged this, mentioning the new midweek Zoom calls he and his brother had in addition to those on Gina's Saturday visits.

Patting her hand, he expressed gratitude for helping him and his brother reconnect. "Priceless," Angelo reflected.

Her demeanor was firm, just as it was with Gus in the apartment. She leaned forward. "Angelo, you know where I come from. We're family. If what I say is out of line, please let me know. Capisce?"

"Dear, bear no burden for me."

"I think Carmelo and Melo may be in danger."

He patted her hand. "What makes you say this?"

"His business partners."

Angelo nodded.

Gina glanced at Gus, his cue to share the details. He cleared his throat and said, "The FBI came to me because I am close to Gina and Carmelo. They're focused on a man named Wolfgang Schnerr. Your name came up."

Angelo's face darkened. "My wife, Emiline, warned me." Head cocked slightly, he said to Gus, "Why did they come to you?"

The old man's genteel demeanor reminded him of Opa, and he knew never to lie to his elders. "The Schnerrs are after me for another reason, so I need to get them before they get me."

Angelo looked up, drained his cup, and said, "Follow me."
~~~

Angelo led them to his apartment, where, upon entering, he instructed Gus to retrieve a brown cardboard box from the floor of his bedroom closet and bring it to his dining room table. He and Gina took their seats and waited.

Angelo patiently flipped through papers, withdrew a stack, and set it to the side where Gus and Gina were seated.

Gus grinned. "Is this what I need?"

Angelo raised his index finger for Gus's patience, then thumbed through the stack, removed a page, and turned it toward him, pointing at lines upside down. "Each line is a different parking garage in the Atlanta area. I have the monthly cash flow and operating statement for every garage. They make a fraction of what the report shows."

"They fabricate income from each parking garage?" Gina asked.

Angelo nodded enthusiastically and lifted his palms, "Miraculously, they are always full—on paper. Emiline insisted I hire a private detective to monitor several garages. I did. He watched them, all day, every day, for months. He counted every car that came in. He took videos. I have it all. At first, I thought it was silly, a waste of time and money, but here you are. She was right."

"You own the land and lease the land to them?" Gina pressed.

"Yes. I have a ninety-nine-year lease and an overage agreement. Standard. If the garage does well, I get a bonus. That's it, there." His thin hand with spotted skin slid a page toward them.

"How many garages?"

"Forty. One per year since '73. Mine was the first. Chip Abernathy came from Boston to attend the University of Georgia in the late 1960s. After graduation, he married a local girl. Gia's son, Wolf, had moved to town. He had a small family. I was in the old place. One night, Wolf brings Chip Abernathy in for dinner, and they start asking about developing my land. I was interested. It was time to get out of the old place."

Angelo smiled, his voice warming with the memory. "Abernathy's father-in-law owned the construction company, and Chip had a keen scheme to add a parking garage between the buildings and give me a ninety-nine-year lease. That's how it started."

"Where did the money come from?" Gus inquired.

"Abernathy's family. They were in pharmaceuticals up north. Chip and his new wife were staying here. He had his sights set on a career in parking garages. I saw an opportunity to bring Carmelo in and use his business degree from UGA.

He managed the books. In the first year, I knew the numbers were off." Angelo smiled. "The parking garage was right there for goodness' sake. Did they think I was blind? It wasn't generating the revenue they reported. Carmelo and I mentioned it, and they said, Take the money. Cash the check. So, I did. My contract stated that we had the first right of refusal on all land for future garages, under the same terms. I used their money to buy the land under every garage. And they all revert to me when the lease expires."

Gus said, "You said Wolfgang Schnerr came from Geneva to open an office here?"

Angelo nodded. "His mother and I were neighbors when we were children. We went to university in Rome before the war."

Gina said, "Was she the one close to Nonno?"

Angelo nodded. "You heard that story?"

Gina nodded. "Some of it."

Angelo stood slowly and moved to a side table, retrieving a faded photograph. "We went to university in Rome in the Fall of 1939." He showed them the picture—young faces, full of hope. "Your grandfather had a soft spot for Gia, but she and the war changed that love story."

"What happened during the war?" Gina asked gently.

Angelo's expression darkened. "A few years later, Gia and Carlo were recruited to assist Nazi spies. The war in Europe ended in May 1945. She returned to our area in the fall of '45, married to her Nazi superior—an SS spy living in Geneva."

Gus felt his chest tighten. The pieces were connecting in ways he didn't want them to.

"She told Stephano she and her husband were sailing to America, destination Atlanta, on business, as Swiss citizens. They left their son with family in Switzerland." Angelo paused, studying Gus's face. "When she arrived home, she learned my older brother and I had already taken passage, and cabled us that she would be in Atlanta."

"Her husband was Schnerr?" Gus asked, his voice barely steady.

Angelo nodded. "At dinner, she told me Schnerr's father owned a chemical plant in Darmstadt—made amphetamines for German soldiers. She said they were in corporate security—tracking stolen documents that belonged to the Reich, documents that had ended up here in Atlanta."

How many chemical plants are in Darmstadt? How many Schnerr families tracked documents to Atlanta? Were these Schnerr's his Schnerr's?

Gus tightened his grip on the table's edge.

Gina said, "Are you ok?"

He managed to nod. "I'll be fine." He wondered if she could see the inward trembling the revelation had created in him?

"Angelo, may I share these documents with the FBI?"

The gentleman nodded, "Please. I want to protect my son and grandson."

Gus lifted the rectangular banker's box, thanked the kind man for his cooperation, and left the apartment slowly.

Gina stayed close by as they returned to the plush lobby.

Danno met them. "Is something wrong?"

"He hasn't said," Gina whispered.

Gus heard her and announced in a tense, controlled, but urgent voice, "Flashbacks."

In the back of the Tahoe, he called Henry, his jaw set with determination.

"Pick up Henry. Pick up." Voicemail.

Did Opa know about the Schnerrs? If he did, why hide them? And more importantly, do the Schnerrs know who HE is?

He then called Udell Suttles. Suttles answered, "What's new, Gus?"

"I have what you asked for."

"The business records?"

"Plus monthly financials, bank statements, and time-stamped video footage of the actual parking garages."

"Let's take a look," Suttles said.

The shifting momentum energized him. "We'll be at Angelos in fifteen minutes to drop off Gina."

Suttles said, "Uh-huh. I'll be out front."

Chapter Forty-Four

The command by Dr. Tanzilla to decipher the source code obtained from Gus Meier left a hollow look on Klaus Schnerr's face. Seated at his desk, his cell phone clutched in his hand on a bent elbow resting on the desktop, he stared out the window at the largest bas-relief in the world on Stone Mountain in the near distance. Three Confederate leaders, appearing somber, caps in hand, with their hands on their hearts. Remorseful or vengeful? Klaus had different plans for how this war ended…and Tanzilla may be a nice casualty.

His cousin Erik, seated at the small conference desk, head hung, was reading the dossier on his target.

Erik closed the folder in a smooth motion and slowly turned to Klaus. Deadpan.

Klaus read his cousin's face and said, "This is war."

Erik set his hand on the folder. "There's no war. He's your brother? And Holly? You're crossing the line."

Klaus walked to the conference desk and leaned on a chair back across from Erik.

Erik lifted his face to frame him perfectly in the surveillance glasses he used to record Donna Sheehan, also known as Holly Abernathy. "The old man has days, a month max. Then I'm in charge. Then I draw the lines and I cross the lines."

"Draw a line down the middle and leave him be."

"You going soft, killer?"

"Your father's about to die, Klaus. You tell me why he lived, cause best I can tell, by my bullet or the grim reaper, dead is dead. Tell me it meant more to you than having everything for yourself."

Klaus smirked and shrugged.

Erik hesitated, then shifted in his seat. "You're in charge. Look me in the eye and give me the order to kill Vinnie and Holly, and I'll set it up."

"Erik, do what's in the dossier."

The assassin's head shook, his steel stare leveled on Klaus. His tone was tight, cold, and distinct. "Say it."

Klaus swallowed. His nasal inhalation was audible.

"Soft?" Erik said.

"Your order is to kill Vinnie and Holly," Klaus said, as the blood drained from his face.

~~~

Along the curb at Angelo's, there was no sign of Dell Suttles.

Danno and Gus walked Gina to the residents' entrance. Gus accompanied her inside.

She pushed the elevator call button and turned to Gus, "Looks like neither one of us knew what we were getting involved in."

He chuckled, "At least you're getting out. I'll bet tomorrow can't come soon enough?"

The elevator doors opened. Gina kept her focus on him rather than stepping inside. The doors closed. She sighed, "I'm glad Angelo was helpful. You both want to be rid of those people." She hesitated. "I'm going home to something similar. Something happened in the past that I was unaware of, and it's a dark secret. If it's exposed, there will be a scandal, and I'm being asked to step in and step up to right the ship."

Gus took her hand. "Families are funny. People I thought I was closest to, but they were here first. Then, I'm going along with my life, just like you are, and out of the blue, a secret from their past is revealed that changes my life."

Gina shook her head slightly. "Isn't that amazing? That is all they have told me! Just, 'Come home. We need you?' I ask, 'Why?' And they say, 'It's a secret. It has nothing to do with you. But it can't get out. We'll tell you when you get here.' They still treat me like I'm the little sister. I'm a girl."

A gentle tug on her hand brought her body to his, their eyes met, his lips found hers, and the long, passionate kiss he'd imagined since he'd left her at the airport ignited between them. He had asked then, and now, it was understood.

"Thank you," Gus said, satisfied and hopeful.

Gina smiled. "When will I see you again?"

A light chuckle, he said, "I can't say for sure, but this is not goodbye."

"Well then, see you later."
~~~

He kissed her forehead. "You go rest. I need to speak with the FBI."

~~~

Exiting the residents' entrance, Suttles's sedan was behind the Tahoe.

He hurried to the Tahoe with Danno in tow. He asked ACE to leave the truck running and wait outside with Danno. She did. He motioned for Suttles to take the rear seat behind the driver.

Inside, Suttle's eyes went to the box on the floor between their seats. Gus loosened the ties on either end and handed Suttles samples that Angelo had shown him.

The detective took his time studying the pages. "This is good. I can take this to the DA."

"Can you shut them down without involving Angelo and Carmelo?" Gus said.

"I'm not a lawyer." Suttles said. "It appears they knew the money was dirty."

"Angelo said he didn't know. He only suspected the money might be dirty."

"Ok. You're not a lawyer, either. Calm down. They'll have their day in court."

"Court?" Gus scoffed. "The Schnerrs aren't going to stop until they are absolutely certain this threat is dead. That's me." Suttles thought for a long moment. "If we had these records and the exact location of their operation, we could get a warrant to go inside."

He flipped the pages in the box. "These are all addressed to Carmelo at the restaurant address. When I get back, I'll go in and ask him."

"Call him. Now. Every minute counts."

Gus called. "Voicemail."

Suttles ordered in a low voice, "Tell him what you want."

He did, and hung up.

Suttles reached for the door handle as Gus's phone vibrated. Carmelo? No, it was Kip. Gus answered, and Kip raced in. "The Governor's press secretary just put out a statement announcing a news conference in one hour. The topic is Georgia Cancer Institute Cancer Center. Period."

He put his phone on speaker.

Suttles became intent.

"What reactions have you seen from the Watchtower?"
~~~

Kip said, "Tanzilla's hair is on fire. He and McIntyre are preparing their own statement. McIntyre issued a press release stating that Dr. Pogue would address the topic from the new wing, following the Governor's remarks. Slayton will essentially say all individuals who appeared anonymously on the testimonials are invited to come forward so their files can be reviewed, and new tests conducted. He's there strictly to calm the hysteria."

Gus said, "What hysteria? Why is the Governor involved?"

"I'd say it was the testimonials that hit after lunch."

"More of the same?"

"Naw. These were gut-wrenching," Kip said in a slow drawl. "Parents. Some kids…miraculous recovery. Others—not so lucky. Those parents laid GCI bare. They wanted to know why. I'd wager they pushed the Governor past the brink."

Gus thanked Kip and ended the call.

His body felt heavy as thoughts shifted to the "Go Dawgs" boy. Was he still alive? Had Gus let him die? Should he have said or done something?

Collected, Gus told Suttles. "The mole is bringing this to light, but if I get killed before it's done, how can I be sure the people who receive my contingency plan will take the risk I have?"

Suttles said, "Let's finish this, and countless families will be spared."

Gus felt his throat tighten despite the air conditioning's cool breeze, his mind drifting back in time. Staring forward, he said in a low voice, "Can I tell you something, detective?"

"Uh-huh."

Gus took in some deep breaths, staring out the window at ACE and Danno standing vigilant in the heat, and confessed, "After the explosion that killed my father, I visited the girl injured during the explosion." He turned to Suttles. "We were in the *same* hospital. Holly Abernathy and I." Turning back, eyes fixed ahead, he continued, "I had skin grafts and had to stay for treatment. They let me attend my father's funeral, then right back. Nurses told me the girl injured in the blast was there, but no one came for her. I could relate. She had no identification. When I could, I went to her room—sat beside her. Her face was covered in bandages. I could see her eyes. Green. Stunning. We never spoke. I told her everything would be ok." He paused to take a breath. "Because no one had come for her, I told her I had lost my mom and my dad, and there was always a silver lining; she had to keep looking for it."

Gus shook his head and turned back to Suttles, "This morning, I knew those eyes. I saw that room and her in that bed. I don't think—she remembered me."

"She didn't find the silver lining."

"From what she said, she never looked."

"Well, I think you keep finding the silver lining cause you keep looking for it. Now, if you find out where her new operation is, we're going to put a silver lining in a lot of lives."

~~~

Helene strolled beside Henry, guiding Opa's wheelchair along the cobblestone promenade on the shore of Lake Geneva. Behind them, the golden lights of **Le Jardin du Lac** spilled onto the stone terrace where elegantly dressed diners lingered over wine. The Jet d'Eau fountain rose against the darkening sky.

Opa seemed energized by the mild evening, his color much improved since Henry made the adjustments Gus recommended to the biofeedback application.

"The duck was perfect, Helene. Excellent choice."

Helene patted his arm, "I'm glad you enjoyed it, Opa."

Henry checked his phone—two missed calls from Gus. The contrast struck him: here, in this pocket of Old World refinement, while thousands of miles away...

He pressed Gus's number.

"Henry? Everything going well?" Gus said from the Tahoe as Suttles returned to his car, and ACE and Danno got in and waited for his direction on the next destination.

"It is. Opa wanted to get out for dinner. Helene is here; we're at the promenade," Henry said.

"May I speak to him?"

"Is everything OK?" Henry's voice carried concern.

"It's getting intense. I'll tell you more later."

"Well, I have some news for you," Henry said.

"What's that?"

"Opa and Helene are going to return to Atlanta with me tomorrow."

"Oh no. Why? Wait. Please wait."

"What brought that on?"
~~~

"You did," Henry said proudly. "Following the Interpol call, they decided to come. But Opa wasn't up to it. Now, he's more optimistic, and I have to get back. He can rest there as well as here."

Gus's voice hardened. "Henry, the whistleblower has turned into a siren."

"Oh. I'm sorry. I should have checked with you," Henry groaned. "They are set on coming…"

"Oh, boy." Gus exhaled. "This is not a good time."

"Don't worry, I'll make sure they stay by the pool, and when time permits, you come to them."

I'll find an opening on my calendar

"Will you put Opa on?"

In the pause where Henry handed the phone to Opa, Carmelo's name appeared on his phone screen. Thank goodness, he'd gotten his message. Did he know Sheehan's location? Gus did not wait for his grandfather and ended the call.

"Carmelo?" Gus asked, turning to his right toward the building where Carmelo lived, as if he'd be able to see him standing by a window overlooking the scene on the street.

Carmelo's voice was low. "Your question…I may know tonight. For sure, in the morning. Gus—Leave this to the police. Think about Gina."

I do think about Gina. Believe me.

Henry's name on his screen interrupted the call.

He said goodbye to Carmelo, eager to ask Opa about the Schnerrs.

Chapter Forty-Five

"Henry. sorry about that," he said, answering his call back. ACE glanced in the rearview mirror and mouthed, "I can't park here."

Gus motioned with his hand to drive around and checked the time. Less than an hour before the Governor's press conference.

"Augustus?" Opa's voice came through—strong.

"Opa. How are you?" Gus said, surprised.

"I'm hopeful, thanks to you."

"Excellent," Gus said, wondering how to begin.

"You wanted to talk to me?"

"Yes…I did. I do…um…" His jaw hardened. "Something I heard today made me think of you."

"Oh. What was that?"

"The name Wolfgang Schnerr."

Silence.

"Opa?"

Silence.

He looked at his phone. The call timer was still running.

"Opa. You know this name?"

His enthusiasm vanished. "Yah."

*Oh my God. These must be my people…**our** people*

ACE turned onto Thirteenth Street and jerked the truck back onto Piedmont upon seeing the media circus in front of Holder.

"Are they, my relatives?"

"Yah."

What don't I know?

"They ordered the explosion?"

"I suspect. But I don't think they know about us."

Know about us?

"I believe they're stalking the device, not you. I questioned the Interpol agent."

Questioned her? Did Henry know?

"You never told me any of this," Gus said. "The agent told us the assassin had two targets in Atlanta…" He froze…two targets…him and Christian or…Vinnie and Sheehan/Holly? Had Klaus brought Erik to Atlanta to…it was unthinkable.

On the upside, they may not know about him…or The Assignment

Gus began again, "Who's Wolfgang Schnerr?"

"My mother's younger brother. As a teenager, he joined the Nazi SS spy service to save his parents and prove his loyalty to the Reich."

"He's the one you told me about in the vault when you explained the Assignment?"

"Yes. A devout Nazi. They regarded the notes as top-secret."

"And your mother and your grandmother secretly corresponded. That's how you knew this?"

"Yah. We'll talk in more detail when I arrive."

ACE pulled into the shade of the Shake Shake on the edge of the park. Danno made a drinking motion to him. He declined.

He pressed on, "You said you always thought Elias was murdered, why?"

"My grandmother told my mother that Wolfgang was obsessed with finding them and the notebook. She said he would turn her and my father in, without hesitation."

Gus said, "If Wolfgang or his son thought Elias had access to the notebook, they would have apprehended him?"

"I think so. To get it back…then kill him."

"After all these years?" Gus said.

"Yes. I took measures…"

"You kept them under surveillance?" Gus asked.

"I had to. I didn't know if they ever figured out what we had done."

"What had you done?"

"After the war, father took us to America to recover the notebook from the American engineer he entrusted it to at a convention in Bern, Harold Holder. While we were there, my mother received a telegram saying Wolfgang was dead. He and his widow had formed a security company to apply what they had learned spying for the SS. Their first task was to find the notebook. She wasn't giving up the hunt. Father used Harold Holder's connections here to get new papers."

"Papers?" Gus said as Danno sipped his drink and ACE drove past Caribou Coffee and the Flying Biscuit again.

"Identification papers. I arrived in America as Heinrich Dreher and left as Lawrence Meier."

"You think his wife and his sons kept looking for someone named Dreher?"

"If they kept looking at all, they should have known by then that we changed our names. When my grandmother died, an attorney tracked down my mother to tell her she had legal rights to her mother's estate. I assumed Gia would have known this."

"Your mother didn't make a claim?"

"No. But she had ways of keeping up with Wolf's wife. She kept the business going and grew it nicely. She groomed her sons to take over. Wolf moved to Atlanta in 1973."

The stories lined up.

"Like Elias, they were after the device. The explosion was business, not personal. Is that what you think?"

"Yes," Opa said.

Gus exhaled, suddenly noticing people out his window as city life carried on. "That makes sense. I'm in the news, on television, social media, with no apparent personal connection."

"That's why I did not believe the explosion was an accident, but a murder rather than an assassination."

Schnerrs don't know who I am. They're protecting their clients. This is business, not personal. That changes things.

~~~

"Too ATRI, please," Gus said to ACE. En route, he texted Kip Richardson, "Coming in to watch the recordings from the glasses."

Kip sent back a thumbs-up.

What had Erik the assassin been doing since he left the Flying Biscuit? Gus replayed Holly Abernathy's plea in the restaurant booth, 'As a parting gift, take out Klaus.' Would that comment send her to prison?
~~~

ACE let Gus and Danno off in the driveway beside ATRI, they walked side by side, Gus more relaxed than he'd been in days. Did he still need protection? Suttles never did report on the men who broke into his place and Christians' last Saturday.

Through security, down one floor to the basement, Gus applied his eye to the retinal scanner, his thumb to the fingerprint pad, and his ID credentials to the reader. Kip and Carley now had six assistants in the space, which was designed for three. Kip anticipated his arrival and motioned Gus to the small office outside the Watchtower to watch what Erik had recorded. Through the Flying Biscuit footage, he stared at the woman he only knew as Donna Sheehan. Her eyes were still captivating. She admitted to her motivation for killing Klaus; she didn't like him, and she and Vinnie had a plan of their own.

Afterward, Gus fast-forwarded through every scene Erik saw on his way to the Consortium Security offices in Stone Mountain. In Klaus's office, he resumed play, with Erik's focus on a sheet of paper where two typed names appeared: Vincent Schnerr and Holly Abernathy. Klaus came toward Erik, looking into the camera and saying, "I am ordering you to kill Vinnie and Holly." After making him say the command explicitly, Erik snubbed his cousin and told him he could find someone else.

Klaus said, "I cleared this with your brother before I invited you."

"I don't believe he would sign off on this. He knows I've pulled my last trigger for him. I've been on the lam as long as Holly, but I built a respectable life."

Klaus laughed, "You're a contract killer."

"And I'm a baker, starting a family."

Klaus pressed keys on his phone. When he finished, he set the phone on the conference desk.

Erik's brother's voice came through. "Yes."

"You need to tell your brother his place."

Erik sat up like a convict awaiting sentencing.

"I'm glad you called. I've been thinking. Rethinking. Erik, it's up to you. Sorry Klaus, he's on his way out. Not the thing he wants to leave on."

"What the fuck is this, Will? You said…"

"I know what I said. I don't give a shit about those people, if you want them taken out, that's your business. But, I'm not leaning on him. He's my brother, and as far as I'm concerned, he's retired."

Erik framed Klaus perfectly. His stunned, blank stare faded to clenched teeth and a simmering rage. Klaus composed himself, "Compromise, kill one, and I'll control the other. Your choice. I'll pay you for two."

Expressionless, Erik said, "I pick. One Million Dollars, up front."

Klaus fails at staring down Erik.

"Cash," Erik said.

Klaus swallowed. Where do I get a million dollars in cash?"

"Ironic, but I got the impression Vinnie and Holly might be a good source."

Klaus snickered. "It is ironic and it's brilliant."

"Deal?"

Klaus nodded.

Erik extended his hand, and Klaus came close to the glasses; they shook. Erik repeated, "Deal?"

Klaus said, "Deal. Make the call, set it up."

Erik scrolled through his contact list and dialed 'Holly.'

She didn't answer. He left a message saying he wanted to meet at her first opportunity to discuss her 'parting gift.'

He stared out the window, toward Stone Mountain. In the background, Klaus interrogated someone on a phone call, "Are you sure? Did you take it apart layer by layer? That's not right. It's there. Keep looking."

Gus hit fast forward, stopping in Erik's hotel room. The glasses were on the nightstand, facing the phone.

He opened the glasses app on his phone, scanned the menus, and taught himself how to send a text to the lens. When Erik woke from his nap and put them on, he'd see the message on the right lens telling him to arrange a meeting with Holly at her new facility. He would assume the command came from the FBI agent who gave him the glasses.

The recording was timestamped: 10:57.

Chapter Forty-Six

An hour later, in the ATRI Watchtower, as the afternoon stretched toward four o'clock, Kip brought up a local TV station on his laptop screen and cast it to a wall monitor.

Gus stood by his side. How much more entangled could this become?

At four o'clock, they listened as the Governor, who had a private hand in getting JCO to suspend Donna Sheehan days earlier, now took his contempt for GCI public. Declaring the most recent testimonials posted were dramatic and heart-wrenching, he said, "When will the leaders of the Georgia Cancer Institute, Medical Center come forward with credible information? Their actions have all the makings of a public scandal. The citizens of Georgia need to know they can trust such venerable institutions as Georgia Cancer Institute.

Kip looked at Gus for a reaction. Gus looked his way, "He's fighting his own battle with GCI. Why?"

"Whatever it is, the wind is at his back," Kips said.

"Scorned," Gus mumbled. "He's settling a score."

With who? He needed a peek at history…behind the scenes, this started a long time ago. One man to call, Cedric.

His phone vibrated in his pocket. Dr. Pogue.

On the same monitor they had watched the Governor, Kip switched to the press room at GCI. Reporters moved briskly to get positioned. The podium displaying the university crest stood in the center, empty.

"Yes."

"Your friend did you no favors."

"Is he settling a score by putting everyone there on notice? I tried to warn you. Remember, 'public scandal?'"

"And I warned you," She said. "They don't back down. What you gave them revealed nothing."

"Like I said…."

"George is about to deliver his statement. He's going to say that you turned over the source code, that you are cooperating to resolve the mystery, and we, his team and mine, will work with any of the anonymous patients who provided testimonials to review their files and look for the catalyst. Would you make a brief video of yourself, saying you support this action and are looking forward to cooperating?"

Gus interrupted, "You want me to…"

Pogue's voice rose to intercept his question, "You don't have to admit to anything. Play dumb if you want. Twenty, maybe thirty seconds, we need to show unification. This is a rare second chance. You know what they are capable of."

"You want me to lie to lend credence to your lie?"

"For the love of God, Gus. Just do it."

"OK. One on condition."

"What?"

"Get Mike Hamilton to Angelo's for dinner in a private room to discuss some new developments."

"Who is that?" Pogue demanded impatiently.

"He's the head of the local FDA office. He's involved in this, or at least he knows who is."

"You want me to call him…and say what?"

"Tell him you have my video to avert a scandal and blow back onto him, and you want his permission to release it."

"Do I?"

"You will. That's no lie."

The moment the call ended, Gus tapped the shoulder of a young man at a surveillance station in the Watchtower and motioned for him to follow him into the supply room, where he picked a blank space on the wall and had the young man record his message. Gus recorded exactly what Pogue needed, honestly. The lie came at the end.

In the Watchtower, Dr. Slayton took the podium. His apologetic tone and his resolve resonated with Gus. Was Tanzilla pulling the strings on Slayton? He stepped out of the Watchtower to call Cedric.

Cedric didn't answer. Hearing his friend's voice assured Gus he wasn't fighting this alone. He had a candid phone transcript between Tanzilla and Hamilton...surely there were emails. Cedric was the only one who could get them.

~~~

He returned to the Watchtower. It was 4:10. On the monitors covering Donna Sheehan's office, while listening to the audio of Dr. Slayton, she stood alone, arms crossed on her chest. He wondered what she was thinking as Slayton's comments came off as sincere, compassionate, and authoritative. She didn't flinch or shift as he made admissions of internal errors on his part and the administration. He professed ignorance of the ongoing mystery regarding clinical outcomes and promised answers in time. For the time being, he pleaded for understanding and cooperation. Cooperation was the cue to mention Gus and Christian by name—everything Pogue had said the script would include. Sheehan didn't budge. CEO Steve James stood as still as a statue a few feet away, visible on camera alongside Dr. Pogue, Dr. Chen, Dr. Tanzilla, and other prominent oncologists. They looked straight ahead. No one moved. When Slayton finished, a camera panning as he and his colleagues exited, showed Communications Director, Josh McIntyre—architect of the script. Reporters shouted questions as McIntyre pulled the press room door shut.

On the monitor, Sheehan made a call. he moved close to the screen to see the number and the name, Vincent Schnerr.

As he reached for a headset and eavesdrop on the Sheehan-Schnerr audio, Dr. Pogue sent a brief text, "6:30" and a thumbs-up emoji. Prompt response— Hamilton was motivated.

Gus sent her his brief video showing his support of Slayton's remarks. She'd like most of his endorsement.

Moments later, Pogue sent back three thumbs-up.

Cedric called. Gus set the headset on the desk, hurried out of the Watchtower to the reception area, and paced in short circles.

"Ced. I need to get back into the GCI system. Are you game?"

His familiar Indian accent was assuring, "You know I am G-man."

"Ok. I'm going to text you what I need. What I'm looking for…do your thing. See what you can find. This is super top-priority."

"Always is when you call," Cedric said.

Gus's eye drifted to the time-of-day in the bottom right corner of the monitor: five-o-five.
~~~

~~~

In the Watchtower with the headset on, Gus rewound the scene in Sheehan's office, her call with Vinnie. She said in a low voice, "I'm through with this place. I want out."

"You've done your time," Vinnie said. "We'll be operational in Florida soon. We can go back and forth at any time. Fly private."

Resignation in her voice, she said, "They won't let me quit. I'm on the selection committee. I have a vote." Sitting at her desk, fidgeting with a pen, Sheehan said, "Klaus gives me ten tons of shit for not seeing this sooner, and look at all the attention that's putting this whole project in jeopardy by a god-damned mole leaking information none of us even have. Is anyone busting his balls?"

"They are, believe me. People are going around him. Calling Wolf directly—he's near death, and those bastards think he can wave a wand. So far, Klaus and his people haven't found anything."

Sheehan bolted up in her chair, "Oh my God."

"What?"

"Clair Pogue came back from meeting with the ATRI guy and said he thought it could all be a hoax. A set up by someone trying to undercut us at the FDA."

"Damn. You think…"

"Maybe they can't find anything because it *is* a set up. If it *is*, I think the Governor's in on it."

"You think he has staged all the social media?"

"No, but he could be in on it?"

"We can't get to him…"

"We can go through his son. He's an addict. A very public addict. I want to plant a ton of pills in his car and tip off the cops?"

Vinnie said, "Wouldn't it be classic if we linked the Governor to the drug ring in the papers all the time?"

Sheehan snickered, "You're mind is corrupt…but that's genius."

~~~

On the desktop beside him, his phone screen lit up, Dr. Chen.

Gus checked the time, 5:37.

More research bombshells?

"Chen?"

"Your device need update."

No time for update

"Talk to my wife," Chen said. "She say you not use best stem cells. She have better cells. Use for pancreas. Pancreas failure trigger many disease. You could prevent many disease beside cancer—cancer too."

Shit—don't tell me this—not now

"That sounds wonderful, but I don't have an extra minute to devote to it."

"In Pacific Rim, where I come from, people change diet. Very bad. Chronic disease unstoppable. Medicine no good. Too late. Need your machine with better stem cells—Wharton's Jelly to save the pancreas."

"Dr. Chen. I believe you, but I…"

"You make your program to update?"

He processed the question…"No. It's static. I didn't plan on all these variations."

"Make dynamic—add Wharton's Jelly. I help you analyze data."

"It's too late."

"Not too late," Chen said. "JCO order must wait."

Gus froze in place, "How do you know about that?"

"Not important. What is important is that I keep your secret. My people need your help more than they need Coca-Cola. Make program where it be upgraded."

"Or?"

"Or I keep your code for myself and take it back to friends in Taiwan and make ours."

Blackmail? Chen?

"Jesus Christ. Don't do that Chen. Don't do this. Not now. Let me get this done, and we'll talk on Monday."

"You right."

"Thank you."

"You need large scale sample. JCO sample perfect. Exactly why must have Wharton's Jelly stem cells for comparison to Mesenchymal stem cells."

This can't be happening. Of all the people…

Chen continued, "Make perfect sense. You good man, Gus Meier. You know I am right."

It did make perfect sense. Could the program be made dynamic? Only Christian would know. But I don't want to ask.

Chapter Forty-Seven

Chen's coercing caught Gus flatfooted, leaving him little room to negotiate.

On his way to the first floor, He texted ACE, "On my way out—heading to Holder."

As he passed through security, he phoned Christian. No answer. He phoned Bobby.

"How's it going over there?" Gus asked.

"Steady. She's not only brilliant, she's a very patient teacher. The whole team is getting a lesson."

"I'm on my way over. Is she available?"

A long pause.

"Hey," Christian said. "We're going to make it."

"Excellent. Thank you. I have a question. Think before you answer."

"Oh, Gus. Damn you."

"Christian, this is critical." He inhaled, "I made the system static, but some functions need to be dynamic."

"Upgrades?"

"Yes. Only a few frequencies. I know where it could be added."

"The fewer the better."

"You want me to come by and walk you through it?"

A long pause on Christian's end. She studied her weary team.

"Christian?"

"The cutoff is six thirty tomorrow morning?"

"Yes."

"Leave it to me—don't come by—and don't call back."

"You can do it—I need to know."

"Yes. The variable is time."

Gus texted Chen, "Making the program dynamic."
Crisis averted. Now to make the bad guys squirm

~~~

ACE pulled into the parking garage on the fourth level near the side entrance to Angelo's. He put on the surveillance glasses Funk delivered to his backpack earlier, added the device to the app on his phone, and walked hastily toward the kitchen.

Inside the swinging double doors, seated at the chef's table overlooking the bustling kitchen operation, he spotted Mike Hamilton and Dr. Pogue. Gus introduced himself to Hamilton and sat across from them both. Hamilton looked dumbfounded, turned to Pogue, perplexed. Gus wrapped his knuckles on the table, hard. The knock blended into the noise around them, but Hamilton snapped to attention.

Pogue leaned forward, her brow furrowed. "Gus, what's this about?"

"Did you see my video?" Gus asked Hamilton.

Hamilton nodded.

"Just a PR charade?"

Hamilton smirked, "What's going on?" He started to stand. Gus met him mid-stance, towering over the unfit bureaucrat. "Sit down."

Pogue's eyes widened, watching the confrontation unfold.

"I have emails and phone transcripts of you and Dr. Slayton, Dr. Tanzilla, Stephen James, and Klaus Schnerr."

Hamilton scoffed. "Why do I care?"

"Because you're in bed with them over this FDA Emergency designation. You'd like to save yourself, and your family."

He opened his phone, scrolled and turned it toward Hamilton. "Enlarge that."

Hamilton spread his fingers on the screen. Pogue leaned in to see.

"That's an order signed by the Attorney General of Georgia authorizing surveillance. Look at the names."

Hamilton scrolled, then swallowed. Pogue's face went pale.

"Two days later, the list expanded to Tanzilla and Schnerr. Have you ever called either one of them? It's recorded."

Hamilton looked at Pogue, who shook her head slightly—she clearly had no idea where this was going. "Over here," Gus said. "You concealed this entire application process."
~~~

Hamilton began to object.

"I realize you were acting under orders, that's why we're here. To help you help me, and Dr. Pogue."

Pogue straightened. "Help me how?"

"Let's take it slow," Gus said to Hamilton. "You don't have to name any names, just help me understand, you did conceal the process?"

Hamilton sat still amid the action surrounding them.

"Phone calls and transcripts are of you—not the people who directed you. So I'm pretty sure you were told to conceal this. Correct?"

Hamilton folded his lower lip under his overbite and nodded.

"That wasn't so hard," Gus said. "You took direction from a superior in Washington. No names. A nod will suffice."

Sweat formed on Hamilton's forehead. He nodded. Pogue watched the exchange, mesmerized.

"You questioned your superior because you're a civil servant with a family to protect."

Hamilton's eyes widened. He agreed.

"Influence like that comes from Georgia's senators. Safe bet?"

Hamilton clenched his teeth. "I can't say anymore."

Gus smiled, "Those are the first words you've said. Nod or shake."

Hamilton nodded.

"Great progress. Thank you. Now," Gus said. "I'm a follow-the-money guy. With this designation, GCI will appoint a committee to vote on emergency approval of a drug. The standards are minimal. No clinical trials. No one to refute the committee's decision?"

Hamilton closed his eyes and nodded.

"This should be easy. Was Dr. Clair Pogue involved in this scheme at any level?"

Without hesitation, Hamilton's head shook. Pogue exhaled quietly.

"To your knowledge—is anyone at GCI aware of, and withholding, a cure for cancer?"

His head shook more vigorously.

"We're almost there, Mike. May I call you Mike?"

Another short nod. Humiliation apparent. Hamilton patted his brow with the cloth napkin.

Gus picked up his phone, pressed the keypad and turned the phone to Hamilton. In seconds the FDA agent looked ashen as his testimony played back.

"Fuck me. Who are you?"

Pogue leaned back, stunned by what she'd just witnessed.

Gus chuckled, "I'm the guy that is going to save you from getting fucked worse than you already are. Listen up, Mike. You and I are the expendable. Your armor is knowing who the companies are. When we finish with the emails you traded with GCI, I may know them too—and I won't need you. I'm looking for backup. I want more."

Hamilton's head began shaking. "Please."

"Relax. I don't want a signed affidavit, Mike. I'm giving you the chance to seek whistleblower protection. One chance. I'm going to reach out to the Attorney General and tell him you'll be calling. Then, with the full protection of the law, you are going to go on record and spill your fucking guts about this operation. No more nodding and shaking. Understand?"

The nod was small. Resignation or relief? Gus wasn't sure.

"When I hear from AG Blakemore, I'll delete this recording. Otherwise, you're on the evening news and in every paper. Your whole life—everyone in it—will be in the crosshairs of the Schnerrs. Think about your wife and kids, Mike. You're getting a second chance. Take it."

Hamilton whispered, "I'll call him."

"Good man." He stood and shook his hand, then turned to Pogue. "I'm sending the number to you. Pass it on to Mike."

He dialed the Attorney General and left a detailed message for Pogue and Hamilton to hear, then said to Hamilton, "Keep your phone close, and enjoy your dinner."

~~~

On the walk to the bar from the kitchen, he felt his shoulders drop about six inches. Resting against the columns near the entrance, he could scan the bar and part of the dining room. No sign of Gina. By the glass doors leading to the Terraza, a lively crowd filled the patio beneath the trellis covered in wisteria and draped with lights. No sign of Gina, but he recalled how many times he'd been the one having fun there. His gaze landed on the table where he and Christian were talking when Carmelo walked up and introduced his second cousin to him.
~~~

He found her in the Capri Dining Room, visible through the glass door. A private party, with tables arranged in a semi-circle, where everyone is seated at extensive place settings. Gina stood in the center with a glass of wine, delivering remarks about the pairings. He watched, admiring her calm confidence. When she noticed him, her face lit up with that smile he was learning to crave.

Carmelo appeared by his side. "She's going to be a while."

"Thanks. I'll wait."

"The party was scheduled exclusively for her to teach wine pairings."

Gus raised his eyebrows.

Carmelo nodded. "First time, ever. Whole new vibe around here. All because of her."

Gus nodded, he felt the same way…whole new vibe, all because of her.

"You should marry her."

Gus deflected.

"You two belong together."

Together, where? I could be on the run forever

The phone in his pocket vibrated—a text from AG Neville Blakemore. "Hamilton is on board. The Governor thanks you."

I'll keep the video in case things change.

He looked back at Gina; his running days may be over.

Still in his hand, his phone vibrated. Cedric texted, "Credentials in your Dropbox. This is explosive. See attached example."

The word 'explosive' made his heart skip a beat. Mustering his composure, he patted Carmelo on the arm and said, "I'm happy for you."

Chapter Forty-Eight

At the end of his day on Thursday, Gus climbed the steps at Henry and Cassie's to find her reclined on the rattan couch beneath the wide paddled fan on the screened-in porch. Cassie had her head propped on a pillow at the end near the lamp on the end table, reading a novel. She declared, "My, my. You're still alive."

"Yeah." He managed a smile, but his mind was elsewhere.

"I need to get cleaned up and check some things in the library."

"Everything alright?"

"I don't even know what alright is anymore."

"Minnie's chicken in the fridge. Orpheus IPA too, if you're interested."

Twenty minutes later, in his pajama bottoms, a T-shirt, and a plate holding fried chicken and an IPA, he powered up Henry's computer in the library.

With the plate of chicken half-eaten, and his beer half drunk, he reread the notes between Tanzilla, Hamilton, Hamilton's boss in Washington, Kenneth Neely, and thought, I'm an amateur compared to these guys. Bewildered, he sat back, ate a bite of chicken, finished the beer, and went to the kitchen for another. This was beyond explosive.

The emails went back two years. The new wing was under construction.

A pharmaceutical representative made the initial proposal to Tanzilla. Private meetings followed. Agendas. Politics. Code names.

The most incriminating was the note outlining what they expected in return for their investment in the emergency use designation.

The scheme was elegant and corrupt: When company XYZ had a cancer drug they wanted introduced without regulatory oversight, Dr. Tanzilla would declare an emergency need. He would write the criteria in minute detail that excluded any competitor drug.

The committee would vote to give emergency use authorization to only the XYZ drug. The pharmaceutical rep's final promise: advance notice for investment purposes to profit from stock price spikes.

But the most chilling email was Tanzilla's response: "Wolf's team has handled 47 US researcher threats since 2019. The EU adopted this protocol in '98. The Consortium there is remarkably effective. Most recently, Barcelona. No one challenges the committee's decisions anymore."

The pharmaceutical rep's reply was equally cold: "Excellent ROI. Our blocked EU competitors lost $27 billion in market value last year. Three are insolvent. We picked up key researchers."

Then came the code names: Senator "Lighthouse" had received $6.3 million in campaign contributions. Congressman "Bulldog" was promised a board position. Governor "Peachtree" was referenced—they didn't want him involved. He was too much of a free thinker.

The final email made Gus's blood run cold: "New priority target identified: device in Pogue's CAM at GCI. Wolf Schnerr et al appear clueless. Potentially catastrophic threat. Recommend immediate containment protocols."

Gus screenshotted the entire thread and texted it to Hile: "Game over. I have people in Holder now. Would you or Suttles send over a show of force?"

Hile's response came within minutes: "We need to bring them in. Thanks for landing Hamilton—and setting up Sheehan with Erik—glasses will become standard. We'll cover your people."

For the first time in weeks, Gus felt like he was winning.

On the porch, he said goodnight to Cassie. She was determined to finish her novel before turning in.

<center>~~~</center>

While Gus was interrogating Hamilton at Angelo's, across town in Stone Mountain, the dining room at Wolf Schnerr's estate felt smaller, weighed down by the pressing crisis against its mahogany walls. Crystal glasses caught the light from the chandelier as servers cleared the remnants of what had been a tense dinner.

Wolf sat at the head of the table, his gaunt frame dwarfed by the high-backed chair. To his right, Klaus picked at his dessert while Vinnie held Holly's hand across from them. Bo Abernathy sat beside his sister, uncomfortable with the family business but trapped by it as the mole Klaus installed in Holder Medical. Erik sat silently at the far end; the surveillance glasses perched naturally on his face—just another pair of reading glasses to anyone watching.

"The FDA may pull out," Wolf said, his voice barely above a whisper. "If that happens, we'll be finished." He looked around the table. "I'm finished either way."

Klaus straightened. "Don't worry, Dad. We'll be fine." His eyes moved to Vinnie, then Holly. The parking garages, the street operation—they had other revenue streams.

Holly shifted uncomfortably. She knew that her focus on expanding the prescription drug network through her family's pharmaceutical connections had let things spiral out of control. The allegiance formed between Wolf and her father in 1973 had been simple then. Now it was a liability.

Wolf turned his hollow eyes to Erik. "You're here to take out the people who got us into this mess?"

Erik saw the irony. Holly's reckless expansion, Klaus's arrogance, Vinnie's street wars—and they wanted him to clean up their mistakes. "Yes."

"Does taking them out change things?"

Wolf looked at Klaus, putting him on the spot. Klaus had been so focused on Vinnie and Holly that he had to recall who the original targets were.

"The girl from Holder, her name is..." Klaus paused, frustrated.

Bo leaned forward. "Christian Lawler. I've been dating her."

"Right. And the guy from ATRI, his name escapes me—"

"Gus Meier," Holly said.

Erik nodded, processing. Then something clicked. He turned to Wolf. "Is he the Meier that was a Dreher?"

Wolf stared blankly.

Erik's voice was terse. "Is he related to the guy killed in the Lake Geneva explosion?"

Silence fell across the room.

Holly broke it. "He's from somewhere over there. Switzerland."

Erik leaned forward, his voice sharp. "The family that stole the notebook." He fixed his eyes on Wolf. "You know—the notebook that launched my Nazi grandparents into this business?"

Wolf perked up, understanding dawning. His eyes darted around the table. "Yeah."

Erik stood slowly and checked his watch. Too late to call home. He said, "Some time after the explosion, we learned the Swiss guy was the grandson of Otto Dreher, who took the notebook from Germany to Switzerland. The kid on the boat was his son." His voice dropped. "The name Gus Meier rings a bell. In the morning, I'll speak to Will, my father, and my grandmother first."

Erik planted his hands on the chair back and leaned in. His eyes shifted between Klaus and Holly, then said, "If he is who I think he is, I can't kill him. He's family."

<p style="text-align:center">~~~</p>

Immersed in her novel, the vibrating phone on the glass top startled Cassie. The security guard at the front gate is calling. A guest. Gina Marchitello.

Minutes later, she appeared at the top of the steps, where a surprised Cassie welcomed her with a hug.

"I'm sorry to intrude, I told them I was here to see Gus."

Cassie waved off the apology. "It's ok. All calls come to me. But Gus is probably fast asleep. He was exhausted."

Unphased, Gina said, "I'm leaving tomorrow, I just wanted to see him if you could tell me where his is."

Cassie hesitated to let Gina add any disclaimers or clarifying remarks. None came, and she led Gina through the kitchen and past the library to the foot of the staircase. "He's in the room on the far right."

Gina flashed a quick, sincere smile and thanked Cassie.

A lamp on the end table by the couch illuminated the common area. The door was shut. She tried the knob. The door opened, and light flowed in, striking his face and the bare portion of his chest and arm outside his cover. She stood still. The light aroused him, he squinted at the sight before him and propped himself on his elbow, "Gina?"

"May I come in?" She said.

"Well…sure."

She unbuttoned her dress, pushed it off her shoulders, and stepped out of it, the lamp highlighting her nakedness.

He adjusted his eyes and sat up. She came to him slowly. His breath stuttered, "Ah…shut the door—lock it."

Chapter Forty-Nine

Friday's dawn brought renewed vigor between Gus and Gina. Fulfilled and exhilarated, she lay flat, he on his side with his arm on her bare abdomen.

In a low voice, he said, "It felt like I had dissolved into you. That was bliss. Pure bliss. You can't leave."

Gina laughed.

He'd never heard her laugh—so freely.

She was happy.

He was astonished.

She said, "I feel like I'm leaving my body."

He chuckled. His chest was rising and falling. "Don't worry, I won't let you go." His breathing began to slow. "Just...maybe don't test that theory right now—because I literally can't move."

An ethereal minute passed. He'd drifted off…

Three soft, successive knocks sounded on the bedroom door.

His eyes snapped open. "What the hell?"

The doorknob tried.

"Gus. Open up."

More knocking, louder, shattered their cocoon of warmth.

"Gus!" Christian's voice, urgent and strained, carried through the wood. "I need to talk to you. Now."

Gina pulled the sheet up to her chin, suddenly self-conscious.

"Just a minute," he called out, reaching for clothes draped on the chair.

"No, now!" She pounded. "This can't wait."

He pulled on his pants, grabbed a T-shirt. "I'm coming."

Gina sat up, clutching the sheet. "Maybe I should—"

"Stay here." He patted the air. "I'll handle this."

But as he turned the lock and opened the door, he realized his mistake. Christian stood in the doorway, her hand still raised to knock again. Her eyes went immediately past him to the rumpled bed, to Gina's bare shoulders visible above the white sheet, to the clothes on the floor.

Her face went white.

"Christian, I—"

She swallowed hard, eyes fixed, composure cracking.

Gus slid in to block her view.

She stayed frozen a long moment and forced herself to look at him. Welling up eyes. She swallowed again, then spoke. Hesitant at first, then more controlled, but he could hear the tremor underneath.

"I..." She cleared her throat, her shoulders rounded, her phone clutched in both hands, focusing on the screen, she said, "I got a hit on the missing unit. Someone's using it—right now."

The words hung in the air like a lifeline she was throwing to herself.

"We should find it," she said, still not meeting his eyes. "Don't you think?"

Numb. His heart felt like a weight in his chest. Three quick nods. "I'll be down in a minute."

Her head bobbed gently.

Neither moved.

He heard himself breathing.

She mumbled, "Okay," and turned away.

The door latch clicked. He turned around. Gina looked at him with wonder.

That hurt

He took in a deep breath and held it a moment, "We've turned the page."

Gina nodded. "I'm sorry…"

He moved to the edge of the bed, his expression softening. "I'm ready for a new chapter in my life."

She grinned, "This mystery just took a twist."

Gus nodded, "Yep, I hope we can rule out this being goodbye-sex."

Gina's smile widened.

"I've got to go," he said.

Gina rolled out of bed, retrieved her dress, and pulled it over her head. "I traveled light."

"I thought I was having a dream—that you had already gone—when you stood there last night."

She looked in the bathroom mirror and dragged his brush through her hair, "Better than a postcard."

Gus smiled, drew her to him, and kissed her.

~~~

Cassie, still in her robe, sipping on coffee, had the Atlanta Journal-Constitution open on the kitchen island.

Christian poured a mug with her back to Gus and Gina entering.

Cassie exaggerated her raised eyebrows. Gus wrinkled his face.

"Good morning," Gina said.

"Buongiorno," Cassie said.

Christian shook her head slightly.

Gus approached her at the coffee maker, pushing through the awkwardness, "Where is it?"

"Bolling Road off East Wesley." He heard the edge in her steady voice. She was trying her best. "Near the Cathedral."

Gus sighed. "That's near my house." He turned to Gina. "By the Cathedral."

His phone dinged. A text from Trish Compton at GMC. He showed it to Christian. "Will you call her?"

"What about the missing unit?" Christian demanded.

Gus raised his phone. "She says she needs to talk to you. Call her first."

He stepped toward the library and called Suttles. Christian went to the porch to call Trish Compton.

Gus said, "Sorry to call so early..." Gus explained the GPS hit on the missing unit. Suttles told him to stay put. They would go together.

A moment later, Kip called, and Cassie warmed everyone's coffee.

"We got a hit on the last unit," Kip announced.

"I'm on it."

Kip added, "Gus, Dr. Slayton's phone and car are at that location."

He checked the time, 8:15.

Oh, Dr. Slayton. Last Friday, he kept his mouth shut. Times have changed

Christian stood in the doorway between the porch and the kitchen. Lips tight. Focused on Gus. "She needs me on site." Christian raised her hands, "I'm going to Dahlonega."
~~~

"What's wrong?" he said.

She hurried past him to the stairs. "Everything."

~~~

Dell Suttles drove his Chrysler through the gate and onto the circular drive, stopping at the wide stone steps.

Gus told ACE and Danno to drive Christian to Dahlonega while he rode with Suttles.

He and Gina descended the front steps hand in hand. Prepared to capture the encounter, he wore Funk's AV glasses.

Gina slid into the rear seat, greeted Suttles, and Gus completed introductions.

Suttles smiled at her, looked at Gus. "Where to?"

"Head to the Cathedral of Christ the King. I'll put in the exact address. When we're finished, we can drop Gina off at Angelo's."

Suttles nodded. "I'm glad you're okay, ma'am."

"Grazie," Gina said.

The hyperlink Christian had texted popped up on his screen. Two miles. Eight minutes. This person was practically a neighbor.

Suttles eased up Bolling Road through the canopy of mature trees.

"It's on the left," Gus pointed. "251."

Suttles pulled to the curb opposite the charming bungalow.

"Adorable," Gina observed, taking in the manicured lawn and flower beds.

"Probably Slayton's ride," Suttles nodded at the white Mercedes S-class.

~~~

A woman in lounge wear answered the door.

Suttles showed his badge. "Ma'am, we're tracking a medical device taken from GCI. The signal is coming from this address."

The woman's warm greeting faded. "There must be some mistake."

Gina approached from the sidewalk. "Are you Annie?"

"Yes."

"Gina. From the Cathedral."

Annie stiffened. "Oh, hi. What are you doing here?"

"I'm with him," Gina motioned to Gus. "How's your daughter? I heard she was ill."

Annie pursed her lips. "She's fine. I'm sorry, you're mistaken about any device." She started to close the door.

Suttles put his foot in the path. "Ma'am, under a surveillance warrant, we're also tracking Dr. George Slayton's vehicle and phone. Both are here. Is he inside?"

"This is bizarre…"

The front door swung wide. Dr. Slayton appeared. "Come in."

~~~

Annie led them through the house to a sunroom overlooking a backyard designed for children—swing set, basketball goal, sandbox. Evidence of a normal family life that Gus was about to shatter.

This feels wrong. But how many other children are dying while he stays silent?

"What's this about?" Annie demanded.

Slayton gestured for them to sit. He said to Annie, "Rosie."

She said, "A detective? These people? What's going on?"

Slayton looked at Gus, his composure cracking. "Rosie is my four-year-old granddaughter. Last year, she developed a neuroblastoma with bone involvement." His voice broke. "I've seen kids die from these brain tumors. I couldn't put her through…" Hands clasped, necktie high and tight, he straightened and exhaled.

Annie put her hand on her father's arm.

Slayton said, "I told Chen. He told me about your device." He shook his head once, face quizzical, "He didn't know how it worked, but it worked."

"You stole a unit," Suttles stated.

"He didn't steal anything," Annie protested.

Suttles pressed. "Did you remove a device from GCI's CAM department?"

Slayton held his head high. "I did." He exhaled, lips pursed, relief on his face. "And Rosie is alive."

Gus felt his chest tighten. He'd found the missing unit, but not the way he'd expected.

He's not evil—he's a desperate, intelligent grandfather. Knowing the options and the odds, he bet his granddaughter's life on Gus.

Intrigued, his breathing getting shallow, Gus said, "You stayed silent— while other children died."
~~~

Slayton scoffed. His stare was defiant, and his eyebrows rose. "Says you. The man lurking in the shadows."

Gus exhaled and put his folded hands on the table. "We share the same nemesis—The Schnerrs?"

Slayton nodded. "They killed your father in 1998."

"You knew?"

"My father told me." Slayton paused. "A year later, he was the Chairman of the Board who installed Donna Sheehan as Compliance Officer. It's all in a ten-page agreement I found in my father's desk after he died. The Schnerrs, on behalf of the pharmaceutical group known as The Consortium, paid a bonus to each member who voted for Sheehan."

How much?" Gus asked.

"One million."

Suttles made notes. "That's a serious allegation."

"It's all in the document. I have it. Locked away for a rainy day."

Suttles looked up, "Is it going to rain today?"

Slayton lifted his chin. "Weather's a funny thing."

What did the Board sell? What did the Consortium buy?

He adjusted his glasses and continued. "Did you figure out how the device works?"

Slayton locked his eyes on Gus. "I don't really care. Rosie's alive."

Precisely. Love does conquer all.

Gus leaned in and drew an arc on the tabletop with his index finger. "Take a Bell Curve." Then made a cleaving motion with his hand on either end. "Why not use it on those cases where your traditional methods fail?

Slayton's eye narrowed. He leaned in and squinted slightly, "What if the middle flattens?"

"Could it?"

Slayton shrugged slightly. "You tell me…I know flatline is never good."

Gus sat tall, swallowed, and prepared his summary. Hile needed evidence. His palms were moist, and his heart raced. "Dr. Slayton, this FDA designation goes against what your father stood for. The Consortium—and a corrupt Board, including your father—paved the way for a prestigious university to be used for covert exploitation. Dr. Tanzilla and the oncology trade union want to lord over the whole industry and look legitimate by placing your father's name on the new wing. And you can't or won't acknowledge the greatest innovation in cancer treatment for fear of your life and your family?"

Annie looked at her father. Eyes wide. Her hand came to her mouth.

Gina sat frozen, her hands on her lap.

Suttles looked on as if he saw this intense exchange every day.

Slayton inhaled, "That's a fair assessment."

Gus withdrew his phone and played back the recording—Annie answering the door, Slayton's confession, everything.

"What is this?" Slayton panicked.

Gus motioned to Suttles. "We're taking down the Consortium and the corruption at Georgia Cancer Institute," Gus said coldly. "Help us, or…I leak this."

I think I have enough. I hate threatening him. But he can seal this deal.

Slayton swallowed, then smiled grimly. "You're dead," he said to Gus, then turned to Gina, "You're dead. Your family is dead." He looked back at Gus, "Maybe you'll get lucky and serve a long prison sentence for the crimes you've committed."

The words hit like a punch to the gut. *He's right. I did commit crimes.*

Gina's eyes widened, her face going pale as the implications sank in.

Suttles raised his eyebrows at Gus.

Gus forced himself to stay focused despite the anxiety clawing at his chest. "I have the sympathy card, you don't. Who will the public side with? Me, or the doctor who stole a device to cure his granddaughter while he lied to the world that any such device existed."

Slayton's confidence wavered.

All in, Gus continued. "Give us something that can't be traced to you."

Silence.

Internal doubts in check, he pushed on. "Something—save yourself—we leave—you keep the device—our little secret."

Slayton considered for a long moment. "The Consortium members funded the FDA Emergency Approval Designation."

"I knew that."

"Donna Sheehan's real name is Holly Abernathy."

"I knew that, too. How did you?"

"It was included in the ten-page document—the whole board signed a non-disclosure agreement."

"What else?" Gus asked.

A deep inhale. Slayton said, "Sheehan orders from her family's company—Abernathy Analgesics. Every month, Georgia Cancer Institute pays for forty percent more doses than my department uses."

Suttles said, "Prove it."

Slayton's voice gained conviction. "I know how she does it. Forty percent never get prescribed. But—we still run out—every single month." He leaned forward. "Those drugs are going somewhere."

Gus felt the pieces clicking into place.

The street operation. That's how they're funding it.

The corners of his mouth turned up. A slight head turn to Suttles—who gave a single approving nod, then back at Dr. Slayton. "Tell us about that."

Chapter Fifty

alking down the curved brick sidewalk outside Annie's house, Gus contained his excitement as he told Suttles, "Hile is going to love this."

Suttles nodded, the ghost of a smile crossing his weathered face. "We got him." He clapped Gus on the shoulder—a brief, professional gesture that carried the weight of shared victory.

"I can have a warrant for forensic accounting at GCI before noon," Suttles added.

Gina's pace quickened beside Gus as they headed down the driveway and across the street. Her hand found his arm, her grip tighter than before. At the car, he opened her door. She stopped and turned to face him.

"That poor man risked everything to save his granddaughter's life—and you convinced him to help you."

Gus nodded. Gripping the top of the door frame. "I shared a story—a vision. He saw every little Rosie that ever came to GCI."

~~~

On the ride to Angelo's, Agent Hile called Suttles. When the call ended, he told Gus, "Erik is meeting Sheehan at the new operation. Hile has the address. They're organizing a SWAT team now.

"Where are Sheehan and Vinnie?" Gus said.

Suttles shook his head. "He didn't say. It was a courtesy call from Hile, to you."

Gina reached forward and touched his shoulder.

He reached for her hand—a brief squeeze.

SWAT team. The end will come too soon. They should die by overdose
~~~

~~~

At a traffic light, an ambulance with sirens blaring ran the red light on the cross street. He wondered about the circumstances of the person inside…was there a person inside? How much had he assumed over the past fifteen years that was wrong? On a deep inhale, he smelled Gina's scent and saw her standing in his doorway last night, and this morning…

Jarred by his vibrating phone, he read, Christian. When he answered, she charged on. "Everything is fine in Dahlonega. The demo can go on. I've told Bobby. He told me to call you. Are you going to be there?"

"What time?"

"Noon. JCO will be there after 11:00."

"Would you prefer I show up for the demo or have your partnership agreement ready to sign?"

"We can handle JCO," Christian said.

"I know you can…and we have something to show them thanks to you. I mean that."

"Thank you…And thank you for including me."

"You're welcome."

~~~

While Gus, Gina, and Detective Suttles were interrogating Dr. Slayton, Erik Schnerr sat at the desk in his hotel room in Stone Mountain, wearing the surveillance glasses, his phone propped against the lamp, speaking to his father and grandmother in Geneva via Zoom.

Wilhelm Schnerr, a husky man with thick, grey hair, sat close to his silver-haired mother, who had gentle creases and a posture that exuded confidence rare in someone ninety-three.

Gia Schnerr deliberated. "You are perceptive and correct—he is family. If reports are accurate," she hesitated, "I want him apprehended, not eliminated."

Erik said, "Klaus is in charge."

"I—am in charge," Gia replied firmly. "And I want whatever he has to use on Wolf."

Will said, "The members won't stand for that."

"This is my decision."

Will added, "And there's the bounty."

"I haven't forgotten," Gia said.

Surprised, Erik said, "What bounty?—

Gia paused. "Wolf joined the SS to find the notebook his sister and brother-in-law had absconded with. After the war, he used them and the notebook as a platform to offer our services to a consortium of drug companies who desperately wanted to protect intellectual property. As an incentive, he placed a bounty on recovering the notebook in our original bylaws. It's still there—mostly for sentiment, but it's substantial."

"What if he hasn't got the notebook?" Erik said. "Anyway, who cares?"

Gia went quiet for a long, anxious moment. "I care."

The words surprised even her.

Silence.

"I spent my life hunting passionate people and their notebooks. They claimed they had a better way to save lives. Threats—we called them." Her voice grew instructive, but softer. "Now my son is dying, and I wonder... what if they were right? What if the people I stopped were the ones who should have had the notebook all along?"

Nodding, Erik said softly, "That's the question I asked myself."

Gia looked at him with recognition. "Another thing the Nazis got wrong."

Will shifted in his chair, his voice sharp. "Our targets were renegades. Have you ever considered their motives? They were radicals wanting nothing more than to disrupt the industry."

"We snuffed out the innovators, Will." Gia's words cut clean. "We were that small group of committed people, not to make the world better, but to make it the way we wanted it, where we profited."

Will's face hardened. "Oh, good God, spare me the sentiments of a forlorn woman staring at her mortality. What is this, a life review? The boy is the end. Protect what you've sworn allegiance to—the people who hired you to do a job. Collect the bounty." He turned to Erik. "We taught you—stay steady, stay focused, pull the trigger. Pull the trigger, Erik."

"No." Gia's voice rang with authority. "DO NOT pull that trigger. I started this company, and I'll end it. Erik, if I die this moment, my directive to you is to spare that young man. Use whatever means you require to keep him alive."

Pensive. Erik nodded.

She paused, looking directly at Will. "Get me his information. I'll call him myself."

Will's voice was flat, dismissive. "Pathetic."

~~~

On the drive back to Angelo's to drop off Gina, Gus and Suttles discussed Dr. Slayton's explanation of how Donna Sheehan skimmed drugs through the medical center's purchasing program. Suttles said it was the perfect place to direct the forensic auditors. Gus conjured a plan to send to Hile regarding a potential takedown at Georgia Cancer Institute later—involving the whistleblower, Atlanta FDA director Mike Hamilton.

At the curb in front of Angelo's Suttles said he'd call the plan into Hile. Gus stepped out, opened Gina's door, and they walked to the side entrance hand in hand.

Inside the resident's entrance, beside the elevator, she turned to him. "I'm not sure what to say."

"About?"

"Well…last night, this morning, where do we go from here?"

Gus sighed, then he chuckled, "I know where I'd like to go, but…"

"I've made things more complicated for you."

He gently drew her to him, kissed her nose, and said, "You are the single most uncomplicated thing in my life—for years."

Gina said, "You and the doctor—that was intense."

He nodded, "That part of my life is about to be over. We're just beginning." Her arms around his waist, she squeezed him and said, "*We* are. And my flight leaves at 11:11 tonight."

"That 11:11 won't be like last night's."

She looked in his eyes, "I don't want to talk about it or think about it. Just go do what you have to do. I'll get ready and I'll see you back here for the party."

This parting kiss was special.

~~~

In the sedan on the curb, Gus texted his attorney to request the documents he needed to have ready by this afternoon and delivered to Holder Medical for Christian and Bobby to sign.

Suttles was still on a call with Hile at his office downtown. Suttles muted the call a moment, "I just got him on the line." Suttles unmuted and put the call on speaker.

Agent Hile confirmed that Mike Hamilton got his whistleblower protection and delivered the evidence Hile needed to make the arrest. Suttles shared what he and Gus got out of Slayton. Hile demanded the recording. Gus announced, "It's on its way."

Hile inserted that the Metro Atlanta SWAT team would strike the Food Truck Commissary at 11:30. The irony they enjoyed is it was one block from the Department of Corrections, across the street from the Public Safety Headquarters. "Get this," Hile said. "One of your snitches on the street works there. He's new, but we brought him and a dozen other undercover agents in, and we think we put it together. The food trucks transport pills to drop-off points in the bottom of garbage bag liners in the receptacles they set beside the truck. Their pusher poses as a neighborhood guy who 'helps' by hauling off their garbage—that's the handoff. Cash comes back the same way. We're moving in once those trucks clear the warehouse."

Suttles said to Hile, "You want me at the Commissary or Georgia Cancer Institute?"

"You're with Gus. This isn't over."

"He has a security detail from Mitch Scales," Suttles said.

"I know, ACE and Danno. But they can't call for backup. You're the badge. Hang with him."

~~~

Outside his Stone Mountain hotel, Erik Schnerr slid into the SUV driven by Klaus's man. No greeting. He punched the address into his phone and set it on his knee for the driver to hear the directions. Holly and Vinnie were waiting at 226 Peachtree Street Southwest. As directed, he had called Klaus and delivered Gia's directive: Gus Meier was to be apprehended, not harmed. Klaus asked if he was family—Erik confirmed they were cousins.

~~~

Assigned to shadow Gus, Suttles pulled his sedan around the corner from Angelo's onto Thirteenth Street.

Less media madness. Maybe they were camped out at GCI? Gus and the detective entered through the second floor of the parking garage. In an empty conference room, he set up his laptop to read the partnership agreements and the purchase order agreement with JCO.

Suttles adjusted the settings on his handheld radio and set it on the table between them. Hile's voice came through—he turned the Commissary operation over to the SWAT Commander. The clock was ticking on Vinnie and Holly... and Erik.

While his computer loaded, Gus told Suttles, "I'm going to take a quick look in the SCIF."

"Leave them alone," Suttles said.

Gus was already in the hall.

Ascending, the 'OCCUPIED' light outside the SCIF showed red. Eclipsing the top step, he froze. The man he'd bumped into leaving Christian's office was sitting on a club chair not normally situated beside the entrance. Alarmed, he backpedaled down the steps. A woman turning the corner to descend said hello to the man and proceed down, acknowledging Gus.

"That guy in the chair. Who is he?"

"Bo Abernathy."

"What's his job?"

"He oversees production."

Impatient Gus walked with her to the second floor. "What...what does that mean?"

She stopped. "He ensures that every product has everything necessary to begin full-scale production. He's quality control."

"Including code."

She nodded, "He's extraordinary at coding."

"Better than Christian?"

She shook her head, "I doubt it."

Gus hurried to the conference room and told Suttles, "He's trying to hack into the SCIF through our WI-FI."

"What now?" Suttles said.

"We have to stop him. Walk up there and...arrest him. Put him in cuffs."

Suttles stood, paused. "He's not going to lay down for me. I'll need backup."

They left together, climbed the steps in time to see the club chair empty and hear the stairwell door click.

Gus called Christian.

"Yes."

Her voice was calm but impatient.

"Are you running the program?"

Irritated, "Yes. We're rehearsing the demo."

Shit. Holly's brother. Klaus's mole. Did he access the source code?

Commotion rang through the atrium when the front doors opened. Gus peered over the railing, then checked his watch, 11:25. Conner Keegan and his JCO entourage were in the house.

The most critical moment in the history of the Assignment, and I'm chasing the infiltrating mole and reviewing contracts.

~~~

Across town in the lobby of the George M. Slayton, Sr Cancer Research Center, the smell of fresh carpet glue mixed with industrial paint hung heavy in the air. Someone had tried to mask it with floral air freshener—the combination was nauseating. Chairs were assembled in neat rows facing the high glass wall as a backdrop, their metal legs scraping against the new flooring. On the stage with nine chairs, technicians tested microphones, the feedback echoing off the two-story glass atrium.

Outside the tinted windows, dark clouds gathered, blocking the morning sun and casting a somber gray light over the lobby. The temperature had dropped ten degrees, and the HVAC system hummed constantly, fighting the humidity.

Communications Director Josh McIntyre paced in the VIP room off the lobby—an open administrative space that still smelled of wet paint and sawdust. Caterers navigated around him, setting up hors d'oeuvres stations, three bars, and high-top tables, their heels clicking sharply on the polished concrete floor. Ice clinked in buckets as thunder rumbled in the distance.

He pulled out his phone. "Hello, Mr. Hamilton. Big day ahead." McIntyre's voice echoed slightly in the unfurnished space as he paced, listening intently. He paused by the floor-to-ceiling windows, watching the storm clouds build. "I'll handle it, Mike. Yes. I understand the timing and sensitivity."
~~~

A jagged bolt of lightning illuminated the gray, gloomy sky as winds pelted the glass with rain, drowning out McIntyre's call. He drove his phone into his pocket, approached the windows, and lifted his head to the heavens.

~~~

At the Fishes and Loaves Commissary, Vinnie Schnerr stood with Erik in his second-floor office, watching the morning deployment.

"Rain or shine—they roll out like clockwork," Vinnie Schnerr gestured to the clock on the wall, 11:20. "And they roll back in between four and five, full of cash."

Erik watched the methodical departure below. Eighty trucks, ten pounds of pills each.

"A hundred and eighty thousand pills per load," Vinnie continued, beaming. "Translates to a million five. On average, each truck moves that in a month."

He gestured toward two large jars of mayonnaise on his desk. "Holly said we go through a lot of mayonnaise around here." Holly laughed from her chair by the window.

Erik shook his head. "Weekends off?"

Vinnie's broad smile remained fixed. "Seven days a week."

"That's a lot of cash to clean," Erik said.

Vinnie looked at Holly, who was still smiling. "We park it."

Holly's laugh was knowing. Erik didn't get it.

She reached for her purse and retrieved her phone. During the call, her face turned pale. When it ended, she stood, clutched her purse, and went to Vinnie. "I have to meet Bo. He thinks they're launching another device. Today."

Vinnie stared back. "Then, go."

Erik said, "Holly. Follow the rules. Apprehend him, don't kill him."

Vinnie hurried to a closet. He returned with a taser gun and handed it to her. She stuffed it in her purse. Vinnie said, "If you have to fire it, use both cartridges. Ten replacements in that sleeve."

Erik's voice dropped. Concerned, he said, "Holly. Be careful." Hearing his voice speak her name, she turned toward him, lips parted in surprise. As Vinnie leaned in for a quick goodbye kiss, her face remained turned toward Erik—no time to pucker, no attempt to return the kiss. Vinnie didn't notice or care; his mind was on the trucks, the pills, the cash. Her eyes never left Erik's.
~~~

Chapter Fifty-One

Friday morning, 11:35am at Holder Medical. Conner Keegan and his entourage exited the elevator on the third floor, their banter lively. Bobby let them into the SCIF.

Suttles stood at the railing on the second floor and radioed in for uniformed police to come to Holder Medical and search for Bo Abernathy.

In the conference room on the second floor, as Gus edited the partnership agreements and purchase order terms for JCO, the time had arrived to decide what he would charge and what he would share. Only his deepest self to consult, he reflected on documentaries of the Manhattan Project—anxious people watching, wondering, anticipating, then devastated by the incomprehension of the moment—that irrevocably cast a pall over every life hence. This moment felt that way.

Ready to launch a revolution. Mankind would never be the same. The Commissary— the fuses had been lit. Georgia Cancer Institute, the dedication—the fuse had been lit. In the SCIF—the fuse had been lit. All that energy in all those lives over all those years compressed— like a harmonic convergence into one day, now. Let there be no pall, no incomprehensible fallout. Please. I am trusting.

Fingers hovering over the keyboard, cursor blinking on the screen, technology awaited his decision. He alone chose which key to strike.

Christian. Bobby. His friends, his companions—names reduced to parties and percentage points in a contract.

I'm editing their lives.

Unsuspecting cancer patients lying in JCO beds…

Criminal? If so, a crime of compassion? Who could be my judge?

The time was now, the place was here, the decision was his. He trusted his decision and typed in the numbers.

A strange intimacy with the moment came up in him—an incomprehensible fallout—it felt cathartic. It felt validating.

Fixed on the laptop screen as he hit 'send' on the email to his attorney, TJ Massey, his phone vibrated on the tabletop.

"Consortium Security."

A last-minute negotiation?

It rang three more times. He stared. Then answered.

"Gus Meier?" A woman said.

Older than Dr. Pogue. Weak. The phonetic inflection of his name was unmistakable—German.

"Yes."

She spoke in his native language. "My name is Gia Schnerr. Do you know who I am?"

The matriarch.

"Yes."

"Would you trade your life for a device that stops cancer?"

She wants to make a deal?

"A question or proposition?"

"Proposition."

She ordered my father killed, and countless researchers to protect pharmaceutical profits, and now she wants mercy from ME?

"You've called the wrong number." He ended the call and stared at his phone, waiting. Two minutes passed. It vibrated in his hand. Same caller.

"Listen," she said.

He didn't cut her off, but he did interrupt as she paused, "Ma'am, either you or someone you care about is dying from cancer, and my device is your only hope."

Silence.

Images of Go Dawg boy, Rosie, and, Opa sent his heart racing.

He glanced at the clock in the corner of his laptop screen, 11:39.

Suttles hurried in, sat on the edge of a chair, and planted the radio between Gus and him. He mouthed, "Commissary."

"Would you hold one moment, please?" Gus said to Gia Schnerr.

<div align="center">~~~</div>

Vinnie and Erik were on the second floor at Fishes and Loaves, observing the last truck leaving and the overhead doors beginning to close, when suddenly individuals in tactical warfare gear stepped into the warehouse, crouched down, and took aim at the support staff. Vinnie rushed for the steps, shouting at Erik to follow. Vinnie ducked into the security closet, grabbed an automatic weapon, and shoved one at Erik. As they ran down the side steps, Erik slowed. Vinnie burst through the ground-floor doors where tactical agents were entering. He instinctively raised his weapon and met a burst of bullets, shuddering his body and shredding his blood-splattered shirt. Erik stayed inside the doorway and shouted out his identification, then stepped into the open with his hands behind his head, and dropped to his knees. The SWAT team acknowledged him and moved on.

<div align="center">~~~</div>

A voice on Suttles's radio announced, "Subject neutralized."

Gus stared at the radio, then at his phone. *Her grandson's blood is still warm on the warehouse floor.* The weight of it hit him—he had set this tsunami in motion, and now there was no stopping it.

His sweaty palm held his phone to his ear. He heard his heartbeat, and his voice carried the finality of a closing tomb.

"The Schnerrs' day of reckoning has begun."

His screen illuminated by Kip Richardson's call from the basement of ATRI.

He accepted the call, ending his conversation with his ominous remark.

"Gus?" Kip said. "Oh, am I glad you picked up. Sheehan is heading there. She got a call from the untraceable phone—also there."

"Kip," Gus blurted. "Where is that phone?"

"I can't tell, specifically. It's just there."

Damn.

"Where is Sheehan?" Gus said.

Kip paused, "One sec…She's sitting still on Ponce DeLeon, by Ponce City Market. Could be a wreck?"

"Ok. Text me updates. Have you checked the recordings from the glasses?"

"When I got here at seven. They were off. But the phones are on fire—lots of tension. Tanzilla, James, and Slayton are promising everyone the FDA deal is a go. They got Mike Hamilton on a conference call a moment ago. He green-lighted it. Tanzilla called both senators, and they gave it the green light. That's what he's passing on to the corporate leaders and their parties. They're all nervous. Like the other shoe is about to drop."

It's not a shoe, it's a boot, or a hammer. Call it what you want, they won't see it coming.

~~~

In the SCIF, Christian Lawler charmed the JCO team during the ice breaker, then dazzled in the demo. Answering questions before they could ask them, they were eating out of her hand. Bobby Blincoe grinned confidently in his chair to Keegan's left, away from the table.

~~~

At Georgia Cancer Institute, the lobby bustled with guests, unwilling to step outside, as the winds battered the newly planted trees and more dark clouds approached. In the VIP room, Mike Hamilton nodded to Josh McIntyre, who cued the wait staff to clear the room, except for the men and women wearing lanyards with the large, pale green GCI and their names. It was precisely 12:45. Josh McIntyre turned on his cordless microphone, called the room to order, and introduced the photographer, who talked over those in the room and those still being ushered out. When the last guest was shown to the lobby, the wait staff shut the doors and stood at attention. The photographer positioned Wolfgang Schnerr's wheelchair at the center, flanked by Dr. Slayton and Stephen James, the CEO. The senators, Tanzilla, Governor Hettich, Clair Pogue, and Klaus Schnerr filled the remaining seats, with the fourteen consortium CEOs and three FDA representatives standing behind them.

Standing behind those seated were the fourteen consortium CEOs and three FDA representatives, including Mike Hamilton—still maintaining his cover as the conspirators' inside man.

The persistent rumbling of thunder and lightning startled the guests in the lobby. The noise rose and fell as the storm got closer. At its peak, the storm provided cover for opening the exterior doors of the VIP room, allowing men and women in blue jackets bearing the gold letters "FBI" to charge toward them. On cue, the dozen metro police officers posing as wait staff closed ranks. There was one agent for each suspect. In short order, each had their hand secured behind their back and was being paraded into the torrential rain toward the Department of Corrections vans. In three minutes, the rear doors closed, a rolling thunder clapped, and the remaining people looked at each other in awe for what had just happened: Governor Hettich, Dr. George Slayton, Jr, Mike Hamilton, Dr. Clair Pogue, Josh McIntyre, and the photographer.

A sturdy rap on the door to the lobby prompted Josh McIntyre to make haste. His hands were actually trembling with excitement as he strode to the podium, unable to suppress the grin spreading across his face.

"Ladies and gentlemen," his voice boomed with barely contained exhilaration, "I want to introduce three champions for everything GCI represents—Dr. George Slayton Jr., Dr. Claire Pogue, and Governor Michael Hettich!"

Dr. Slayton practically bounced up the steps, his usual reserved demeanor replaced by pure joy. In the front row, he paused to hug Annie. Beside her, standing on her chair, a pink and white sundress with a matching bow in her hair, he embraced Rosie. Dr. Pogue's eyes were bright with tears of vindication, her shoulders thrown back with pride. Governor Hettich pumped his fist once before catching himself, then beamed as he waved to the crowd.

The three of them met at center stage, clasping hands and raising them together like victorious prizefighters. The applause thundered through the lobby—the energy was infectious.

Dr. Pogue leaned into the microphone, her voice ringing with triumph: "What has happened here today has been a very, very long time in coming. This new wing marks a new beginning, a fresh start. Our moment of redemption. All for one and one for all!"

Chapter Fifty-Two

Over the past few hours, in the second-floor conference room, Gus and Detective Suttles heard the transmissions from the Fishes and Loaves and the sting at GCI. Gus leaned back, closed his eyes, and exhaled slowly—the fuses he'd lit had found their targets. Hamilton had executed his plan perfectly, assembling all the dignitaries in one place for Hile's agents to take them down efficiently.

In the SCIF one floor above him, unaware of the coordinated takedowns, Christian finished her demo and answered all the pertinent questions. When Bobby rose to close the demo portion and ask if any compelling concerns would preclude the presentation of the purchase agreement Gus had prepared, Conner Keegan raised his hand to say he would be acting in that capacity. With that, Gus's attorney, Mr. TJ Massey, approached, and they adjourned to the conference room where Gus and Suttles were. Keegan thanked Gus profusely for his guidance from the previous week. Gus said, "I hope your appreciation extends to our revised pricing." TJ Massey showed him the sales agreement. Keegan looked at the sheet. His eyes widened. He looked at Gus. "Modest?" Gus sat expressionless, then said. "You were the one who said they were hemorrhaging money. You admit the product is far superior."

"It is, undoubtedly…"

Gus raised his hand to spare Keegan, "What do I need to do to make you happy?"

Keegan hesitated, "Ten, maybe fifteen percent."

"How about twenty—would that get this done and give you a win?"

Keegan's head nodded excitedly, he thrust his hand to Gus and shook it until Gus had to stop him."

Massey adjusted the numbers, Keegan wrote the check, and the deal was done. Shipping would commence on Monday.

Bobby, Christian, Gus, and Suttles stood on the railing as the elated entourage exited the front entrance, no longer congested with media madness.

They returned to the conference room, congratulated one another, and sat down to execute the partnership agreements.

TJ Massey said to Gus, "Is there a notary on staff?"

Gus looked at Christian and mentioned a name. "She is, but she's on vacation."

Bobby made a call. That person was gone.

Gus called Carmelo. A lady in his business office could notarize the documents. They all rose to walk to Angelo's when Kip Richardson texted Gus. "She's on the move. ETA eighteen minutes."

~~~

Out of Holder Medical's second-floor exit, they walked across to the public stairwell to the fourth level, where Gus punched in the code to access the entrance.

The business office was on the third floor. Ah, ahead, he spotted Carmelo and Gina. Gus avoided a casual remark and asked directly, "Where is the business office?" Gina offered to escort them via the main elevators in the lobby and used her access card.

~~~

Donna Sheehan pulled in the parking garage. She texted Bo. "Where are you. I'm here."

Bo called. She answered, "Do you have it?"

Bo said, "I can't tell. I got interrupted. I might. I might not."

"Shit, Bo."

"Let's just grab him," Bo said.

"Where are you?"

"In my office in the production area. They'll be in production on Monday."

"I need this now. This is my peace offering to Klaus and Tanzilla. We can't risk this getting out, whatever it is."

"You won't know if you don't nab him," Bo said.

"Where is he?"

"They went next door."

"For the party. It's too early?"

"That's where they are. I checked with someone on the second floor."

"Alright, I'm going to Angelo's. Bring what you have. We might be able to bluff him into coming quietly."

~~~

She walked east of Thirteenth Street toward the park and turned left. She passed the residential entrance, then turned left again, to the bank of elevators on the left before the entrance to Izzy's. She rode to the fourth floor. The ornate lobby was dim and empty. Staff were active behind the inside bar. She could see through to the Terazza, where more staff were setting up.

~~~

In the business office, Gina and two clerks cleared space for everyone to sit. Gus then asked her and the clerks to wait outside until he needed the notary. Suttles excused himself to stand guard at the entrance. TJ Massey then passed out documents and reviewed the pertinent terms. No questions were asked. Handshakes, hugs, and tears followed. Massey summons the notary.

Gus checked his phone. No text from Kip.

He texted Kip. "Where is she?"

Massey and the notary returned. The documents were signed. The deal was done. Partners.

Kip texted, "She's on Thirteenth Street, heading to Angelo's."

"Where's the other phone?"

"Inside Holder."

Anxious for their safety, Gus urged Bobby and Christian to the stairwell, shook Bobby's hand and hugged Christian, thanked them and said he call soon.

~~~

When Sheehan entered the stairwell, she had the option of up to her left or down to her right. Voices to the right. One step down, Gina turned the corner below.

Two steps up she and Sheehan locked eyes.
~~~

Gina stopped. Took a step down. Sheehan drew the taser and aimed it at her and stepped toward her slowly.

"What do you want?" Gina said.

"Where is he?" Sheehan said.

Silence.

Sheehan motioned with the taser for Gina to back up. "He's in the business office."

"No. He left. They took the elevator."

"Take me to the business office," Sheehan said.

As Sheehan came down each step, Gina matched.

At the third-floor landing, Gina's eyes gave him away. Still above them by ten steps, Sheehan said, "If you're there, Gus, come out."

Silence.

"I'm going to shoot her where she stands."

Gus turned the corner. Gina backed toward the corner, her back against the wall.

Sheehan aimed the taser at him. "Come with me and nobody gets hurt."

"It's over, Holly," Gus said.

Her eyes narrowed, her jaw hardened.

Gus motioned for Gina to move behind him.

"Stay where you are," Sheehan shouted.

"Holly," Gus pleaded. Does she know it's over?

"You come with me, or I'll shoot her. Is that what you want?"

He raised his hands—I'm unarmed. "Holly. I'm the one who visited you in Geneva. I know you didn't mean to set off the bomb."

Her phone buzzed insistently in her purse. Then again.

Frustrated, she glanced at the screen-Bo.

Gus lunged for the taser, but she reflexively fired both cartridges into his chest. Fifty thousand volts coursing through his body, seizing uncontrollably. He crumpled to the landing in front of Gina.

Gina gasped, enraged.

Sheehan and Gina's eyes locked.

Sheehan lunged at Gina from three steps above, leading with her outstretched arms, trampling Gus, pinning Gina against the wall, and releasing primal screams. Her thumbs landed on Gina's throat, clutching her windpipe.

Gina gasped. Her eyes bulged, her flailing hands frantically found and clutched Sheehan's head. She drove her fingernails into her eye sockets ferociously.

Sheehan screamed louder.

Gina gasped more.

Sheehan shifted her feet on Gus, all her mass shifted to Gina, and she screamed at Gina to let go.

Instinctively, Gina tucked her knees to her chest, working her feet as far up Sheehan's torso as possible, her thumbs unrelenting, blood pouring from the eye sockets.

From above, Udell Suttles appeared. "Stop. Stop," he said, rushing to them.

When his hands drew Sheehan up, Gina shifted her feet and drove them into Sheehan's chest as hard as she could, sending her into the side wall.

Disoriented, blinded, Sheehan misstepped and somersaulted backward to the landing, her momentum thrusting her torso into the wall and whipping her head into the concrete—the impact echoing through the stairwell—like a melon dropped from ten feet.

Stunned silence.

Gus moaned and rolled to his side. Panting, holding her throat, Gina kneeled behind him, resting her arms on his side. Suttles stood bent over them, his hands on his knees, breathing hard from his rush down the stairwell. Donna Sheehan, seated, eyes sockets streaming red tears, her jaw drooped, as a crimson band flowed across the concrete beneath her.

Chapter Fifty-Three

Two Fulton County ambulances lined the curb beside the resident's entrance. Paramedics secured the gurney carrying Gina Marchitello in the first one. As they stepped out to close the doors, Gus urgently stepped in, kissed her forehead, assured her she was going to be fine, and said he'd follow as soon as possible. The paramedics closed the doors and drove away with the siren wailing into Friday afternoon traffic on Piedmont Avenue.

My heart feels like it's driving away with her.

Gus climbed into the other ambulance and removed his shirt. An EMT bandaged his puncture wounds.

Yellow crime scene tape cordoned off the scene. Metro police officers directed traffic, pedestrians, and vehicles. Suttles and Hile stood together in conversation.

Twenty feet away, at the edge of the police barricade, a black body bag was carried out the side door and loaded into the medical examiner's van. Holly's twin, Bo, handcuffed, was led to a police cruiser and driven away.

Bobby and Christian approached the back of the ambulance, both looking shell-shocked.

"Gus," Bobby leaned into the truck and extended his hand as the lady EMT attended to his wound. "Man, I don't know what to say."

Gus shook Bobby's hand, then offered his hand to Christian. She clasped it for a long moment.

"What a nightmare," Gus said.

Christian swallowed, her eyes welling. "Thank God, it's over."

Gus raised his eyebrows. "*This* is—but," he looked past them for anyone eavesdropping. "*It* may not be—*It* may be just about to begin. Stay tuned once the JCO mats go online."

Bobby nodded. "That'll be a while."

Christian said, "Take a vacation. Well deserved."

"And," Bobby added, "I have to find a new production man—we lost Bo."

Christian shook her head and raised her hands to urge restraint. "Nobody say a word. This is a fragile moment. Let's observe that. I'll take my licks later."

Bobby smiled. "I'll handle it," he said to Gus. "Don't worry."

Gus shrugged. "Ok. I won't. I'll be in touch. TJ will record everything on Monday." He looked between them. "You two are running things now. Holder is in the loop and on board."

A weary smile crossed Christian's face. "Partners," she declared while Gus buttoned his shirt and stepped to the street. She gave him a quick hug. "Thank you...partner. We've got this."

Carmelo appeared at Gus's side, his face ashen. "Will she be okay?"

He nodded and said, "She will. I'm heading to the hospital now."

"May I ride with you? We should swing by and get Angelo. He'll want to be there. We'll call her parents."

They piled in the Tahoe. ACE drove, Danno rode shotgun.

A Metro cop stopped traffic for ACE. Two more stood on the crime scene tape for her to pass.

Carmelo said in a low voice as they drove away, "When she called and asked to visit, you were the first person I thought of. I never dreamed...this—" He gestured at the chaos behind them.

"It had to end, Carmelo. I'm glad you asked me."

"Destino," Carmelo said. "Fate."

The afternoon sun cast long shadows as they headed to Angelo's then to Piedmont Hospital.

Gus rode in the third row, cramped. Angelo rode behind ACE, quiet. He'd made it clear when he got in that NOTHING BAD could come to his Regina.

Under the portico at Piedmont Hospital, ACE pulled the Tahoe behind a grey Mercedes SUV, where Henry was helping Opa from the back seat. Helene exited the rear passenger door. Cassie sat behind the wheel.

ACE parked behind them. She and Danno stepped out and opened the rear doors. When Carmelo and Angelo were out, she unlocked the rear seat to let Gus out. She extended her hand. "It was an honor, sir." When they shook, she added, "Most people under protection are happy to survive. You and G-Mar found something worth protecting."

"Ditto," Danno agreed with a slight smile. He offered his hand. "If there's a silver lining. You two are it."

Gus nodded, suddenly understanding that beneath Danno's professional distance had been genuine concern.

"Take care of yourself," ACE said, her formal tone softening as she stepped back.

Gus watched them return to the Tahoe, carrying a chapter of his life that was closing. He turned toward the hospital entrance where his family waited.

Helene rushed to him, between ambulances, crying when they embraced. "Cassie told us."

"Today was the day of reckoning," Gus mumbled. "It's great to see you."

He and Helene walked arm in arm to Opa.

"You hate to miss the action." Gus chuckled and hugged his grandfather.

Henry and Gus shook hands. "You've had a busy week," Henry said.

Gus nodded. "Bizarre."

Henry's expression grew serious. "Gus, I'm proud of you—I admire you. I wish your mom and dad were here."

Gus looked at Henry, then turned to Helene. "My mom is here." He embraced Helene, who squeezed him tightly.

"You need some downtime around the pool with us," Helene said softly.

He draped his arm on Cassie's shoulder. "And Cassie runs a nice bed-and-breakfast."

She smiled as Gus re-introduced Carmelo and the group moved into the ER lobby.

Gus approached the reception desk. "We're here to see Gina Marchitello."

The receptionist said she was having scans.

He returned to his family, filled with gratitude, and sat beside Opa. He whispered to his grandfather, "The Assignment lives." Opa put his hand on Gus's.

"Augustus, I have a confession. That Sunday morning that we went to the vault—I debated taking you there. I considered what happened to your father and all you had going on." Opa paused. "A voice in me said, 'He's ready.'"

Gus shifted toward Opa. "Really?"

The old man's eyes took on that faraway look—his gaze fixed on the middle distance where present and past seemed to merge, where his mind rummaged through old filing cabinets of GCI. His voice carried the gentle weight of accumulated wisdom and regret.

"You and I had different visions," Opa said. "You were coming back to a calculated, privileged life. I saw an untested boy in a man's body." He paused, swallowing with effort as though the truth required physical strength to release after all these years.

"That notebook had no special code that your father and I could tell. It spawned some good ideas, which we capitalized on, but you—" his voice cracked slightly, "—you found things in there we never imagined."

His eyes refocused briefly on Gus. "Had you stayed here a year or two and decided you found nothing, I would have welcomed you home. I want you to know that."

Gus sensed the urgency and remorse in his words.

"But, you found what David Primack wanted us all to find. You dug deeper. You tried harder. You created the Holy Grail he imagined." Opa sighed, "You gave his life meaning."

Gus nodded, the weight of his grandfather's confession settling between them.

A fragile smile touched Opa's lips. "I wasn't deceiving you, Augustus. Not in my heart." He reached tentatively toward Gus's hand. "I did not know if you could sustain the life you were coming into." Opa turned to Gus and smiled. "You exceeded every expectation."

The sliding doors to the ER opened, and George Slayton and Clair Pogue walked in, their faces a mixture of concern and determination. Gus excused himself and went to them.

Handshakes and hugs exchanged. Slayton said, "Are you still recording?"

Gus motioned to remove his invisible glasses.

Slayton smiled.

Gus and Clair Pogue hugged again.

"Thank you," Pogue said.

Before Gus could respond, Josh McIntyre and a woman Gus presumed was his wife walked in.

Josh came to Gus with an outstretched arm. They shook hands, and Josh quickly introduced his wife.

"I'm honored to meet you," Debbie McIntyre said.

Josh motioned for Gus to step outside, his expression suggesting urgency.

Josh said, "Debbie used your device."

Gus wrinkled his face.

Slayton and Pogue stepped out to join them, exchanging knowing glances.

Josh continued, "She had pancreatic cancer. She doesn't anymore."

Gus looked at Slayton and Pogue.

"I just found out today," Clair Pogue admitted.

"I told him what results Chen was getting," Slayton added.

Josh's expression grew serious. "Chen said I should take it home. When I saw what it did for her, I followed everyone who used your device at home, tracking their progress. Then, I recorded their testimonials."

"You?" Gus stared at him, then whispered, "You leaked them."

Josh nodded. "The entire campaign." His voice gained strength. "I was inside listening to what Tanzilla and Sheehan were doing—I knew the world needed to know."

"But the risk to your career..."

Josh said. "My wife was dying, then she wasn't. How could I not say something?"

"What about the people at CNN? They knew plenty."

Josh looked at his wife.

"That was me." Debbie McIntyre said. "I work there. Anita was covering for me. I'm the regular producer of New Day."

Gus smiled and shook his head. "You all knew more about my device than I did." The pieces finally connected in a way he hadn't anticipated.

Suttles and Hile approached from across the lobby. Hile's face showed exhaustion mixed with gratitude.

"Gus," Hile extended his hand. "I can't thank you enough. What you pulled off today—" He shook his head. "We got everything we wanted and more."

"Any word on Wolf?" Gus asked.

Hile's expression sobered. "We took him to Grady Memorial. He's in his final days." He paused. "Klaus broke down when we separated them."

"And the assassin?" Gus said.

"Still in custody. Interpol arrested his brother, father, and grandmother."

Gus shook his head. "Is Agent Baumann satisfied?"

Hile smiled and nodded.

Suttles stepped forward. "Gus, I enjoyed working with you. Learned a lot."

Gus looked surprised. "Seriously?"

"Uh-huh," Suttles nodded with a slight smile.

Gus's phone dinged. Kip texted. "Are you okay?"

Gus texted back three thumbs up.

Cedric texted, "I saw the news. G-man. U good?"

Gus chuckled, "Good, Ced. Talk soon. Thanks."

Helene came to the ER entrance. "Gus."

Inside, Gina sat in a wheelchair. A small gauze bandage covered her throat, and dark bruises formed a ring around her neck where Holly's hands had gripped her windpipe. A doctor stood by her side. Gus took her hand, relieved.

The doctor explained, "The blunt force to her trachea has caused fractures and tears to the cartilage. She can speak when the swelling subsides."

Carmelo approached from across the waiting area, putting his phone away. "I spoke to your father and mother," he said to Gina. "Do you want to keep your plans?"

Gina nodded.

He looked at Gus. "I told them about your family connections to charter planes."

Helene spoke up, "There's one at PDK right now. You're welcome to it."

Carmelo looked at Gus. "She shouldn't travel alone. They asked if you would accompany her."

Gus's eyes widened. He looked at her. She smiled, nodded, and gave a thumbs-up.

Gus leaned over and kissed her forehead. "You are my new assignment."

Her eyes welled up. She brought his hand to her mouth and kissed it.

About The Author

Dr. Craig Mueller is a Doctor of Chiropractic with over four decades of clinical experience. During his career, he utilized a version of Electronic Acupuncture according to Voll (EAV) and implemented protocols developed by renowned researcher Dr. Donald Kelly. Having witnessed firsthand some miraculous changes in people with chronic diseases, Dr. Mueller conceived *The Assignment*, his debut thriller. This fictional account explores what might happen if revolutionary healing science were ever made available to the masses, and the forces that would try to stop it.

Visit the author's web site:
www.drcraigmuellerbooks.com